The Boath

The Scottish Highlands Series

Winter in the Scottish Highlands

The Secrets of the Glen

Return to the Lake House

The Boathouse by the Loch

Coming Home to Aviemore

AUTHOR'S NOTE

This series is best read sequentially to enjoy the story arc as it was intended.

The Boathouse by the Loch is the fourth book.

The Boathouse by the Loch

The Scottish Highlands Series

Book IV

ELISE DARCY

Penny Lane Press

ISBN 978-1-913147-35-8

"Your life does not get better by chance, it gets better by change."–*Jim Rohn*

1

'I didn't expect to see you back so soon.' Gayle looked as surprised as she sounded, and it was little wonder; Jake had only checked out of his room that morning and had been heading for the airport to catch a flight back to London. Now, here he was, just a few hours later – back on the doorstep of her guesthouse, Lark Lodge, in Aviemore.

'Change of plan,' said Jake, hoping she still had vacancies. He should have been returning home. It had been agreed that he'd step into Marcus's shoes and head up the Ross Corporation while Marcus checked himself into rehab. It was only temporary. Jake had previously been a corporate lawyer, running the family business with Marcus, but after the accident up in the Cairngorms the previous Christmas, he'd left all that behind to train as a teacher in an inner-city school in London.

After what had happened to Jake's wife, Eleanor Campbell-Ross, the media interest had been intense. It had been all over the news – the tragic accident involving William Ross's two children, Marcus and Eleanor, and son-in-law, Jake, during their annual Christmas holiday to their beloved holiday home, The Lake House, in Aviemore.

Eleanor had been airlifted to hospital, and that had been the last detail regarding the accident that the press had been privy to. In the immediate aftermath, the family had refused to issue a press release or engage with anyone outside the family. They had all been uncontactable. They'd closed ranks to protect themselves; to protect Eleanor.

Jake would have done anything to swap places with her, but he couldn't, and the press could only speculate as to what had happened to her.

They'd all had different coping mechanisms after the tragedy. Marcus's father, William Ross, the head of the Ross Corporation and the man who had taken Jake in after he'd been orphaned as a child, had withdrawn from work, avoiding the boardroom. He was now spending most of his time on the golf course.

Marcus had stepped into his father's shoes, which hadn't surprised Jake. What had surprised him was finding out that Marcus's recreational use of drugs had turned into something far more serious as he soldiered on with running the company single-handedly while dealing with what Jake believed was his guilt over what had happened to Eleanor on the ski slopes. A freak avalanche had caused the accident, and Marcus had chosen to dig Jake, his best friend, out of the snow before Eleanor.

Of course, Marcus had denied it. He'd always maintained that there was someone else up on the ski slopes with them. Someone else had dug Jake out first. Because of that, Jake had walked away from the accident on Christmas Day unscathed, but Eleanor had not.

'How are the hands?' Gayle asked.

Jake looked at his bandaged hands as he stepped into the hallway. They were a reminder of how he'd come to be in that part of the world. 'Better,' replied Jake. He was meant to be finishing his first year of teacher training in London. It had been the last week of the summer term, and he'd found himself off work.

It had all been going so well until he'd got another one of those phone calls from Lydia, Marcus's fiancée, to say he hadn't come home the previous night. Jake had discovered Marcus at his own house. Marcus had tried to break in, leaving shattered glass in Jake's hallway, which Jake had slipped on, landing hands-down on the glass.

Marcus had wanted to know where Jake had been that night, why he wasn't home. Jake did not want Marcus to jump to conclusions, but he'd stayed the night at the house of a woman. Faye. She was a work colleague, deputy-head of the school where he worked, and Jake's mentor. Faye was a single parent, and Jake had been babysitting her daughter while she was on a course, training to be a headteacher. Over the course of the school year, Jake had got to know Faye, and he knew he'd been growing too attached both to Faye and to her daughter, Natty.

He'd fallen for Faye, although she was aware of that. But he'd nearly lost her friendship – lost both her and Natty – when Faye had discovered he'd been spoiling Natty. Whatever she'd wanted, he'd bought for her. He had the money. Not from his trainee teaching salary; the Ross Corporation still deposited his salary into his bank account. William Ross had ensured he was still on the board, and was expecting he'd be back. Marcus had said the same; that when Jake had come to terms with what had happened to Eleanor, he'd return.

Jake felt that William and Marcus were acting as though he was having some sort of mental breakdown because of his decision to leave the company and train to be a teacher. But he knew they were wrong to see his decision that way. He loved his new job. It was worlds away from the Ross Corporation, but if it hadn't been for Eleanor's accident, he'd never have left.

He'd felt enormous guilt over the fact that it had taken such a tragedy for him to find the life where he truly felt he belonged. Whilst he knew he'd made the right decision to leave, it was true that he had had a breakdown of sorts. He'd convinced himself that Eleanor had died. It was the only way he'd been able to cope with what had happened.

Jake had finally come to terms with the reality of Eleanor's situation. She wasn't dead, but to him, she might as well have been after the injuries she'd sustained. He hadn't visited her since the accident, and neither had Marcus. Jake had put Marcus's reluctance down to guilt over what had happened on the mountain. Jake felt guilt too – that he hadn't been able to save his wife or somehow prevent the accident. But it was more than that. He was afraid to see her, to face the fact that she wasn't the same anymore. He was barely able to acknowledge that their life together was over.

Jake was back in Aviemore to find out the truth about what had really happened on the ski slopes the previous Christmas. If Marcus had been telling the truth all along, and someone else really had been up there with them, Jake's plan was to return to The Lake House to find them..

2

As Gayle ushered him inside, Jake decided not to mention that he hadn't intended to return to Lark Lodge. He'd driven straight to The Lake House, which backed on to Gayle's house, intending to stay there. But when he'd arrived, he'd discovered that the house was in the middle of being decorated. There was no one there, but he'd discovered paint pots in the bedrooms, along with rolls of wallpaper.

He'd visited the house just that morning, doing a quick circuit of the rooms and making sure the place was as the family had left it, with dust sheets covering the furniture. The Lake House, where the Ross family had always spent Christmas together, had in fact been his childhood home until his parents had died. It was still his house; his to do with as he wanted. And the previous day, after his visit, he had started seriously contemplating letting go of the place and selling up. He had thought about employing a local interior designer to spruce the place up to sell.

He'd seen the designer's outlet on the way into town. On passing Gillespie's General Store, he'd caught sight of one of the shop's windows, which had a lovely display of soft furnishings and materials that he knew Eleanor would have loved. He recalled the sign over that window – Robyn's Interior Design.

And now he wondered if Robyn was working on The Lake House already. If it was her, she must have already started work, but in Jake's haste to whip around the house the previous day and check every room, he had missed the decorating paraphernalia. He'd only opened the doors and glanced in, quickly checking that the furniture was still covered with dustsheets and there was no evidence of squatters.

But on returning from the airport that afternoon, ready to move into his house for a few days, he had been less preoccupied. He'd noticed the evidence that someone was redecorating.

He hadn't employed her. He hadn't employed anybody, even though he'd considered it. There was only one other person who would have done so, even though that person never visited Scotland; one person who had the remit to do such a thing. Aubrey. William Ross's right-hand man. They were close, Jake and Aubrey; always had been. Jake wouldn't have been surprised if Aubrey had stepped in to take care of the property. After all, the Ross Corporation took care of everything.

Jake managed a smile as he stepped into Lark Lodge. He hadn't expected to be back so soon either. He headed straight for the stairs with his bag to the room he had been staying in just the previous day. He had originally booked two nights, even though he'd told Gayle just that morning that he was leaving and wouldn't need the room for the second night.

He heard Gayle close the front door.

'That room is taken,' Gayle called after him.

Jake stopped abruptly and turned around with a puzzled look on his face. He hadn't expected her to rent the room out so quickly.

'That's right.' She noted Jake's bewildered expression and

pointed to the stairs. 'There's an attic room,' she said. 'It's bright and airy, with good views of the Cairngorms,' she added.

Jake noticed that she hadn't mentioned the rest of the view. Her guesthouse backed on to The Lake House.

'You just want to show off your rooms,' Jake chided, not fully believing that his room had gone in the space of a few hours, especially when there were other, bigger rooms available in the guesthouse. He recalled that the room he'd stayed in was the most expensive. Gayle had said she didn't normally rent it out, as it was reserved for friends only. She had made an exception for him and Marcus. Had she made an exception for someone else, or did she have friends staying?

He wondered if Robyn had returned to the guesthouse. He recalled mentioning to Gayle that he'd like to meet her, and she had said that Robyn popped in from time to time. She had lived with Gayle for a time. They were good friends. Perhaps she'd moved back.

Gayle who was normally chatty, didn't volunteer who was staying in that room, and Jake didn't ask.

Reluctantly, Jake followed Gayle up the stairs.

Gayle said, 'You're in luck again.'

He frowned at her back. 'Really? How's that?' He didn't feel particularly lucky as he followed her up to the attic room.

'You know yesterday, when you turned up for two nights, and I told you that apart from my two longer-term guests …'

Of course, Jake remembered Nick Addison, the site manager who worked on a new development in town. He'd bumped into Nick on a piece of land outside town, where Jake remembered an old lodge had stood. Jake had originally thought of staying there for a couple of nights. It was Nick who had suggested Lark Lodge guesthouse when Jake had seen that the old lodge in the woods had been demolished. And that was where he'd discovered the other long-term lodger at the guesthouse – Marty, the gardener who looked after the garden at The Lake House.

And now another friend had moved in, robbing him of his room. Jake silently berated himself for being so childish. It was not his personal room. In fact, he suddenly recalled that he was sure Gayle had told him that apart from these two nights, the guesthouse had been fully booked. So how come this attic room was free?

He had a feeling he was about to find out.

'I told you that you were lucky because my last bookings, who were on a five-night break, left yesterday, leaving two nights free – last night and tonight.'

'Yes.' Jake raised an eyebrow. 'I thought you said it was busy again from Friday onwards, apart from the single room being vacant.' Jake remembered that she did special offers on three, five, and seven-night breaks, which attracted a lot of guests.

'I'm more than happy with a single room on a lower floor, if it's vacant.'

'How long are you anticipating staying this time? You see, my seven-night stay in the attic unexpectedly cancelled.'

'Ah. That's handy.' Although he'd promised Marcus and Faye he'd be back as soon as possible, he really didn't know how much time he'd need to find out exactly what had happened on that mountain the previous Christmas. He didn't want to be there indefinitely, so he booked a return flight, which meant he had six more days, if he needed them. He'd change his flight if he could return sooner. 'Does that mean the attic room is available for the next six nights?'

'It certainly is.' Gayle threw a smile over her shoulder.

Jake grinned. 'Perfect. Then I'll take it.'

Gayle halted at the top of the stairs, outside one of the two attic bedrooms, and turned around.

Jake caught her expression. 'What's the matter?'

'I will reserve the room for you for the next six nights.'

'Great. Of course I'll pay upfront.'

'Now, that's the problem.'

'Huh? How come?'

Gayle cocked her head to one side. 'May I be blunt, Mr Campbell-Ross?'

'Please, call me Jake.' He thought they'd dispensed with the formalities already. He had stayed the night, and they'd been on first-name basis then.

'Well, we both know you are not here on holiday. You have … family affairs to sort out, I'm sure.' Her eyes drifted to the skylight window.

Jake knew exactly what she was looking at. His eyes drifted to the rooftop of The Lake House too.

'Obviously, that's none of my beeswax …'

Jake smiled at the expression.

'But I am not taking your money for the full six-night stay.'

'But—'

'No buts,' she said, sternly folding her arms.

Jake lowered his eyes. He understood. He'd paid for two nights, and had left after only one night, telling her to keep the money. It was the wrong thing to say to someone like Gayle. He'd offended her. She knew he was made of money. He was a Ross, after all. When he and Eleanor had married, they'd agreed she'd take his name and keep the Ross name too. And Jake had been so inextricably linked with the Rosses since childhood that he'd had no qualms about joining their surnames into a double-barrelled married name.

Now, he wished he hadn't. Everywhere he went, the name Ross, and what had happened to William Ross's daughter, followed in his wake. And yet he knew he couldn't drop his married name. It would upset William and Marcus.

But what would happen if I were to remarry? he wondered. That thought had never crossed his mind before.

'You don't agree,' said Gayle flatly, keeping hold of the door key to the vacant attic bedroom.

'Oh, er. Of course, of course. I'll … um … pay when I leave then?'

'Yes, that's what I would prefer.'

'All right.'

'Good. That's settled then.' Gayle smiled as she handed him the key to the room with the view of The Lake House. He remembered the faux pas Gayle had committed when she'd mentioned the attic rooms at the start of his previous stay. She'd said that there were lovely views from those rooms of the Cairngorms, the famous mountain range in Scotland. Of course, that was where they'd had the ski accident. But worse still, she'd added, you'll get a glimpse of the Rosses' holiday home too.

Jake remembered that Gayle had been mortified, apologising profusely. Jake had just waved the comment away, realising she'd said it on autopilot because that was what she said to all her guests. She'd even admitted as much. The Rosses, with their global construction empire, were one of the wealthiest families in the country. It stood to reason that people might be interested to catch a glimpse of the family in the flesh; they'd only normally see them if they popped up on the news. Unfortunately, after the accident at Christmas, and the news stories about the tragedy, Jake imagined that bookings at the guesthouse – especially for the attic rooms overlooking the Rosses' holiday home – had increased.

If Gayle had told any of her guests that a member of the Ross family was actually staying there, they probably wouldn't believe it. 'Can we stick to being on a first-name basis?' Jake suddenly blurted.

Perhaps it was just as well he would be staying up in the attic, away from prying eyes – although he knew Gayle would not be telling all and sundry just who he was.

Gayle offered him an understanding nod. 'Of course we can.'

Even so, he had it on the tip of his tongue to ask to swap rooms if there was a guest in one of the single rooms on the lower floor, and let them have an upgrade at his expense, but he decided against it. Gayle had told him she did not accept charity, and he imagined she wasn't expecting her guests to either. Besides, it suddenly occurred to him that they might want to know which one of the guests was being so generous as to pay for their upgrade. That was a surefire way of getting noticed by the other guests.

Instead, he asked, 'Where's Olive?' He looked down the stairs, expecting her to bound up to greet him at any moment, wagging her shaggy tail. He looked at Gayle. 'You shut her in the kitchen this time, didn't you?' Jake smiled knowingly. When they'd arrived the previous day, the huge dog had come belting towards them, scaring Marcus, who'd clung to the banister for dear life.

Jake had been more than happy to give the exuberant puppy dog, an Old English Sheepdog called Olive, a fuss. He'd thought she was adorable. But, seeing Marcus's reaction, Gayle had promptly taken her to the kitchen and shut the door.

'Oh, she's not in the kitchen.'

Jake imagined that Nick had taken her out for a walk. She was his dog, after all – not Gayle's.

Meeting Olive had reminded Jake that Natty had been on at him about getting a puppy. Of course, he couldn't buy her one without Faye's say-so. After all, who was going to look after it? Natty had begged, and pleaded, saying that she would take care of it. But she was only nine. Jake knew, without even asking, that her mum did not have the time or resources to take on a puppy. But Jake did. He had thought that he could buy a puppy for Natty, and just have it at his house for when she visited. But that plan had gone straight out of the window when Faye had found, in his house, all the toys he'd been buying Natty for when she stayed over. He hadn't realised what a fool he'd been. Faye shouldn't have had to tell him that he should not be giving Natty the idea that she could have whatever she wanted, whenever she wanted it. It wasn't the way Faye was bringing her up. And besides, she just didn't have the money to spoil her like that, even if she'd wanted to.

'Everything all right?'

Jake looked at Gayle.

She said, 'Oh, you asked me about Olive. She's at the shop.'

'The shop?'

'Mr Gillespie's General Store.'

Jake frowned. 'What's she doing there?' Then a thought suddenly occurred to him. 'Oh, god – she's not for sale, is she?' If so, Jake was ready to drive on over to town and buy her.

Gayle burst out laughing. 'Oh, goodness me! What a thought. Mr Gillespie selling puppies down aisle number three! Although I'm sure, knowing his fastidiousness, he'd be sure to put the puppies down the dog food aisle.'

Jake smiled. 'Ah, you mean he is looking after Olive.'

Gayle shook her head. 'Ah, no – she's in Robyn's side of the shop. Doggy daycare alternates between here and a rather large comfy cushion that Olive loves lounging on in Robyn's part of the shop. I think Olive is rather fond of Annie's little girl, Evie. I know Evie is very fond of Olive. She loves that her mum, who works for Robyn, brings Olive to collect her after school before they both return to the shop. Evie loves reading to Olive after school.'

Jake said, 'How old is Evie?'

'She's six.'

Once again, Jake was thinking of Natty and how much she'd love a dog. Evie wasn't that much younger that Natty. Perhaps Natty would read to her dog after school, like Evie did.

Gayle added, 'I heard Evie had been badgering her parents for a puppy …'

Jake nodded, not at all surprised.

'But now she's been badgering her parents for an Olive!'

Jake laughed.

'Unfortunately, an Old English Sheepdog in their two-bedroomed house … well, there just isn't the space.'

Jake nodded.

'I think they're worried what will happen when Nick's job finishes at the new development in Aviemore, and he leaves, taking Olive with him.'

Jake remembered meeting Nick in that clearing. They were building something in the woods. He hadn't sounded sure what exactly would be built there, even though he had been tasked with overseeing the preparations for building work to commence. Jake said, 'I'm sure he'll be around for some time yet.'

Gayle said, 'Let's hope so. I've kind of got used to having him around. Both him and Marty, actually.'

Jake pursed his lips, recalling what he'd done for Marty when he'd met him gardening in the grounds of The Lake House and had discovered that the Ross Corporation hadn't been paying him for his work since he'd taken on his father's gardening business when his father had retired. Unbelievably, it had turned out that Robyn had been paying for him to continue looking after the grounds of The Lake House.

But he'd wanted to set things straight, and give Marty backpay for his work, and a bonus. He'd ended up giving him more than that. Marty clearly hadn't yet told Gayle about his conversation with Jake, and Jake's decision to buy Marty the show home on the new housing development where Nick was site manager.

William was still paying Jake handsomely for the work he was not now doing at the Ross Corporation. It wasn't that Jake was in the habit of just giving money away. But Marty was effectively an employee of the Ross Corporation. William always looked after his own, but this time he hadn't. Nobody had. Even though Marty had been being paid by Robyn – he wouldn't have been able to continue the work if nobody had paid him at all – Jake still felt he owed him. And Marty, who had effectively been made homeless after his parents had retired and moved away, and a room in a friend's house had fallen through, hadn't had a hope of getting on the housing ladder. Now he had a home of his own. He just had to tell his friend Gayle that, some time soon, he would be moving out of the guesthouse.

Jake changed the subject. 'I'd still like to meet Robyn.' Jake had said that the last time he'd been there. He still wondered if it was Robyn who had moved back into Lark Lodge.

Gayle said, 'And I'm sure you will. Now, why don't you get settled in?'

Jake nodded, but he did have a question. 'You want to show me around the house sometime?' After seeing Eleanor's old doll's house in the basement of The Lake House, and noticing the striking similarities with Lark Lodge, Jake was very interested to see just how much more of her design had been used by Robyn in the restoration of Lark Lodge.

In answer to his question, Gayle flashed Jake a smile.

Jake took that as an affirmative. 'I'll hold you to that,' he said. He walked into the room and put his bag on the bed. He was still intrigued as to who was now in the room he'd been staying in only the previous day – the one that was usually reserved for friends.

Jake walked over to the attic window and looked across Gayle's gorgeous back garden, which was a smaller version of his own garden, over her garden wall. The grounds of The Lake House. He stared at the familiar house.

He hadn't planned on sticking around Aviemore any longer than he had to. Scotland was a big place. There were plenty of other areas to explore that wouldn't come with painful memories of the previous Christmas. But Jake had a plan. To move on with his life, it was time to put the past, and what had happened that Christmas, well and truly behind him.

A knock on the door startled Jake out of his reverie. He turned around and walked to the door, opening it.

Gayle pointed. 'I forgot to ask. Do want some ice for that?'

Jake's hand involuntarily moved to the side of his face – it felt tender and hot to the touch where Marcus had punched him in the face. He'd hoped Gayle wouldn't notice. But how could she not? He hadn't looked in a mirror, but he didn't have to. He knew he'd have a black eye in the morning. He'd felt the welt getting bigger on the side of his face where Marcus's knuckle had caught him during the blow. Jake didn't blame him. He just wished Marcus had punched him in the face months ago. Of course, it was over Eleanor, and Jake refusal to come to terms with the fact that she hadn't died on that mountain. What had happened had been far worse.

Jake momentarily closed his eyes, as if that would erase the memory.

'I'll be right back.' Gayle closed the door.

3

Jake opened the drawers in the sideboard and unzipped his bag. He was going to unpack this time. He deposited his clothes neatly in the deep drawers and folded his jacket over the easy chair by the window, by which time Gayle had reappeared. It had turned out that there was no ice. Jake closed the bedroom door and sat down on the end of the bed. He put the small pack of frozen peas wrapped in a cloth to the side of his face and winced. A few moments later, he put the peas down and picked up his mobile phone. He was not looking forward to this conversation.

She answered straight away.

'Faye.' Jake sighed; it was good to hear her voice, even though he'd only spoken to her an hour earlier on his way back there from the airport. She hadn't been answering his calls, so Marcus had said he'd sort it out. Jake hadn't expected that Marcus would be able to get her to phone him. But he had. He'd told Faye that Jake was returning to the Ross Corporation. She'd been straight on the phone to him, shocked. Marcus hadn't told her that it was only for one or two weeks, the summer at most, while Marcus checked into the rehab clinic. Jake had reassured her he'd be back to school for the start of the new academic year in September.

What he'd failed to tell her was that he probably wasn't going to be flying home the next day. He'd promised he was only staying another night, but after his conversation with Marcus, Jake had a feeling he'd need more time. He'd also told her something else he shouldn't have – at least not over the phone. It was concerning what he and Marcus intended to do as soon as Marcus got out of rehab. They were going to go and see Eleanor. It had just slipped out in conversation.

He could tell Faye thought he'd lost his mind when he'd told her Eleanor had survived the skiing accident. All along, she had been under the misapprehension that he was a widower. He'd also told her he didn't want to go into specifics over the phone. Fortunately, Natty had been in the background, haranguing her mum to let her speak to him, so he hadn't had to. The last thing Faye had said to him earlier was that she missed him terribly and that he had better be coming back very soon.

Jake sighed heavily down the phone.

Unfortunately, Faye heard him. 'Is everything all right? Don't tell me that your flight tomorrow has been cancelled.'

'Look, about that—'

'You're not coming back, are you?' Faye said flatly.

Jake took a deep breath. 'Not tomorrow, no. Look I need more time.'

'It's about Eleanor, isn't it?'

'Yes,' Jake said in a small voice. 'You know I said I didn't want to go into specifics about the accident over the phone. But the fact is, Marcus and I … well, we had a huge falling-out over what happened up on that mountain at the time. He was convinced someone else was up there with us when we were skiing off-piste. I didn't believe him.'

'Why was that fact so important?' Faye asked gently.

'There was an avalanche. There was no warning of one when we went skiing up there, no hint that anything of that nature would occur, otherwise we would not have skied on Christmas Day. Then it happened, and we got buried in the snow – well, Eleanor and I did. But Marcus dug me out first. That's what I'd assumed. How could I not? If only he'd dug her out first, then she wouldn't be—'

Jake halted. 'All along, he said there was someone else up there with them, must have been, because he said it wasn't him who dug me out and then Eleanor.'

'And you didn't believe him.'

'Of course not. He was just lying. At least that's what I thought all along, until …' Jake picked up the peas and held them to his sore eye again. 'Well, until Marcus made me see sense. Eleanor was … is … his sister, after all. Although he and I, we're best friends, like brothers, Eleanor is his family, his sister. He'd have dug her out first, I just know it.' Jake sighed. 'I think I just needed someone to blame, when I really should blame myself for not stopping her going skiing.'

There was an uncomfortable silence.

Faye said, 'Take as much time as you need. I'll tell Natty something came up, and you won't be back as soon as we hoped.'

'Oh, god! I forgot about Natty.'

'She'll be fine. As long as you're coming back …' She let the sentence hang.

'Of course I'm coming back. I just need a few days. I've booked in here for six nights, but I'll be back sooner, if I can.'

'Is there anything I can do?'

Jake smiled. The fact that she'd answered her phone to him was more than enough, and she'd been understanding that he'd reneged on his promise to return to London when he said he would.

'You've done more than enough.'

Faye disagreed. 'But I haven't done anything.'

'You've been understanding. Especially after I blurted what I did about Eleanor.'

'It's okay, Jake. We all deal with grief in different ways. Someone doesn't have to die to mourn the life that was taken away from you.'

Jake nodded. Of course she understood. He imagined she was talking from experience. She'd been in love with Natty's father, Yousaf, and although they'd never married, she'd thought she'd have a life with him, there in England. He'd been a foreign student from a wealthy family in Oman, but Faye hadn't wanted to return with him to live in his country. She'd had a life, a career, and wanted to bring up their toddler daughter in England.

Unfortunately, the pressure to return home to his family abroad had clearly been too much for Yousaf, so he had returned, but not before attempting to take Natty with him, ostensibly just to visit his family. Jake had been so angry when Faye had told him she'd discovered Yousaf had bought one-way tickets for himself and Natty. He hadn't been intending to bring her back. The trip with his daughter had not gone ahead, and he had returned to Oman alone. Inevitably, the relationship between them had broken down completely. Correspondence followed in which Yousaf apologised profusely for what his family had forced him to do. Although Faye had forgiven him, Yousaf had not seen his daughter since she was three – six years earlier.

Jake thought that it was for the best. What if it happened again? Yousaf had promised it wouldn't, but that hadn't stopped Faye moving around, in the beginning, so he wouldn't find them if he returned to England. All that was now behind them, though, and they were settled in their house. Natty was settled in her school, and Faye in her job.

Thinking of school, and missing the last few days of term, Jake asked Faye how things were going at work.

'I'm suffocating under a mountain of paperwork,' she said sullenly, 'and it's not even mine!'

Jake pursed his lips. He knew what she was referring to. He remembered the state of his in-tray. As his mentor while he was training, she was responsible for his work. 'Well, I wanted to make sure you were too busy to miss me while I'm away.'

'Don't worry – I'll make sure I return the favour,' said Faye, 'with knobs on.'

Jake kicked off his shoes and threw his legs onto the bed, enjoying the banter. God, I miss her, he thought. He smiled, then plumped a cushion and leaned back into it. 'Is Natty okay?'

'She's fine. It's the last day of term tomorrow, so I expect she's going to enjoy the fact that there won't be much schoolwork going on, just fun and games, and a movie in the hall for the whole primary school in the afternoon.'

'Sounds fun,' Jake said, smiling.

There was an awkward silence. 'Look I've got a lot to do at work, so …' she trailed off.

Jake noticed that the easy familiar banter had disappeared at the mention of Natty. She was obviously still a sore point. So, he'd bought her too many toys, and had been thinking of getting her a puppy, although he'd kept that thought to himself. Although Jake knew he had been spoiling her, he couldn't help thinking it really was no big deal. It was definitely a big deal for Faye, though. She had never had to share her daughter's affections until now, and Jake was wondering what the consequences of that would be.

They hadn't properly cleared the air regarding that debacle. It wasn't something Jake wanted to bring up over the phone. But he did want to talk about that elephant in the room, because he was still afraid of losing Faye and Natty.

He did want to be completely honest with Faye from that point on. No more hiding things. 'Look, there's another reason I need to stay here for a bit.'

'Jake, it's fine. You don't have to tell me what—'

'I want to. I need to,' Jake blurted. He frowned, thinking, do I sound desperate? Desperate to remain in her good books, for fear of losing her again? Damn right he did – and he knew it.

He said, 'This guy phoned me out of the blue asking me to help him. Martha had some letters. Turns out she needed help finding her son. That's how I ended up deciding to come back here in the first place.'

'Who?'

Jake didn't want to get into the fact that this guy had been impersonating Martha's husband. Instead, he said, 'It turns out that Martha is Aubrey's sister.'

'Aubrey. He's a bit of an enigma, isn't he?'

Jake raised his eyebrows. That was certainly one way of putting it. Faye had only met him once, but she'd cottoned on to that too. With Aubrey, you never really got to the truth of who he was – his background. All Jake had known about him was that he'd worked for the Rosses for decades, and it had turned out his name, Aubrey Jones, was fictitious. Jake told Faye that.

'Now, why does that not surprise me in the least?'

Jake's mouth curled up in a smile. He hadn't been smiling,

though, when he'd realised that after he'd left the Ross Corporation, William had told Aubrey to babysit him, follow him around, check he was okay. After his initial annoyance, he'd reasoned that it was understandable. Jake was now working in a tough inner-city school, biking to work through not overly salubrious areas of London. William was worried for him, for his safety. After what had happened to Eleanor, he didn't want to lose Jake too.

Jake suddenly had a thought. What if Faye knew about Aubrey's activities? After all, she had spent some time talking to Marcus in his house, and then Aubrey had arrived. If she'd found out that Aubrey had been following Jake around, she would know that he might have been following him when he was looking after Natty, taking her to the park, to his house. She didn't know who this guy was. He was harmless – on paper. Just a sweet old guy who had known Jake since he was a child, and who Jake was very, very fond of. But Faye didn't know him from Adam, and he could just imagine she would not take kindly at all to the discovery.

Jake didn't want to think about that. The fact was that if Aubrey had been following him around, he hadn't followed him to Scotland. It was the one place that Aubrey refused to return to. And now Jake knew why. Ralph Delaney, or Aubrey Jones as he was now known, had fallen out with his father, Angus Delaney, many, many years earlier, and never returned to claim his inheritance – the mansion, Cedar Grove.

'His real name is Ralph Delaney.'

'Oh, okay. Have you asked him?'

'Who?'

'Aubrey – about his nephew? He might know where Martha's son is.'

That had occurred to Jake. When he'd visited Martha, who had Alzheimer's and only had rare lucid moments, he'd thought that Aubrey must know about her son – where he was, where Jake could find him. But of course, he'd thought, things were never that simple.

Jake sighed. 'I'm afraid it might be a little bit more complicated than that. You see, Martha never married Ralph's father. I think she gave him up as a baby.'

'Ah, so you're saying Aubrey might never have known about him.'

'That is a possibility.'

'Well, the only way to find out is to ask him.'

Jake nodded. That was true. But it was sensitive. It wasn't something he wanted to broach over the phone. He'd have to meet up with Aubrey in person to raise that sort of delicate subject. What if he'd never known he had a nephew?

'I could ask Marcus to speak to Aubrey,' suggested Faye.

'No. Don't do that. I'd rather talk to him myself when I return to London.'

'Can you do anything for Martha about finding her son in the meantime, while you're in Scotland?'

Jake thought about that. 'I can return to visit her.' He was hoping he might catch her during one of her more lucid moments, and with luck she might be able to tell him more about her son and her brother.

'I'm sure she'd like to see you again. I imagine having visitors is very important at that age, stuck in a care home.'

Jake chose not to go into detail regarding the fact that although it was a care home, she had an apartment all to herself, decorated as though it was still the home she'd grown up in.

Somebody had had the idea to turn part of the house into expensive apartments for those that could afford them.

Jake agreed with Faye's sentiments, although he doubted that Martha would remember his visits. But he did have another idea.

Jake winced in anticipation of the backlash. 'Actually, Faye, I need a favour.'

'Which is?' Faye said slowly.

'I have a photograph, presumably of her son, Ralph. I could do with finding out if it can be dated. Really, any information about the photo would be helpful.' Jake had an idea that Martha's son was in his thirties, but even so, he was hoping Faye's father could take a look. Perhaps he could shed some light on Martha's son. Although he was retired from the police force, Jake imagined he still had friends in the police who might do him a favour.

The problem was that Faye was estranged from her father, Patrick. Jake sat there, holding his breath, wondering what Faye would say to his request. She hadn't spoken to Patrick in a long time and refused to let him see her daughter. It all stemmed from the fact that Patrick and Faye had fallen out over her break-up with Yousaf, whom Patrick had got on very well with, apparently. Furthermore, he'd thought Faye was overreacting, and didn't believe Yousaf would have attempted to take Natty.

'Jake. I know you made a promise to Martha. But you need to get some rest and relaxation too – that's what you're supposed to be doing on holiday.'

Jake wondered if she was avoiding the subject of contacting Patrick on his behalf. Or perhaps she didn't realise that was what he was asking of her.

She fell silent for a moment before exclaiming, 'Hold on. Are you asking me to contact …' she trailed off.

Jake hesitated and took a deep breath before he spoke. Now he expected Faye would just hang up on him once she realised who he was going to ask her to contact. 'Your father.'

'You remember I'm barely on speaking terms with him?'

Now she was whispering down the phone, and Jake could just about hear her over the din of the staffroom. It was late afternoon, and she'd be there for some time yet, catching up on paperwork while Natty was in an after-school club.

'Yes, of course I remember.'

'I'll ask one of his friends who still works in the police to see if he can help.'

'Really? I didn't know you kept in touch with your father's friends.'

'Of course I do. Just because I've fallen out with my dad, it doesn't mean I'm not on speaking terms with some of his friends from work. They've known me my whole life.'

Jake grinned. 'Great, thank you.'

'The guy I know has been in the force for years. He is our police liaison officer for the area – and comes into the school on a regular basis to talk to the kids about drugs and gangs. I suppose he could look into it as a missing person's case. I'm not sure. I presume he'd have to ask his boss.'

Jake hesitated. He hadn't expected Faye to say yes. Now he was having doubts as to whether he should be involving the police. He fell silent, debating what to do. Martha's son, the boy in the photo, was called Ralph, clearly named after his uncle, but Aubrey was using a false name – had done for years. Jake could only speculate as to his reasons. Perhaps it was simply the case that he'd fallen out with his father and, having chosen to disappear, he'd had to change his name so the executors of his father's will could not track him down. Perhaps he just wanted a fresh start and to leave his past behind. The problem was that Jake didn't know what he'd done with the intervening years between leaving the boarding school and hooking up with William and the Ross Corporation.

Although Jake was curious himself, did he really want to arouse the curiosity of the police? Who knew what they might find if they started digging around into Martha's past, and by extension, her brother's? He didn't want them to do that; just to see if they could find the whereabouts of her son.

Faye said, 'Obviously he might not be able to help if it's not really a missing person case. You did say you think her son was adopted as a baby. Wouldn't that be social services, or some adoption register that would hold those details?'

Jake hadn't thought of that.

'You said you had a photo. If you text me the photo I will ask him when I see him next, see what he says.'

On the one hand, Jake thought that for the sake of the company, for the sake of William and Marcus, he couldn't afford whatever dodgy past Aubrey might be concealing to come out now, just when things might finally be getting back to some semblance of normality. But what if this boy, Ralph, was a missing person, and was in some police database? However unlikely that was, it was still worth a try. Jake had enough on his plate, both with trying to find out what had really happened when they had been skiing the previous Christmas, and with the promise he'd made to Marcus to return to the Ross Corporation while he checked into rehab. He could have done without having Martha's wish to find her son on his plate too.

Jake made up his mind. 'I'll text you the photo.' She said, 'I can't make any promises—'

'It's fine, Faye. I appreciate it's the end of term, and you've got a million things to get done before the summer holidays …'

'I'll find the time to give him a call. I'll let you know what, if anything, he can do.'

'Thank you, Faye.' He didn't really anticipate that Martha's son would show up on a police database. He just hoped Martha's brother didn't show up on a police database instead. Jake frowned, wishing Martha's son and brother didn't have the same name. He didn't want to think about that. Faye was probably right. By the sound of things, it was more likely Martha's son had been registered with an adoption agency, and it had involved the family courts. Jake wasn't family. He wouldn't have access to what he imagined were closed adoption records. So far, Faye's contact was the only official channel he had access to, and he reasoned that it might be a shot in the dark, but it was worth a try.

'I just hope this doesn't get back to my dad,' Jake heard her mumble.

Jake acted like he hadn't heard that comment. He imagined she would not want her father thinking that because she'd been in contact with one of his old friends, that opened the door to resuming their relationship. He hoped she didn't change her mind about the favour.

'Is Marcus with you?' She'd only met him one time, but the slight inflection in her voice gave her away; her concern for Marcus was evident.

The question surprised him. 'No,' he said gruffly. It still got his hackles up – this apparent interest in Marcus. 'I thought he told you that he was checking into a rehab clinic?'

'Yes. I just wasn't sure when.'

Jake said irritably. 'In fact,' he glanced at his watch, 'at this very moment he's on the flight to London.' Jake didn't know why he was telling her all this. 'Look,' Jake picked up the pack of peas, which were now soggy, and put them down again. His head was still throbbing, but the peas weren't going to do any good. 'Why all the sudden interest in Marcus? You only met him at my house the other day.' Of all the people he could have turned to for help when he was arrested and thrown in a cell, why had Marcus phoned Faye?

Jake though that they must have hit it off. Now things made sense, like the way Marcus had turned up at his house, aware of his intended holiday. There was only one possible explanation. 'You told him, didn't you?' said Jake irritably. 'You told him about my holiday.' Jake didn't know why he was suddenly making a big deal about it. After all, Marcus had already told him that fact. And if it wasn't for Marcus giving her a call, he realised he wouldn't be on the phone to her at all. She'd still be avoiding his calls. Jake bit his lip, wishing he hadn't said anything.

'Marcus looked so unhappy.'

'You saw Marcus again?' Jake said in surprise. 'When?'

'It was later that day, after you'd found Marcus at your house, and you slipped on the glass from the broken door. You know … when I returned to work without you.'

Jake shook his head. How could he forget? That was why he was on an enforced holiday before the end of the school term.

'Yes, we kind of bumped into each other and he said he really needed to see you, Jake, speak to you, but you wouldn't return his calls.'

'You bumped into each other,' Jake said flatly, thinking sarcastically that it was a likely story. Of course he believed Faye, but Marcus didn't just bump into people.

Faye said, 'It was after school. He drove past as I was leaving work. He waved and pulled over.'

Jake sighed heavily. Since when did the route from the Ross Corporation's skyscraper building in the city – where employees of the Ross Corporation, including the executive directors, lived – to the London head office in Canary Wharf take you past an inner-city school?

Jake couldn't believe Marcus had been trying to get to him through Faye. He'd succeeded: Faye had told him that Jake was going on holiday. The thought had crossed his mind that perhaps there was nothing going on between them. Instead, Marcus was just using her to get to him. He didn't like either scenario.

'So, I just thought I was doing you and Marcus a favour.'

'Me and Marcus … or just Marcus?' said Jake with an edge to his voice.

'What are you talking about, Jake?' Her voice sounded more reasonable than he deserved.

He wished he'd shut his mouth. He was afraid that his friendship with Faye was slipping away under Marcus's influence. Marcus and Faye talking to one another was bugging him, big time.

Jake raised his eyebrows, wondering why he was feeling jealous. Marcus had a fiancée – Lydia.

He closed his eyes, his hand grasping his mobile phone, and had a revelation; Marcus had taken Eleanor away from him and now he was going to take Faye from him too. 'I've got to go,' he said. He put the phone down.

He had the sudden urge to haul himself to the airport, get on the first flight back to London and confront Marcus. Instead, the urge passed as quickly as it had come. Jake calmed down. He was overreacting. It had been one hell of a long day, and he was exhausted. He stood up and walked over to the window. He stared at Gayle's back garden, his eyes roving to the rooftop of The Lake House. He shook his head. 'I'm an idiot.' Marcus wasn't trying to take Faye away from him. Marcus was the one who had promised him he'd get Faye to call. And it had worked.

'And now like the idiot I am, I've ruined my chance.' He hoped that wasn't the case. He had an impulse to call her back right away and apologise. The trouble was that he was afraid she wouldn't answer the phone to him after his rude outburst.

Just phone her.

His thoughts drifted to Marcus instead as he stared out of the window, his attention drawn to Cairngorm Mountain. Even in summer, the peak could be snow-capped, but this summer, although he could still see snow, it was patchy rather than the traditional snow-capped mountain he was used to.

The mountain reminded him what he was still doing there. All along, he'd thought Marcus had taken Eleanor away from him by choosing to dig him out of the snow first, but now Marcus had almost convinced him there had been someone else up there. He was determined to find out if Marcus had been telling the truth all along.

4

Jake heard someone knocking on his bedroom door. His eyes shot open. He looked at his phone, which was still in his hand, to check the time. He'd only sat down on his bed and closed his eyes for a moment, but had then felt himself sinking back into the very soft, feathery pillows. That had obviously been a mistake. He imagined the knock was Gayle, asking him to join her for dinner.

'Just a sec.'

'Mr Campbell-Ross?' A man's voice called back.

Jake raised his eyebrows. He pulled on his shoes, walked to the door and opened it.

'You remember me? From the forest on the edge of town?' The young guy smiled at Jake as he held out his hand. 'Nick Addison.'

'I remember,' said Jake wearily, grasping the man's hand. He was in no mood to be in the company of some bright-eyed, bushy-tailed, life-is-oh-so-wonderful young man. Although he knew Nick had been staying at the guesthouse the previous night when he was there too, before he had left for the airport, Jake had missed dinner in Gayle's kitchen with the rest of the house guests, and he'd missed breakfast too. It meant that he hadn't actually seen Nick since bumping into him in the woods, when he'd suggested that Jake could stay at Lark Lodge. Nick had been wearing a smart suit and a yellow hard hat then. This evening, he was in jogging bottoms and a grey sweatshirt with the name of a university emblazoned on the front.

Jake looked past him, expecting Olive to be bounding up the stairs. 'Where's Olive?'

'Oh, she's shut in the kitchen with Gayle. Muddy paws. I couldn't have her bounding up the stairs after me, leaving muddy paw prints on Gayle's new carpet. And you know what my dog is like. She would have had muddy paws all over you too. We can't have that, can we?'

'Of course not,' Jake said, although he wouldn't have really minded seeing Nick's shaggy sheepdog bounding up the stairs, greeting him as though she hadn't seen him in an age, when it had only been a matter of hours.

'Ooo … that looks nasty,' Nick pointed.

Jake wasn't surprised that Nick had spotted the large welt forming on his temple, and the black eye. 'I walked into a door.'

'Of course you did.' Nick grinned. He wasn't fooled. It was obvious Jake had walked into a fist. 'Gayle was out of ice; I suggested the frozen peas – any good?'

'Kind of,' said Jake, feeling upset that Gayle had shared his unfortunate comeuppance even though she didn't know the details.

'I expect you'll see Olive at dinner time.'

Jake smiled at the thought.

'Please tell her off if she begs at the table.'

I'll do no such thing, Jake thought. In fact, he probably wouldn't be able to resist feeding her scraps from the table. He kept that thought to himself.

'On that note, Gayle sent me up to see if you're wanting dinner here this evening.' He leaned towards Jake, whispering, 'I wouldn't recommend it myself.'

'Why?' Jake wasn't in the mood for polite conversation, so he was going to make every effort not to be congenial.

'Oh, right. I didn't realise you hadn't dined here yet.'

Jake had eaten dinner at the guesthouse just the previous night, but Nick did not know that. As he'd arrived back at the guesthouse late, after the other guests had dined, he'd had dinner with Gayle instead. She'd waited for him to return and had then served up a ready meal from the freezer. He already knew that home cooking wasn't Gayle's forte.

'No ready meals this evening,' Nick elaborated. 'She's cooking tonight.' He pulled a grimace and then laughed infectiously.

Jake, despite his foul mood, felt the corners of his mouth twitch. He slowly shook his head at the young man, excited about everything and nothing – about life. Jake remembered what that felt like – just. He managed a smile. 'So, I take it you've experienced the delights of her cooking before?'

'Oh yes. And once is quite enough, I can tell you.' He peered at Jake. 'So, are you still up for it, or do you want to grab a takeaway with me?'

Jake shuddered at the thought of fast food. Besides, given the way he was feeling, he thought his brain would melt if he had to keep up with young Mr Addison. Jake declined. 'I think I'll risk it.'

'Brave man,' Nick replied. He turned to go, but almost as an afterthought, he glanced back at Jake and asked, 'Was I right – about the guesthouse being nice and all?'

Jake nodded. 'You just neglected to mention the food.'

'Well, enjoy your meal.' He gave Jake a knowing wink. 'I'll let

Gayle know you'll be joining them for dinner. Oh, and if you need anything, just knock,' he said. 'I'm right next door.'

Jake watched him enter the attic bedroom next door and emerge two seconds later wearing a coat. 'I'm going to get that takeaway in Aviemore. Dinner is at seven, by the way.'

Jake watched him dash down the stairs. Seeing Nick reminded him that there was another reason Marcus had been anxious to return to London. When they'd bumped into Nick in a clearing in the forest where the old lodge with rooms to rent had once stood, they'd discovered he was preparing the site so that building could start. Bizarrely, Nick hadn't even been sure what was being built. But what had really piqued both Jake's and Marcus's interest was that apparently the Ross Corporation was building something 'hush hush' on the land. But Nick Addison did not work for the Ross Corporation.

Perhaps they'd contracted out to another company, which would be most unusual. Or perhaps it was just a local rumour that someone had started. After all, it was Lawrence, the receptionist at Cedar Lodge, who had mentioned it. But it was something neither of them could ignore. Nothing went ahead without Marcus's say-so. If the Ross Corporation was building something without Marcus's knowledge, it meant only one thing – Marcus was losing his grip.

Marcus was checking his side of things back in London, but Jake decided to go on his own fact-finding mission and see if he couldn't wheedle more information out of young Nick Addison; see what he now knew about what was planned for the building site. And this was his opportunity to do just that. Jake decided that the information might be worth risking an evening meal consisting of fast food.

'Wait!' Jake rushed forward and looked over the banister. He heard the front door click shut; Nick was already gone. His throbbing head told him that dashing down the stairs after him was not an option. Questioning Nick would have to wait. Jake turned into his room and closed the door. His attention was drawn back to his phone.

He picked it up off the bed, debating whether to ring Faye back and apologise for his unreasonable behaviour on the phone. But was it unreasonable? Had Faye and Marcus been talking about him behind his back? He couldn't decide. He sat for a long moment in the limbo land of indecision, staring at his phone. Then he sighed and put the phone on the bedside cabinet. Apologies led to explanations, and Jake decided he wasn't in the mood for either.

He put his feet up on the bed and leaned into the plump feather pillow cushioning his back. He yawned and stretched his arms wide. He looked at his watch; he had half an hour until dinner. He was going to keep his eyes open this time.

From his vantage point on the bed, Jake took a good look around his new quarters. The room was vastly different to the one downstairs; it was light, bright and airy, with white walls and modern furniture suggesting a minimalist approach. Jake tried to recall the detail of the tiny rooms in the doll's house, but he doubted that this room was based on Eleanor's designs.

It was all conjecture anyway, whether Robyn had copied designs from the doll's house – whether she had even seen it. It could have been a coincidence. But thinking of Marty, Jake doubted that very much. It made perfect sense; what other reason would a complete stranger pay for Marty to look after the gardens of his house? She was feeling guilty for copying those intricate interiors that Eleanor had fashioned as a child when she'd ripped out the interior of her doll's house and set about redesigning it.

He turned his head, catching a glimpse of the gardens and, off to the right, the roofline of his own house. It made him think about the business he had there the next day. It made him think about Marcus. 'Maybe I should have got on that plane with him.' Jake closed his eyes.

Marcus. The same questions were swirling around his head like a broken record. What if Marcus had been right and there had been someone else with them on that mountain on that day? What if someone else had in fact made the choice of who to dig out first, just as Marcus had been saying all along? But if that were true, then who were they? And why hadn't they come forward and made their presence known? It wasn't as if they hadn't had plenty of opportunity; the place was literally buzzing with news journalists citing a 'freak' avalanche, reporting in their terse journalistic prose, printing their sensationalist, attention-grabbing headlines: Ski tragedy strikes construction entrepreneur's family – in the full knowledge that money and tragedy combined well to sell newspapers.

Didn't everybody want their five minutes of fame? Surely, if somebody else had been there, had dug them out from the snow, they'd have come forward to take the credit. He could see the headline: Local hero saves the Rosses! Why hadn't they? Why hadn't they made themselves known in anticipation of some financial reward? The newspapers would have paid handsomely for their side of the story. It didn't make any sense.

Jake felt himself drifting off in a sea of confusion.

5

'Jake.' A gentle tapping at the door followed his name.

'Yeah,' Jake opened his eyes.

'Dinner will be in ten,' Gayle called from behind the closed door.

Jake sat up and tossed his legs over the edge of the bed. He rubbed his eyes, wishing he hadn't told Nick he was joining Gayle for dinner. He felt like crawling under the covers and calling it a night. He dragged himself to the bathroom. He splashed cold water on his face and looked in the mirror. His short, cropped blonde hair was standing on end on the side he'd lain on while napping. Jake patted his hair with his sopping wet bandage.

He unwound both bandages. The scabs showed they were finally healing; he'd just have to be careful not to open them up again. Jake had a fresh roll of bandages and carefully bandaged them again. Hopefully it wouldn't be long before he could dispense with the bandages altogether.

Jake patted his hair one last time, tutting at his reflection in the mirror. He looked at the shower, then at his watch. It was too late to have a shower; he was already late for dinner.

Jake hastily closed the bedroom door behind him and rushed

down the stairs, gearing up to apologise profusely to Gayle. After all, she was going out of her way to cook that night.

Approaching the bottom of the stairs, he heard voices, male and female, coming from the kitchen. Jake instinctively slowed.

'I think you should just tell her how you feel.' Gayle's voice carried from the kitchen.

'But it's never the right time. Besides, it's probably nothing.'

'Probably nothing?' Gayle said haughtily. 'Then why are you here, asking me if she's spoken to me, and wondering if there's something going on she hasn't told you about?'

Jake frowned. Was Gayle talking to Nick? Jake thought he'd left to get a takeaway in Aviemore. Surely, he couldn't have been and come back so quickly.

Jake walked slowly down the last few stairs. He hoped a stair would creak loudly to announce his presence. Failing that, he'd have to fake a coughing fit, because by the sound of it they were talking about problems in his personal life.

'Look, I'm sure everything is fine. She's got a commission to do a job in London, that's all.'

'Yes, I know. But why did she have to take it? She's got plenty of work around here. I thought once we moved into the boathouse together ...'

'Look, I'm sure you're reading way too much into those trips. You're not thinking she's meeting up with someone else, are you? She's in love with you.'

Jake resorted to the coughing fit, hoping he hadn't overdone it. The conversation in the kitchen stopped abruptly.

'Changed your mind about that takeaway?' said Jake, walking into the kitchen, trying to act as though he hadn't heard a word. He stopped in the doorway and looked at Gayle, standing by the stove with a wooden spoon in her hand and a bright apron tied around her waist, and then at the unfamiliar man seated at the table.

They were both staring back at him in silence.

'Excuse me,' said Jake feeling very embarrassed. 'I heard voices as I walked down the stairs, and I assumed Nick had changed his mind and decided to join us for dinner.'

Gayle waved her spoon at the table, sending a spray of brownish sauce in the air. 'Jake, meet David,' she said nonchalantly. She turned her attention back to the contents of a large saucepan simmering on the stove.

Jake held out his hand to a guy who was around about his own age. David clasped his hand briefly and then lowered his head, staring forlornly at the table.

Jake sat down opposite him. David. He recognised the name. He was Gayle's friend, and Robyn's fiancé. By the sound of the conversation he'd just overheard, they were having relationship issues.

Jake's thoughts turned to Faye. Now he wished he'd called her straight back after ending the call so abruptly.

Determining that the guy wasn't in the mood for polite conversation, Jake turned in his chair. 'Sorry I'm late for dinner, Gayle. Can you believe I must have dozed off?'

Gayle glanced over her shoulder. 'I guess it took more out of you than you thought, coming back here.'

'I guess it did,' said Jake, catching Gayle glance past him with an almost imperceptible shake of the head. Jake turned back to find that David was frowning at Gayle with a look of incomprehension on his face.

'My wife had a tragic accident here.' Jake raised his eyebrows, surprised he'd found himself telling David that.

'I'm sorry for your loss,' said David sincerely.

Jake opened his mouth to explain but simply said, 'It was some time ago now,' in a lame attempt to wave it away. He did not want to cast a mood over dinner, although looking at David, Jake felt that the mood was already cast, and it was very black indeed.

'Time doesn't heal, no matter what they say,' David said glumly, dark eyes staring fixedly at Jake.

'No, it doesn't.' Jake held David's gaze, wondering what exactly he was referring to. Seeing as everybody seemed to be in the spirit of sharing all of a sudden, Jake threw caution to the wind and ventured a guess out loud. 'Your wife?'

In the uncomfortable silence that followed, Jake realised that the spirit of sharing had obviously taken flight at such a direct question, but that he had nevertheless hit the nail on the head. Jake opened his mouth to attempt a pathetic back-track.

Gayle intervened to stop him making a complete fool of himself. 'David and Robyn are having some relationship issues. At least, that's what David thinks …'

David frowned at her. 'Thank you, Gayle, for sharing that with all and sundry.'

'Well, it's true, isn't it?' Gayle shot back.

'I'm sorry,' Jake said meekly, really wishing he hadn't opened his big mouth. Now Jake understood why the room that Gayle reserved for her friends was occupied. It sounded as though Robyn was in London, and David had made an impromptu visit to speak to Gayle. He was having dinner. He must be staying the night.

'OK, yeah, I think Robyn and I are having some relationship issues, as you put it.' David suddenly stood up from the table. 'But that doesn't mean it's my fault.'

'I didn't say it was,' said Gayle. 'However, maybe it wouldn't hurt to—'

'Don't start with the self-help psycho-babble crap!' David exclaimed. 'I am not interested in using that room!' He sat back down and pointed his finger towards the kitchen door.

Jake cast his eyes in the direction of the hallway. He knew exactly what David was referring to. Gayle had turned her late father's study – this had been her childhood home – into a room for relaxation, meditation, and reading from her extensive collection of self-help books.

Gayle put her hands on her hips. 'What's wrong with that room?'

'Urrgh. Next, you'll be turning this place into some sort of wellness retreat.'

'The thought had crossed my mind.'

'You're joking.'

'No. The house is in a lovely setting, in gorgeous grounds, thanks to Marty …'

Jake looked about him, wondering where Marty was. Perhaps he was late for dinner too. Or maybe he was all too familiar with Gayle's cooking, and had decided on a takeaway too.

'But a wellness centre, for god's sake. What's wrong with it being a guesthouse?'

'Who said I was going to stop running the guesthouse?'

'But you just said …'

Jake looked from one to the other and decided to forego dinner. This was getting awkward. Jake got up.

'Sit down.' Gayle waved the wooden spoon at Jake.

He sat obediently.

'Now look here,' she pointed the spoon at David, 'you need

to speak to Robyn, tell her how you feel. I'm sure there's nothing going on apart from your imagination running wild.'

Jake looked at David, wondering why – if Jake was guessing correctly – he'd got it into his head that Robyn could be cheating on him.

'I don't need to tell her anything,' said David defiantly. 'She needs to talk to me. That's what I keep telling you. She needs to tell me what's going on.' He paused. 'Because there is something going on, Gayle. She keeps making these trips to London.'

Gale sighed. 'We just spoke about this. You know she's getting offered commissions all over the place. I've got to say, I can't believe how her business has taken off so quickly.'

Jake looked at Gayle, thinking of her friend's small interior design outlet in Mr Gillespie's store. Robyn certainly had done well. It couldn't have been open long. He didn't recall Robyn's Interior Design in Aviemore the previous Christmas.

'Yes, I know,' David said glumly. 'I can't understand it.'

'I can. There're a lot of second homes around these parts, a fair few of them owned by wealthy individuals who I imagine live in London.'

Jake felt like slinking down in his seat when David's eyes roved over to him. He avoided David's gaze.

Gayle continued, 'They've obviously liked her interior design work and given her commissions to work on their London homes.'

David's attention shifted back to Gayle, standing at the oven. Jake thought that whatever she was stirring in the big pot on the stove smelled really rather good.

'I thought we'd be spending time together in the boathouse, you know, after …'

Gayle glanced over her shoulder and grinned. 'I know. She told me all about it.' Gayle glanced at Jake. 'David and Robyn are engaged. David proposed on bended knee on the balcony of his boathouse that overlooks the loch. It's so romantic.'

Jake stole a glance at David. The look on his face said he wasn't in the mood to talk about it. Jake bet he wished she hadn't brought it up.

David shook his head. 'I thought that after that, we'd start planning our wedding, but she's more out than in. Now I wish she hadn't set up her outlet in Dad's shop.'

Jake raised his eyebrows. So, David was Mr Gillespie's son. He wondered if that was how David and Robyn had met, through his father's shop.

'Don't begrudge her this success. Just because you're—' She stopped abruptly.

David sat back in his chair and folded his arms. 'Just because I'm what?'

Gayle heaved a sigh. 'Just because your ice hockey career went south after your injury.'

Jake looked at the kitchen door, wishing Marty would get a move on and walk in. He was feeling very uncomfortable.

'David, you know she's been to London before to meet up with clients in their homes. Why are you making it such a big deal?'

'Because as you well know, I always go with her,' said David through clenched teeth. 'But just lately she's insisted on going to London alone. She doesn't want me with her. And these trips are getting more frequent, and …' He stopped abruptly.

Jake stole a glance at David; he was staring miserably at Gayle. His dark, wavy hair, swept back from his face, revealed equally dark eyes. 'I'm losing her, Gayle,' he said quietly, 'and I don't even know why.'

Gayle turned around to say something as David got up from the table. 'I'm not hungry,' he said, and abruptly left the room.

Jake and Gayle stared after him in silence. Jake heard the front door open, as did Gayle.

'David!' Gayle flew out of the room.

Jake stayed where he was, sitting alone in the kitchen listening to the hushed voices of Gayle and David in the hallway. He couldn't make out what they were saying, and he didn't want to. He had enough of his own problems. Jake picked up the wooden spoon from the table where Gayle had discarded it on her way out. He looked in the direction of the hallway, then got up and meandered over to the stove. He plunged the wooden spoon into the hotpot and stirred. A feeling of calm descended on him.

He missed home. He missed the pleasures of cooking in his own kitchen while listening to the radio – it was a great way to relax and unwind after a tough teaching day. Jake scooped up a little of the thick mixture in the wooden spoon and bent his head slightly to taste it. It wasn't as bad as Nick made out. Jake took another slurp. But then it wasn't that great either. Jake left the wooden spoon in the pot and quietly opened some cupboards. He knew what he was looking for. He just hoped she had some. Three cupboards along, Jake found the spices and sauces. Hunting through, he took out the condiments that might add a little flavour to Gayle's rather bland stew.

'What are you doing?' Gayle's voice startled Jake.

He turned to look at Gayle, wishing his arms weren't laden with bottles and jars.

Gayle was standing in the kitchen doorway, her arms folded. 'Were you going to mess with my stew? That's a special recipe, you know.'

Jake started to put them back in her cupboard. 'You can tell a lot about a person by the contents of their kitchen, do you know that?' said Jake, trying to lighten the mood.

'Is that a fact?' said Gayle.

Her deadpan tone of voice told Jake she was in no mood for banter. 'Gayle, I'm sorry about David. I don't think my presence helped.' Jake was one of those rich people from London.

'It's got nothing to do with you, Jake.'

Jake wasn't sure whether she meant it was none of his business or that it wasn't his fault her friend was upset. 'Do you still want my company for dinner?'

'Of course I do.' Gayle was adamant. 'Now give me those condiments.'

Jake handed them over and watched her put them back in the cupboard herself.

Jake sat back down at the table. He watched Gayle ladle the stew onto two large plates. She brought them over to the table one at a time.

Gayle sat and picked up her spoon. 'What's wrong?' Gayle noticed Jake hadn't touched his stew.

'I don't want David to miss this delicious meal on my account.' Jake looked up from his plate. 'I'll take this upstairs to eat. You call David back.' Jake got up.

'Will you just sit down and eat.' Gayle waved her spoon at him.

Jake sat and picked up his spoon.

'Besides he'll be back.'

'He will?' Jake moved his spoon back and forward in the thick stew, making tiny ripples.

'He's staying here – in the room you were in just last night.'

'Robyn's room?' said Jake, although he'd already guessed as

much. He just wasn't sure if David had changed his mind and decided not to stay at the guesthouse for the night after all.

'That's right; they normally stay there when they visit, even though they don't live far down the road. Except this time, he's alone.'

'Is she really in London?' Jake blurted, wondering if Gayle knew more than she was letting on and was covering for Robyn. The question was out of order, and he realised he was on first-name basis with somebody he hadn't even met. It was none of his business.

He was about to say as much when Gayle said, 'What makes you say that?'

Just rubbed his forehead. 'I'm sorry, just ignore me. It's been a long day.'

'For your information, yes, she is in London. I'm not covering for her, if that's what you think.'

Jake opened his mouth, but thought the better of saying anything further and putting his foot in it. 'Sorry,' he said in a small voice, and continued eating his stew.

Unfortunately, Gayle wasn't finished. 'She'll be back from London quite soon, I imagine.'

Jake recalled part of the conversation he had overheard coming down the stairs – something about Robyn setting off to London unexpectedly.

'Although she left in rather a hurry, according to David.' Gayle stared into space, thinking aloud. 'Little wonder David thought there was something going on because he's right, they usually go together. But by the sound of it, she was insistent she took the trip alone. I have no idea why.'

Jake continued eating his stew, keeping his thoughts to himself.

Namely, that she must be meeting someone that she didn't want David to know about.

'I expect her back in town sometime this week.'

'Really?' Jake was very pleased by this unexpected news; maybe he'd get to meet her.

Gayle pointed at her stew. 'I think I've surpassed myself this time. It's actually rather good.' Gayle was clearly surprised.

Jake put the spoon to his lips. 'Mmm … now this is a tasty stew.' Jake smiled. The condiments had worked.

6

Jake sipped his coffee and looked around the lounge. It was comfortably furnished with an assortment of soft furnishings and antiques that didn't match but made the room feel homely. It reminded Jake of the lounge in his own house, The Lake House, that the Rosses used as a holiday home, and where they all spent Christmas each year. It made him wonder what would happen next Christmas.

Fortunately, he didn't have to think about that. It was months away. But one thing he was certain of was that nobody would be spending Christmas in that house. Like at Gayle's house, the lounge at The Lake House overlooked the garden and contained odd bits of archaic furniture that had been passed down the generations on his father's side, almost making the lounge into a museum piece.

Jake's eyes settled on Gayle's mother, who was dozing in an armchair by the window. He could hear the occasional clatter of cutlery and crockery coming from the kitchen. Gayle had insisted that he should take his coffee into the lounge and leave her to do the dishes. He sipped his coffee and waited for Gayle to join him.

'There, that didn't take long.' Gayle appeared at the lounge doorway, her apron gone, a cup of coffee in hand.

'Now, where were we?' Gayle sat on the sofa opposite Jake.

'Marty,' Jake reminded her. He had asked Gayle where the young gardener was who was currently living at her guesthouse. It turned out he was having a night out with friends. 'I was telling you that I met up with Marty before I left for the airport. Then you booted me out of the kitchen.' Jake sounded hurt. 'I only offered to wipe up.'

'You're my guest, Jake.' Gayle rolled her eyes. 'Next you'll be helping me prepare the meals.'

Jake pursed his lips, thinking of the condiments he had surreptitiously added to her stew. 'So, like I said,' he said, moving swiftly on. 'I saw Marty, and apparently he is getting paid for the gardening.' Jake was unsure just how much Gayle was feigning ignorance because it involved her friend.

Gayle brought the cup to her lips and took a sip of coffee without comment.

Jake continued, 'Marty is paid to maintain the gardens by your friend Robyn.'

'I know,' Gayle said simply, picking up her teaspoon and slowly stirring her coffee. 'I didn't tell you before because I didn't want to get her in any sort of trouble. Sorry.' She cast a furtive glance at him.

'Don't be,' Jake reassured her. 'It's no trouble.'

'Well, that's what I said to her; I didn't see why she would get into trouble for doing a good deed. She wasn't sure how your family would feel about it, or about the fact that Marty took her on a tour of the house. I told her that if anything, you'd be grateful. It's not like she was taking anything that wasn't hers.'

Jake stared at Gayle.

Gayle stopped stirring her coffee, conscious of Jake's frozen glare. 'She didn't, did she?'

'No, no,' Jake's eyes dropped to his coffee cup. 'There's nothing missing.' Not in the tangible sense, anyway, he thought. She hadn't actually removed anything. Borrowing an idea didn't count, did it? Jake was thinking again of the old doll's house in the basement of The Lake House. It had been quite a shock to discover that some of the décor in Lark Lodge was eerily similar to the miniature rooms in the doll's house that Eleanor had decorated as a child.

When Marcus had discovered this, he'd been very angry. Jake didn't see the harm in it, or in the fact that Marty had clearly shown Robyn around The Lake House. He must have found the spare door key under the flowerpot. Or was it the doormat? Jake couldn't remember.

Marcus had thought that Robyn must have been paying Marty to look after the gardens because she'd felt guilty for stealing Eleanor's designs from her old doll's house. Jake was inclined to agree with Marcus, but he wasn't bothered. He didn't begrudge Marty a hot drink if he wanted to use the kitchen while he worked on the gardens, and he understood Robyn's curiosity about the Rosses, and why she'd want to take a look around the house.

The question was, had her generosity – paying Marty to look after the gardens of his house – extended to redecorating too? Jake didn't think so. She surely didn't have the time to redecorate his house for free, never mind the money for the materials.

Jake admitted, 'I was intending to return to The Lake House and stay there, but—'

'It holds too many memories from past.'

'Well, yes. But that wasn't the reason I'm not staying there this time. On a more practical note, it's in the throes of being redecorated.'

'Oh, yes of course. Robyn said she'd been instructed to redecorate the house. I remember Annie mentioning to me that Robyn was so nervous about meeting a Ross that she even asked Annie if she would go to the house in her place.'

'How strange,' Jake said, rubbing his chin.

Gayle shook her head. 'Not really. The Rosses, and I'm including you, are practically celebrities, you know. Because you're so wealthy. Not that you splash your wealth around, or anything.'

Jake bit his lower lip, wondering what she would make of the fact that he'd bought Marty a house. And not just any house. The rather lovely show home, which was one of the most expensive houses on the new development where Nick worked.

Jake decided not to share that fact just then. Instead, he asked, 'So, did she meet one of the Rosses at the house? It wasn't me, if she did,' he quickly added. At least if Gayle could tell him who it was, then it would clear up the little mystery over who exactly had employed her. Of course, it wouldn't clear up the why. Although that was obvious; after months and months of standing empty without a soul visiting, apart from Marty making himself a cuppa while he was gardening, the place was starting to deteriorate at an alarming rate.

'No, she did not. Nobody turned up. Which surprised her. Surprised me too. I think the remit was just to use her judgement. Which I think is a good call, knowing Robyn's interior design skills.' Gayle paused. 'Have you been back to the house?'

Jake nodded, lost in thought. He knew Eleanor's father, William Ross, was on a golf course somewhere. Marcus was always too busy with work, or finding his next drug score. And Grace

Ross, Eleanor's mother, was always too wrapped up in herself to care about anyone or anything else.

That left Aubrey. Jake looked at Gayle, and knew the only explanation was that Aubrey had hired her. He didn't want to get into that.

'Do you like it? What's she's done so far?'

As far as Jake could see, she'd bought materials, but hadn't actually started yet. He supposed that didn't stop him from moving back in for a few days. But he didn't want to hold her up, if her intention was to crack on with it when she returned from London.

'Yes, it's great,' Jake replied reassuringly, catching the worried look on Gayle's face. Even though Robyn hadn't started, going by what she'd done to Gayle's guesthouse, Jake was confident that whatever she chose to do would be a vast improvement. In fact, he hoped she changed the décor completely. Then it wouldn't remind him of—

'What I can't figure out is why she would do such a thing.' Gayle cut across his thoughts.

It took a few seconds for it to register that Gayle was referring to Robyn's trip to London without David.

'And another thing …' Gayle put her teaspoon on the saucer and looked at Jake thoughtfully. 'She didn't tell me herself, you know. I had to hear it from Marty.'

'About her trip to London?' Jake furrowed his brow, wondering why she'd told Marty.

'No. I'm talking about paying him to work on your garden.'

'Oh, right.'

Gayle continued, 'I expect she knew I might have a thing or two to say about her generosity. I don't really understand why all the interest in The Lake House – do you?'

That thought had crossed Jake's mind. What if he was way off beam and there was more to it than copying the miniature room designs in the doll's house? It made him wonder if Robyn knew Eleanor. He looked at Gayle. Perhaps she'd know.

'Did Robyn know my wife, Eleanor?'

'I don't know.' Gayle shrugged. 'Although it would certainly explain why she has a fondness for your garden.'

'She hasn't said anything to you?' Jake paused in anticipation. '… About Eleanor?'

Gayle put her empty cup on the wooden coffee table between them. 'It would appear there's a lot she hasn't told me, lately.'

Thinking of these illicit trips to London that had David wound up like a tight coil, it seemed to Jake that Robyn had a few secrets of her own. Would she have shared any of these with Eleanor? What would Eleanor have shared in return?

Jake thought of David's parting words, I'm losing her, and I don't even know why. Those words mirrored Jake's own feelings on his final days with Eleanor just before Christmas. There had been something wrong, something bugging her. It should have been the best holiday of their married life together. She had finally become pregnant. They had been looking forward to telling her parents. At least, Jake had been. He had wanted it to be their Christmas present to her parents and to Marcus. But everything she had done had been out of character. She hadn't wanted to spend the holiday with her family at The Lake House. That had been so unlike her.

When Jake had insisted on their going anyway, she'd avoided him, going shopping alone in Aviemore instead. She hardly ever went shopping in Aviemore. She'd been out when he'd arrived late at The Lake House from work on Christmas Eve. They hadn't travelled up together to Scotland that Christmas, which was another first. Then, after Christmas dinner, she'd disappeared out again into Aviemore. He'd had a strong suspicion she was meeting somebody. But she didn't know anybody locally; none of them did. He was hoping Robyn might be able to help him answer these questions, which had plagued him these past seven months.

Robyn. It was vital that he spoke to her before he left. He thought he could just wander into her shop in Aviemore any time, but her busy work commitments meant she might not be there.

He hoped she'd be back in the next few days. In the meantime, he had plenty to occupy his time; there were two other things to get done before he left. With that in mind, Jake put his hand in his jacket pocket.

'I've got something I'd like to show you.' Jake passed Gayle the photograph of Martha's son. 'Do you recognise him?'

'Should I?' said Gayle studying the photograph before turning it over and reading the name on the back. Gayle looked up. 'Who's Ralph?'

Jake didn't really expect that Gayle would have the answers he was looking for. 'There's a lady called Martha. I'm searching for her son. This is the only photo I have.'

'You're searching for a missing child?'

Jake shook his head. 'No. This photo was taken some years ago. Look, there's a date on the back. That would make him in his thirties.'

Jake sighed when he caught Gayle staring at him blankly. It wasn't all that surprising that she didn't know him. Aviemore might be a small community, but that didn't mean everybody knew everybody else.

'I shouldn't have promised Martha Delaney I'd find her son.'

'Delaney?'

'That's her surname. I believe she was not married when she had her son, which meant he would have been Ralph Delaney before he was adopted.'

Gayle said, 'The name Delaney rings a bell. Is there any connection to Cedar Grove, by any chance?'

'Yes, yes. Martha's father, Angus Delaney, left Cedar Grove in a trust when his son failed to materialise to claim his inheritance.'

'It's a care home now,' said Gayle.

'You know it?'

Gayle frowned. 'My brothers and sister were planning to send my mother there.'

'Oh, I see,' Jake said, trying to hide his disappointment. For a moment, he'd thought Gayle might be able to help him in his search.

'I looked it up online. It is a lovely place, but I just didn't want to send her away.'

Send her away. Jake remembered chatting to the receptionist at Cedar Lodge, whose father had been an amateur local historian. He had speculated as to the reasons why Angus Delaney's son, Ralph Delaney, also known as Aubrey Jones, had run away from his boarding school and never returned. Angus had sent his wife away; had had her committed to a psychiatric hospital. Sadly, back then that had been a common approach to treating people with mental health conditions, which were often considered nervous disorders.

Jake wondered as to the reasons Ralph had run away and had, at some point, changed his name to Aubrey. The receptionist had speculated that maybe he had been afraid that his father might send him away too. Maybe he had been a shy, introspective child who was very close to his mother, and had been worried that this would be enough for his father to consider sending him to an institution.

Gayle passed the photo back to Jake. 'Sorry I can't be of any help.'

Jake put the photo back in his wallet. He changed the subject. 'So, do you know when Robyn is due home?'

'Friday, I think.'

'Tomorrow?'

'Yes, I think so. That's what David said. She's travelling back from London tomorrow, so they'll have the whole weekend together. But I'm afraid you won't see her then.'

'Oh. How come? She doesn't work in her shop on Saturdays?' Jake was visibly disappointed. He thought that as a retail shop, it would be open at the weekend.

'No, her shop is open, and she does work on a Saturday, but David has arranged with his sister-in-law, Annie, who works part-time in the shop, to work tomorrow and over the weekend. David told me he's heading into Aviemore to book a stay in a five-star hotel with an evening meal included in their à-la-carte restaurant. There wouldn't be any point if she had to get up early the next morning for work.'

Jake could see the point regarding work the next morning, but he did wonder why David didn't just give the hotel a call.

'Because it's tomorrow, and he couldn't get through on the phone, he's driven there now to book a room in case they all go. I imagine Friday nights are popular. He's got it into his head that if they just spent some time together, with no distractions, then he might get to the bottom of whatever was going on in London.'

Gayle shook her head as if to say she thought his chances were slim. Either that, or there really was nothing going on in London, and Robyn was just meeting up with clients like Gayle had said.

'He was going to pick her up from the train station and bring her back here.'

Jake would have preferred that; then he would have got to meet her sooner.

'He had thought staying the night together in their old room here at the guesthouse, where he felt they were happiest, was a good idea. Perhaps even the whole weekend too. It just seems to me, and David voiced this too, that since she left here and moved into the boathouse, she hasn't been her normal self.'

Jake nodded, wondering whether Gayle should be sharing all this personal information about her friends.

'David thought, and so did I, that when he popped the question, that would change. He's beginning to regret asking her to move in with him. I think he did confront her at one point, asking her if she wished she hadn't moved in with him, but just as I expected, she said of course it wasn't him. I chatted to her just recently, asking if everything was okay, if she was okay, and she reassured me she was.'

'But you still think there's something up.'

Gayle sighed heavily. 'If it's not David – and she was over the moon when he proposed, showing me the ring – then we're both thinking perhaps she's not happy in the boathouse for some reason. The problem is that the boathouse is David's home. And it is a gorgeous house. I really thought she'd love it there. I suspect David thought that if they spent the night together back here, then perhaps he could get to the bottom of what was really going on with her. He's prepared to move back in here with her – start again, so to speak.'

'But he's booking a hotel room.'

'Yeah. I suppose it's like the old adage – you can never go back.'

Jake didn't understand.

Gayle caught his expression. She explained, 'They lived here before it was a proper guesthouse. Obviously their old room is just as they left it. But it's not just Nick and Marty here now.'

'Oh, sorry. Is that why David left in a hurry to book the hotel room – because I'm here?'

'No. Well ... yes. Don't take it personally, Jake. This is a guesthouse now. David knows that. He and Robyn can't expect to have the place virtually to themselves. I told him that he should check into a hotel if he wants to spend time together with Robyn, just the two of them.'

'But there will be other guests in a hotel.'

'Yes, that's true. But it's more impersonal, and there's more space, so they can dine together, just the two of them.'

Jake understood.

'And besides. I'm not sure whether it's a good idea for them to return here. If something is going on with Robyn, what if she decided not to return with David to the boathouse? I'd feel terrible if that happened, like it was all my fault.'

'But it wouldn't be, Gayle.'

Gayle smiled. 'I know. But it's my guesthouse, and it was my suggestion that they return here, so I'd kind of feel responsible.'

'But who says that's going to happen?'

'Well, it certainly isn't, because Robyn won't be staying the night here.'

'Unless when she returns she decides she's leaving David.'

'Don't say that!' Gayle shook her head vehemently. 'She's happy with David.'

Jake understood. They were both Gayle's friends, and the last thing she'd want to see was them splitting up.

'So, there has to be a reason she's not happy living in the boathouse.'

'But I just don't see why that would be the case – do you?'

Jake was just shrugging his shoulders when he heard the front door. He tensed. It might be David. What if he hadn't managed to book the hotel room? It was no wonder David hadn't exactly been pleased to see him at dinner; he was yet another guest, there reminding David that Lark Lodge was a guesthouse and that he couldn't turn back the clock to the way things had been when he and Robyn had lived there and it had still been just a home.

Jake was just about to rise from his chair, thinking that if it was indeed David, he'd retreat to his room, when something large and shaggy and slobbery came bounding into the room.

Jake grinned. 'Olive!'

Olive furiously wagged her tail and made a beeline for him, her tail taking an unintentional swipe at the cup in Gayle's hand. Fortunately, it was empty.

'Hey, girl! Where did you appear from?' Jake said, giving her a big fuss and a scratch behind the ears that he knew from experience she loved.

Nick appeared in the doorway, holding two white plastic bags. Jake could smell Chinese takeaway.

Nick said, 'Hey, what's that amazing smell?'

Jake stopped stroking Olive and looked up at Nick curiously. 'Your Chinese takeaway.'

He looked at the plastic bags. 'No, I don't mean my takeaway.'

Gayle grinned. 'Ah, that will be my stew.' She tapped her nose. 'It's a secret recipe.'

Jake gave Gayle a sideways glance but kept his mouth shut.

'Do you want some?' Gayle asked. 'There's still plenty left.'

'Do I ever!' Nick licked his lips, then clearly remembered his Chinese. He held up the plastic bags. 'What am I meant to do with this?'

'Stick your takeaway in the fridge. I'm sure it will be fine for tomorrow.

'Both bags?' Nick asked.

'Yes, there's room in the fridge.'

Jake thought that it looked as though he'd bought far too much takeaway food for one person.

As if reading Jake's mind, Nick said, 'I bought extra in case anybody wanted to join me.'

'Well, I'm sure myself, Marty and Jake won't object to Chinese tomorrow night.'

After he'd smelt the takeaway, Jake thought why not?

Nick said, 'I'm not sure I've bought enough to go around. Although I could order more in, Gayle.'

Gayle shook her head. 'I'm sure there will be enough. The pan with the stew is on the stove. You just need to heat it up.'

'Anyone joining me?' Nick asked.

'No, we've both eaten.'

'What about David?'

'He might when he gets back.'

'Gets back? Is he picking Robyn up from the station?'

'Not until tomorrow. But they're not staying here after all – change of plan.'

Nick nodded. 'That's a shame. I was looking forward to seeing her. Since she moved into the boathouse, she doesn't come round half as much as I thought she would.'

Gayle sighed. 'I know.'

Nick added. 'I know why. She misses the place so much, she doesn't want to come visit in case she has the urge to move back.'

'Did she say something?' Gayle asked.

Jake started to feel uncomfortable again, hoping it didn't get back onto the subject of David and Robyn's personal life.

Nick shook his head. 'It was just a joke, Gayle.'

'Oh, right. Of course. Silly me.'

'Why would she move back into her room here when she's got a gorgeous boathouse to live in? No offence, Gayle.'

'None taken,' Gayle replied.

'Right, well, I'll go and put these bags in the fridge and heat up that stew. If it tastes half as good as it smells …' Nick's voice trailed off as he crossed the hall to the kitchen.

Jake caught Gayle smiling after him, obviously feeling chuffed that her stew was going down a treat.

Nick's head appeared round the door. 'Olive, be good!'

Olive was sitting next to Jake. He patted her on the head. 'Good girl.' Thinking of Robyn, he turned to Gayle. 'Is Robyn coming here some time over the weekend, do you think?' he said.

'Yes, I was expecting to see her when she got back from London tomorrow, but if things go according to plan for David, then I guess she might pop in to say hello on Sunday instead. I do cook a Sunday roast. They know they're welcome any time.'

Sunday it is, then, thought Jake, not without some trepidation; what was he likely to find out about Eleanor, and would it be good news or bad?

7

Jake sat on the bed, picked up his mobile and phoned Faye.

A child's voice gave a wary hello down the phone.

Jake smiled. 'Hello, cherub.'

'Jake!' Natty shouted excitedly. Then her tone changed abruptly. 'No!' she whined, 'I'm speaking to Jake.' Her voice sounded muffled this time, and Jake guessed Faye was trying to wrestle the phone out of her hand – without much luck, by the sound of it.

'Is that Mummy?' Jake spoke down the phone.

'Yes, but I got here first. It's my turn first,' Natty shouted, evidently still asserting her right to keep hold of the phone.

Jake heard Faye acquiesce in the background. 'Five minutes. It's well past your bedtime.'

'Where are you?' Natty said down the phone.

Jake smiled. It wasn't so much a question as a demand. She made it sound like he was absconding from babysitting duties without her permission.

'I'm in Scotland.' His leave from work had been sudden, and with a pang of guilt Jake realised he hadn't even told Natty he was taking a holiday. He hoped Faye had put her in the picture. The last thing he wanted was for Natty to think he was walking out of her life – like it would seem to her that her father and grandfather had done.

'You remember, your mummy told you I was going on a little holiday?' Jake hoped this was true.

'Yes,' said Natty, 'I remember. But where are you? Scotland's a big place. I saw it on a map. So where exactly?'

'I'm in the Cairngorms. You can google it.'

Hearing Natty's voice made Jake realise how much he was missing the kid; he missed taking her to the park. He missed their shopping trips to Hamleys in Regent Street to buy new toys – the trips that had got him into so much trouble with Faye. He even missed the bottomless pit of questions that she seemed to store up just to drive him nuts when he was on babysitting duty in the evening after a long day at work.

'Natty?' The line had gone quiet. Jake called her name several times. On the fourth try, she answered.

'Say it again, the place where you are?' Natty demanded.

'The Cairngorms.'

The line went quiet again her end.

'What are you up to, Natty?'

'I've found it, I've found it. But where is the town?'

'Are you looking at a map?'

'Yes. I've got Mummy's old map. She won't let me use her laptop.' There was a pause during which Jake heard the rustling of paper. He imagined she was unfolding the map on the kitchen table. He heard Natty say, 'We are here, in London, and you are … are … hmm.'

It sounded to Jake as though she hadn't been able to locate Aviemore.

'It's in Scotland – right?'

'Yes, that's right. I'm staying in a lovely guesthouse called Lark Lodge, in Aviemore.

'Hey, I've found the Cairngorms. It says it on the map.'

Jake smiled. 'Well done!' He pictured her hunched over the map, her mum's mobile phone in one hand, and a little finger tracing the distance between them. Finally, she said, 'It's a long way away.'

Jake sighed. 'I know.' Since arriving in Aviemore, he'd discovered he wasn't particularly missing London. He'd forgotten how at home he always felt in this beautiful part of the world. But he was missing the two people he'd discovered he couldn't live without. That was the reason he was keen for Robyn to get on with redecorating The Lake House. He knew that in his heart, when he'd thought he'd lost them, that he couldn't possibly consider returning to live in his house. They were in London, and there was nowhere else he'd rather be than back there with them.

'I don't think you're going to find Aviemore on that map, sweetheart.' The village was too small for her to locate it on a map of the UK.

'Oh.' She sounded disappointed.

'Jake?'

'Yes?'

Jake heard Faye's voice in the background.

'Just one more minute!' shouted Natty, 'I want to ask Jake one more question.'

Jake stifled a laugh. Natty with another question! Who would have thought? He felt like asking her – only the one? But the sarcasm would have gone right over her head. Besides, she didn't need any encouragement.

'Only one, I promise!' Natty yelled at her mother.

Jake shook in silent laughter. Faye knew her daughter too well.

When he had sufficiently recovered – Natty would be very cross indeed if she thought for one second he wasn't being serious – Jake put the phone to his ear.

Her little voice said, 'Jake.'

'Yes, Natty?'

'When are you coming home?'

Jake thought about this. The answer was that he didn't know exactly. His return flight was in six days, but he might need more time. Then again, he might not, and might even rearrange his flight to return sooner. So, he used the classic adult ruse. 'Soon,' he said, dragging the word out, knowing that it wasn't going to wash. 'In a few days, maybe.'

There was a silence. Jake waited for the usual battery of questions that followed a vague answer he could never hope to get away with.

'I miss you.'

Blown away by Natty's unexpected reply, Jake was momentarily lost for words.

'I miss you too, honey monster.'

'I am not a honey monster,' her tone very serious.

Jake could picture her standing right in front of him, folding her arms theatrically, cocking her head to one side and giving him that silent ticking-off that said, You're not to call me honey monster; I am not a baby.

But to Jake, she was. He just wished she was his baby, his child. 'I know you're not a honey monster,' Jake conceded with a sigh.

'Well, that's good to hear,' Faye's voice answered.

'Oh, I didn't realise …'

'She'd be on the phone all day if I didn't rescue you,' Faye sounded exasperated. 'God help us when she's a teenager.'

Jake was surprised by the use of the word us. It made them sound like a family. Next, they'd be grilling her first boyfriend and debating where those university fees were coming from. Jake shook his head. Faye had simply used a figure of speech, and there he was making the leap from being a colleague, a friend, the babysitter she relied on – to what? A ten-year relationship behind them and a kid of university age? It was no wonder Natty was confused. It confused the hell out of him. And the truth was, it scared the hell out of him too.

'Jake – are you still there?'

'Yes, look I wanted to apologise for hanging up on you the last time we spoke.'

'It's all right, Jake. I get it. You've got a lot on your mind.'

Jake didn't think that excused his behaviour, but even so he was so relieved she'd taken his call. Now Jake was trying desperately to remember why he had rung Faye; he had completely forgotten.

'Have you sent the photograph?' Faye reminded him.

'The photograph,' Jake said hurriedly, feeling like a drowning man snatching at a life raft. 'Of course, the photo. Right, er …' Jake was having a problem piecing his thoughts together. 'What did you just say?'

'I said have … you … sent … the … photograph? You know that little favour you asked for?'

'Ah! Yes. I mean no.'

'Well, which is it?' she paused. 'Are you alright, Jake?'

No, he was not alright. He felt awkward. He felt tongue-tied. He felt like a teenager trying to arrange a first date. It was weird, because suddenly he was having a really tough time holding an ordinary conversation with Faye. Normally, he could talk to her about anything and everything, and here he was clamming up. Maybe Faye was right: he'd needed a holiday more than he thought. Just not in Aviemore. Jake frowned. 'I think maybe coming here has made me a little out of sorts. I'll text you a copy of the photo.' Hearing Faye's voice again and speaking to Natty made Jake realise that he couldn't wait to wrap things up and head back to London. He told Faye he couldn't wait to return.

'Then you'll keep your promise to Marcus, and return to the Ross Corporation while he's … away?'

Jake rolled his eyes. Marcus. It seemed that every time he spoke to Faye, Marcus cropped up somewhere in the conversation. He noted the euphemism, away. Natty was probably listening in on her mother's conversation. Faye didn't want her overhearing her talking about Marcus going to the clinic. 'Look, I know you had the best intentions when you told Marcus about my holiday, but the thing is,' Jake paused. He didn't want it to sound like he wanted her to butt out. But, in fact, he did. 'There are things going on between Marcus and me that—'

'Are you talking about Eleanor?'

'Marcus didn't tell you?'

'Tell me what, exactly, Jake? Do I have to tell you every word that passes between me and your brother?' she said testily.

Jake was inclined to say yes, but kept his mouth shut.

There was a silence down the phone until Faye asked, 'When you get back, will you tell me about Eleanor? About what really happened?' she said softly.

Jake had promised her he would, just not over the phone, but he was changing his mind about waiting until he got back. What if she bumped into Marcus again, or more likely spoke with him on the phone – and Marcus said something? For that reason, Jake made up his mind to tell Faye what had really happened to Eleanor.

'I want you to hear this from me Faye, before you hear it from …' he paused, thinking of Marcus, 'somebody else.' Jake was positive Marcus had told Lydia; it was obvious from Lydia's attitude towards Jake when they spoke on the phone. Which meant that in time, Marcus might tell Faye.

He couldn't imagine Marcus would just phone Faye up and start talking about Eleanor's accident on the ski slopes, but what if it just came out in conversation? Faye was a good listener. That was the problem. Before Marcus knew it, he might just find himself telling Faye his life story, and that would include just what he and Marcus had had a massive falling-out over – namely what really happened on that mountain in the aftermath of the accident.

8

'I haven't told anybody this – not friends, not family. It's just been between Marcus and me.' Jake thought of Marcus's fiancée, Lydia. 'Whether he has said anything to anybody else, I'm not certain.' Jake continued before he could change his mind. 'It was a skiing accident, but obviously you know that.'

'It was in the newspapers and splashed all over the news,' Faye affirmed.

'Yes, the press always makes a big deal out of a wealthy family tragedy. Guess they think you can't have wealth and happiness, but you can, Faye.' He paused. 'It was just a stupid, stupid accident.'

'Jake – tell me what happened up there on the ski slopes.'

He took a deep breath, trying to stave off a panic attack as he recalled the events of the previous Christmas. 'Marcus always goaded Eleanor to join us on the slopes. She never really liked skiing; it was never her thing – know what I mean?'

'Not really. I've never set foot on a ski slope in my life,' Faye commented.

Jake sighed. He wasn't surprised in the least at Faye's comment. Skiing was an expensive pastime. The destinations were expensive, the ski passes, the cost of the gear to go skiing.

'Marcus wouldn't let up until she came with us. I always joined in for my own selfish reasons because I wanted her to come. It just wouldn't be the same without her.' Jake closed his eyes thinking back to that day. 'Every Christmas at The Lake House was the same rigmarole; we teased, she relented, and the three of us skied.'

Faye said, 'I see.'

'But last year was different. She was adamant that she wasn't going. I knew that it probably marked the end of our traditional afternoon Christmas Day ski, once she missed one, but I was in total agreement; there was no way I wanted her to ski.' Jake spoke softly. 'Not in her condition.'

'… condition?' Faye prompted.

The words she was pregnant caught painfully in his throat. 'I was going to be a father.'

'Oh, Jake. I had no idea.'

'Nobody knew. It was our secret. Telling her parents was to be our Christmas present to William and Grace – a grandchild, you see; their first grandchild. Marcus didn't know, and still doesn't, that he was going to be an uncle.' Jake closed his eyes at the painful memory of such a joyous occasion cruelly dashed.

'So, what made her change her mind?' Faye ventured.

Marcus. Jake opened his eyes. 'I'd already told Marcus to back off; Ellie was not coming with us, and that was final. Of course, he didn't know the reason, and being Marcus, he wouldn't let it go. I just wish we'd told him. I found out afterwards what he had been whispering to her that evening at the dinner table. He told her that we had skied off-piste when she wasn't with us and that this time, we'd take her.'

'Off-piste? What does that mean, exactly?' Faye asked, interrupting Jake before he could explain what had happened next.

'Oh, right.' Jake had momentarily forgotten that he was talking to a non-skier. 'Basically ski pistes are ski slopes that have been prepared for skiing.'

'Prepared – how?' Faye asked.

'Well, there's trail poles each side which mark out the route to take down the slopes. Then the slopes are prepared with something called grooming machines that smooth the surface of the snow for skiing the next day. And of course there's the full-time ski patrol up there too who look after piste safety as well as the markers, and they are on hand in case of an emergency.'

'I think I'm getting the picture,' said Faye. 'So presumably if you ski off-piste, the slopes are not prepared, which makes skiing harder. There's no trail markers to identify the route down, and you're unlikely to have ski patrols either on hand if something goes wrong.'

'Unfortunately, you've hit the nail on the head.' Jake sighed heavily. 'There's lots of reasons it's not advisable.'

'So, why do you do it?'

'I have to say it's something Marcus and I have only done a handful of times, and with a qualified guide who knows the terrain and is aware of avalanche risks.'

'So you were with a qualified guide when you all went skiing off-piste?'

'No.'

'Why not, if that's what you'd done in the past?'

'Well, here's the thing. We had no intention of skiing off-piste that time. I don't know what made Marcus say that because it wasn't true; we had never skied off-piste before in Scotland.' The poor snowfall usually meant there were no thrills to be had skiing off-piste in the Cairngorms. How ironic that the conditions had been ripe for some adventurous skiing that year.

It suddenly occurred to Jake that perhaps Marcus had seen the weather forecast and had realised that the heavy snowfall forecast that day could mean some serious skiing. Was it possible that rather than trying to persuade Ellie to go, Marcus had in fact been trying, for his own selfish reasons, to do the exact opposite; to dissuade his sister from joining them on the ski slopes and spoiling the fun?

Jake remembered asking Marcus what he had told Ellie to change her mind, furious with him for refusing to let the matter rest and allow her to remain behind just that once.

'You would have thought it was the last thing he should have said to try and persuade her to go,' Jake was thinking aloud. Why hadn't he realised that before?

'Maybe she found the excitement of it appealing?' Faye ventured a guess.

'No way. She always stuck to the same route, the same mountain pass, because that's where she felt safest.' The more Jake thought about it, the more it rang true that Marcus would not have wanted her with them. It wasn't his fault she had inexplicably turned up despite Marcus's warning that they were not intending to take their usual route down.

'But that's all water under the bridge now, isn't it, Jake?' Faye said gently. 'Something persuaded her to go.'

'She went shopping,' said Jake.

'Why do you think she changed her mind?'

'I wish I knew. She just turned up, decked out in her ski stuff.' Jake turned his head and stared out of the bedroom window towards the roofline of his house. 'I guess she was pulling one last surprise.'

'Surprise?' Faye repeated down the phone.

'It was, like, a game we used to play.' Jake paused, not sure whether he should be telling Faye something so personal, so private about their relationship. Still, Eleanor wouldn't mind – not anymore. 'Eleanor liked pulling pranks. Well, in fairness, we both used to do it, to each other.' Jake paused. 'In the beginning.'

'In the beginning?'

In the beginning, thought Jake, we were just kids. Jake couldn't quite believe how young they had been when they made the biggest commitment of their adult lives – they were just in their teens when they promised one another they would marry.

Had they been young and foolish? Maybe. After all, Eleanor had floated the idea of giving up going to university to study interior design in order to marry him. Jake had refused to hear of it. She hadn't needed to do that, although he'd been afraid that if she went off to college, he'd risk losing her to a new way of life – a new love, perhaps. But that hadn't happened. They had been young and in love. They'd known each other long enough to know they were perfect for each other.

Jake tried not to think about how much he missed Faye, how much he wished she was in the room with him instead of in London, on the end of the phone. He wondered if she was sitting on her bed in nothing but a towel, not long out of the shower, her skin still glistening with drops of water.

'For god's sake!'

'Jake, is everything okay?'

He put his hand to his mouth. He hadn't meant to admonish himself out loud for thinking about Faye like that. He rubbed his temple, wishing that the particular memory of Faye hadn't come to mind. He'd stayed over, babysitting Natty. He'd slept on the couch in the lounge and had accidentally seen Faye on the landing upstairs, exiting the shower room in nothing but a small white towel.

There he was, trying to have a conversation about Eleanor, and all he could think of was Faye, semi-naked. Jake shook his head and focused on the rooftop of The Lake House through the attic window, his thoughts turning again to the previous Christmas.

'In the beginning,' Jake remembered, 'when we were first married, Eleanor was determined that we weren't going to turn into some boring couple who were just comfortable in each other's company. She used to say that just because we'd done something very grown-up and got married, it didn't mean we had to suddenly be all grown-up and sensible.' Jake smiled at that. 'So, she used to get up to things …'

'What sort of things?'

'Sometimes …' Jake smiled at the memory, 'Sometimes she'd ring up my secretary and book an appointment, pretending to be a business client, just so she could see me during the day. It was my own fault. I'd joked that if she wanted to see me during the day, she'd have to book an appointment. I remember I was meant to have a business lunch. There I was, sitting at a table in a restaurant, thinking I had some important new business client, and my wife turns up instead, saying she missed me and just had to see me, even though I'd only left for work three hours earlier! God, I was stunned. Then I started to feel faintly amused, and then I was laughing, great whoops of laughter in the middle of a top London restaurant where the business elite were quietly conducting important power lunches.'

Jake remembered that those lunch dates had become a regular occurrence. They were not always power lunches. Jake enjoyed the packed lunches she'd bring along with her in the nice weather, so that they could sit in one of the London parks together.

'I swear my secretary was in on it.' Eleanor's appointments for lunch always coincided with the free spots in his calendar when he wasn't having meetings or business lunches with real clients. Jake laughed at the absurdity of it all. 'I remember pulling one or two surprises on her, but they were never quite as amusing or inventive as hers. She was always the creative one in the family.' Jake's smile faded. 'Then it happened.' He fell silent.

'What happened, Jake?'

'We turned into that boring couple who were just comfortable in each other's company. You see, we changed, we matured, and the time for childish games had passed.' Jake thought about the trips to London, the visits to Harley Street because they were having problems conceiving the child he'd thought they both so desperately wanted. Then there was the time they'd spent in America while he was following new American contracts. How Eleanor had loathed America. How much she had missed England, missed London.

Jake recalled those regular trips to Harley Street, and how unhappy Eleanor had been when the time had come to leave London and return to America. Jake had begun to see a picture emerging of what the future held for them both, and that picture was beginning to look an awful lot like Eleanor's parents: William working in different countries, and Grace choosing to stay in London – together but apart, married but separated. What kind of future was that? And what did that mean for their children?

Jake had made the decision not to return to America and to remain based in London. He wished he'd listened to Eleanor again when she'd told him she did not want to spend Christmas at The Lake House.

He breathed a heavy sigh, telling Faye, 'I should have listened to her when I had the chance. She wanted to stay in London, just the two of us, last Christmas. We'd been trying for so long, and all I wanted to do was tell everyone the news, but in hindsight I realise now that Eleanor needed time. She hadn't had a chance to forge her own career, which I know she desperately wanted after university. My job at the Ross Corporation came first – always had. I'd told her we'd figure it out. But what I could see in our future was that I'd continue working wherever in the world the company needed me, and she would eventually stop travelling with me. Which meant we'd end up leading separate lives, with her in London, where I'm sure she wanted to open a shop.'

'But what about when you had children?'

'I hadn't really considered the implications until she got pregnant, because after years of trying, it was as though it would never happen. Then I guess I thought until they started school, we could still lead that life, living and working away.'

'But things changed.'

'Yes, Faye, they did. I stopped travelling, and she started to focus on what she wanted to do.'

'Opening a shop?'

'Interior design, that was her thing. But then it happened.'

'What happened – the accident?'

'No, Eleanor falling pregnant. God, you should have seen me.' Jake remembered walking out on the balcony of their penthouse suite in London, when he'd found out, and literally shouting from the rooftops that they were having a baby. Eleanor wasn't with him. She'd taken herself off to bed. Jake had convinced himself she was just tired, and emotional, after the incredible news they'd been waiting so long to hear.

But he wasn't blind. He'd known what was going on; just when he'd decided to stay in London permanently, and she'd finally be able to focus on herself, her career, she'd fallen pregnant. He just wished he'd talked to her. And now he would never be able to.

9

'Jake – are you still there?'

If only he'd listened to Ellie at Christmas. But I wasn't listening, was I? he thought. I didn't hear her unhappiness. I didn't see her need for me to put her first over the family, over the company.

He had thought he'd done that already by choosing to be based in London. But he hadn't considered how she must have felt about being pregnant when she'd thought it was never going to happen.

Jake didn't think badly of her when he thought about her not being overjoyed at the news. She'd just needed time to figure out how she was going to balance doing what she wanted for herself with being a mother, and perhaps figure out what she wanted for them as a family.

Jake said bitterly. 'It never occurred to me that she might want us to make a life for ourselves independently of the family business.'

He'd chosen to stay in London, but for how long would it have lasted? As much as he had wanted to plan a life around staying in London with Eleanor and the baby, the reality was that it might not have been possible in the long run. The company always came first, and he didn't know what that would have meant for their future.

'Is that what she said?'

'Not in so many words.' But Jake knew his wife. There had been things going on with her at Christmas. He was back to wishing that he hadn't been so hellbent on sticking to their normal routine and spending Christmas with the Rosses in the Cairngorms. In hindsight, it felt like it had been a test – would he put her or the family first? He'd failed, and the cost had been—

Suddenly Jake wished he wasn't having this conversation over the phone. *Why didn't I just get on that plane with Marcus?* he thought. Then he could be telling Faye this in person. He stared up out of the attic window, up at the Cairngorms.

Jake had had many months to dwell on the events surrounding that fateful Christmas Day. He had eventually arrived at the real crux of the matter. 'I realise now that she wanted us to stay together in London. Not just over Christmas; she was asking for something more. She was asking me not to make her choose.'

Jake took a deep breath and confided, 'She would have left me, Faye. One way or another, I would have lost her, because she knew I could never walk out on Marcus, William or the company.' The irony wasn't lost on Jake that he had ended up doing just that.

'I think she needed to pursue her own career without the shadow of her father's company bearing down on her and squashing her personal achievements.' Jake thought of the abandoned doll's house in the basement of his house. 'It just never occurred to me until it was too late.'

'Too late?' Faye halted. 'But she's alive – isn't she?'

Jake said, 'Yes,' in a small voice. 'I just wished she hadn't pulled one last surprise,' he mumbled.

'Everyone in school assumed you were a widower.'

Jake heaved a sigh. 'I know. I'm sorry.'

'Don't be!' Faye quickly replied. 'You don't have to apologise.'

'What the Rosses wanted, what I wanted, was to keep the press out of our personal affairs, away from Eleanor, and her … recovery.'

'Recovery? Does that mean you'll leave teaching and go back to working for the Rosses? No, wait – you thought that was not what she wanted; that she wanted you to leave the corporation. Is that true? What did she say about that? Perhaps she'll be okay with you teaching in London. Perhaps she'll open her shop here?'

'Oh, Faye. If only that were true.'

'Which part? You staying in teaching or her opening her shop?' Faye paused and said in a small voice. 'I thought she'd died after that accident. I thought you were … single.'

'She did. I am.'

'What? Jake – what are you talking about? You said you're not a widower, and she's recovering. I don't understand …'

Recovery. Jake realised that was the wrong word. 'She's not—' Jake halted. How could he explain? He hadn't seen her himself. In all these months, he hadn't visited. But he didn't have to. How could he forget what the doctors had told them?

'She's never going to be what she once was.'

'Oh, Jake. People change, and when you've had an accident, it's bound to take time to—'

'No. You don't understand. She's gone, Faye. She may recover physically, but—' Jake thought of the doll's house Eleanor had once loved in the basement of the house. She'd never design anything now. All she would be able to do was to play with it like a three-year-old. Jake suddenly had a thought. Perhaps when he visited, he'd organise having it shipped so she could.

'Oh, Jake.' Faye interrupted his thoughts. 'I'm so sorry. I had no idea …'

'No, neither does anyone else, apart from close family.' Close family. Jake scoffed. So close, that none of them, including himself, had visited her in all these months. Well, he was resolved to change that. As soon as he returned to London.

'I promise,' Faye said, sounding very earnest, 'that what you told me will never leave my lips.'

'Thank you, Faye.'

'I don't know what it's like to suffer that sort of loss.' She breathed deeply, 'but I can imagine …'

Jake sat up and thought about the little girl who had answered the phone. 'You're talking about Natty.'

'If anything happened to her, I think I'd go crazy.'

There was a pause. Jake imagined what had crossed her mind at that moment. When Natty had been a toddler, and she'd nearly been taken by Natty's father, Yousaf, to meet his family in Oman, he might not have brought her home. And Faye might never have seen her daughter again. Jake shuddered at the thought.

'You know I wouldn't let anything happen to her,' Jake reassured her.

'I'll just go check on her. Won't be a minute.'

'It's alright. You do that,' said Jake, as much for his own peace of mind as for hers. Suddenly, he was feeling the distance between them; his powerlessness to do anything if Yousaf should try anything again.

'Stupid, huh?' Faye was back on the phone within seconds.

'Not at all,' said Jake, just relieved that Faye had come back on the line and that everything was OK at her end.

'So, tell me Jake, about that one last surprise?'

'One last surprise?'

'Yes, you said she'd pulled one last surprise.'

'Yes, she did.'

Jake took a deep breath and exhaled before continuing. 'She must have arrived at the slopes before us. I saw her up ahead, waiting in the queue for the next ski lift. At first, I thought it wasn't her; I thought I was mistaken because she had cleverly convinced us she was not coming. Don't you see? She had it planned from the start – the surprise show at the slopes.' Jake paused. 'I just wish she'd gone shopping like she said.'

'She said she was going shopping?'

'Yes, that's what she said.' Jake frowned. It was beginning to dawn on him that she would have needed help to pull off her little surprise, turning up on the ski slopes unexpectedly. She would have needed somewhere to keep her ski stuff, to change into. And someone to drive her there too. Their driver had taken her into town, but Jake knew he'd returned.

'It turned out that the surprise, discovering she'd come after all, was just the start.'

'How do you mean?'

'Remember I told you about skiing off-piste a moment ago?'

'Of course. Is that what you and Marcus did? And Eleanor followed?'

'No, not at all.' Jake sat there, shaking his head. He still couldn't believe what had happened next. 'It was Eleanor who, to our amazement, went skiing off-piste.'

'So you two followed her.'

'That's right.'

'I don't think it's all that surprising,' said Faye. 'I mean, Marcus had goaded her, said you were going skiing off-piste.'

'Yes, I know. But I would have thought that was the last thing she'd want to do. In fact, I thought at the time, if Marcus was trying to persuade her to come with us by goading her about skiing off-piste, then he was going about it the wrong way. As I said before, skiing wasn't her thing. Why would she do that, especially in her condition?'

'I think I know,' said Faye, surprising Jake.

'How could you possibly know?'

'Well, no, you're right, how could I know? But from what you've said, the fact that she enjoyed surprising you … that's just what she did, doing something you'd never imagine she would.'

'And look what happened.'

'I'm sorry, Jake.'

'It's Marcus who ought to be sorry,' Jake blurted.

There was an uncomfortable silence.

'Tell me,' said Faye. 'Tell me what happened up there to make you hate Marcus.'

'Is that what he told you?'

'He said you'll never stop blaming him, that you'll always believe it was his fault.'

'I don't hate him, Faye. I hate what he did. I wish it had been me and not her. I wish she had walked away unscathed.'

'But you can't blame Marcus for the avalanche.'

'You want to bet?' Jake knew he sounded heartless, but he had every right to blame Marcus. 'He chose me, Faye, over his own sister.'

He had wanted to believe Marcus when he'd said there had been someone else up there on that mountain with them; someone else who had chosen to leave Eleanor trapped in the snow after the avalanche and dig Jake out first. Jake hadn't seen anyone else skiing off-piste with them. Part of him still thought it more likely that it was Marcus's way of coping with what he'd done; to block it out and convince himself someone else had made that decision.

'Up there on the ski slopes …' Jake got up off the bed and stood by the window, staring at the snow-capped mountains beyond the house. 'Up there, he made the wrong choice.'

10

Jake closed his eyes, trying to blank out the memory, trying to control his already shallow breathing. He wasn't winning; the memory was coming straight at him, bringing fear and panic in its wake. 'We were having a good time. Eleanor was skiing with a confidence I'd never seen before, and I was doing all I could just to keep up. Marcus was following close behind.' The words tumbled out; he couldn't hold back. 'I looked over my shoulder to see a massive grin on his face and remember thinking that he'd noticed the improvement in her skiing too. Then it began to snow – hard.'

Jake opened his eyes. 'This only added to the enjoyment, the exhilaration, the sheer thrill that the three of us were experiencing skiing in formation down that mountainside. I tell you, it was like something out of a bloody James Bond movie.' Jake shook his head in amazement.

'Then the weather closed in. More snow, less visibility.' Still standing by the window, Jake couldn't take his eyes off the snow-covered peak of the Cairngorm Mountain beyond The Lake House. 'Eleanor, she was skiing like the wind.' At first, it had been exhilarating, but Jake recalled that the faster she skied, the more concerned Jake became for her safety. 'I was struggling to keep up with her. So was Marcus. I could hear Marcus behind me yelling at her to slow down. Of course, she couldn't hear him. Then I had a terrible thought, Faye. I started to think she was doing it on purpose, scaring me for making her go there and share our news with the family. Then it got worse, then my thoughts turned really bad; was she trying to kill our baby?'

'No, surely not!' Faye cut in.

'That's when she disappeared straight over a precipice.'

Jake heard Faye take a sharp intake of breath.

'Marcus was beside me, grabbing at me, trying to stop me following her. We'd both stopped at the edge. There was no way I was going to let her go first. It had never been my plan. I couldn't face being a widower. So I punched him, Faye, with such force that I must have knocked him out. Then I went after her, launching myself over that precipice like I was on some sort of suicide mission.' Jake stopped.

'Jake?' There was concern in Faye's voice.

'There she was,' Jake said, his voice distant, 'quite still, just a few feet away. She was standing under a snowy ledge, out of the driving wind and snow, sideways on, looking my way. And under those goggles and scarf, I could imagine that knowing smile, those dancing eyes. She'd done it again, Faye; she'd tricked me one last time. I'd dropped just two or three feet over what turned out to be a shallow incline. She must have known. God knows how, but she must have known what she was doing all along. But that's when it happened.'

Jake left the window and sat on the bed. 'It was on my approach. I must have … it must have been …'

He knew that this would be hard to tell; that it would be hard to admit to being the cause of the accident.

Faye's soft voice filtered down the phone, encouraging him to continue.

'I don't know how it happened, I don't know what I did, Faye, but as I skied under that ledge to meet her – maybe it was the sound of my skis, maybe I was going too fast – it collapsed.'

'Oh no.'

'I found out afterwards there had been an avalanche. All I knew then was that one minute I was skiing towards her, feeling a mixture of blessed relief and complete outrage, wondering which emotion was going to win out, and the next I …' Jake couldn't go on. He couldn't speak of it. The panic, the breathlessness was setting in now.

'You were buried alive.'

'Yes,' Jake croaked. His throat felt dry. He felt cold, yet his skin felt clammy and hot. He closed his eyes.

He was back.

It was the sudden darkness that scared him most; the bright white world taken from him in an instant by the snow enveloping him, crushing him, until he couldn't breathe, couldn't move, couldn't escape back to the light, realising that it was all over sooner that he could ever have imagined.

He wanted his last thoughts to be good, to be true. He didn't want his last moments to be wasted in a futile struggle against the inevitable. So, he tried to recall with as much vivid detail as possible the people he loved, so he could at least feel he wasn't making that final journey alone and perhaps could leave the world enveloped in a kind of peace.

'Remember that night you stayed over at my house?' said Faye.

Jake opened his eyes. Of course he did. He'd been babysitting

Natty while Faye was on her course that day, training towards her headship qualification. She'd been stuck in traffic on the way home, and hadn't got in until very late. Natty had already been in bed, and was asleep. Jake had stayed over, sleeping on the couch. Natty had woken up at a silly hour that morning while Faye was fast asleep. She'd come down for a drink of water and had snuggled with Jake on the sofa, eventually falling asleep.

'I heard you, Jake.' He listened as Faye recounted what had happened that night. She'd been woken by a noise downstairs. It had been around midnight. She had got out of bed and automatically checked her daughter's room. Finding it empty, she'd expected Natty to be in the kitchen making a racket as well as a glass of water. But the kitchen had been empty, the lights off, and Faye had begun to feel anxious.

She always locked every door, checked every window; her little ritual twice around the house before lights out. But that night, unexpected company in the form of Jake crashing on her sofa had thrown her little ritual into disarray; she had forgotten it.

Jake's voice had pierced the silent stillness. He'd sounded agitated; she'd thought he had called out her name. She'd bounded through the lounge door. 'What is it?' she remembered asking as she approached the sofa. She had found Jake still asleep but sweating profusely – great beads of sweat were on his forehead, like he had a fever. And he seemed to be having trouble breathing.

'I thought you were having an asthma attack. You were really bad, Jake. But when I called your name, and you woke up, you were fine.'

'I can control it during the day, Faye, when I don't think about it. But at night …'

At night, it was out of control, and Faye was right; it was really bad. Jake hadn't had an uninterrupted night's sleep since the accident. Every night he was back. He couldn't move, he couldn't see, he couldn't breathe; trapped in a snow-white coffin, paralysed with fear, until a movement above, snow shifting, light, blinding, dazzling, beautiful light.

But the nightmare didn't end there. It never ended there.

'At night, I constantly relive that moment.' The moment when Jake's relief at being freed from the darkness, being able to breathe in that crisp white air, turned to horror at the thought of Eleanor just a few feet away, so close, yet so alone in her own snow-white coffin.

'As soon as my lungs were filled with air, I was screaming at Marcus to leave me and find Eleanor, get her out. He left me. Then he returned, asking me if I was OK – asking me what happened, as if he hadn't heard a single word I had just said. Christ, I felt so helpless.'

Jake remembered that overwhelming sense of helplessness at being trapped in the snow, unable to help rescue Eleanor. 'He left me again. I was still trapped, but at least I could breathe. But I was desperate to know what was happening. Had he found her? Was she alright? Please, god, tell me she's alright, I prayed. But Marcus wouldn't tell me anything. All I could hear was his voice repeating her name over and over.'

Jake took a moment to remember to breathe, trying to stave off a panic attack as the memories came flooding back.

'Then they arrived out of nowhere.' Jake recalled the thumping sound of the rescue helicopter appearing overhead, whipping up a mini snowstorm around them, threatening to bury them again. He remembered looking up through the driving snow and seeing a man in bright colours being winched down beside a metal cage. He looked back and wondered at how quickly they'd been found.

'They took her first. I insisted. After they had resuscitated her, I wanted them to get her to the hospital fast; I didn't want to run the risk of losing her again.'

Jake's attempts to convince a sceptical rescuer that he was alright so that they would leave without him wasn't helped by Marcus's constant interference with the words, 'You don't look alright.' At Marcus insistence, they checked him over. There was some bruising, but no broken bones. Jake even got to his feet to prove he was alright, which he wasn't – not really. He was suffering from shock. He was shaking so badly that he didn't know how he was going to make it off the mountain. But he did, because all he could think of was being reunited with Eleanor.

'I saw her. We both did.' She was nearly free of that white tomb. 'I remembered thinking …' Jake shook his head, 'why her? I should have done something more to stop her.'

'You can't blame yourself.'

Jake cut across Faye's protestations that it wasn't his fault. He knew what she was going to say; it had started to snow hard, and it was just a coincidence the way that ledge had collapsed on his approach. It wasn't his fault there had been an avalanche.

Jake wasn't having any of it. 'I remember standing there staring as they flew her straight to hospital, thinking it should have been Eleanor that Marcus dug out first.'

Jake stared through the window at The Lake House. If they hadn't rowed, if he'd only listened, Eleanor wouldn't have felt the need to prove a point, and she wouldn't have been standing under that ledge. They'd have spent Christmas in London instead. And Marcus wouldn't have been forced to make an impossible choice he would have to live with for the rest of his life.

Ultimately, Jake knew, by hating Marcus, by punishing Marcus, by withdrawing his friendship, his love, he was really punishing himself for being the cause of it all. Until Jake could forgive himself for his part in the tragedy, how could he hope to forgive Marcus?

'Up there, he made the wrong choice,' Jake said again.

Jake expected Faye to make sympathetic noises, say something, anything. 'Faye, are you still there?'

'He told me you'd say that.'

Jake's eyebrows shot up. So he had told her! Marcus perpetrating the lie, making Jake look bad in front of Faye. Making himself out to be the innocent party, the wronged man. No wonder Faye had told Marcus about his holiday. No wonder she was mad at him for getting Marcus thrown in jail when he'd followed Jake on holiday to Scotland, and Jake had informed the local police he might have brought drugs on the flight with him.

'He says you've got it all wrong.'

Jake didn't need this. How many times had Marcus told him this same absurd lie? Even though he was there in Scotland to find out the truth about whether someone had been up there off-piste with them, Jake had to acknowledge that deep down, he just didn't believe it was true.

'He says it wasn't him.'

Jake had seen nobody else on that run. Who did Marcus think it was? The ghost of bloody Christmas future?

'He says you knocked him unconscious, and when he came around. it was your voice he could hear shouting out. That's when he realised you were okay; you weren't buried like Eleanor. So he started digging her out. He says when he found you, your face was already clear of the snow; somebody had got to you first. He says there must have been somebody else up there with you.'

'What do you believe?' Jake's tone was curt.

'I don't know what to think,' said Faye haltingly.

That wasn't good enough. 'I've got to go,' Jake said abruptly. 'I've got things to do.' He couldn't wait to get back to London and have it out with Marcus – once and for all. He'd been foolishly persuaded that Marcus might, just might be telling the truth. But if somebody else had been up there with them, then why hadn't they come forward? He'd asked himself that question once before, but this time he had the answer: no one had come forward for the simple reason that no one else had been up there with them.

'Jake, Jake, I didn't mean …'

Jake slammed the phone down.

11

Jake parked in front of Gillespie's General Store next to a battered green van with the faded words Gillespie Deliveries on the side. He'd arrived just as the shop was opening. As he approached the entrance, he was forced to do a quick sidestep out of the way of a young man leaving the store, his arms laden with three crates. He looked familiar. Jake waited while the guy loaded the van, then accosted him as he approached.

'David?' said Jake, stepping in front of him and blocking his way into the store. Jake noted the disconcerted look that flickered across his face. 'We met yesterday at Gayle's,' Jake clarified. 'At dinner. Well, you didn't end up staying for dinner …' Jake looked at him expectantly, wondering if David would tell him whether the previous day he'd managed to book that hotel room for tonight, to surprise Robyn when she returned from London today. Perhaps he was planning for them to stay more than one night.

'Yes, I remember,' he said slowly, a guarded look in his eyes.

Jake knew it was none of his business, but he wanted to meet Robyn before he left, hoping she wouldn't be too busy catching up with her boyfriend in a posh suite in a hotel to visit Gayle at Lark Lodge. That was assuming David had booked a room. There was another reason for Jake's interest – he wanted David's room at Lark Lodge. Jake appreciated that he'd been in luck when Gayle had told him that the seven-night booking for the attic room had been cancelled. It meant he could stay on at Lark Lodge for six more nights, if he wished. The problem was that Jake didn't want to remain in the attic room – the one with the view of The Lake House.

Jake had an idea. If they got into conversation about something else, maybe he could drop in the question about whether David was staying on at Gayle's. He'd asked Gayle that morning, but David had left early for work, and she hadn't had a chance to speak to him.

Jake opted to show him the photograph of Martha's son; it would be a way in. He was their generation. Perhaps her son had been adopted by a local couple, and he had gone to school with David. It was a long shot, but anything was possible.

'I've got something to show you.'

He was about to explain how he came by the photo, and how he had met the boy's mother, but when he got out his wallet, he couldn't find the photo. He put his hand in his coat pocket and came up empty. He was momentarily thrown. He held up a finger. 'Just one second.' He checked the other pocket.

'Look, some people have to work around here,' said David as he pushed past him, the sarcasm in his voice unmistakable.

Jake was left standing outside the store, frantically searching all his pockets until he remembered: the previous evening, after his conversation with Faye, which he'd ended rather abruptly, he had taken the photo out of his wallet to try and focus on something else. He must have left the photo on his bedside table and had forgotten to put it back in his wallet.

Jake sighed, his thoughts turning to Faye. He should have phoned her straight back and apologised for being so rude, but he hadn't. That morning, when he'd woken, he'd known she'd be getting herself and Natty ready for the last day of term. He'd decided he would either phone her later, when she'd returned from work, or on Saturday morning, and would have to hope she would answer her phone. She wouldn't have had time to listen to his lame apologies that morning, which was just as well, because Jake had wanted to leave early for Mr Gillespie's store. He'd had something pressing on his mind. However, it wasn't catching up with David.

David reappeared with another load of crates and gave Jake a black look on his way to the van. He deposited the crates on the pavement and loaded them into the van one at a time.

Jake sidled up to the van, conscious of the fact that this had not got off to a good start. 'Look,' he said, 'I have something to show you that might be of interest.' He was aware he was sounding like some dodgy salesman, or worse, a dealer offering David something illegal. Jake wished Marcus hadn't come to mind at that moment. He pressed on. 'Can we talk?'

'I'm busy.' David loaded the last box into the back of the van.

'OK.' Jake hadn't expected this to be easy. 'It doesn't have to be now.' Jake would still rather have the photograph, something with which to open the lines of communication. 'Later, perhaps, at Gayle's …' Jake was fishing. He waited to see what David would say to that.

David finished loading the van, passing Jake several times as he entered the shop, returning with more goods for the van, making him wait for an answer. Finally, he slammed the back door shut, wiped his dusty hands down the front of his jeans, and came over to Jake. 'I won't be back till late – very late.'

Jake pursed his lips. So he hadn't booked a hotel room. Damn! There went that room at Gayle's that Jake wanted to move into. On the other hand, perhaps it was good news. He wondered if David was picking Robyn up from the train station. Maybe they were having a meal together and then staying over together at Gayle's. That could be a possibility. Jake bit his lip. He couldn't very well ask him. He didn't even know Robyn. Their relationship was none of his business. He guessed he'd just have to wait and see if she was there at breakfast on Saturday morning.

'I see.' Jake was not perturbed.

He watched David climb into the van. Jake turned towards the store.

'I'll be at The Winky.'

Jake turned back. David was sitting in the driver's seat, his window wound down.

'The Winky?'

'You know, The Winking Owl.'

'Sorry, I don't know what that is.'

'It's a pub.' David shot him a look. 'I can tell you're not a local, despite your accent.'

Jake shot him a look. Of course David knew he wasn't a local – he was Jake Campbell-Ross.

But he hadn't always been a part of the Ross family. 'I used to live here once, years ago, when I was a boy.' Jake could hear the sadness in his voice, the ache for what might have been. He might have grown up in this small community in Aviemore if his parents hadn't died. Perhaps he'd have known David all his life, gone to school with him, and called The Winking Owl The Winky, like the locals obviously did.

Jake glanced at Mr Gillespie's store. Perhaps his mother had shopped there. He wouldn't be surprised. The large chain supermarkets had only been in the town for around ten years. Until then, this store had been the main grocery store unless you travelled further afield. Jake could just imagine his mother taking him shopping there as a child. Jake hadn't been in the store since. It made him wonder if David's father would remember him – the little kid whose father was in the RAF.

Although Jake and his mother could have travelled with his father, and lived abroad during his postings, his mother loved Scotland, and her home town of Aviemore, and The Lake House – their home. So they'd lived there, the two of them, while his father was away.

'I don't think I've ever been in that pub,' Jake thought aloud. He hadn't really ventured into Aviemore much over the years, even though he'd been there every winter for Christmas.

'It's up the road there, right in the centre of town.' David pointed. 'I'll be drowning my sorrows,' he said, 'so don't expect too much coherent conversation. But you're welcome to join me for a drink and … well, whatever it is you want to show me.' He offered Jake an unexpected grin.

David was out to get plastered tonight, and he'd invited Jake along for the ride, although Jake intended to stick to soft drinks.

'I'll be there,' Jake said, surprised by the invitation.

Jake watched David start the engine.

David's plans to book into a fancy hotel and patch things up with Robyn had presumably gone awry. That morning, at breakfast, Jake had noticed that Gayle was unusually subdued. She hadn't said why. Now Jake guessed that Robyn had phoned her and told her as much. Perhaps Robyn was staying in London for the weekend. Or maybe she was coming home, but didn't want to see David.

'Lost my girl …' said David.

Jake nodded knowingly.

'And I haven't even got a proper job.'

Jake looked back at the store, then back at the truck.

David read his mind. 'I'm helping out the old man, just temporarily – I hope.'

Jake lost his chance to ask David about his plans for the future by the appearance of Mr Gillespie at the door, casting a disapproving glare in his son's direction and shouting, 'You still here?'

'Speak of the devil,' said David, starting the engine. He looked out of the window at Jake. 'I'll be in the pub 'til closing time most probably. I'll buy you a pint,' he said. 'It's the strong stuff, mind, none of that wishy-washy English rubbish.'

'I'll be there, but I'm not drinking—' Jake's voice was drowned out over the rumble of the engine. There was a crunch as David put the truck into gear.

Jake stepped back and watched the van drive off, feeling sorry for David. It sounded as though things had been going great one minute – he and Robyn had got engaged, and had moved into his boathouse – and then something had suddenly happened, and everything had changed.

He swallowed hard at the thought of how life really could turn on a dime. He'd heard that phrase when he was working in America, and he'd had to ask his American colleague, who had recently suffered an unexpected bereavement, what he'd meant by that. He'd told him it was a figure of speech, meaning the course of a person's life could change direction very quickly.

Jake could empathise. It had happened to him as a child. But he'd had no clue back then that it would happen to him again.

Eleanor.

Jake breathed a heavy sigh, remembering what he had gone there to do.

He turned around to find Mr Gillespie senior still standing outside his shop, arms folded over his chest, eyeing Jake suspiciously. 'Can I help you?'

'Yes, as a matter of fact, you can,' said Jake, following him into the shop. 'I need a sledgehammer.'

12

'You want what?'

'A sledgehammer.'

'May I ask what you need the sledgehammer for?'

'No, you may not,' said Jake, opening his wallet and wondering how much the tourist rip-off premium was this season.

'We don't sell 'em.'

'Excuse me?' Jaked looked at the sledgehammer that Mr Gillespie had just deposited on the counter right in front of him.

'That's mine, from my workshop.'

Jake sighed heavily. 'How much?' He closed his fingers around a big wad of cash.

'Put it away, son, for goodness' sake.'

Jake looked up, perplexed.

'You can borrow it; just as long as you remember to bring it back when you're done doing whatever it is needs doing.'

Jake took his fingers out of his wallet. He didn't know what had surprised him most – the fact that Mr Gillespie was going to lend him the thing, no questions asked, or the fact that he wasn't charging for it.

Mr Gillespie handed Jake the tool. 'And I'll have you know I don't fleece tourists.'

Jake rolled his eyes. He was sick to death of being called a stranger in his hometown, the place of his birth, the place he had lived quite happily until an ill wind brought forced change. 'And I'll have you know I'm not a bloody tourist,' Jake answered back.

Mr Gillespie raised his eyebrows. 'You sure act like one.'

Jake blushed; it was true, he'd always breezed into town on vacation like a tourist, throwing money around, acting like he owned the place while doing his utmost to steer clear of the locals – and that went for local establishments too. Everything was catered for, ready for their arrival; good food and fine wines sent ahead from London. He never had reason to visit Mr Gillespie's store, even though it was just a short ride or a reasonable walk from his house.

His mother may well have brought him to this store all those years earlier, but Jake had not stepped inside the place since. Mr Gillespie was right; although he had been born there, and he had property there, he was now just a stranger – one of many tourists visiting the town.

Perhaps it was time he got reacquainted.

'I own The Lake House,' said Jake by way of introducing his credentials as a fully paid-up member of the community.

'Do you, now?' Mr Gillespie nodded. 'Vacation home, is it?' His disapproval was glaringly obvious.

Jake blinked. He had assumed Mr Gillespie knew The Lake House was the Rosses' holiday home. Maybe he did, and he was just making a point that it was of no consequence to him. Jake got the idea that Mr Gillespie was not someone he should underestimate. After all, he'd sublet part of his store to Robyn, and the shop was buzzing – not just in Robyn's Interior Design, but in the original grocery side of the business too.

Jake glanced over his shoulder at the interior design outlet and debated whether he should wander over to the other side of the store and talk to Robyn's assistant, who was working there that day. He recalled Gayle mentioning that David had arranged with his sister-in-law, Annie, that she would work on Friday and over the weekend.

Perhaps he'd wait and see if Robyn arrived at the guesthouse first before he ventured over there.

Jake looked at the sledgehammer in his hand. Perhaps it wasn't the right moment to introduce himself. Besides, he did have something much more pressing he wanted to do.

'The house used to belong to a Royal Air Force officer. Nice fellow. His wife was born and raised here. Know what I'm saying?'

Jake turned back to Mr Gillespie, and nodded. Jake did know what he was saying, loud and clear; Mr Gillespie had mistaken him for one of the city-dwellers who were buying up local property as weekend homes, taking advantage of the scenery, the skiing, and giving little back in return, stripping away entire communities to leave them practically deserted ghost towns. He was guilty of that, it was true, but not through choice. Circumstance had dictated he had not been able to grow up in that house, in this community, but thanks to William, at least he had retained some links to his past, however tenuous.

'I'm his son,' said Jake.

'Pardon me?' Mr Gillespie was evidently surprised.

'The RAF officer. I'm his son.' Jake watched the man's surprise turn to embarrassment at his obvious gaffe. 'I was born here too, in Aviemore, but did not have the good fortune to grow up here.' Jake's voice was tight.

'Yes, I remember.'

Jake didn't doubt that; small towns had long memories.

'You're Rosemary's boy.' Mr Gillespie's eyes danced around Jake.

'I remember your mother bringing you into this shop while she was shopping.' He paused. 'You've been away a while.'

Jake looked at him quizzically; it was a strange way of looking at things. It made it sound as though Jake had just returned from a trip rather than having been gone twenty-five years, apart from his annual holiday. It made Jake feel strangely homesick, but not, as he would have expected, for England. 'I live in London now.'

'I would never have guessed.' The corner of Mr Gillespie's mouth twitched.

Jake gave him a sideways glance as he picked the sledgehammer off the counter. It felt satisfyingly heavy, like he could do some serious damage – just what he wanted.

'Are you coming back – to live perhaps?'

'Maybe,' Jake frowned. Where had that come from? He had absolutely no intention of returning to live there. So, what the hell had he said that for? Jake walked to the door, pondering the question.

'It's what I've been telling them all along.'

Jake stopped short of the door. He turned to look at the old man. 'Telling who?'

'The young ones like yourself who leave for the bright lights of the big cities. I tell them that they'll come back. They always come back. Can't help themselves. You see, it's the place – The Highlands – it haunts you. When you leave, your soul doesn't want to go with you; it wants to stay here with the mountains and the lochs. There's no place in the world like it.'

Jake stood by the door in contemplative silence, broken by Mr Gillespie beating a fist on the counter. 'It's those damn weekenders,' he said vehemently, 'stealing the houses from our children. Means they can't come back, doesn't it? You should count yourself lucky, son. Never sell, lad. Never sell. Keep it for your children.'

'I have no children,' Jake said stiffly. He opened the door.

'Yes – I remember now,' Mr Gillespie spoke softly. 'It was your wife that had that terrible accident up there last Christmas.'

Jake nodded.

'An unfortunate set of circumstances.'

'Yes.' Jake agreed that it was. Last year had been exceptional, both in terms of snowfall and the potentially dangerous conditions it had brought about, one of which Jake was now well-acquainted with – overhangs; snow and ice hanging precariously over precipices, waiting to be dislodged, creating mini-avalanches to bury alive unsuspecting skiers passing underneath. And they would not have become those unsuspecting skiers if it hadn't been for Eleanor's bizarre decision to lead them all off-piste. Marcus may have mentioned skiing off-piste, but nobody would have expected Eleanor to take him seriously. Not for nothing was skiing off-piste considered a hazardous pursuit; in some circumstances, it was illegal. But in Scotland, under normal conditions, it would have been fine. That unfortunate set of circumstances would haunt Jake for the rest of his life.

Jake looked at the sledgehammer in his hands. It was time to face up to what had happened and put it behind him.

13

'Are you alright, son?'

Jake's breathing was shallow; he was about to exit the shop, but he was having a problem catching his breath.

'Yes, of course. I'm fine, Mr Gillespie – really.' He knew he didn't sound fine, each word spoken in between laboured breaths.

In the beginning, he had thought he'd developed asthma. He'd never suffered from it before, but apparently it was possible to get adult onset of the condition. Thorough medical tests had revealed it wasn't asthma, pneumonia, a bronchial infection or anything of a physical nature; it was all in his mind. A psychological problem, Jake wasn't pleased to hear, manifesting itself in panic attacks triggered by confined spaces and a very specific memory of an event. If he avoided the triggers, he avoided situations like now. But sometimes there was no way of avoiding enclosed spaces, like the lifts at the school where he worked. Instead, Jake had learned to control it.

But this wasn't one of those situations. The shop floor was spacious. He wasn't confined. So what had brought it on? Jake suddenly had a brainwave. It wasn't the actual physical spaces that brought on anxiety attacks, but the memory they elicited. He'd learned to control thinking about it, and at school in those lifts, he was too busy with work to think of anything else.

Here was the proof. He wasn't even in an enclosed space, but he was thinking of what had happened on that mountain.

'Do you need to sit down?' Mr Gillespie appeared from behind the counter, carrying a stool.

Jake held up his hand. 'No, really. I'll be alright.' He stood by the door, holding the door handle, steadying himself, Mr Gillespie hovering nearby with the stool at the ready. The less Jake thought about the memory, the more he improved.

In the beginning, this had been next to impossible, as his every waking hour had been consumed by that one event. What he had come to realise was that he needed two things: time and distance. He needed plenty of both. He had created distance – emotional distance – by leaving the firm and trying to divorce himself from the family. He had created physical distance – the easy part – by remaining right where he was in London; as far away from Scotland as possible.

The time issue was the tricky part. He had needed a job, and he'd needed it to be one that would keep him on mental high alert, with no time to think, to reflect, to question, to argue, to rage with his tormentor – the past. Becoming a teacher had fitted the bill perfectly. Not only did he expend all his energies on acquiring the new skills needed to become a teacher – it could be tough working in an inner-city school – he also had a mentor and a class of students he could not fail by not being one hundred per cent dedicated to his job.

From the very beginning, when he'd got the teacher training position in the school, he'd known that the only downside of the job would be the long school summer holiday. But when he'd started in the autumn term, that had been months and months away. However, the time had passed in the blink of an eye, with the summer holidays looming ever closer. So Jake had made a plan – he would volunteer for every summer club run by the school, and if he couldn't do that, then he'd volunteer somewhere else, like a summer camp in America.

That had been the plan. He certainly had not expected to find himself out of work before the end of term, at a loose end, and told to go on a holiday. He looked at his bandaged hands. Soon the bandages would come off. But now he didn't want to volunteer for summer clubs, or go away to work in a summer camp. All he wanted was to fast-forward to September so that he could spend as much time at work as possible – not only because he loved his job, but because Faye was there. And once they were back at work, he could resume babysitting duties for Natty.

But he couldn't fast-forward to September. That day, the school was breaking up, and no doubt Faye had plans for the summer. If only he could spend the summer with them. Jake raised his eyebrows. How would that happen? What was he going to do – invite them to his holiday home in Scotland for the summer?

Jake raised his eyes even further. Could he? More to the point, even if she were to accept the invitation, would it work for Faye to come to The Lake House, even though they were just friends?

Jake knew what the problem was – he wanted more than just friendship; he wanted her. And the guilt of falling in love with someone else so soon after what had happened to Eleanor was—

'I'm glad, though, that at least when the snow thawed, they found the person who fired off that shot.' Mr Gillespie cut straight across Jake's thoughts with a bombshell.

'What?' Jake let go of the door. It slammed shut. 'What did

you just say?'

'The person who fired off that pistol shot – more than likely started that avalanche and brought down the heap of snow that buried … Oh!' Mr Gillespie registered Jake's shock. 'You didn't know?'

Now Jake needed that stool. He sat down on it by the counter. He could barely speak.

Mr Gillespie turned around and ushered some surprised customers out of his shop, telling them to leave their baskets by the door and come back later. He put the closed sign in the door, and locked it.

There were just two customers, a young couple, in the interior design outlet. They were too busy choosing curtains to notice that the grocery store customers had suddenly been kicked out.

Jake could feel the anger welling up again about what happened to Eleanor, to all three of them. 'It wasn't a freak act of nature?' he said in a hoarse voice.

Mr Gillespie shook his head. 'I'm afraid it doesn't look like it was. I once read that it's a myth that a noise can trigger an avalanche—'

Jake looked at him sharply. 'But you just said—'

'Let me finish.'

Jake shut his mouth.

'It sounds to me as though that gunshot did cause a shelf of snow to shift, and, well, you know what happened next.'

'It started off as a rumour among us locals. Somebody – who was it now?' Mr Gillespie scratched his chin. 'I forget who first said they'd heard a shot up there that Christmas, but it got around town like wildfire. Then more people started saying they'd heard something, but others hadn't. It was the talk of the town, what with the skiing accident up there that same afternoon.' He studied Jake. 'Of course, you can't be sure what you hear up there. It's the wind, you see – it could carry a sound you thought you heard right next to you from miles away, and it makes it so that a sound could come from any direction, any distance.'

Jake found his voice. 'I don't remember hearing a gunshot.' But then at the point when Jake had skied over that edge, and caught up with Eleanor, all he could hear was Marcus yelling at his sister to slow down, unaware she'd come to a halt under the overhang.

'There you go. You see, a lot of people didn't. Then again, a lot of people did. I guess it depended on where you were – downwind of the shot or not. But what was certain was that it came from the area where you were skiing off-piste.'

'How could you possibly know that?'

'Someone came forward, anonymously; someone else who'd been off-piste that afternoon too, claiming there had definitely been a gunshot.'

Jake nearly fell off his stool. 'Are you saying someone else was up there with us?'

'Two people, apparently. Mr Anonymous who heard the shot, and the person who took the shot.'

Jake narrowed his eyes. 'How did they know it wasn't one and the same person?'

'Ah, because the person who made the call to the police was very much alive, obviously.'

'Huh?'

'They found him – poor guy.'

'The shooter?' Jake stared at him.

'That's right, when the snow thawed.'

'Dead?'

'Very. Suicide.' Mr Gillespie put two fingers to his temple. 'Bullet right here.'

Jake was, quite frankly, astounded; how could he not know this?

'It was in the spring,' Mr Gillespie continued. 'Some walkers found him, raised the alarm. It was suicide, plain and simple. Only thing they couldn't figure was why he was wearing skiing gear. If that was what his intention was, then why did he go to the bother of taking his skis?'

'Perhaps he was just having one last ski for old times' sake,' Jake said in a small voice.

'Perhaps. In any case, they confirmed the time of death. Puts him right there that day.'

Jake stared at Mr Gillespie, taking all this in.

'They found his car at a little-used Forestry Commission car park. Hell of a hike from there to the ski runs.'

Jake didn't think so; perhaps he wanted some peace and quiet, some solitude, before he departed the world. Jake had thought about it often enough – in the beginning. A person could do the craziest things, if they were pushed. A person could lose all rational thought and do a thing no sane person would even contemplate. Jake's hands closed around the sledgehammer.

'But you know what the craziest part was?'

Jake shook his head.

'He'd gone and bought a ticket, a car parking ticket out of the machine. That's how they could pinpoint the exact date and time of death, because those things are dated and time-stamped. Now, tell me,' he paused, staring at Jake intently, 'does that sound like a man intent on taking his own life?'

Jake didn't know what to say.

'Of course, us locals put two and two together; your skiing accident was most likely caused by the sound of gunfire dislodging the snow, but it wasn't a matter for the police. There was no crime committed there. It wasn't as though he was shooting at you.'

Jake stirred uneasily.

'As I said, an unfortunate set of circumstances. If he'd been there any other day, then who knows? Perhaps …' he trailed off.

Perhaps the accident would never have happened, thought Jake.

'Who was he?' Jake wanted to know the name of this man who had taken not one, but two lives that Christmas.

Mr Gillespie thought hard. 'I don't recall … but my son might remember.'

'David?'

'Yes, I'll be sure to tell him to stop by on the way to his next delivery – The Lake House, wasn't it?'

'No.' Jake hesitated. 'I'm staying at Lark Lodge, actually.'

Mr Gillespie nodded solemnly. 'I understand.'

Jake doubted that he did. He thanked Mr Gillespie.

'Call me Duncan.'

Jake nodded and turned to go. Then he had a thought. 'Duncan … you don't have to worry about asking David to stop by Lark Lodge. He'll be there later. But he said he'd be in The Winky this evening, so I'll expect I'll see him there first.'

'What do you mean – he'll be back there?' Duncan frowned. 'He hasn't got any deliveries at Lark Lodge today.'

'Well, no. He's staying at the lodge.' Jake realised he'd put his foot in it. David and Robyn's relationship was none of his business, but now he had to tell Duncan something was up. Or perhaps he didn't have to. 'Look, it sounds like David is stopping at Gayle's while Robyn is in London.'

Duncan's frown deepened. 'What do you mean – stopping at Gayle's?'

'You know, he's taken a room.'

'In her guesthouse?'

'Well … yes.'

'What's wrong with his boathouse?'

Jake knew there was nothing wrong with the boathouse, apart from the fact that Robyn wasn't there.

'What is going on?' Duncan's frown deepened.

Jake stood up from the stool and looked at the door.

'Annie!' Duncan shouted across the shop.

It didn't sound like a request; more like an order. Jake remained rooted to the spot, eyes wide, wishing he could just leave. He did not want to get drawn into whatever was going on between two people he barely knew, or in the case of Robyn, didn't know at all. Jake's followed Duncan's gaze to the interior design outlet.

A slim young woman, dressed in tailored trousers and a blouse, left her customers to report to Duncan at the desk. She looked from Duncan to Jake. 'I'll be with you in a minute,' she said to Jake, mistaking him for one of her customers.

'He is not one of your customers,' Duncan said.

'Then what is it, Duncan? I'm busy.'

'It's David. Jake here says he's staying at Lark Lodge, apparently.'

Jake looked at Annie. This was awkward. He'd thought Duncan would introduce him. 'I'm Jake.' He held out his hand. 'I'm staying at Lark Lodge too. That's where I met him.'

Annie shook his hand. 'Um … pleased to meet you, Jake.' She paused. 'Have we met before? Your face seems familiar.'

'No, no – we haven't met before.' Jake really didn't want to divulge his full name.

'Of course his face is familiar,' Duncan boomed. 'His name is Jake Campbell-Ross.'

Jake rolled his eyes at Duncan. As he did so, he caught sight of the young couple who had been choosing curtains, oblivious to the conversation in Duncan's grocery shop. Now they were looking in his direction, all ears.

Jake heaved a sigh. 'Well, it's been very nice meeting you, but I really ought to get going …' He looked at Duncan, who had the keys to the locked shop door in his hand.

Duncan ignored him and turned to Annie. 'So, did you know he'd moved out of the boathouse?'

'He hasn't moved out. He's just staying with Gayle for—'

'Oh, so you did know.'

Jake pursed his lips, looking over at the door and wishing he could escape the awkward conversation.

'Have David and Robyn split up? I knew he shouldn't have got together with an out-of-towner.'

'Look, do we have to do this now?' She glanced over at her customers.

Jake noted they'd quickly returned to looking through the curtains samples, probably feeling as embarrassed as he did at overhearing the conversation.

'I warned him he knew nothing about her. She appears out of nowhere on Christmas Day…'

Jake looked at him.

Duncan continued. 'And why has David moved out of the boathouse? Why hasn't she?'

'She's not at the boathouse. And David hasn't moved out. He's just staying with Gayle for a bit.'

'As good as,' Duncan scoffed. 'So, where is she?'

'In London on another assignment.'

'Oh, right. Another assignment.' Duncan slowly shook his head from side to side. 'A likely story. David obviously doesn't believe that either.'

Jake stole a glance at Duncan's deepening frown. He was just wondering how long he'd have to stand there, listening to their personal problems, when the young couple walked over. The woman sheepishly said, 'Um, we'll come back later.'

Annie said, 'No, don't go! I'll be right over.'

'Nah, it's fine.' The young couple exchanged a glance. 'We'll, um … pop back later. Promise.'

Jake guessed they probably would not.

Annie folded her arms and threw Duncan a black look as they walked to the shop door. Jake heard one of them say, 'The door's stuck.'

'Just give it a yank. I want to go.'

Annie said, 'Did you lock the shop door?' looking at Duncan in surprise.

Jake caught her looking around the shop floor. 'Where did all your customers go?'

Before he could answer that question, she held out her hand. 'I can't believe you chucked your customers out. For goodness' sake. It's no big deal. They're just going through a little rocky patch, that's all. You're making a drama where there isn't. I can't believe you shut the shop over this.'

Jake bit his bottom lip, really hoping that Duncan did not correct her and tell her the real reason he'd got rid of his customers and locked the shop. Jake did not want to get drawn into talking about his personal issues with a total stranger.

Duncan glanced at Jake and kept his mouth shut as Annie took the keys. She unlocked the door, and the young couple hurriedly exited the shop. As soon as they were out of the door, the customers who'd been in the middle of shopping when Duncan had unceremoniously kicked them out stepped straight in and picked up their shopping baskets. They'd obviously been waiting outside.

Jake took that as his cue to leave.

Duncan called after him, 'Remember, have a word with David. Perhaps he can tell you who was up there.'

Jake paused at the door and nodded. He was just stepping outside when he heard Duncan call after him, 'And Jake – welcome home.'

'I'm not—' Jake turned around to find the door closed and Mr Gillespie standing inside the shop, his hand still on the doorknob, having words with Annie. Jake heard him say, 'All these trips to London … do you think she's meeting someone from her past? Is that what David thinks?'

Jake couldn't have heard Annie's response or the rest of the conversation even if he'd wanted to. Another customer had walked up to the door. Jake stepped aside and walked back to his car, thinking about what Duncan had said about Robyn: She appears out of nowhere on Christmas Day …

Jake shook his head. That was none of his concern.

He deposited the sledgehammer on the back seat and drove home.

14

Jake took off his jacket, folded it once and placed it beside him on the stone bench. He picked up the roll of bandages – he had come prepared – and rolled up his sleeves. He wound a layer of bandages first around his left hand, then his right hand, making sure to secure them tightly at the wrist. The cuts to his hands were healing nicely, and if he opened them up, then so be it – this had to be done. Jake was ready. He stood. He picked up the sledgehammer and took five paces forward. He stopped.

He swung.

The memorial stone shattered.

The date went first, then her name, Eleanor, and finally that word – Chosen. Three more swings and it was down to a mere stump; the rest would have to be dug up. But it was good enough for Jake. He'd done exactly what he'd gone back to do. He stood there for a moment, looking at the debris of the memorial stone he'd had erected in the small side-garden of The Lake House and thinking of his state of mind soon after the accident, when he'd convinced himself she was dead. She might as well be, thought Jake again. But even so, she wasn't, and it was a terrible thing to have erected a memorial. It was why Marcus had followed him there. Marcus was worried about him. Why wouldn't he be, after he'd found out about the stone? Jake shook his head. This was part of his journey to acceptance of what had happened. The memorial stone was gone, and with it the delusion that Eleanor was gone too. And when he got back to London, as soon as Marcus had cleaned himself up, and was out of rehab, Jake knew he'd have to face up to the next challenge, which was going to be an awful lot harder than taking a sledgehammer to a piece of granite – facing Eleanor for the first time since the accident.

How could I have left visiting her all these months – not seeing her once?

Jake didn't want to go on that guilt trip right now. He still had one more thing to do before joining Marcus in London – find Martha's son. He hoped her son had been adopted locally, if that was what had happened, and that David knew him. He hoped it would be that easy; needed it to be so. He was going to get the photo of the little boy called Ralph, which he had left in his room at Lark Lodge, and meet David at The Winky to show him the photo. David would tell him, 'Hey, that's a kid I went to school with. And do you know, he still lives and works in Aviemore.'

Jake sighed. He didn't think there was a chance he would be that lucky. It occurred to him that he could have asked Mr Gillespie if he knew Martha. It was another long shot, but he had obviously lived in the area for years and years. Their paths might have crossed. He resolved to return to Mr Gillespie's store to find out. In the meantime, perhaps when David had loosened up after a few drinks, he might be ready to talk. Jake just hoped he didn't spend all night talking about Robyn, rather than what Jake was going to be there for – finding Martha's son.

Jake was still holding back from asking the one person who

was closest to Martha – her brother – the question that was still on his mind. What if Aubrey had never known that Martha had a son – that he had a nephew? It still wasn't a conversation he wanted to have with Aubrey over the phone.

Jake's thoughts were interrupted by someone shouting his name from the main garden. He dropped the sledgehammer, rolled down his sleeves, picked up his coat and noted with some satisfaction that the bandages were still clean.

Jake walked through the gap in the hedge, feeling pretty good about things, just as Marty skidded to a halt in front of him, grabbing his sleeve. 'Jake!' He was breathless, as though he'd been running. 'It's Gayle.'

Jake immediately registered the alarm on Marty's face. 'What happened?'

'She sent me to find you. You'd better come quick. There's some woman on the phone for you, hysterical, can't get a sane word out of her.'

'Oh, god – it's Lydia!' Jake's heart pounded. His pace quickened. By the time he got to the car, he was running full pelt and too psyched-up to stop.

He ran past the car and across the lawn. He hurled himself through a tiny gap in the privet hedge where once, as children, he and Marcus had sneaked into the neighbouring property. He ran towards Gayle, who was standing on the porch, looking down the driveway, not expecting Jake to arrive from another direction. Jake reached her, panting like a dog.

She guided him to the phone in the study, her face urgent.

Jake picked up the phone as Gayle pulled the door closed, leaving him alone to take the call.

He hesitated.

Was this the call he'd been dreading? Time and again, it had been Lydia ringing him up, and he had tried to reassure her that everything would be alright; that he'd go and find Marcus. But no, not this time; this time it would be Lydia telling him that everything wouldn't be alright – ever, because it was too late. That Marcus was dying. Or that he was dead in a gutter before Jake had a chance to reach him. Why hadn't he got on that plane with Marcus? Why now, when everything seemed to be coming together? Jake closed his eyes as he brought the phone to his ear. He didn't think he could bear to lose them both. 'Lydia?' Bile was rising in his throat; he thought he was going to be sick.

'Jake? Oh, Jake! Oh, god!'

Jake opened his eyes. 'Faye?'

'Oh, god! Jake, I don't … I can't …' She was hysterical. This wasn't the Faye he knew. Jake had never, ever known her to act this way.

'Faye.' Jake repeated her name several times as he fought for control of his own voice, because there was only one thing that could send her off the rails like this. Jake's heart at that moment was pounding in fear as he said, 'Faye – tell me what happened to Natty.'

Jake was forced to wait an excruciating few seconds for Faye's sobs to subside enough for her to manage, 'She's gone, Jake – they took her.'

'They?

❖

'You're leaving? But you've only just arrived. I thought you came back because you had unfinished business.'

Gayle was standing in the doorway of the attic bedroom. She'd popped upstairs, clearly concerned after Jake had got off the phone and raced up the stairs like a herd of elephants, the old stairs creaking loudly under his heavy footfalls as he took them two at a time.

He'd heard Gayle call after him, but he hadn't had time to pause on the stairs and explain what was going on. He'd barely had time to shove his stuff in his overnight bag. He wasn't surprised that Gayle had followed.

Jake turned around. 'I'm sorry, Gayle. I know I booked for six nights, but—'

'Oh, Jake. I'm not fussed about that. I'm sure I'll rent the room out.'

'Even so. I want to pay for—'

Gayle wagged a finger at him. 'Now, we are not going through that again. You're only paying for the night you stayed, do you hear me?'

'Yes, Gayle. Loud and clear.'

'What happened, Jake?'

'It's Natty, my friend's daughter. She's … missing.' Jake did not want to get into the specifics of exactly what Faye had told him: They took her.

'Oh, goodness. How old is she?'

'She's only nine. I have to get back to London.'

'Of course, of course. Will you get a flight at such short notice?'

Jake stopped and stared at her. 'God, I'd forgotten I've got to book a flight.' Jake picked up the keys to his hire car. 'You know what? If it comes to it, I'll have to drive.'

'That will take hours!'

'I know. But I can't sit around doing nothing, waiting several days, or god forbid, for my return flight in five days' time.'

He stuffed one last shirt in his bag and tried zipping it up. 'Dammit!' The shirt got stuck in the zip. 'You know what? Why am I even packing? I don't need to take this bag with me.'

Gayle stepped into the room. 'Here, let me zip it up while you make that call, see if you can get a flight back to London today.' She put a hand over Jake's arm. 'Take a breath, Jake. Everything is going to be okay.'

Jake took a deep breath, realising he wasn't thinking straight. He should have sorted a flight first.

It didn't take long for Jake to sort the flight. He didn't even have to make a call. He turned to Gayle with a sigh of relief, holding up his mobile phone. 'I've booked the next flight online. It leaves this afternoon.' Now he knew why Faye had phoned the guesthouse. His phone had been on silent. Thank goodness he'd told Natty about staying at Lark Lodge in Aviemore. She must have told her mum.

Gayle handed Jake his bag. 'You're leaving right now?' Gayle asked as she followed him out of the door.

'Yes.' Jake hurried down the stairs. Although there was plenty of time to drive the airport, he didn't want there to be any chance he'd get caught in a traffic jam and miss his flight.

They stopped at the front door. 'Feels like déjà vu,' commented Gayle.

Jake knew what she was talking about – just the previous morning, he'd been standing at her front door, with Marcus waiting in the car, heading off, much to Gayle's surprise.

And to add to the feeling of déjà vu, Olive suddenly appeared out of nowhere, running down the hallway towards him. Jake gave her a fuss. He looked at Gayle. 'Sorry to do this again.'

'Really, don't be. I'm just relieved you got a seat on the next flight to London.'

'So am I.' Jake looked at his watch, even though there was no point. He had plenty of time. Even so, he didn't want to stand and chat.

Gayle grabbed Olive by the collar. 'Come on, Olive. Jake can't stand here all day, petting you.'

Olive whined.

Jake looked at Gayle. 'Thank you.'

'You'll come back, won't you, Jake?'

He managed a smile. 'You know, I'd love to bring Faye and Natty here, show them Scotland.'

'Well, you know what? I've got a grand idea. You're going to pay me for the attic room, those five more nights?'

Jake looked at her. 'Pardon?'

'Then when you get back to London, and you find Natty – which you will today, I just know it – then wouldn't it be lovely if you all came back here, for a holiday, to Lark Lodge? I'll keep the room reserved. You know, it's a family room.'

'But—' Jake didn't have time to explain that her plan wouldn't work. He wasn't in a relationship with Faye. But it did buoy him up, the thought that as soon as he reached London, he'd find Natty, if Faye hadn't already, and he could tell her about the guesthouse, and see whether she'd entertain the idea of the three of them having a holiday together. 'All right.'

'Good, good. That's settled then.'

Jake looked at her, and thought it wasn't, not really. He had no idea whether Faye would come away with him to Scotland, and if she wanted to, when that would be? Perhaps Gayle wouldn't even have vacancies. He thought aloud, 'I could stay with them in The

Lake House, if you get a last-minute booking tonight for the attic room.' There were also a lot more bedrooms, so he wouldn't have to worry where he would sleep.

'But it's being decorated, remember?'

'Not if Robyn's staying in London,' Jake blurted. On second thoughts, he didn't want to return to The Lake House – not with all those memories of Eleanor there.

Gayle looked at him.

'Sorry, I know it's none of my business, but I bumped into David this morning at Mr Gillespie's store, and it didn't sound as though he booked that hotel for the two of them for tonight, and he's staying here on his own instead. He's going to The Winky to drown his sorrows.'

'Is he, now?' said Gayle with a twinkle in her eye. 'I don't think he is.' Gayle grinned and lowered her voice, even though, apart from Olive, there was nobody else in the house. 'I'll tell you a little secret. She's coming back today, but she wants to surprise him. They're going to stay in their room here for one night, for old times' sake. I had a conversation with Robyn, told her what's been going on with David, how he feels. I didn't want to interfere …'

Jake doubted that very much. They were her friends. Of course she'd want to interfere.

'But I had to say something. When I told her he was afraid he was losing her, especially after this last trip to London when she didn't want him to accompany her, and that he'd wanted to book a night in fancy hotel in Aviemore as a surprise when she returned, she told me she was going to play a little trick on him.

'A trick?'

'Yes, you know … a prank.'

Jake frowned. It reminded him of Eleanor. It sounded just like something she'd do.

'Sorry, you haven't got time to listen to this.'

Jake shook his head. 'It's all right.' He wanted to hear this, despite being anxious to get on his way. 'Go on.'

'She told me to tell him she was staying in London for the rest of the weekend. But unbeknown to David, she's travelling home today, and she'll be waiting in their room upstairs to surprise him.'

Jake cast a glance upstairs.

'Oh, she's not back yet. But she's going to arrive before he gets in from work.'

For a moment, Jake's thoughts turned to Robyn, wishing he wasn't going to miss seeing her. He really wanted to meet her. Even more so, after what Gayle had just told him.

'Look, don't let me keep you. Now, remember that when you've found her, you're most welcome to head on over to my place for a few days' holiday.'

Jake smiled. She made it sound like they were locals, not coming all the way from London.

'I'll have the room prepared.'

Jake smiled. 'All right. I'd love to come back, and bring them with me.'

'Good.' Gayle glanced at Olive. 'Do you hear that? You might get to meet some more very nice people who will give you lots of fusses. Who knows, perhaps Natty would like to put some ribbons in your fur, and make you all pretty.'

Olive barked excitedly.

'I thought you'd like that idea.'

Jake walked to the car.

Gayle called out, 'Don't worry. I wouldn't be surprised if by the time you arrive in London, she's home safe and well.'

Jake prayed that was the case. He raised his hand to wave.

'See you soon, Jake. All of you.'

Jake stood there for a moment, wishing he could fast-forward this moment, and Faye and Natty were with him, and they'd just arrived in Scotland all together, and this episode with Natty going missing was well and truly behind them.

He took one more look at Gayle's beautiful Scottish home. As soon as he got in the car, he had to remember to breathe, like Gayle had said. He was wound up like a tight coil. All his anxieties over what might have happened to Natty came flooding back.

Thankfully the flight wasn't a long one; otherwise he didn't know how he'd stand it. Getting to the airport and waiting around for the afternoon flight was going to be bad enough. But it was still quicker than driving all the way back from Scotland.

As he set off in the car, he was relieved he hadn't had to stand and listen to Gayle make suggestions as to what might have happened to Natty – she might have got lost, or run away from home – because the last thing he wanted to tell her was that Natty might have been taken, and by those closest to her – her father and grandfather.

It might be innocent enough; perhaps Yousaf was back in the country, and he had wanted to see his daughter. That wouldn't surprise Jake. It wouldn't surprise Faye either. That was what she'd told Jake she imagined had happened. Rather than ask her if he could see Natty, he'd got in contact with her father Patrick, whom, according to Faye, he had always got on with very well. Faye believed that together they'd hatched a plan for Yousaf to see Natty without her mother. Those were Faye's thoughts when she'd told Jake, *she's gone – they took her*. And now Jake was on his way to get her back.

15

'What are you doing up here?' Gayle reached the top of the second flight of stairs to discover that David was standing on the landing, knocking at the door. She hadn't heard him come in. Olive had got out into the garden and had brought muddy paws back into the kitchen. Gayle realised she'd been so busy mopping the kitchen floor that she hadn't heard David walk into the house and straight up the stairs.

'Here – let me take those,' said David, wrestling the clean sheets and towels out of her hands. He looked from the fresh-smelling sheets to the door. 'Hey, I don't get my bedclothes changed every day.'

Gayle glanced down the stairs. 'Um, have you just got in?'

'Yes, I came straight up here.'

Gayle smiled to herself. He was in for quite a surprise. She'd got the call mid-afternoon from Robyn, who had said that she was nearly home. They had arranged for Gayle to pick her up from the train station, and Gayle had been home, anticipating her call.

She'd bundled Olive into the back of her car. Olive loved a car ride and had jumped in and out excitedly several times before Gayle had managed to close the back door.

Olive's green Bentley, inherited from her parents, did not enjoy Olive – or more to the point, the green Bentley's owner preferred not to take her out in the car. She slobbered everywhere and left fur all over the upholstered seats.

But that afternoon, it had been a small price to pay to make sure Robyn was picked up from the train station in Aviemore and brought back to Lark Lodge to surprise David and hopefully sort out what was really going on. Gayle didn't want to think about the fact that there was definitely something the matter with her friend. It troubled Gayle that Robyn had avoided telling her what it was that had happened. She knew that Robyn's London trips had become more frequent. Robyn usually had David in tow, and as far as he was aware, she visited clients. Although he did not go with her, she'd told him where she was each time. The last time, he'd tagged along uninvited, watching from a discreet distance. Unfortunately, it was not discreet enough. Robyn had discovered him: she'd exited the house through the back door and had reappeared down the street of the extensive property, only to catch her fiancé standing on the street corner, looking up at the house and watching the front door. Robyn had seen him take off at pace down the street when her clients had suddenly opened the front door.

Of course, she'd told Gayle all this. And the next thing Gayle had known, Robyn had decided to go up to London without him. Gayle's first thought when she'd told her this was that Robyn had been annoyed with David for spying on her and had decided to teach him a lesson.

When she'd first found out that David wasn't going, Gayle had broached the possibility that if he had decided to follow her at any point when she was meeting up with clients – Gayle was careful it didn't appear that she and Robyn had been talking about that episode behind his back – she might have decided next time he wasn't going with her. But he'd dismissed the possibility, saying there was no way she'd have spotted him, surprising Gayle by not denying it.

But she had spotted him. Gayle just couldn't tell him that. Now she looked at him and wished she had. Then perhaps he wouldn't have got it into his head that there was something more going on.

The problem was that if he asked Gayle whether everything was okay with Robyn, as far as she knew – and it was nothing more than her being ticked off with him for following her – she wouldn't be able to give David what he wanted: a reassuring answer. Gayle had a strong feeling Robyn was keeping something from her, from both of them, and that it had something to do with those visits. The fact that Robyn was surprising David, in a good way, should have convinced Gayle that she was just imagining things. The trouble was that it just felt to Gayle like Robyn was over-compensating for something. Especially when she'd collected her from the train station, and her arms had been laden with presents from London for her and Olive – Gayle had had to hide them in a kitchen cupboard until David knew she was back. There were presents for Annie, and her husband, David's brother Joe. And of course David's little niece, Evie, whom Robyn had grown quite attached to.

Of course, Gayle had thanked her for the expensive perfume from Harrods, joking that she must have a very rich client. Robyn's face had slipped when she'd said, 'How did you know?' And there it was, once again – the feeling that there was definitely something up. Robyn was hiding something.

'Everything all right?' David asked.

Gayle realised that he must have caught her expression as she was thinking all this. She tried to put it to the back of her mind. It was spoiling her joy at the thought of the wonderful surprise in store for David when he discovered that Robyn was waiting for him in their room at Lark Lodge, and that she'd bought him something very special home with her from London.

Gayle grinned, thinking of the surprise in store. 'I'm fine,' she said, and opened the door. Her smile slipped when she wondered what Robyn might have been covering up during her trips to London. They'd known each other for months – since Christmas Day, when Gayle had been visiting her late father and had spotted Robyn in a hospital bed after a car accident. Robyn had lost her memory. After all these months, as far as Gayle was aware, it hadn't come back – or had it?

Perhaps David was right, and there was more to her trips to London than meeting clients – perhaps she was meeting someone from her past.

But she hadn't shared that fact with Gayle, and they were best friends. Gayle gave David a sideways glance as he put the sheets and towels down on the unmade bed.

The trouble was that if Robyn wasn't being truthful now, what would happen down the line if she was found out? Gayle hadn't mentioned what was on her mind when she'd picked her up from the train station because she hadn't wanted to spoil Robyn's evening – or David's. And besides, Gayle rather hoped she was going to share with David that night what she had been doing in London, if there was something else going on. Maybe that was the surprise.

Gayle suddenly had the most extraordinary thought. Was

Robyn pregnant? Was that it? Maybe she was seeing a doctor in London. But why travel all the way there, when there were plenty of good doctors and hospitals right there in Scotland?

'What's wrong with you?' David said, catching the look of surprise on her face.

'Oh, er … nothing.'

'Alright. So don't tell me,' David said sulkily.

'No, really – it's nothing.' She decided it was wishful thinking. Robyn didn't look tired, or peaky. And didn't have morning sickness. She was sure Annie would have noticed and said something. And Robyn had had a big bottle of bubbly in her hands when she'd got off the train, and had joked that she wouldn't be drinking it all herself.

Gayle had asked, 'What's the special occasion?'

Robyn had replied, 'Wouldn't you like to know!' Then she had put her arm through Gayle's and had said, 'Just celebrating a big contract in London.'

Gayle sighed. Perhaps that really was all there was to it.

She looked at the unmade bed.

David followed her gaze, then looked around the room and caught sight of the empty wardrobe. 'Jake's left already?'

'Yes, I'm afraid so.'

'Damn.'

'You were calling on him?' Gayle asked, walking into the room, followed by David carrying the freshly laundered sheets and towels.

'Where did my drinking buddy go?'

'He had to head back to London – had an emergency.' Gayle's head swivelled in his direction when she realised what he'd said. 'Drinking buddy?'

'Yeah, I invited him to join me at The Winky. I did warn him, though, that I was drowning my sorrows, so he might not get a coherent word out of me.'

'Yes, shame that the idea of the plush hotel in town didn't work out.' Gayle turned around and smiled to herself. 'So, before you head out,' Gayle said, keeping up the pretence that he'd be going anywhere that night, 'You must join me for some stew.'

'Stew?'

She caught David's eyes widening. 'You know what? I was going to grab a takeaway. Don't want you to go to any trouble.'

'It's no trouble.' Gayle knew he was only being kind. 'I insist.' He'd tasted her stew, and probably didn't want to again. 'I have a new recipe.' Gayle really couldn't take the credit. She'd memorised the condiments she'd caught Jake putting back in the cupboard. He'd spared her feelings by not mentioning that he'd added them when she'd nipped out of the kitchen the previous evening to catch David before he left. But she was happy that the addition had made it delicious.

She hadn't decided whether David had been avoiding Jake or her food the previous evening. She'd guessed a little of both. He hadn't been in the mood for company, or her stew.

This evening was going to turn out very differently. Jake was gone, unexpectedly. Although she would never wish anyone ill, and certainly hadn't liked hearing that Natty was missing, she was convinced the little girl would turn up safe and well. She'd also thought Jake's leaving was for the best. Marty was out with college friends. Gayle had had a word with Nick, telling him to make himself scarce.

Gayle had set up the dining room for a romantic meal for two. She had lit two candles on the dining room table and had put low-wattage bulbs in both the standard lamp with the large, old-fashioned flowered lampshade in the corner and in the small lamp on the bookshelves in one alcove. She had lit the log fire. Easy chairs were placed either side of the fire for guests to sit and enjoy reading in front of the open fire after dinner. Gayle was going to make herself scarce in case Robyn and David wanted to sit in the cosy lounge across the hall instead. She'd put coal on the open fire in there too. When the temperature dropped in the evenings, even in summer, it could be quite chilly in the large, old house. Although she did wonder if she was overdoing it a bit, lighting two fires.

The rooms downstairs – the lounge, dining room and kitchen – were free for guests to use if they wished. But tonight, with no tourists staying the night, and only Marty and Nick in residence, both of whom had been told to make themselves scarce, the guest house harked back to before it was Lark Lodge, and there had just been Gayle and her mother, Nick, Marty, and of course Robyn.

Gayle said, 'Feels like old times.'

David was just putting the fresh towels in the bathroom and collecting the used ones. 'What was that?' He stepped back into the bedroom.

'Oh, nothing.' Gayle tried to contain her grin. 'Here, let me take those.' Gayle put the towels into her linen basket, along with the sheets she'd just stripped from the bed.

'Shall I carry this downstairs?'

'Good idea.'

David was about to take the basket out of her hands when his eyes drifted over to the bed. 'Hey, what's that?'

Gayle turned around, holding the linen basket in two hands.

David dived on to the bed and reached for something on the bedside table. He held up a small photo of a young boy. 'I think he left this behind.'

He turned over the photo. 'Ralph. The boy's name is Ralph.'

Gayle put the linen basket on the bed. 'Let me see.'

David passed her the photo. 'He said he had something he wanted to show me,' commented David. 'I'm wondering if it was this photo. I'm not sure why it would be, though.'

'Ah, I recognise this.' Gayle nodded. 'Jake showed me this photo. He asked me if I recognised the child.'

'Ralph.'

Gayle glanced at David. 'Yes, according to what is written on the back of the photo.'

'Did you recognise the boy?'

Gayle remembered the conversation. Jake had looked at her expectantly, as though she knew everyone in Aviemore, which she did not. In fact, when she'd turned the photo over, and had spotted the name Ralph, she'd asked Jake who the boy in the photo was.

'Martha's son.' Gayle remembered.

'Who?'

'Oh, it's a long story. A lady called Martha who lives locally is searching for her son, and Jake is trying to help. Sounds like she gave the child up for adoption. At first, I assumed he was searching for a missing child, but it turns out this photo was taken some years ago.'

'I spotted the date on the back,' commented David.

'I guess he's in his thirties now.'

'So, he was going to ask me if I knew or had known him.'

Gayle nodded. 'I expect so.'

'Nope, never known a Ralph.'

Gayle said, 'Me neither.'

David took the photo out of her hand. 'Looks like him, though.'

Gayle was just about to pocket the photo for when Jake returned, in case it got lost or, heaven forbid, Olive got in the room and nabbed it. She looked up sharply. 'Huh?'

'Jake. The kid looks just like him.'

Gayle frowned. 'Give that here.' This time she put on her glasses. 'Well, I'll be … how strange.'

Gayle studied it some more. She took off her glasses and looked at David. 'Sometimes people fail to see what's right in front of their noses.'

'Or they don't want to believe it,' he replied sullenly.

Gayle had an idea that David was no longer talking about the photo. But was he in for a surprise very soon.

He handed the photo to Gayle. 'I guess you'd better contact him, let him know he left this behind. Otherwise he might be searching for it.'

'I think he's got more important issues on his plate right now than an old photo.'

'Woman trouble?' David asked knowingly.

Gayle thought of Natty. She didn't elaborate. 'Yeah – that.'

David sighed heavily. 'Well, I expect he won't be coming back.'

'Oh, I hope he does. He's paid upfront for the room for the rest of the week, although I said I'd put the money towards another week if he can't make it. But I really hope he can, and he brings the ladies with him.

'Ladies!' David chuckled. 'Wow.'

'Oh, David! It's not what you think. It's a colleague who works at the school where he is teacher training and her young daughter.'

'Hmm, colleague. The trouble is that if they come here, by the time they leave they'll undoubtedly be more than just colleagues, or friends.'

Gayle didn't have to ask what had made him say that. She smiled knowingly. He was talking from experience.

'It's once people leave. That's the problem.'

Gayle's smile faltered. Gayle knew he was talking about himself and Robyn.

She looked about her. It might not be The Ritz or one of the fancy local hotels, but the house had a special place in Robyn's heart – and David's. She was thrilled that Robyn had returned, although she had made Robyn promise that it was only for one night. It was not that Gayle wanted to see the back of her – not at all. She was just afraid that if Robyn got too comfortable back at Lark Lodge, she might not want to leave. Gayle didn't want that. Robyn and David were a young couple with their lives to lead. Whatever had been going on with Robyn since she'd moved into the boathouse, Gayle hoped this surprise marked the end of it. The only thing she had to make sure of was that David didn't go out.

'Right – let's get this lot downstairs, and in the wash. Then I can get that stew on.' She dumped the wash basket in David's hands.

'Seriously, don't worry about it. I'm heading out anyway.'

Gayle turned around at the bedroom door. 'Now?'

He nodded.

'Oh, so you don't like my cooking?' Gayle joked, feigning shock.

'Oh, of course I like … love it.'

'Good, I'm glad you're staying.' She turned away.

'Do I have a choice?' she heard David mumble to her back.

Gayle paused at the door, glancing at the photo before she slipped it into her pocket.

She was back to thinking how people so often failed to see what was right under their noses, for one reason or another. However, she thought David had hit the nail on the head when he suggested it wasn't the case that they failed to see it, but that they didn't want to.

'What's up with Olive?' David got to the bottom of the stairs that led to the attic room and caught Olive outside his bedroom door, sniffing along the bottom of the door.

Behind David, Gayle looked over the banister and grinned.

Olive woofed.

David walked along the corridor towards her. 'Hey, girl – what's got into you? Ah, I know what it is. You think Robyn has come back too.'

'Here, give me that.'

'Don't you want me to take it down to the kitchen?'

'No, I'll do that. Why don't you freshen up for dinner.' She caught David frowning at the door. 'You know what? I'd rather come downstairs, if you don't mind.'

Gayle guessed that his idea to stay at the guesthouse while Robyn was away in London hadn't worked out how he'd expected. She guessed the room just reminded him of happier times. But then again, he hadn't wanted to stay at the boathouse without Robyn either.

'Do you want some help making the stew, or sorting out the room upstairs? Or—'

Gayle held up her hand. 'No thank you.' She motioned at the door.

David sighed. 'Well, I suppose it wouldn't hurt if I freshened up after spending all day out on deliveries.'

'Good.'

'At least I'll have some company.'

They both looked at Olive. Gayle frowned. She could just imagine that the surprise – Robyn lying seductively on the bed in a new see-through chiffon nightdress might be somewhat spoilt by a large over-exuberant Old English Sheepdog racing into the room and bounding onto the bed, giving her lots of sloppy doggy kisses.

Gayle had no idea what was going on behind that door right now. It was probably not at all what she had just imagined. But even so, Olive would definitely cause a bit of a ruckus and would get in the way of the big surprise reunion.

'I'll take her.'

'No, don't do that.'

'I insist. I don't want her in the bedrooms.'

David raised his eyebrows. 'Since when?'

Gayle took hold of her collar. 'Since now.'

She saw David's shoulders sag in resignation. 'All right.' He turned to the door.

Gayle resisted the urge to hang back and witness the surprise. 'I'll be downstairs, getting the dinner on. It will be ready at seven.'

'Seven! What am I going to do until then?'

Gayle was already heading for the stairs, the basket balanced in the crook of her arm, one hand on Olive's collar, pulling the reluctant dog with her. She whispered, 'Dog treat.' Olive shot forward and raced down the stairs. Gayle whispered, 'Clever dog.' Olive knew where her favourite treats were, in the kitchen cupboard.

As she got to the bottom step, she heard a whoop from David. Robyn? You're back? No way! When did you … how … was Gayle in on this?'

Gayle paused on the bottom step and heard Robyn say, 'Get over here.' The next thing she heard was the bedroom door shut and the key turn in the lock.

16

Jake was offered a glass of champagne, which he refused.

'Would you prefer a non-alcoholic beverage?'

No, I would not. I would prefer to be left alone. He smiled tightly at the member of the cabin crew, who was only doing his job, and said, 'No, thank you,' not bothering to point out that he'd been offered a drink countless times by several of the flight attendants during the short flight, and had turned down all of them. When were they going to get the message?

Jake knew there were countless other freebies in business class, but the young man thankfully didn't offer Jake anything else. He would have preferred not to be sitting in one of the most expensive seats on board, but it had been the only way home on this flight. He couldn't have cared less if he was flying back in the hold. But the fact remained that he had the money to fly business class; more money than he knew what to do with. And he would use every penny to get Natty back.

Jake looked at his watch, feeling relief as the plane descended into London City Airport. The flight had been delayed, adding to his anxiety. It crossed his mind that if he hadn't got that call from Faye, he'd still be at Lark Lodge. He imagined that David had arrived back at Lark Lodge after work and was wondering where his drinking buddy was.

He'd been looking forward to finding out if David knew anything about the man who had been found dead off-piste when the snow had thawed. Jake suddenly remembered the photo. He had also been going to show David the photo of the boy called Ralph and ask him if he recognised the child, who'd be the same sort of age as them now. However slight the possibility was that the boy had stayed in the area, and David had known him, it was worth a shot to ask.

Jake frowned when he recalled that he'd searched his wallet, and pockets for the photo. He was sure he had left it back at Gayle's guest house, but even so he sat forward, checking his coat pocket before getting out his wallet. He disturbed the young woman sitting next to him when he accidentally nudged her. 'Sorry.'

She briefly looked up from the magazine she was reading and gave him a passing glance.

Jake opened his wallet and still couldn't find the photo. 'Damn!' he said under his breath. He'd definitely left the photo on the bedside table in the attic bedroom. At least nobody would be checking into that room, as Gayle was expecting him back.

Jake slowly closed his wallet. The photo wasn't important. What was important was finding Natty. The thought of the three of them returning to Lark Lodge, all together for a family holiday – if Faye would agree to come – warmed his heart.

Family holiday? Jake raised his eyebrows at the thought that Faye and Natty weren't his family. He knew that he wanted them to be.

He looked at his watch, desperate to get off the plane and find Natty.

It had felt like an interminable afternoon once he'd arrived at the airport – and that was before he'd discovered the flight was delayed. At first, he'd been unable to check in and go through security because he had been early, which meant being stuck in limbo, drinking copious amounts of coffee and keeping an eye on his phone for any word from Faye. He somehow resisted the urge to keep calling her. But he knew that as soon as Faye found her daughter, she'd call. That didn't stop him picking up his phone every few minutes, willing it to ring or beep with a text.

As soon as he could, he checked in, walked through security, and arrived at the departure lounge. It was no ordinary departure lounge; it was for the privileged few who flew first class. Jake didn't usually do that anymore.

There had been absolutely nothing he could do after that but wait. He'd paced the small, comfortable lounge, getting looks from other passengers, who were probably wishing he'd stop. He was making them uncomfortable.

Jake had sighed and sat down in one of the leather chairs. A waitress had immediately appeared. Jake had waved her away. He didn't need any more coffee. He was hyper enough as it was. Jake had looked at his knee, which was bobbing up and down in nervous agitation. He'd slapped it, trying to keep still. It was killing him, not being with Faye, not being able to do something.

And then the news that the flight was delayed had come, and had left Jake with a huge dilemma. There was scant information about how long the flight would be delayed, which meant that after all those hours in the airport, he had to decide whether to return to his car and drive all the way back to London.

As the plane finally descended into London, he thanked god he had not decided to abandon his plan to fly back. If he'd driven, he'd still be on the road, with hours to go, and still unable to do a damn thing about finding Natty.

Jake suddenly had an idea. Perhaps there was something he could do as soon as the plane landed and he could switch on his phone. Why hadn't he thought of it before? Aubrey had been following him around since he'd left the Ross Corporation. At least, that was what he assumed had been going on when he'd discovered Aubrey in his house after his run-in with Marcus.

Jake recalled hearing Aubrey's voice in his hallway and realising that Aubrey had arrived at his house far too fast for someone who had been called by Marcus to help clear up the mess he'd caused.

Aubrey must have been in the vicinity, in his car, keeping an eye on Jake as he arrived home.

Jake got out his phone in readiness. The plane was now taxiing to a halt on the runway. He thought that if anyone could find Natty, it was Aubrey. Jake affectionately thought of him as the fixer. No one really knew what his job title was at the Ross Corporation. He just seemed to deal with the difficult jobs – he very occasionally turfed people out of the Ross Corporation's grace-and-favour apartments in the building owned by the Rosses in the heart of London. Jake had witnessed it himself, just the previous Christmas Eve. An employee had been shown the door, having lost his job. It must be a tough call, Jake knew, having to kick someone out, but somebody had to do it. And that somebody was Aubrey.

He was William's best friend, his right-hand man. He did the jobs no one else wanted. And that seemed to include following Jake around.

The seatbelt sign switched off and the cabin occupants sprang to life, unbuckling their seatbelts and getting bags down from the luggage compartments. Jake jumped out of his seat, anxious to get off the plane as soon as possible. He switched on his phone. While he queued in the aisle, he scrolled through his contacts, looking for Aubrey's phone number. A question sprang to mind. Why would Aubrey have any clue where Natty was? The last thing Jake would have thought of was to ask Aubrey to keep an eye on them. Why would he? They had nothing to do with the company.

But they have everything to do with me, Jake thought.

Aubrey might well have agreed if he'd asked him. He'd always felt that of the three of them – Marcus, Eleanor, and himself – Aubrey had a soft spot for him. That had been borne out when he'd discovered something – Aubrey had been living in the penthouse apartment, the very top floor of the Ross apartment building for employees, and the very apartment that was reserved for William. Access to that top floor apartment was by a different lift, with a keypad. A code was necessary to use that lift. Jake had discovered the code was actually his own birthdate.

Jake brushed thoughts of where Aubrey had been living aside. He stared at his phone. He wished he could go back in time and ask Aubrey to keep an eye on the two people who meant the world to him. He realised belatedly that it wasn't the job that had got him up in the mornings and had given him a purpose since the accident; although he loved his job, it was Faye and Natty who had given him a purpose and the strength to keep going despite what he'd been through.

Jake didn't call Aubrey. He'd have no idea where Natty was. But he might want to know where Jake was. Jake did not want to get into that over the phone, or get Aubrey involved in finding Natty. As much as he wanted to make that call, and ask if he could help find her, he thought he'd have to ask Faye's permission first. Natty was her daughter, not his.

Jake had already learned his lesson from overstepping boundaries; he had not thought there was anything wrong with buying Natty whatever toys she wanted – not until Faye had discovered he was spoiling her rotten. He'd also realised something else. He and Natty, they had a rapport. They were best buddies. And maybe there had been more to Faye being upset about the toys. After all those years as a single parent, despite a relationship here and there, it had always been just her and Natty. She'd never introduced those liaisons to Natty, or brought anyone home. Jake guessed that had been her golden rule until she'd realised too late she'd slipped up; she'd brought into Natty's life that which she sought never to do – a man Natty had grown very fond of, but a man nonetheless who was not her father and who could walk out of her life at any time.

He'd babysat when the sitter had let Faye down, answering her call when none of the other contacts she had could help. And then it had gone from there. Jake had been reliable, always there at a drop of a hat. And then he realised he had become a fixture in their lives, in Natty's life. He imagined Faye was afraid that if he met someone, one day, he'd have better things to do than see Natty.

But I'm not going anywhere, he wanted to tell Faye.

Of course, that train of thought didn't help him now. And neither did standing in the queue, feeling increasingly worked up, waiting what seemed like an age for the crew to open the cabin doors. He checked for any missed calls and text messages. There was still no news.

Even if Faye had phoned him back almost immediately as he was heading out of Lark Lodge, and had told him that it was a false alarm, he'd still have caught the first flight back. He needed to see Faye, see both of them. He missed them.

Jake shook his head as he followed the snaking queue of people leaving the plane. What had he been thinking, not catching that flight with Marcus? He should never have stayed behind in Scotland. Perhaps if he hadn't, Natty wouldn't be missing right now.

This isn't my fault.

Telling himself that did not help the situation. If he had been around, maybe he would have been looking after Natty, and she wouldn't have gone missing. Jake swallowed. No way would he say that to Faye when he spoke to her. That was tantamount to blaming her for Natty's disappearance. Jake didn't know exactly what had happened, but from what Faye had told him – and it hadn't been much, in her hysterical state – she believed Natty's father was back. And he'd taken her. She's gone, Jake – they took her.

They? Jake remembered asking, but that had been the end of the conversation. All he'd been able to do was promise he'd be on the first flight back to London. But he'd had enough time waiting for his delayed flight to figure out exactly whom Faye had meant, besides her ex, when she'd said *they*.

17

Jake stood in the line for passport control. He called Faye's number. He couldn't stand it any longer. He had to know what was going on. It went to voicemail. She was too busy to answer his call. Too busy being reunited with her daughter, he hoped. Then his phone rang. His heart missed a beat when he heard Faye's voice.

'Have you found her?'

Jake listened, his heart pounding at every word. They hadn't found her. Faye was frantically searching the streets with friends. One friend had been left behind to wait at her flat in case Natty turned up. The police wanted Faye to stay home, but Jake completely understood; Faye had to be out there, doing something.

'I'm coming right over. There's just something I need to do first.'

'I'm not at the flat, Jake, I told you.'

'Of course, of course.' Jake wasn't thinking straight. Faye said, 'Look I haven't got time to talk. Would you go straight to the flat? Obviously my friend is there. But it would be so much better if you were there when Natty gets home.'

Jake felt slightly better, hearing those words – when Natty gets home. It made things sound normal, like she'd just popped out, or gone out on a playdate; not like she was missing. Jake understood – Faye had to convince herself Natty would be back, otherwise she'd go crazy with worry.

'I just wanted to tell you that—'

'Jake – whatever it is, this just isn't the time! Just go to the flat, will you?'

'But it's about—'

Faye rang off.

Jake pushed his way through the queue, getting grumbles from those waiting in line, until security stopped him. 'What do you think you're doing?'

'Look, it's an emergency,' Jake pleased.

'Yeah, yeah.' He shook his head.

'No, you don't understand, Natty is missing. I'm trying to get home to help Faye find her.'

'Hold on. Who is Natty? Is she your child?'

Jake could hardly speak, he was so anxious to get through security and on his way. He just nodded.

'She's missing, you say?'

Jake nodded again.

'Have you called the police?'

'Her mother has. I was away in Scotland. She phoned me and—'

He waved his hand at Jake. 'Okay, all right. Come with me.'

Jake followed security past the long queue and watched him ask someone who was about to step up to one of the ePassport gates to step aside.

Jake stepped outside the airport terminal and immediately hailed a taxi. He wasn't going straight to Faye's. There was somewhere he needed to go first. He had something to pick up that he hoped he'd find in Aubrey's apartment. Jake asked the taxi driver to wait as the car pulled up outside the Ross Corporation's apartment building. He barely acknowledged the porter on the door as he raced inside. The concierge at the front desk recognised Jake, looking surprised to see him again in the space of just a few days.

The concierge hurried over to ask Jake if he had any luggage.

'I'm not staying. Just a flying visit.'

The concierge returned to his desk.

Jake got in the lift that took him straight to William's top floor apartment, where Aubrey was living. He needed something that he was sure Aubrey would have. And it wasn't the speciality teas that Aubrey was so fond of.

He paused in the bright white, airy hallway, listening. He didn't call out Aubrey's name. He hoped Aubrey wasn't in. All Jake could hear was his own heavy breathing. Nobody was home. He sighed with relief. Aubrey would not let him have what he had gone there to take without a very, very good explanation. But Jake was not about to tell anyone what he had it in his mind to do to get Natty back.

He raced to the study. Aubrey had told him once where he kept just what Jake was after. Jake was making an educated guess that wherever Aubrey was residing, he'd keep it in the same place – a desk drawer of a study.

'Aha!' Jake grabbed the small black case and slammed the desk drawer shut. Thrusting the case into his jacket pocket, he retraced his steps to the lift and waited impatiently as it made its way to the ground floor. His usual panic in lifts had not troubled him this time; he was too focused on his task.

Jake sprinted past reception and a bemused concierge and

straight out of the door to the waiting taxi. He told the driver his next destination and then slumped into the back seat, catching his breath, staring out of the window as the taxi manoeuvred into the late afternoon traffic outside the apartment building. Jake frowned. Rush hour had already started. He hoped the London traffic did not hold them up.

Jake looked at his phone. He was still praying that Faye would call him and say the search had been called off because they had found her; that the nightmare was over. Jake had watched enough police procedurals with the same old line – the first twenty-four hours were crucial, and after that, the chances of finding a missing person fell dramatically. It was all tosh – wasn't it? And if there was some basis in fact, Jake wasn't going to be unduly worried that he had just a short time to find her, because he knew exactly where to look. And more importantly, he had exactly what he needed when he got there. Jake had the small black case in his hand at the ready.

18

The flat was located in a large complex of purpose-built flats on a busy main road. Jake had to google the address. The complex was a lot bigger than Jake had thought – huge, with two different entrances, and several concrete squares with small play areas. At first he'd been thrown by the sheer scale of it. Fortunately, the taxi driver had said that he had a friend who had lived there decades earlier, so he knew which entrance to aim for. The driver had explained that the place was not like a modern apartment building with one foyer and lifts up to the different floors. There were five floors. The complex had no lifts, but rather lots of entrances to stairwells that rose to the flats in that part of the block. The trick was to know which part of the block the flat number was located in.

Unlike in the Ross apartment building, there was no concierge and no reception desk, and to Jake's relief, there wasn't even a buzzer system – he could just walk right in off the street, through the gates.

He stood in a large inner concrete courtyard and thought that if the taxi driver hadn't been able to direct him to the right entrance, he could have been walking around for hours.

He walked around the courtyard and found the entrance to the hallway and stairwell for the flat. 'Damn!' he said. He recalled the taxi driver saying he hadn't been there for years. Things had obviously changed. The driver had said that Jake could just walk into one of the hallways. There would be two flats located on the ground floor, but if he was visiting someone on a higher floor, then he just took the concrete stairwell. There were outer doors on the entrances to the hallways. Whilst he'd been able to walk into the courtyard from the street, he couldn't get near the flats uninvited and unannounced, which was exactly what he had intended to do.

Jake looked around at the red-brick building, at the upper floors with small concrete balconies. It had been built back in the fifties by the Catholic church – most of the residents back then had been Catholic. The huge complex had later become council flats. He knew that most, if not all of them, would now be privately owned and worth around half a million.

Jake shuddered. It wasn't the sort of place he'd want to live. He understood its appeal. It was close to the shops in Kilburn High Road, and he could imagine it was a nice, friendly community in which to live, and so close to central London. The taxi ride from the Ross Corporation building had been very short. They'd passed a park on the way that the taxi driver remembered his friend had fondly called The Rec.

But coming from Aviemore, with its lochs, mountains and wide-open spaces, and his beautiful garden at The Lake House, the contrast with where he was standing couldn't have been any more stark. In fact, Jake had noticed something when he'd returned to London from Scotland – something that, for some reason, he hadn't really noticed before; how much he hated the crowds, the noise, the hustle and bustle of city life, and the traffic. When he'd stepped through the gates of the complex, he'd found that the inner courtyard was so much quieter away from the main street outside, full of traffic. He realised how tired of it he was.

He stood there, appreciating the surprising oasis of quiet and calm, away from the noise, and the traffic, and the people outside those gates. He longed to return to Scotland. He'd never felt that longing before, not after any of the trips he'd made to The Lake House for Christmas. Perhaps it was that he'd been too busy wrapped up in his life working for the Ross Corporation to even notice that he wasn't happy, to even care, because supposedly he had it all. And he'd had nothing to complain about. Although there had been times he'd questioned whether it was truly the life for him.

But I'm busy now, with my teaching job, so why am I feeling this way, this unhappy? What has changed? What Jake realised, staring at the door he couldn't get through, was that without Faye and Natty, he just couldn't stay in London. They made it palatable. They made his life here worthwhile, complete – almost.

If only he could take them with him back to Scotland. Then his life would be just about perfect.

Jake shook his head. What a stupid thought. They weren't a couple, a family. And besides, he knew that would never, ever happen, even if he and Faye were together; he remembered the reason Faye had split up with Natty's father, Yousaf. He had wanted her to return with him to live in his home country. Granted, Scotland wasn't as far away as Oman, where Yousaf's family were from, but it would still mean taking Natty out of her school, and Faye changing her job, and leaving the little rental they called home.

Jake glared at the door. He didn't have time to stand around imagining a life that would never be.

Thinking of Natty's father reminded Jake why it was imperative he got through the door into the block.

'Hey, there. Are you okay?'

Jake froze and looked about him, wondering where the voice had come from.

'I'm up here.'

Jake looked up, scanning the concrete balconies. Some had little washing lines with clothes hanging out to dry. There were others with planting boxes full of summer flowers.

Shielding his face from the late afternoon sunshine, he spied a young man sitting at a folding table on a balcony two floors up.

Jake waved.

The young man stood up. 'I was just wondering if you're locked out?'

'Yes, er … I am.'

'Oh dear. Hold on, I'll buzz you up.'

Jake smiled to himself. What a stroke of good luck. He hadn't wanted to randomly buzz one of the flats because he'd imagined that unless he was known to the flat owner, they'd be suspicious and wouldn't buzz him in.

The young man appeared a second later without buzzing him in. He leaned over the railing. 'What flat number did you say you lived in?'

Jake frowned. Of course it wouldn't be that easy.

'Sorry to be a pain, but I don't recognise you.'

Jake was getting irritated. He didn't have time for this. Since when did everyone know everyone else in a block of flats? He imagined most people nowadays barely knew their next-door neighbours.

As if he'd read Jake's mind, the man said, 'We're a friendly lot. Even when you don't know everyone, you see the same faces in and out of your block.'

Jake realised he'd been caught out. 'Well, the thing is, I don't actually live here. I've come to see a friend.'

'Oh, all right. Who's the friend?'

Jake sighed. He wasn't exactly a friend, but he did know him. Well that wasn't exactly true. He knew of him. Jake gave him the name, along with the flat number, and what this so-called friend used to do for living. He stopped short of giving a description. He couldn't do that. He'd never met the man in person, although he knew his age, or thereabouts.

'Ah, yeah. I know him.'

Jake looked at the young man and prayed he wasn't going to ask him something about the occupant of the flat that would raise suspicions. He just hoped he was in. It was something that had only occurred to him now he was here. Once again, Jake realised he wasn't really thinking straight.

'Come for the game?'

Jake almost put his foot in it when he'd nearly said, what game? 'Oh, yeah – sure.' he said. 'Looking forward to it.' He made a show of looking at his watch. 'The thing is I'm late, so I'd really appreciate if you could—'

'Why don't you just ring the buzzer. He'll let you in.'

Oh, no he won't, thought Jake. Not with this. He thought of the case containing the gun in his coat pocket.

He smiled tightly. He quickly thought of an excuse. Lying through his teeth, he said, 'Look, I don't want to interrupt the game.'

'But you'll interrupt it when you bang on the door.'

Jake rubbed his forehead. This was getting really tiresome. 'Look, he's not expecting me to turn up, so I wanted it to be a surprise.' Jake winced. That was, in actual fact, completely true.

The young man grinned. 'One sec. I'll buzz you in.'

Jake was by now so convinced the young man wouldn't let him in that he stood rooted to the spot for a moment before launching himself at the door just before the buzzer died.

He headed up the stairs and stood outside apartment number six on the third floor. He had the impulse just to ram the door in, but resisted; he didn't want some interfering neighbour calling the police before he made his move. Jake felt in his pocket for the gun and then knocked once on the apartment door.

The door opened.

'I've got more money than I know what to do with in my bank account,' said Jake, holding up a wad of cash, as much as he'd been able to withdraw from several different bank accounts, using an ATM which he'd spotted on the way in the taxi.

'And there's plenty more where that came from.' He could get more, a lot more, but that would mean a visit to his bank in person. He hadn't had time for that. But if emptying his bank accounts wasn't enough to get Natty back, then he'd just have to go to William Ross. But he didn't want to play that trump card just yet.

Jake glared at the old man. He was smaller and thinner than Jake had expected, but Jake wasn't fooled by his timid exterior. He remained on his guard because if Aubrey had taught him anything, it was that appearances can be deceptive.

'Well, aren't you going to invite me in?'

The old man stared at him blankly. For Jake, this was a good sign, a sign that his presence or the money or both had caught him by surprise. Jake was now ahead of the game.

'Who is it, Virgil?' another man's voice came from inside the room.

'Virgil?' repeated Jake, re-checking the number on the door to verify that in his haste he hadn't knocked at the wrong apartment.

Virgil turned away from Jake and walked into the room, leaving the door ajar. He called out, 'Paddy, is there something you've been holding out on from your mates?'

Jake opened the door wide and looked past Virgil into the room. The front door to the flat opened directly into the kitchen. To Jake's surprise, there were three other men seated around a small circular table – so small, in fact, that their elbows were almost touching. One was smoking a cigar, and they were each holding a hand of cards. The guy smoking the cigar tossed a plastic chip onto the pile already accumulated in the centre of the table.

Jake had not anticipated company. He'd assumed when the young man on the balcony said the game, he was talking about watching the football on the TV.

Jake stepped into the room.

'This is a friendly game of poker,' said the guy with the cigar, pointing at his cards as he threw a plastic chip on to the pile in the middle of the table. He looked up at Jake and pointed his cigar at him. 'I don't know where you've got the idea that this is some den of iniquity, and we are gambling for real, but you can take your money and find another venue.'

Jake looked around the table as Virgil took his seat, studying each man in turn. They had all resumed the game, ignoring Jake completely. He had wrongly assumed the old, retired police officer would be at home alone, not playing cards with three other equally old, equally retired, fellow police officers.

This was not a good start.

If things turned nasty, there would be four very highly respected and reliable witnesses to testify to Jake's threatening behaviour and, if things really turned nasty, assault with a deadly weapon.

Jake hoped it would not come to that. Not because he was afraid of losing his new teaching job – that didn't matter a jot – but because he was afraid of losing Faye and Natty, which would certainly be the case if he was sent to jail and lost his liberty. However, he was there to find Natty, he reminded himself, whatever the cost. The question he was asking himself now was: which one was Patrick? He looked around the table until his eyes settled on an empty chair. At that moment, somewhere in the apartment, a toilet flushed and a door opened.

Everybody turned in the direction of the door.

Patrick Ames stopped in the doorway, momentarily disconcerted by Jake's presence. He looked over at the men seated at the table. 'Who is he?' he said in a strong Irish brogue.

Jake had found his man.

Virgil answered, 'How the hell should we know? I called out to you, but you didn't answer. I thought you must have invited him.'

Jake stared at the short, stout man with the harsh army crew cut and the deep-set, suspicious hazel eyes. This was exactly what Jake had imagined Faye's father to look like in the flesh.

The man with the cigar spoke up in a deep baritone voice, 'Says he's got a wad of cash. Have you finally crossed over the thin blue line and gone to the other side, Paddy?'

'Guess we're going to have to arrest you,' said Virgil. This was followed by a collective chuckle from around the table.

'Pension not enough, Paddy?' said the third man as he selected a card from his hand and placed it face up on the table.

'How about cutting us in for a bit of the action?' said the fourth man, smiling broadly at the other men and laying his cards face up on the table in front of them. 'I've got full house, gentlemen.' He reached for the large pile of chips in the centre of the table.

'Wait a minute. I recognise you,' said Patrick Ames as he walked into the room, eyeing Jake. 'You're Jake Campbell-Ross. I've seen your picture in the newspaper.'

Jake knew that having married into such a wealthy family made him recognisable, like some sort of minor celebrity. Not everyone recognised him, of course, or if they did think he looked familiar, they couldn't put a name to his face. Trust Patrick Ames to do just that.

Patrick's four friends turned in their seats to scrutinise Jake.

'Lost your wife last Christmas.'

Jake's frown deepened.

'Thought he looked familiar,' said Virgil.

The other three chimed in too, in agreement, one adding, 'He's better-looking in real life.'

Jake rolled his eyes in their direction.

'Down on your luck, lad? Heard you quit the Ross Corporation.'

'I am not down on my luck, thank you very much.' He looked at the wad of cash in his hands and suddenly realised what it looked like. They thought he was there to gamble at cards. 'I have a very lovely job training to be a teacher. Faye is my teaching mentor.' Jake had no idea why he was telling Faye's father all this.

Patrick said, 'More than that, I heard.'

Jake actually blushed. 'Really?' Had Faye said something to him? He'd thought they weren't on speaking terms.

'You babysit my granddaughter.'

'How do you know that?'

'WhatsApp. I asked her if she needed any babysitting. I know she's attending courses training for a headship.'

'She told you about me?'

'Not specifically, but I've seen you with Natty in the park.'

Jake wasn't surprised he was keeping an eye on his granddaughter from afar.

'WhatsApp?' said Virgil, turning in his chair to look at his friend.

'Yeah. I message her.' He frowned. 'She still won't engage with me much, though, apart from the odd photo of Natty and little titbits here and there. I'm just relieved she hasn't blocked me.'

The old guy with the cigar said, 'I haven't a clue what you're on about, Paddy, with the WhatsApp malarkey. Will you come and rejoin the game?'

Paddy stood by his chair, about to sit. He looked Jake up and down. 'What are you doing here?'

Jake was just about to answer that question when Patrick's eyes suddenly went wide. He clutched his chest, looking as though he was having a heart attack. Patrick exclaimed, 'Oh god! What's happened? Has something happened to Faye? Tell me she's okay.'

Jake fixed him with a cold stare. 'Don't mess with me. You know perfectly well nothing has happened to Faye!' Jake threw the money at his feet. 'Where is she?' Jake opened a door to his right and poked his head into the lounge. It was empty. 'Is she in here?' He pointed at another door which he discovered led into a bedroom.

'I don't know what you're on about.'

'Here?' Jake shoved passed him to look in the bathroom.

'What's he looking for?' Virgil asked.

'Beats the hell out of me,' said Patrick, and Jake thought he might just do that. 'Right where did you take her?' demanded Jake as he emerged from the second bedroom, realising he had exhausted the possibilities of the small apartment.

'Are you hiding a woman in here, Paddy?' said Virgil, raising another collective chuckle.

Jake rounded on the men at the table. 'This is not a joke!' He wanted to tell the lot of them to go home, but he knew they were liable to call the police. Instead, he shoved Patrick into the corner of the room. 'Look, I am deadly serious.' As if to prove the point Jake drew the gun.

19

Jake was intending to play it cool. He was going to stay calm, but coming up against five men – even if they were all well into retirement – was making Jake nervous. He held up the gun.

'Patrick!' one of the men exclaimed. 'What the hell have you got yourself into?' Inexplicably, they were all still sitting at the table, holding their cards as if at any moment the game would resume, and Jake would just go away.

'On the floor, all of you.' Jake waved the gun at them as if to say he meant business.

No one moved.

'Now, look here son,' Virgil began.

'NOW!' Jake tipped the table over for effect to show them he was serious. He'd seen it countless times in the movies; make a bit of noise, do some violence to an inanimate object – it soon got people going.

Slowly, with much complaining about arthritis and ailments Jake had never even heard of, they got on their knees.

'Not you.' Jake pointed the gun at Patrick Ames.

'You'd better have a very good reason for pointing that gun at me,' he said coolly.

'Ask him where he got the gun,' said Virgil. 'This isn't bloody America. You can't just walk into a gun shop and buy one.'

'Is it even real?' asked another guy, who was still smoking his cigar.

'Of course it's bloody real,' said Jake, hoping they didn't catch the waver in his voice. Jake had never seen a real gun, let alone handled one.

Jake couldn't believe the nerve of them all, throwing questions around when he was meant to be in charge. He was the one with the gun. He focused on Patrick.

In the corner of his eye Jake noticed movement. He swivelled his head and caught one of Patrick's friends try to get up. 'Stay sitting down and put your hands behind your heads.'

One by one they obeyed.

Jake waited until they all complied then he turned his attention back to Patrick. 'Now I want to know what you have done with Natty.'

'I still don't know what …' he stopped abruptly. 'What are you talking about?' His eyes suddenly darted around his apartment, where Jake had flung open all the internal doors, searching his flat.

'She's missing? My granddaughter is missing? You've got to tell me what happened. We've got to go find her.'

'Stop bullshitting me,' Jake spat. He had expected this; he had expected him to plead for his life, but not to start trying to save his own neck by telling such abject lies. 'Tell me where she is – goddamn you! Tell me.'

The silent promise he had made to himself that he would return to Faye's flat with her daughter was ringing louder in his ears with each passing moment. The possibility of losing them both was becoming painfully clear. He would never forgive himself if he didn't get her back.

Jake started to go over his last conversation with Natty, when he'd spoken to her over the phone the previous evening; perhaps if he had told her when he planned to return from Scotland, instead of just replying with a vague soon, he wouldn't be there right now; she wouldn't be gone. Of course, he knew that was absurd. It wouldn't have made any difference. It had nothing to do with him going away. But for some reason, he still felt responsible, and that it was up to him to find her.

'Now I'm going to ask the question just one last time, and so help me if I don't get an answer …'

One of the men on the floor spoke up. 'Tell him, Patrick. For god's sake, tell him where she is.'

'I can't. You know I haven't seen my granddaughter in an absolute age – through no fault of my own, I might add.'

Jake shook his head. 'You're lying.'

'Why do you think I follow my daughter on Facebook? For any snippet of information I might get about my own granddaughter. But she rarely posts anything, and certainly no photos – nothing about Natty. Except that one time just recently about her headteacher training course, and how she wouldn't have been able to continue it if it wasn't for her new, and very reliable, wonderful babysitter, Jake. That's you, isn't it?'

'It's true,' said Virgil. 'He doesn't see his own grandchild.' The other men joined in voicing their agreement.

Jake couldn't think straight with the cacophony of voices. 'SHUT UP!' he shouted. He knew what he had come here to do; it should be straightforward. So why wasn't Patrick telling him where she was?

'Can you tell me how long she's been missing?' said Patrick, his even tone of voice not hinting at his current predicament.

'May I remind you that I'm the one holding the gun? I'm the one in control,' said Jake, aware that his unnaturally high-pitched tone of voice was betraying his true feelings; he did not feel fully in control of the situation. From the very start, things had not gone according to plan. 'And I don't have to answer your questions.' All the same, Jake did a quick mental calculation; he'd got the call from Faye mid-morning. It was the last day of the school summer term. She'd said something about dropping Natty off at breakfast club, which she did every day before work. But then she'd had a call from the school a while later because Natty had failed to turn up at breakfast club. Jake momentarily forgot about the gun in his hand, and looked at his watch. It was six pm. She'd been gone ten hours. Ten hours!

'Oh god! She'd been missing ten hours!'

Suddenly the men on the floor were all talking at once, saying something about being around the kitchen table all day, give or take lunch, and breaks – especially toilet breaks. Bladders weren't what they once were. It was one of their weekly marathon sessions.

Jake didn't believe a word of it. 'You're friends of his. You'd cover for him,' he barked.

'That's right,' said Virgil, 'we are all friends of his. Friends that go way back. Friends that don't want to see him get hurt. But,' he paused, 'just because we're retired from the force doesn't mean we have any less regard for truth and justice. Believe me, son, if we knew Paddy had done something wrong, had taken his granddaughter like you say, we would tell you in a heartbeat.'

Jake regarded each of the men nodding their heads, each of the men's earnest expressions. They obviously didn't know why Paddy was estranged from his daughter – because he was good friends with her ex, Natty's father Yousaf, and had taken his side when they'd split up, choosing not to believe Faye when she'd told him that Yousaf had attempted to take her daughter.

He needed to think. If what they were saying was true, that Patrick had been there all day, then Yousaf had taken Natty himself. But he must have got the information on the whereabouts of her school and her routine from her grandfather. Something didn't ring true, though. Yousaf was a kind, gentle soul, according to Faye. He didn't sound like the kind of man who would snatch Natty. That would be very different from trying to take her away with him before they were estranged. Natty didn't know her father now. She wouldn't have gone willingly with a stranger.

Jake was getting tired of excuses. It still had to be Patrick. Maybe he'd said he had to nip out for the morning paper. That was more plausible. But even as he thought it, it sounded ridiculous. How long would it have taken him through rush hour traffic to get to the school, grab Natty, take her to wherever her father was, and then rejoin the game?

He was back to thinking about Natty's father. 'Who took her – was it Yousaf?' said Jake. 'Who did you arrange to be outside her school when Faye dropped her off this morning – who was it?'

'What the hell are you talking about?' exclaimed Patrick. 'If she's missing, why aren't you out pounding the streets looking for her, for Christ's sake, instead of in here waving a gun around interrogating me? What in heaven's name has Faye been telling you?'

'She told me that you wouldn't believe her when she broke it off with Yousaf because he'd attempted to take Natty away.'

'You mean that visit to Oman so his family could meet his daughter?'

'Yes,' said Jake, seething.

'He'd have brought her back.'

'On a one-way ticket?'

Patrick sighed heavily. 'Look, Yousaf wouldn't do that. She was mistaken.'

'Then why is she convinced those plane tickets she saw were one-way? Why can't you believe her that she wasn't mistaken?'

Patrick frowned. 'But he's such a nice guy.'

'Didn't you consider for a moment that your friendship with him clouded your judgement? Maybe he is, as you said, a nice guy, but it sounds as though he was pressured by his family to—'

'Oh, god!' Patrick interrupted Jake. 'Are you saying he's back? That he took Natty?'

Jake stared at him. 'You really have no idea who took Natty, where she is – do you?'

'Of course I don't! I wouldn't consider for one second helping Yousaf take Natty away from us. I haven't seen or heard from the man in years. All I have left is my daughter and granddaughter, and now I don't even have them because Faye won't forgive me. Why did I put my friendship with Yousaf before my own daughter? I'm an idiot. Now I'm just a sad old man with this lot for company.'

There were murmurs of agreement from the floor.

'Know this,' said Patrick. 'I had nothing to do with Natty's disappearance. Nothing.' He looked Jake in the eye. 'I miss them like a man dying of thirst misses water, with all my heart and soul, and I don't care what you believe. My granddaughter is at this very moment out there somewhere, quite possibly with her father, a man she doesn't know. You'd better shoot me now and be done with it, so at least you can stop wasting time and get out of my apartment and find her.' He pointed at the door.

Virgil commented, 'I'm sure it's a fake gun, Patrick.'

Jake dropped his arm to his side and stepped back. His thoughts were not on the man in front of him, but somewhere else – a place that terrified him. He'd been so convinced that he'd find Natty there with her grandfather, not helping Yousaf take her away, but simply facilitating a reunion that he knew Faye would not want. What he'd never considered was the possibility that Natty was gone – and would never be found.

20

Jake loosened his grip on the gun.

'NO!' somebody shouted. 'Don't drop it!'

Jake wasn't listening. Then just as he dropped it, someone crashed into him, knocking him sideways. The gun went off. Jake felt a sting to his temple, like a paper cut. He was lying flat on his stomach, and somebody was holding his hands in a vice-like grip behind his back, pinning him to the floor.

A voice, muffled, was asking, 'Is everyone alright?'

Jake recognised Patrick's voice, and he could see, with his head turned sideways, the other men struggling to get up.

'We're OK,' said Virgil, 'but he isn't. Look – he's bleeding.'

Patrick loosened his grip. 'Are you alright, Jake?'

Jake could feel a trickle of blood from his temple.

'Are you alright?' Virgil asked Patrick. 'That was quite a move at your age.'

'I'm fine. I had a soft landing.'

'Get off me,' Jake struggled, but Patrick had him in a police lock; the more he struggled, the more it felt like his arms were being pulled out of his sockets.

'Easy, son,' said Patrick. 'Virgil, pick up that gun.'

Jake watched Virgil pick up the gun and pass it to Patrick.

'Get up slowly and take a seat,' said Patrick in a slow, deliberate tone. 'Do you understand?'

Jake nodded. He felt his hands being released and the weight being withdrawn from his back. Jake slowly got up and saw Virgil pass the gun to Patrick. Jake did exactly what the man pointing the gun at him told him to do; he sat in the chair. He looked anxiously from Patrick to the four other men in the room and wondered what they were going to do to him. But Patrick's friends were more concerned with the overturned table.

He watched them pick up the table and scoop up the chips and cards from the floor. Every now and then, Jake glanced at Patrick. Jake was hoping that Patrick's attention might wander so that he could bolt for the door. While he waited, he was forced to listen to the old men complaining about stiff joints and bad backs after their spell on the floor.

Jake turned his head, first left, then right, noticing the distinct change in noise level as he did so. He rubbed his right ear and realised he'd lost his hearing on that side. He was silently debating if it was a burst eardrum or whether the gun going off had left him permanently deaf, when Patrick shouted out, 'What are you doing?'

Jake was just about to explain that he was feeling absurdly emotional over his new-found disability, when he realised Patrick wasn't looking in his direction.

'What are you doing?' snapped Patrick for the second time.

Jake followed his gaze.

One of his friends had picked up the phone on the kitchen counter. 'I'm dialling the police. He can't get away with barging in and ruining our game. I can't even remember my hand.'

Jake felt like launching himself at the man; a young girl was missing and all he could think about was his card game?

'Put the phone down,' said Patrick.

'Say what?'

'Put it down. I'll deal with him myself.'

Jake slowly turned his head to look up at Patrick, who was standing there coolly, still pointing the gun in his direction.

'Go home, all of you.'

'But …' they objected, 'we're not leaving you alone with this lunatic.'

'He's not a lunatic.'

Jake stared at Patrick.

They all shuffled to the door. 'Do you want us to help you look for your granddaughter?'

Patrick shook his head. The police must be out there right now, looking for her. I'll let you know if – when – we've found her …' He trailed off.

Jake put his head in his hands.

'Are you sure you'll be OK?' said Virgil.

'Go.'

Virgil turned to Jake before he headed off. 'You know, he just saved your life. That gun could have landed on the butt and fired a shot right between your eyes.'

Jake touched his forehead. 'You thought the gun was fake. So, why did Patrick do that – push me out of the way of the gun?'

Virgil said, 'Second nature. After all those years on the force, your training just kicks in, and you react accordingly.'

Patrick nodded.

Jake resumed holding his head in his hands, consumed with thoughts of Natty and where she might be. He felt helpless.

The front door clicked shut and the voices grew faint as Patrick's friends walked down the hall.

Patrick pulled up a chair and sat. He held out a clean white handkerchief. 'Here. Go on, take it.' He thrust a handkerchief at Jake. 'Clean that up.'

Jake reluctantly took it and carelessly dabbed at his temple, wiping the blood from the side of his face.

'What are you doing here?'

Jake was surprised by the question. 'What do you mean – what am I doing here? I thought I made that clear. I came to find Natty.'

Patrick said, 'Have you got a thing for my daughter?'

'Pardon me?'

'Faye.'

Jake dropped his eyes to the floor.

'Oh dear. That's going to be a problem.'

Jake looked up sharply. 'Why – is she still in love with Yousaf?' he blurted.

'I wouldn't know about that. In fact, I very much doubt it, not after what she alleged he'd done.'

Alleged. So he still doesn't believe her, Jake thought. Still, he was relieved to hear that Patrick doubted she still held a candle for Natty's father. But he had to ask, 'Why is it a problem, then?'

He looked Jake up and down, and said, 'You're young and good-looking.' Patrick waved the gun, pointing at Jake with the firearm. 'You're not some sad, lonely old fart like me. You could find someone else.'

Jake glared at Patrick. He didn't want someone else. He wanted her.

'And from what I hear, you're not short of a bob or two.'

Jake slowly shook his head in dismay. Why was it when you

were rich, your bank balance seemed to be everybody's business? Even by training to teach, he couldn't escape his past. 'Who told you that?' said Jake coldly.

'You did,' said Patrick, casting his gaze down to the floor, which was littered with Jake's wad of bank notes.

'So, if I'm so young, good-looking and rich, why are my feeling towards Faye a problem? Do you think she won't be interested in me, in that way?'

'Oh, that's not what I'm saying.'

'Then what are you saying?'

'After Yousaf, Faye is committed not to have a relationship, you know that – right? Of course, she has date nights, but nothing will ever lead anywhere. She doesn't want men in and out of her life who won't be sticking around.'

'Who says I won't stick around?' Jake's attention was drawn to the gun. He wanted to leave, get out of there, resume the search for Natty. What were they sitting around talking for?

Patrick's hand might be resting lazily in his lap, but Jake wasn't fooled; it was still pointed in Jake's direction, with Patrick's trigger finger at the ready.

Patrick followed Jake's gaze. 'I'm keeping hold of this, if you don't mind,' he said, lifting the gun off his lap and aiming it at Jake. Perhaps you'd like to tell me where you got it from.'

Jake shifted nervously in his seat. 'No, I would not.' He was in enough trouble as it was, without implicating Aubrey. At first, Jake had thought it was a good sign that Patrick had stopped his friend from calling the police. Now he wasn't so sure.

'I see.' Patrick regarded him for a long moment before changing the subject. 'I want to know everything that's happened so far in relation to my granddaughter's disappearance.'

'Give me one good reason.'

'I thought I already had.' he waved the gun at Jake. 'I'm assuming you had nothing to do with it.'

Jake was out of his chair like a shot. 'Have you lost your mind? Why on earth would I take her?'

'Because you've grown very fond of Faye, and she might not feel the same way.'

He waved the gun at Jake to sit back down.

Now Jake understood what he was still doing there. He was a suspect. 'This is insane.' Jake added through clenched teeth, 'I was in Scotland. I flew back as soon as I heard.' Jake put his hand in his jacket pocket.

Patrick slowly stood. 'What are you doing?'

'Getting out my boarding pass to show you.' Jake put his hand straight on the boarding pass, and threw it at Patrick. 'There. And just for your information, I would never take Natty away from her mother, or let any harm come to her. I bloody swear. I just want them both to be okay.'

Patrick pointed the gun. 'Where do you think you're going?'

Jake turned around. 'I'm going to find Natty.' His gaze dropped to the gun. 'Are you going to shoot me with that thing, or can I have it back?' Jake looked past Patrick at the card table. He was about to find out whether his hunch was right and Patrick, like himself, had been bluffing.

A minute's stand-off ended with Patrick handing over the gun. 'I guess you haven't got a licence for that thing.'

Jake didn't answer that.

Patrick lowered the gun and said, 'Let me help you find her.'

Jake sighed. 'Natty talks about you.'

Patrick looked taken aback. 'She does?'

'Natty asked me why she doesn't see her granddaddy anymore.'

The old man's pained face at this news confirmed that he was sincere. But the fact that Patrick knew nothing about his granddaughter's disappearance hours earlier meant only one thing: Faye hadn't contacted him. She didn't want him involved.

Jake stared at Patrick, at a loss as to what to do next. He'd been convinced he'd find her there. He turned to the door. He could still smell something. 'What is that smell?'

Patrick said, 'It's the gun. The smell of sulphur from the gunpowder lingers for some time after a gun is fired. It would be on your skin too, if you'd actually fired it.'

Jake pulled a face. 'It smells rank.' He wondered how long the smell would linger, and whether Aubrey would guess the gun had been fired – that was, assuming he could sneak it back undetected.

Jake opened the door, trying to think what he should do next. When he'd spoken with Faye, as soon as he'd landed at London City Airport, she'd asked him to make his way straight to her flat, in case Natty turned up. Although she had a friend there, Faye must have realised that it would be him who Natty wanted, after her mother, if she were to suddenly reappear.

Jake suddenly realised where he needed to be. Where Faye needed him to be. 'I've got to go.'

'I'm coming with you,' said Patrick.

'No, you can't.' Jake's voice was insistent. What would Faye think if she returned home to find Patrick there? And worse, that Jake had gone to see him and brought him back to her flat.

Jake opened the apartment door, about to leave, when Patrick said, 'I made a mistake! I didn't believe her about Yousaf.'

You still don't. Jake was thinking of that word he'd used – alleged.

'She won't give me a second chance.'

Jake turned around and looked at the old man. 'Maybe you need to earn her trust.'

Patrick walked over to the kitchen table. He stood fingering a playing card. He looked across the room at Jake. 'You're right. After what she said Yousaf tried to do, she didn't trust me because of my friendship with Yousaf.' Patrick bent down and picked up an overturned chair. 'At the time, her reaction was completely understandable.' He picked up the cards and shuffled them into a pile. 'It coincided with her addiction problem.'

'Addiction problem?'

'She was afraid of losing her job, her only means of support. And afraid that social services would step in and take her daughter.'

Jake thought back to something Faye had said about Marcus. Let's just say we have something in common.

'Drugs?' whispered Jake, not quite believing it. Even so, he involuntarily closed the door to the apartment, as though a neighbour might overhear.

Patrick shook his head. 'Thank god, no – alcohol.'

Jake knew Faye didn't keep alcohol in the house – not even wine vinegar for cooking. It made sense.

'She got over the addiction, but she never got over her fear that someone would come and take her daughter away.'

Jake stared at Patrick. Was it possible that Faye had got it wrong, and that Yousaf wasn't trying to take her daughter away from her? Had Patrick had been right all along, and she was just being paranoid? Jake didn't want to believe him, but everything he'd said so far made sense; although she'd sworn she'd seen two one-way tickets back to Yousaf's home country – one for him, and one for Natty.

Patrick stopped shuffling cards. He looked up at Jake. 'Have you ever said something, done something in the heat of the moment that …' He shook his head. 'Oh never mind, you'd wouldn't understand.'

Jake understood perfectly. 'That you wish you could take back?'

Patrick regarded him thoughtfully. 'I don't think Faye will ever forgive me for telling her she was just paranoid, and for taking Yousaf's side. She's my daughter. I should have listened.' He cast the playing cards aside. 'I miss them like you couldn't even begin to imagine.'

You wanna bet, Jake felt like saying, but he kept his mouth shut. Instead he walked over to the table and looked the old man in the eye. 'Can you assure me that you have had no contact with Natty's father since he left the country?'

Patrick studied the pack of cards in his hands intently.

Jake raised his eyebrows when he realised why Patrick wasn't responding to his question. 'You have got to be kidding me! After all you've just said …'

Patrick shot him a look. 'It's not what you think. He owes Faye money – child support for his first-born.'

'First-born?'

'He married. His new family knows nothing about Natasha's existence, and he wants to keep it that way.'

'How do you know all this?' said Jake, surprised by this revelation.

'I told you – child support. We were coming to an arrangement of sorts; he pays up and …'

'… and you don't let his new family into his past,' Jake concluded. 'What does Faye think about this arrangement?'

Patrick hesitated. 'I have the cheques right here.' He pointed at a kitchen drawer. 'I've left her messages. She won't take the money, even though I'm sure she could do with it.' He lowered his head. 'I think I've made things worse between us, if that's possible.'

'Because you've been in contact with him.'

'Yes.'

Jake could understand that. 'How did it come about that you got in contact with him after all these years?'

'I saw him in London.'

'He's here?' Jake said in alarm.

'No, he's not. He was on holiday with his family. I spotted a familiar face at a museum on a Sunday afternoon. Of course I wanted to talk to him, find out why he was back. Was he in London to see my granddaughter? That's when I found out the truth, and asked him for child support, backdated too, for Natty.'

'I thought I was doing the right thing. All I want to do is help my daughter out. I've seen the cheques. They are very, very generous.'

Jake bet they were. Yousaf was from a wealthy family.

'After I messaged her about it, she actually phoned me.'

Jake wasn't surprised.

'She thinks he is just doing it to make her feel guilty about not letting him see his child. But she didn't give me a chance to explain the situation. She didn't question why, after all these years, he'd suddenly offered to pay child support. Unfortunately, it's not what she thinks.' His voice faltered.

'You're telling me she doesn't know he married?'

Patrick started to pace. 'She believed the money was just the start; she was expecting him to walk back into Natasha's life and demand his parental rights, afraid he might even attempt to take her away. I think that's why she wouldn't have me come round with those cheques, let alone cash them.'

Jake knew why Natty's father couldn't send the cheques direct to Faye. She'd moved house and put Natty in a different school.

'You didn't tell Yousaf when he got back in contact with you where Faye was – did you?'

'Of course not. But she was still in London, so I suppose if he'd really wanted to track her and Natty down, he could have. But that's the point. He's got a new life now. I told you. He doesn't want his wife to find out about Faye and Natty.'

Jake stared at him. He suddenly felt lightheaded and grabbed onto a chair back. This meant only one thing. 'It wasn't Yousaf that took her.'

'Of course it wasn't.'

Jake's mobile phone rang. He didn't know how to tell Faye that he had been wrong; her daughter wasn't at her father's, and he had no bloody idea where she was.

He breathed in heavily when she told him there was still no news. 'No, sorry, I haven't arrived at your flat yet. But I'll be there very soon.' Jake closed his eyes. He could tell by the tremor in her voice that she was afraid and close to tears. 'I'm coming home too,' said Faye.

Jake guessed she was exhausted.

'The police said I need to go home, get some rest. But how can I rest, Jake?'

'Is it my daughter? Let me speak to her.'

Jake turned his back on Patrick and walked to the door, praying that Faye hadn't heard her father's voice.

'I'm never going to see her again, am I?'

'No, don't say that. We'll find her, Faye, I swear it. I'm coming right now and …' Jake opened the door to the apartment, 'I've enlisted some help … who? Somebody who can be trusted.'

Jake signed off and turned around to find Patrick staring at him, wide-eyed. Jake hoped to god he was doing the right thing. 'Well get your coat, man, if you're going to help me find Natty.'

Patrick grabbed his car keys off the sideboard. He didn't bother with a coat.

21

'What is he doing here?' A tearful and exhausted Faye answered the door to her flat and immediately spotted her father standing behind Jake. 'Is this some kind of joke?'

'Please, Faye. Just hear me out,' said Jake, cupping his hands together.

'He's not coming in,' said Faye, her tone of voice stressing that the subject was not open for debate.

'Faye, he only wants to help.'

'No one can help,' said Faye. 'This is all my fault.' She left the front door ajar and walked into the house.

Jake followed her inside. 'What are you talking about?'

She turned around to face Jake. 'We had a row and I think … I think she ran away.'

'Ran away? Why didn't you tell me this before I—' Jake stopped abruptly. He felt too embarrassed to divulge just what had taken place at Patrick's apartment, thinking it was him who'd had a hand in abducting Natty; it had been like something out of a Tarantino movie.

'I didn't tell you this before,' continued Faye, 'because it only just occurred to me when I saw you at the door.'

'What's it got to do with me?'

'It's got everything to do with you, Jake. I told her she couldn't see you anymore.'

'You did what?' Jake was shocked. He grabbed Faye's arm. 'Why did you tell her that? I was only on holiday. You knew I was coming back.'

'You're hurting me, Jake.'

'Sorry.' Jake hastily let go of her arm. 'But I don't understand!'

'It wasn't about your holiday. Things were getting too … too …'

'Complicated?' suggested Patrick as he walked past them both and popped his head around the door to the lounge.

'I thought I told you that you're not welcome here,' Faye glared at Patrick.

'Faye,' Jake touched her arm gently. 'Tell me what I've done wrong. Everything seemed okay between us, chatting on the phone when I was away in Scotland.'

'When you were away, I had time to think.'

Jake did not like the sound of that.

Faye looked at Jake for a long moment. Finally, she said, 'Natty was just getting too attached to you, Jake. Look what she said to you the other day; she called you Daddy.'

Patrick, who had been scouting around the lounge, overheard Faye. He reappeared in the hall and stared at Jake. 'She really called you her daddy?'

Faye turned to her father and said, 'It's none of your business.'

'Since when is my granddaughter none of my business?'

'Since you sided with Yousaf when I broke up with him, you moron.'

Everyone fell silent.

Jake and Patrick exchanged surprised glances. Even Faye looked shocked at her own outburst. It was obvious that she was completely stressed out, and Jake, her father, and the whole world were in the firing line until she got her daughter back safe.

'Alright,' said Patrick, holding up his hands in an effort to defuse the situation. 'Suppose I go have a look upstairs.' It wasn't a question because he was already heading for the stairs.

'I thought I told you to leave.'

'Did you check to see if anything was missing?' said Patrick. 'Perhaps she took something with her this morning that she would not normally take to school. It might give us a lead.'

The look on Faye's face said she hadn't thought of that.

Patrick said, 'Didn't one of the police officers ask to see her room?'

'I don't know,' Faye said in a small voice. 'I wasn't here. I left a friend here. I was out searching for my daughter.'

'Well, I'm here now,' said Patrick taking charge. 'Let's find her.'

All three of them scooted up the stairs. Patrick followed Faye along the landing into Natty's bedroom. Faye set to work opening cupboards and drawers, rummaging through her daughter's stuff.

Jake stood in the centre of the room, at a loss as to what he could do to help. If he had been searching through Natty's stuff at his house, he would know if something was missing, but not in her bedroom at home.

'Now, what have we here?' Patrick was on his hands and knees, peering under the bed. 'What do you suppose she was doing with this?' He pulled out a map.

Jake and Faye came over as he spread it out on the bed.

'It's my old road map of Great Britain,' said Faye. She must have been looking at it when she was on the phone to you.'

'Yes' said Jake thoughtfully. 'When I spoke to Natty on the phone from Scotland, she asked me where I was on holiday, said she had a map. Now I come to think of it, she was asking a lot of really specific questions.' Jake paused to look at the map realising she must have been looking at it in secret in her room while they were chatting, before Faye returned to take her phone back.

'What sort of questions?' asked Faye.

Patrick added, 'Tell us as much as you can remember from that conversation.'

Jake nodded. He recalled she'd asked where he was, and he'd told her he was in the Cairngorms. But when she'd asked which town, he'd said it was so small, she might not find it on a map of Great Britain, which is what he had gleaned she was looking at when he'd heard the distinct sound of the rustling of paper. He'd asked her if she was looking at a map.

'So, it turned out that it was your old map,' said Jake, glancing at Faye, who clearly wasn't happy with what he'd said.

Jake moved swiftly on. 'Anyways, by the sound of it, she traced with her finger where she was in London all the way to the Cairngorms, which she told me she'd found on the map. She said it was a long way away.'

The three of them stood there, eyeing the map.

'She wanted to know where I was, the name of the place in Scotland. Isn't that just like her?' added Jake. 'Wants to know every last detail.'

They all fell silent. It had become glaringly obvious; Natty had been trying to locate him on the map. Faye had told her she wasn't seeing him anymore, so Natty had decided to go and see him by herself. She was out there on the streets all alone.

Faye turned wide-eyed to look at him and said, 'And you didn't talk her out of it?'

'Talk her out of what?'

'Why – coming to find you, of course.'

Jake wished the ground would swallow him up. It was all his fault.

Patrick stepped in. 'Are you sure you told her you were in Aviemore?'

Jake thought hard. 'Yes, I'm pretty sure.' But there was no marking of any kind on the map to indicate where Natty was off to, if indeed she had decided she was somehow going to attempt that journey. But knowing Faye's stubborn, headstrong, and very bright little daughter, Jake guessed she wouldn't have put a mark on the map, just in case her mum found it. That didn't mean she hadn't somehow got it into her head that she was off to Scotland, even though she wouldn't get very far travelling on public transport before someone alerted the authorities, surely.

'I discovered her iPad is missing,' said Faye. 'She always takes that if she's going on a long journey.'

Patrick raised his eyebrows. 'So, that's where she thinks she's going,' he said, stabbing the map with a stubby forefinger, right dab in the middle of the Scottish Highlands.

'This is all your fault,' Faye turned on Jake.

Jake said in a small voice, 'I never meant for any of this to happen …'

'Faye, I don't think you can blame it on—' Patrick began.

'You stay out of this.' She pointed a finger at Patrick, then turned her attention swiftly back to Jake. 'Actually, this isn't your fault; this is my fault for not seeing the signs earlier. I kept all my dates out of Natty's life so she wouldn't get attached to another man who would walk out of her life at a drop of a hat, like her father, like her grandfather …'

'Now, Faye, that's not fair …' began Patrick.

'I said, will you stay out of this!' She rounded on her father. 'Can't you see what's happening here? I had it all figured out. Guys could come and go so long as I stuck to one simple rule; there were no instant families here. That way she wouldn't get close, she wouldn't get hurt.'

'Who are we really talking about here?' interrupted Patrick. 'Natasha or you?'

She fell silent.

Jake scrutinised her closely because that was an interesting question. She'd had a number of dates with one particular guy who, according to Faye, wasn't willing to commit. This seemed a tad confusing to Jake when he considered the conversation he'd overheard on the doorstep of her house one night during babysitting duties.

Faye had just arrived home after an evening out. Jake had just nipped upstairs to check on Natty, who was fast asleep. He was walking back down the stairs when she'd opened the front door and he'd overheard a snippet of conversation between Faye and her then beau. The gist of it was that he was serious about her and wanted them to take the relationship to the next level. He owned some plush city apartment, and he wanted them to move in together. He'd even taken the liberty of hiring a personal shopper to set up a child's bedroom, along with a playroom as a surprise for Natty. 'I'd love to meet her, you know.' Jake distinctly remembered that line. He'd hated the thought of another guy in their lives.

Jake never heard mention of the guy again.

At the time, this had pleased Jake no end, not because he didn't like the guy – he didn't even know him – but because he liked things just the way they were. Jake knew that in time, he would have to face up to the possibility that Faye would get into a relationship that turned serious. But still, he found himself absurdly fretting over each new guy, wondering if he was the one she'd fall head-over-heels in love with, unaware, until Patrick had made that comment, that Faye was committed not to have a relationship, that she had been playing the field with no intention of letting anything get serious; with no intention of letting anybody get close.

Jake should have recognised the signs; after all, he had been just as guilty of playing that game himself these past few months. This should have made him feel relieved. Instead, it made him feel uneasy because he realised that he had become that guy with the apartment, that guy who had taken the liberty of setting up the bedroom and playroom for Natty. Jake had got too close, and like that guy, Faye was cutting him loose.

'Everything was working just fine until you came along.' Faye stabbed a finger into Jake's chest. She turned to her father. 'He'll get promoted,' she said. 'Then he'll be transferred to another school. Oh no, wait – you're going back to the Ross Corporation.'

Patrick turned to look at Jake in surprise. 'Really?'

'No. Not permanently.'

'Never say never!' Faye spat. She turned to her father. 'And he's never short of female company.'

'That does not surprise me.'

Jake frowned at Patrick. He wasn't helping.

Faye was on a roll. 'And babysitting Natty will go out of the window as soon as one of them turns serious.'

Jake was just about to object when Patrick cut in with four

words. It shocked Jake to hear them out loud.

'He loves you, Faye.'

Jake stood there, open-mouthed. Had he just said that?

Faye stared at her father. 'What did you just say?'

'I said he's in love with you. My God, you should have seen him at my apartment. I think he would rather have killed himself than come back here and tell you he hadn't found your daughter.'

'You're serious, aren't you?' said Faye, turning to look at Jake. She regarded him for a moment. 'You're very quiet all of a sudden. Aren't you going to tell my father what a blithering idiot he is?'

Jake looked across at Patrick. What he wanted was to tell Patrick to shut the hell up. But it was his own fault. He hadn't told him outright that he was in love with Faye, but he might as well have. Jake thought about the conversation back at Patrick's flat. Patrick knew he was in love with Faye, but Jake hadn't anticipated he'd come right out and say it – the fool. Now, because of him, any chance he might have had with Faye was lost; it was over before it had even started. Patrick had said it himself: Faye was committed not to have a relationship. Now she really would steer clear of him, if that was what she thought he was after.

He could feel Faye's eyes boring into him, the impatient tap of her foot on the carpet, signalling that she was waiting for a response. Jake continued to look at the floor, the ceiling, anywhere but directly at Faye.

'Jake?'

After that revelation, courtesy of Patrick, just for a moment, he imagined a fantastical scenario whereby she simply fell into his arms and expressed the same hidden feelings about him. Over the past few months, he'd thought he'd picked up a vibe that she might just feel the same way about him. And she had told him she missed him terribly when he was in Scotland. Or had it all just been wishful thinking on his part? He loved Natty like she was his own child. And he loved Faye. Didn't those things count for something?

Apparently not.

To Jake's dismay, she just stood there and stared at him like he was some village idiot who deserved to be ridiculed. He couldn't think of a worse way to find out he'd been wrong.

He was saved from the excruciating embarrassment of it all by Faye exclaiming, 'God, what am I standing around here for, talking to you two? I need to find my child.' Jake was the first out of the bedroom door. The knowledge that Natty had run away just so she could go and see him was weighing heavy on his shoulders. Faye was right: this was his fault.

As he raced down the stairs, wondering how exactly Natty thought she was going to get all the way from London to Scotland, he was surprised by the sound of Faye's telephone in the downstairs hall. Jake stopped halfway down the stairs. He looked behind him. Faye and Patrick had stopped dead too. They were all pinned to the spot, unable to move, afraid what it meant. Then, suddenly, all three were hot-footing it down the stairs, making a mad dash for the phone, all thinking the same thing – why weren't they calling Faye on her mobile?

Jake got there first and held out the receiver to Faye. She looked at the phone, and shook her head, motioning for Jake to answer. Jake put the receiver to his ear, his hand shaking, and listened. Everybody was holding their breath in anticipation of some news. The second Jake heard the words he repeated them to Faye. 'They found her. She's fine.'

Faye fell into her father's arms, great sobs of relief bellowing into his shoulder.

22

After the initial wave of relief that Natty had been found came the questions, Faye and Patrick firing them off at Jake while Faye, in her desperation to get answers, kept reaching for the phone in Jake's hand.

'Calm down, both of you,' Jake ordered, because they were drowning out the woman on the end of the line. Jake had assumed he was talking to a police officer, but it turned out the young woman was an employee at the coach company, working in the ticket office. She had noticed a young girl hanging around Victoria Coach Station in Belgravia.

'She's where?' said Jake. 'All right. We're on our way.'

'Where is she?' Faye asked.

'Victoria Coach Station.'

Jake was just relieved she hadn't got on a bus to Scotland. But she had bought a ticket.

'She what?' said Patrick.

Faye asked, 'Why did they ring my house phone?'

Patrick said, 'Either she remembered your home phone number, or they used directory enquiries.'

'She kept asking for a mobile phone, and I said no. If she'd had one, she'd have had my number in her phone, and I would have been able to contact her.'

'And track her phone,' commented Patrick.

Jake held up his hand for them to quieten down while he listened. Natty had bought a ticket to Edinburgh. How she'd planned to get from there to Aviemore, Jake had no clue; the coaches didn't go all the way to Natty's destination. Of course, the company wouldn't sell tickets to a lone child, but Natty had walked up to the ticket booth on her own and had explained that her parents were letting her buy her own ticket. She'd pointed at a young couple who were sitting together, waiting for a bus, and had sat down on the seat next to them after she'd bought her ticket. It would be a long wait.

When the young woman started her shift, she'd noticed the young girl sitting on her own with an iPad and a backpack. That was when her colleague told her he'd sold her a ticket because her parents had said she could buy it herself.

'So, where are the parents?' she'd asked, getting suspicious, wondering if the girl was running away from home. The young woman had told Natty a fib, that the bus was cancelled, and that she'd refund her ticket, and was there someone she could call to collect her from the station because she couldn't stay there all night until the next bus in the morning.

Jake listened as the young woman said it was quite something for someone so young to plan a journey all the way to Scotland, and she'd found the cheapest route.

A smile flitted across his lips. 'That's what I keep telling her mother,' said Jake, eyeing Faye.

'What – tell me?' said Faye, who was still clinging to her father's arm.

'That she's a very smart young lady,' said Jake, passing the phone to Faye. 'She's just finishing eating a hot meal in their staff canteen.'

Faye shook her head. 'Tell them I'm on my way.'

Jake nodded. 'All right.' He did just that and put the phone down. Jake explained, 'Sounds like she had a plan. She bought a bus ticket to Scotland.'

'How the hell did she do that?' said Patrick. 'They know kids are not allowed to travel alone. I'm going to get hold of the person who issued the ticket to a lone nine-year-old kid and …'

'Apparently Natty knew about that little rule as well,' said Jake eyeing Patrick. He could well imagine what Patrick would do to that ticket officer. 'Somehow she made him think she was travelling with a young couple.'

Patrick raised his eyebrows. 'How'd she do that?'

Jake told them what the young woman had said. 'Natty must have been aware she wouldn't be able to travel alone, so she sat down in the waiting area next to a young couple. Now the man in the ticket booth sees them together, so when Natty comes up to buy her ticket she tells him that her mummy – at this point she makes a show of turning around and waving at the young woman – has let her be all grown-up and buy a ticket all by herself as long as the nice ticket man will let her.'

Jake could imagine those dark, mischievous eyes staring dolefully at the poor man in the ticket booth; he didn't have a chance.

'I don't believe it!' said Faye.

Patrick chuckled.

Faye turned to her father. 'This isn't funny!'

He tempered his smile, and said, 'Ahem, no, of course not.'

Patrick got out his mobile phone and dialled the police as he walked to the door. 'Hello, yes. I'm phoning about a missing child – Natasha Ames. We found her.'

❖

As Faye hurriedly slipped on a coat, Jake followed her to the front door and said, 'I'm sorry about all this.' She was right: it was his fault. 'I should have guessed what she was up to.'

Faye surprised him when she replied, 'You had no way of knowing she'd do something like this.'

Jake smiled in relief. Was all forgiven? Could they go back to the way things had been? Might he be in with a chance with Faye after all?

'There's just one thing that puzzles me,' mused Faye. 'Where did she find the money to catch a bus in the first place? She only gets a couple of pounds a week pocket money, and I know for a fact she spends that on sweets.'

Oh, dear. Jake pursed his lips. I think she must have used her GoHenry account.'

'Her what?' said Faye.

'It's a savings account with a pre-paid debit card for youngsters aged between six and eighteen.' Jake added, 'It's not just parents who can open one for children, grandparents and close family friends can … too.'

The look on Faye's face said he'd done the wrong thing.

Faye asked, 'Whose idea was that?'

'Actually, it was hers.' Jake wasn't passing the buck, but it was true. 'She said all her friends had one and it made her feel grown-up. You can use it to pay for the … bus.' Jake frowned.

'Why didn't she ask me?'

Jake would really rather not answer that question.

'Well?'

'She said Mummy never has any money so there was no point having the card if she couldn't have more than two pounds.'

'I don't believe this,' said Faye.

'Now, don't get mad,' Patrick intervened. 'It sounds like a good idea to me.' He turned to Jake. 'Does that mean I can deposit some money into her GoHenry account?'

'Of course. You can transfer some money, and even set up a recurring transfer too. I'd just need to add you to—'

'Urrgh!' Faye cut across Jake. 'I can't believe you went behind my back and opened an account in my daughter's name.'

'It was only recently. I was going to tell you. We wanted it to be a surprise.'

'Oh, so now you're both keeping secrets from me.'

Patrick came to Jake's defence. 'Now come on Faye, don't you think that's a little harsh?'

'Now you're taking his side. Well, what a surprise!'

Jake said, 'It's a really good account, comes with an app that teaches them about managing money, budgeting, and saving—'

'Teaches them money management! That's a fine one coming from you,' she scoffed. Faye turned to her father. 'Do you know how much stuff he buys her? It's like a regular toy store at his house. He buys her whatever she wants. And now he's going to give her whatever money she wants too.'

'No, I wouldn't do that! Look Faye, I didn't mean …' began Jake, but he was cut short by the phone ringing.

Faye leapt to the phone. She said anxiously, 'Hello? Yes, yes, that's me,' said Faye down the phone. 'She wants to speak to me before I come and get her? I was just walking out of the door. Is she okay? Oh, she just wants to speak to me. Of course, yes put her on …' She waited a second or two then, 'Natty? Oh, sweetheart, it's so good to hear your voice … no, you're not in trouble … no, I'm not mad at you …' She laughed. 'No, not even an insy bit … of course I still love you … oh, I shouldn't have said that about Jake. I'm sorry.' Faye turned to look at Jake. 'Of course you can see him again.'

Jake sighed in relief. It didn't mean all was forgiven, but at least he was still in their lives – for the time, being at least.

'When?' Faye said, clearly repeating what Natty had asked. 'He's here with me right now. Yes, it's true. He came straight back from Scotland when he found out you were missing.'

Faye frowned. 'All right.' She reluctantly handed him the phone.

'Natty, sweetheart. No, I'm not angry with you …' Jake reassured her, smiling when he realised he was almost repeating verbatim what Faye had just said to Natty a moment earlier before he handed the phone back to Faye.

She said, 'Right, I'm on my way.' Faye looked at Jake. 'No, it's just me coming to collect you.'

Jake stepped forward, about to protest, but Patrick caught his arm and shook his head. Jake backed down. In that moment, he realised no matter how close he felt to Natty, no matter how much he would be honoured to be her daddy, the simple fact was that he had no rights there. It was all up to Faye, and from her reaction to what Patrick had foolishly blurted earlier, or maybe to the GoHenry card, or just to the fact that Natty had wanted to speak to Jake, or just everything right now, it looked like he'd never get the chance to be anything more than a friend. Perhaps not even that.

This was exactly the reason he could barely acknowledge his own feelings, let alone tell Faye how he really felt about her; he was scared of rocking the boat in case Faye threw him overboard. He would rather things remained just the way they were without any possibility of taking their relationship further, just as long as they both stayed in his life. Now it looked as though the chances of that were slim to none, unless she had other plans. Unless she was planning a surprise for Natty. He could picture the scene; Faye arriving to fetch Natty, surprising her by bringing along both Jake and her grandfather – a happy family reunion. And the icing on the cake would be Faye telling Natty that she loved Jake and she wanted to marry him.

By the time Faye had put the phone down and rushed to the door, picking up her coat and car keys along the way, Jake was right behind her with a big grin on his face, convinced she was going to change her mind and let them go too. Glancing behind him, Patrick was hot on his heels, similarly smiling from ear to ear with, Jake imagined, the same thought running through his mind.

Faye opened the front door, stepped outside, and stopped abruptly, forcing Jake to a halt at the door and sending Patrick careering into Jake's back.

'Sorry,' said Patrick. He glanced at Faye. 'Have we forgotten something?'

Faye turned around and stared at her father. 'You're not coming.'

Jake turned to look at Patrick. The expression on his face spoke volumes; the word disappointment didn't begin to describe the pain etched on the old man's face at the realisation that he wasn't invited on this trip.

Jake turned back to Faye. He wanted to object. He wanted

Patrick to come too, but he knew it wasn't his call, his decision. Jake accepted that fact and took a step forward.

Faye didn't move. Instead, she focused her attention on Jake.

'What?' said Jake in surprise. 'I can't come either?'

She shook her head. 'Didn't you hear me on the phone? I told Natty it's just me coming to collect her.'

'But I thought—'

'You thought what? There'd be some, like, big family reunion or something?'

'Now look …' Jake began.

'I SAID NO!' She whirled on her heel and darted down the pathway to her car.

Jake was too taken aback by the ferocity of her retort to argue with her or even chase her to the car to ask her to reconsider. Instead, he just stood there and said nothing.

And, standing in that open doorway, watching the woman he loved leaving him on such a bitter, unresolved note, left him with something else – a terrible sense of déjà vu. He hadn't gone after her either, after Eleanor when she'd said she was going out on Christmas Day. He'd just stood there. A voice in his head had said, go after her, but like an idiot, he hadn't, believing mistakenly that there was always a second chance.

Suddenly, Jake was running down the pathway towards her car, waving frantically and shouting, 'Faye! No! Wait!' as the car engine revved up.

She drove off just as he reached the kerb.

'NO!' He stopped and watched the car disappear into the distance. 'No!' he said, 'not again.'

Jake felt a hand on his shoulder.

'Let her go.' Patrick was standing beside him. 'She needs to see her daughter alone, just the two of them, the way it used to be – at least for now.'

'You don't understand,' said Jake, feeling immensely agitated. 'I've done it again. I let somebody else go like this and she never came back. The person I knew, the person I loved, never came back.' He grasped Patrick's shoulders. 'Don't you see? If I'd just run after her, if I'd just opened my damn mouth and said something, then maybe … maybe …' Jake's shoulders began to heave.

Patrick pulled him close in a bear hug. Jake began to cry, great big heaving sobs into the shoulder of a man he barely knew.

'It's alright, son,' he said soothingly. 'It's going to be alright.' Patrick patted him on the back.

'There's nothing to see here!' Patrick shouted suddenly. Neighbouring porch doors shut with a rackety clap. 'Jake, why don't we go back inside?' Patrick gave him one last affectionate pat on the back and released him.

Jake wiped his nose on his sleeve.

'She'll be back. You'll see,' Patrick said reassuringly. 'Faye and Natty will be back. She just needs a bit of time, that's all.' He put an arm around Jake's shoulder and guided him towards the house.

At the front door, Jake stopped. 'She doesn't want me, Patrick, does she?'

'Let's go inside, eh?'

'You didn't answer my question.' Jake stared into his hazel eyes. They were the same colour as the eyes he had looked into nearly every single day for the last few months, since he'd first met Faye. She had her father's eyes.

'Who knows what is going through my daughter's mind at this moment? She's just found out that Natty is safe and well after hours of going through fear and anxiety like you couldn't imagine. Then she finds out that the man she has been trying her utmost to keep at arm's length is in love with her.' Patrick peered at Jake. 'I think that's a lot to take on board all in one day – don't you?'

They both turned at the sound of the house phone.

'Maybe that's her,' said Patrick, skipping up the front steps into the house.

Jake hovered on the doorstep and left Patrick to take the call.

He stared up at the night sky, a sky that in the city never got completely dark. Not like in the Highlands of Scotland, where no lights could be seen for miles and where the night sky was so black, you couldn't see your hand in front of your face. Where people didn't go out at three in the morning and buy a cappuccino or shop at a twenty-four-hour convenience store, but did what they should be doing at night – sleeping.

Jake stood outside, listening to the sounds of cars and people and the neighbourhood, and had a longing like he'd never felt before; a longing to return home. Perhaps he wouldn't feel this way if he hadn't returned briefly to Scotland. Maybe that was his mistake. But he had a feeling that Mr Gillespie was right about the place; it was in his soul, pulling him back like a piece of taut elastic waiting to be released. Now, that pull felt stronger than ever.

And that pull was raising serious doubts about the choices he had made in his life these past few months. Maybe he had got it wrong. Maybe this wasn't meant to be his new life, his new beginning. Maybe it was just a phase, a stage, a transient place; somewhere he was just passing through on his way to coming to terms with what had happened, on his way towards – he knew now – something better, something right for him. He thought of Faye and Natty; maybe, however much it hurt, he had to come to terms with the fact that he was only passing through their lives too.

But I don't want it to be that way, thought Jake. He realised it didn't matter what he wanted. The ball was firmly in Faye's court. After what had happened with Natty, he seriously doubted whether things between him and Faye would ever be the same again.

A little voice in his head said, perhaps it's for the best.

He'd thought he had it figured out – living in London, getting a new job, teaching – but at the back of his mind, he realised it had always been there, festering; the possibility that this might not be the rest of his life. That was why, he now realised, he had been so careful not to get emotionally involved with anyone else, not to risk getting hurt again, because when the time came to leave, as he believed it had, he knew he most probably would not be able to physically uproot those attachments and take them with him.

However much it hurt Jake, maybe the fact that Faye didn't want him was for the best; it meant he was free to start over again, properly this time, not deceiving himself any more about what had happened to his wife, able to move on now to a permanent place – home.

'Jake! It's Faye.'

Jake turned around and took a tentative step into the house. He looked at the phone in Patrick's hand. 'She wants to speak to me?'

He nodded. Jake wasn't sure he wanted to speak to her and get another earful. But the look on Patrick's face – he was smiling, and winking at Jake – made him wonder … she wasn't phoning to apologise to him, surely?

'Faye?'

'Don't say anything, just listen …'

Jake listened. His mouth dropped open. 'I'm sorry, did I hear you correctly?' He stared at Patrick, who was bouncing from one foot to the other, clearly dying to know what exactly was going on. 'What do I think?' Jake didn't know what to think. He couldn't have been more surprised. 'I … I … of course I want to come … Yes, Marcus will be okay. He'll just have to wait until I get back to check into the clinic.'

Jake slowly put the phone down.

Patrick said, 'Well – what did she say? Is she coming back to collect you and take you to the bus station to collect Natty?'

Jake slowly shook his head from side to side. 'No.'

'So, what's going on?'

'She wants to take Natty to Scotland for a holiday, and she wants me to come too. She's going to tell Natty the plan.'

Patrick grinned, and slapped Jake affectionately on the back. 'Well, there you go. All's well that ends well.'

'But will it?'

'Will it what?'

'End well?'

'You mean you and Faye getting together?'

Jake meant more than that. Could he convince Faye to start a new life with him in Scotland? She'd nearly finished her headship qualification. She could be a headteacher in Scotland, couldn't she? He could get a teaching job too. He'd have to show her all the great things Scotland had to offer, make sure it was a holiday to remember.

Jake frowned when he had a sudden thought. Did she have an ulterior motive? Was this their final hurrah, letting Natty see him, taking her on a trip to Scotland together, before bowing out of his life completely? She wouldn't do that – would she?

Jake stared at Patrick.

Patrick shrugged. 'Do not ask me what is going through my daughter's mind. The only thing you can do is go to Scotland, make sure they have a bloody good time, get back in her good books, and lastly …'

'And lastly?' Jake asked, hanging on his every world.

'Don't screw it up.'

23

'Just like old times.'

Robyn turned her head and looked at David. He was smiling. He turned on his side, head resting on his elbow, and smiled at her. 'How long have you been awake?'

Robyn was still nestled under the duvet. She'd been lying awake for some time, watching David sleep, her mind elsewhere. She turned to look at the ceiling. 'Just a little while.'

'Why didn't you wake me?'

She turned on her side to face him. 'Why would I do that? You were fast asleep.'

'I wish you had. I don't want to miss a second of your company now you're back.' He paused. 'You are back – right? You're not returning to London, are you?'

She gave him a reassuring smile and leaned in to kiss him. When she drew back, she noticed he seemed quiet. 'I already said I wasn't going back to London, if that's what you're worried about.'

'Do you mean right now? Or … you know … for the foreseeable?'

Robyn sighed and sat up in bed, smoothing down the black lace nightie she'd bought from London as part of her surprise the previous evening. Gayle had phoned her, telling her that David was staying over at Lark Lodge while she was away. That had surprised her at first. Then Gayle had told her the reason for her call. It wasn't just to tell her that. David was concerned about what was going on in London. Robyn had asked her what she'd said to David, and all Gayle had told him was what she knew: Robyn had another interior design contract. She didn't want to interfere in their relationship, but she'd told Robyn that because this time he couldn't go with her, he was worried about what was going on.

Gayle told her that David suspected she was meeting up with someone from her past. Gayle hadn't asked her outright. All she'd said was that if that were the case, she'd know, because Gayle was her best friend, and Robyn told her everything.

Robyn thought – not everything. The good thing that had come out of that conversation was that Gayle had told her she'd tried to reassure David that there was nothing going on, but then had let slip to Robyn his plan to book a fancy hotel as a surprise for when she returned. Gayle wasn't happy that she'd accidentally told Robyn that. But Robyn was happy.

Robyn glanced at David. The last thing she wanted was for him to spend money on a fancy hotel when she'd much rather stay at Lark Lodge for a night. She'd told Gayle as much; that Lark Lodge was a hundred times better than any fancy five-star hotel. And then Robyn had had the most amazing idea. David had been expecting her home on Saturday, but Robyn had decided she'd get home the day before and surprise him.

Her new interior design commission was going well. She'd told Gayle that too. But she didn't want to tell Gayle everything that was going on in London. She couldn't. Not straight away. Not if she didn't want to risk the life she had made for herself in

Aviemore with her new friends, with David. The only thing that wasn't working for her was the boathouse. She didn't want to think about returning there. She'd have to, though. She couldn't stay at Lark Lodge indefinitely. What would David think if she told him she wanted to stay there? Would he think that she regretted moving in with him? She did not. The boathouse was a gorgeous place to live – right on the loch, in the middle of the highland countryside, at the end of a long single-track road with very few properties, surrounded by pine forests. What was not to like?

Nothing apart from her past. Robyn was still having issues with her memory loss after her car accident. Arriving at the boathouse for the first time, before they'd moved in together, had triggered a memory that, quite ironically, she'd rather had not surfaced.

Every time she turned up at the boathouse, she remembered turning up there once before, in a car, after dark. She didn't know when that had been, or whose car she had been in, or who she had been with. But she did remember feeling afraid. All she had wanted to do was run away. That feeling was still with her every single time they arrived at the boathouse. She wished it would go away, but it would not. She guessed the only way for that to happen was for her memories to come back. Then she'd know what she'd been so afraid of. The question on her mind was what she had even been doing there. She wouldn't have known David. They'd only met after their car accident.

She didn't want to tell David that the reason she'd started taking commissions in London – from wealthy home owners who had holiday homes in Aviemore but who wanted work done on their main homes – was to get away from the boathouse. She loved her life in the Highlands, and had sworn she'd never want to leave

– until they'd moved in together.

Robyn cast the duvet aside and swung her legs off the bed. She felt David catch her hand. He said, 'Oh, don't get up yet. Let's have a lie-in.'

Robyn glanced over her shoulder at him. He was still holding her hand, squeezing it gently. 'I couldn't believe it when I walked into the bedroom last night, and you were here.'

Robyn smiled. 'I know.'

'We had a wonderful evening together, didn't we?' said David, sitting up in bed.

Robyn nodded and smiled. 'Yes, we did. Thanks to Gayle.'

David grinned. 'She knew all along about your little ruse, keeping it a secret that you were returning yesterday instead of today. You know, I realised in hindsight that there were little tell-tale signs yesterday when I returned from work.'

Robyn turned around on the bed and sat crossed-legged, facing David. 'Like what?' She was interested to know.

'Oh, Olive for one.'

'Olive?'

'Yes. I caught her sniffing and whining outside the bedroom.' David glanced towards their bedroom door. 'Gayle grabbed her and dragged her downstairs. I did think it was a bit odd, but now I come to think of it, Olive knew.'

Robyn grinned. 'I heard her. I really, really wanted to let her in. But I knew that if I did, she'd totally give the game away. She'd start barking with excitement, and the whole house would know I was here.'

David grinned too. 'Yep, I can just imagine.'

'I thought of opening the door, and giving her a quick fuss, and then sending her on her way.'

David shook his head. 'Nah, that would not have worked.'

'Yes, we both know what she's like. If I'd closed the door on her, she'd have howled. I had to keep as quiet as a mouse and hope she just went away.' Robyn had heard Gayle taking Olive downstairs just before David opened the bedroom door.

David said, 'I wanted to go out last night, get a takeaway, and drown my sorrows.'

Robyn didn't have to ask what he meant by drown his sorrows. She knew he hadn't managed to book the fancy hotel room, which had disappointed him immensely. But it hadn't just been that. He'd been worried that he was losing her. She'd come back the previous night to surprise him and reassure him that it was not the case. He wasn't losing her. It was just … Robyn thought about her trips to London. Things had got complicated. Just what she was afraid of had happened – she'd discovered someone from her past. But the last thing she'd wanted to do was ruin her wonderful evening with David by bringing that up.

She said, 'I bet you're glad you didn't go out last night.'

'I am. If I'd known you were just a few feet away, hiding in the bedroom, Gayle would not have had to go to lengths to try and persuade me to stay and have dinner. The trouble was I never much liked her stew.'

Robyn wriggled her nose. 'No, me neither. Not until last night.'

'It was just delicious, wasn't it?'

'Oh, yes. I don't know what she's added, but she really went to town to make our evening together at Lark Lodge special, didn't she?'

Robyn smiled, thinking back to the previous night …

❖

They walked, hand in hand, down to the dining room. Gayle had knocked on their door and told them to head down there when they were ready. Robyn noticed that Olive was nowhere to be seen and guessed she was upstairs with Nick in his room. She heard the television on in Nick's room as they passed by, and smelled a rather lovely Chinese takeaway wafting in the hallway. She realised that Nick must have taken it up to his room before they emerged. She smiled. She could just imagine Olive begging for some food.

Robyn and David walked into the kitchen to a frown from Gayle. She turned around and waved a wooden spoon at them. 'What are you doing in here?'

David quipped. 'It's the kitchen. We always eat in here.'

Robyn nodded in agreement. She loved Gayle's country kitchen, with its old-fashioned, oak-fronted kitchen cupboards, Aga, and large oak table in the centre of the room. She grown to love it when she went to live at Gayle's after her accident on Christmas Day, when she'd had nowhere else to go and no one to turn to. She knew she'd be forever grateful to Gayle for taking in a stranger and giving her a home just when she'd needed it.

Robyn had such fond memories of sitting at the table with Marty, Nick and Gayle's mother, Doris – with Olive being very naughty and begging at the table. To repay Gayle for her kindness, Robyn had redecorated her house, keeping many of the original features and adding some of her own ideas.

Strictly speaking, they weren't her own ideas. She'd copied them from the intricately designed doll's house she'd found under a dustsheet in the basement of The Lake House. She wouldn't have been in that house if Marty hadn't taken her on a tour. He had found a key under the doormat by the back door. She'd taken a keen interest in the house, although she didn't know why.

Perhaps it was because she had something in common with the wealthy heiress, Eleanor Campbell-Ross; they'd both been involved in an accident on Christmas Day. Or perhaps it was that the house had been abandoned soon after. She doubted the family would return. And who could blame them? That was why she'd been surprised to be asked to revamp the interior of the house.

Annie had suggested that the family wanted it refurbished because they were going to sell the place. Robyn remembered feeling strangely protective of The Lake House, telling Annie that she felt they'd never do that. But when she'd got the commission, she had become absurdly anxious about meeting the family. Annie had told her not to get overwhelmed or intimidated just because the Rosses were so wealthy. But it wasn't that she was worried about. She'd used the designs from the doll's house at Lark Lodge. What if they found out? She wasn't sure how they would react. Would she lose the commission? Or worse, had she done something illegal by stealing Eleanor's ideas?

'I told you both that dinner is in the dining room this evening,' Gayle said. She walked towards them, waving her spoon. 'Now scoot.'

They both backed out of the kitchen as Robyn said, 'Hi, Doris.' Gayle's mother was sitting at the kitchen table.

'Something smells delicious – doesn't it?' commented David.

When Robyn didn't answer, David turned to her. 'Everything all right, Robyn?'

'Oh, yes – of course. Why wouldn't it be?'

'You look a bit preoccupied.'

Robyn didn't want to tell him that she had a lot on her mind; not least the thought of returning to the boathouse. She wondered what David would think if she suggested staying the weekend at

Lark Lodge. Perhaps Gayle didn't have any new guests arriving.

'I know what you're thinking,' David said, pausing outside the dining room.

Robyn doubted that very much.

'You want to stay here for the weekend.'

Robyn's mouth dropped open. 'How did you know?'

David lowered his voice. 'Look, I'm not blind. I don't know why but for some reason we … you were happier here.'

'I wanted to move in together.'

'Then what is it?' He leaned against the dining room doorway and stared at her. 'It's me – isn't it? Since we moved in together, you've changed your mind. That's why you keep going to Lon—'

'Oh, my god. Of course it's not you. How can you say that after …?'

David nodded knowingly. They both knew what she was talking about. As soon as he'd stepped into their room and discovered her there, they had been mad for each other. It was as though they'd been apart for weeks, months even, and they'd just found their way back to one another. It didn't make sense. She'd only been gone a few days. Or perhaps it did. Robyn raised her eyebrows. They hadn't spent such a passionate night together since they'd set up home at David's boathouse in June a month earlier.

Robyn knew – and she guessed David knew too – that they'd been drifting apart. She knew that was why her trips to London, especially the latest one, when she'd insisted on going alone, were worrying him no end. The fact that he'd said they could spend the whole weekend at Gayle's suggested he understood that she'd been unhappy since moving into the boathouse.

David said, 'It's my boathouse – isn't it?'

Robyn caught Gayle standing in the kitchen doorway with

folded arms. 'And why aren't you two in the dining room like I told you? Stop hanging around in the doorway.'

Robyn grabbed David's shirt sleeve. 'Come on.'

They walked in. 'It's a bit dark in here.'

'Oh look. Gayle has lit some candles.' Robyn walked up to the dining table in the centre of the room. It was smaller, more intimate than the kitchen table. Gayle had removed the other two chairs, so there were now just two chairs, one at each end of the smooth chestnut oval table.

David suddenly rushed towards Robyn. She wondered what he was up to. Then he said, 'Here – let me.' David pulled out the chair for her.

Robyn smiled at him as she took a seat. She watched him take a seat opposite her. He undid his top shirt button and glanced at the fire in the grate. 'Why did she light that on a summer's evening?'

'For atmosphere.'

'Oh, right.' He rolled up his shirt sleeves.

Robyn couldn't believe how thoughtful Gayle had been. She recognised the tablecloth as Gayle's favourite. The she glanced around the room. She rarely ventured into it; she'd spent most of her time in the lounge or the kitchen when she'd lived there. The dining room felt like a rather posh room for special occasions, which apparently was how Gayle's parents had thought of it – sort of like a parlour, in old-fashioned parlance.

The times she had gone into the room had been when she had redecorated and furnished it. The interior design had come from the doll's house; the matching cosy armchairs in a floral print either side of the fireplace, the standard lamp in the corner, the bookshelves in one alcove with a lamp on one shelf. The lamp had a low-wattage bulb and a pretty porcelain lampshade, and Gayle had thoughtfully switched it on; it gave off a warm yellow glow.

'What are you thinking?' David asked.

'I'm thinking I agree with you. The stew smells delicious,' said Robyn. She picked up the napkin that was neatly arranged in a champagne glass.

'No, I meant what I said about the boathouse.'

Robyn put the napkin on her lap. She did not want to talk about the fact that it wasn't the boathouse itself, but something in her past. She looked across the table and said instead, 'Yes, I'd love to stay on here for the weekend.'

David frowned at her. 'It is the boathouse, then.'

Robyn was saved from having to respond by Gayle appearing in the doorway. 'Dinner is served.'

Robyn turned in her chair. 'That smells delicious, Gayle.'

Gayle smiled as she walked in, carrying a tray. She set it down on the table and picked up a plate and the ladle in the casserole dish. Robyn avoided David's gaze as Gayle passed them a large bowl of stew each. She put a plate with crusty bread and butter on the table.

Robyn looked at the stew. 'It's so lovely of you to go to all this trouble.'

'Not at all. What are friends for?'

Gayle's other friends, Marty and Nick, had obviously been told to make themselves scarce. Robyn said as much.

Gayle nodded. 'It's true. I couldn't very well have them turn up while you two are having a romantic meal together.' Gayle looked from Gayle to David. 'That is what's going on here, isn't it?'

David frowned.

Robyn avoided Gayle's gaze.

David said, 'Robyn wants to stay for the weekend.'

Gayle turned to look at her.

'Yes, I do. If that's all right with you?' Robyn was aware that although Gayle had said in the past she liked to keep their room aside in case they came to stay, the reality was that she was running a guesthouse, and the room wouldn't always be free.

'All right,' she said slowly. 'Is that just you?'

Robyn looked across the table. 'No, David too.'

He managed a smile.

Gayle looked relieved. 'Good, that's good. I have to say I do miss you guys.' She looked at Robyn. 'Hey, you know what? You might get to meet one of the Rosses.'

Robyn had just picked up her spoon and was about to taste the stew. She looked up sharply. 'Pardon me? Did you just say—?'

'Oh, you mean Jake is coming back?' David asked nonchalantly before tasting the stew.

'Yes, hopefully,' Gayle replied.

Robyn looked from one to the other. 'I'm sorry, but what are you talking about? I didn't think you had any guests at the moment.'

Gayle passed David some crusty bread and opened a bottle of wine. 'No, not this weekend. Well, I did have Jake Campbell-Ross here. He had several nights booked, but had to leave unexpectedly with an emergency.'

Robyn nearly choked on her stew. She spluttered, 'Jake Campbell-Ross, as in—'

'The guy whose wife, Eleanor, had that accident here last Christmas.'

Robyn sucked in a breath. 'A Ross was right here, in this guesthouse?'

Gayle smiled. 'Oh, yes. I'm afraid you just missed meeting him.'

Robyn stared at her, open-mouthed, then turned to David, remembering what he'd just said. 'You've met him – haven't you?'

He shrugged. 'Yeah.'

'And you're on a first-name basis with him already?'

'We were going to have a drink together at the—'

Gayle added, 'He left this morning before you arrived.'

Although she'd got a new commission in London, Robyn was still committed to working on The Lake House too. The problem was that she hadn't met any of the Rosses to discuss the finer details. She wasn't even sure which Ross had actually commissioned her to do it, as the email had come from the company – the Ross Corporation – selecting her little interior design company to do the work, and was obviously signed by one of their employees; a Mr Aubrey Jones. Whoever that was. Various searches on the internet had produced absolutely no results whatsoever, and she'd started to get concerned that the email might be some sort of scam – especially when Marty, the gardener who worked in the grounds of The Lake House, had told her he had not put in a good word for her with the Rosses as she'd assumed.

So where had the commission come from? She'd wanted to meet one of them, or at least contact them to find out. But getting hold of one of the Rosses personally was impossible.

She should have been disappointed to hear she'd just missed meeting one of them, but she felt a huge relief. She felt absurdly anxious about the prospect. Once again, she recalled that Annie had told her not to be intimidated at the thought of meeting them just because they were very rich.

But it wasn't that. Robyn's thoughts turned again to the doll's house. She could feel her face growing bright red at the thought that Jake Campbell-Ross had actually been right there in Lark Lodge. Did he remember the old doll's house in the basement of The Lake House? Did he see the resemblance to some of the rooms she'd decorated?

'Are you all right?' Gayle asked. 'Your face has gone bright pink.'

'It's, um—'

'Rather hot in here,' David said.

'Oh, I did wonder if lighting the fire was overdoing it a bit on a summer's evening. I just thought it added a bit of ambience,' Gayle said. She poured them both a glass of bubbly. 'I expect him back soon.'

'He's coming back?'

'I hope so. I've kept the attic room available for his return.'

'When?' Robyn looked over at the door, as though he'd walk in at any moment. 'Tonight?'

'Oh, not tonight. He only left this morning. I'd expect the earliest would be tomorrow. He could turn up at any time.'

'Any time?'

'Yes, as I said, the room is ready. He's paid upfront for several more days, so I'm hoping he'll return, otherwise I'm going to refund him the money or put it towards another week if he wants to postpone his trip.' She put the bottle of bubbly down. 'Well, I'll leave you two lovebirds in peace.'

'I've changed my mind about staying the weekend.' Robyn caught David raising his eyebrows in surprise.

'Oh, you have?' said Gayle, looking equally surprised. 'I thought you said—' She paused. 'Ah, I understand. It's Jake Campbell-Ross.'

'Why do you say that?' Robyn could feel the colour rising in her cheeks again.

'I didn't mean it's him in particular. I understand it's not quite the same with other guests staying here, not like it was before, with just you, Marty and Nick.'

Robyn nodded. 'Sorry.'

'Oh, don't be, Robyn. I'm just so happy things are working out and you're both going back to the boathouse.'

Robyn caught David smiling and forced a smile too. The problem was that she didn't want to go back to the boathouse the next day. She wanted to stay at Lark Lodge for the weekend so that she had more time to gather her thoughts. She knew she couldn't carry on with an absurd feeling of dread every time she returned there. But the thought of ending up face to face with Jake Campbell-Ross meant she had no choice. If there was any possibility he might return over the weekend, she had to leave. She knew it was irrational, but she just had to. She just wished she didn't have to return to the boathouse.

Gayle said, 'Well, it's not the same with other guests here, obviously. Right now, it's like old times – isn't it? But you know, it's a guesthouse now, and you two want time to yourselves.' She paused. 'Well, on that note, I'll leave you to enjoy your dinner.' Gayle turned on her heel and headed back to the kitchen.

Robyn put her spoon in her stew. She'd been so surprised when David had mentioned staying there for the weekend. She had been looking forward to it. Now, after that conversation, she was leaving first thing in the morning instead.

David said, 'I'm so pleased we're going back to the boathouse. It's rather silly, but I was afraid that after you surprised me here, and you'd arranged for us to stay the night, you might not want to leave.'

Robyn let out a little laugh as she plunged her spoon into the stew, avoiding eye contact.

Robyn resolved to enjoy the rest of her evening and not think about returning to the boathouse.

❖

Sitting on the end of the bed, recalling the previous night, Robyn had put her worries to the back of her mind so that they could enjoy their evening together. But now all she could think about was returning to the boathouse.

She suddenly had a thought. She didn't want to face what might be in her past. She'd been avoiding it, hoping all her memories didn't come back – especially, for some reason, the memory she had of sitting in a car in the dark at the boathouse, wanting to leave, to run. But what if it wasn't as bad as all that? What if there was just some innocent explanation as to why she had been there? She'd only know for sure if she remembered everything.

Robyn picked up one of the cushions they'd hastily tossed to the end of the bed and onto the floor amidst their urgent love-making the previous night. David was still holding her hand. Robyn was sitting cross-legged on the bed, facing him.

He asked, 'What is it, Robyn?'

'I'm thinking of going to see Dr Jamieson.'

'Dr Jamieson?'

'You know, the doctor at the hospital who treated me when I was taken in after the accident last Christmas.'

David looked at her, wide-eyed. 'Is something wrong?'

Robyn frowned. Of course there was something wrong. Her memories still hadn't come back. He knew that. But Robyn didn't want to be sarcastic. It wasn't his fault. 'It's just the memory thing. Maybe she can help.'

'Your memory loss? I thought you said you didn't want your memories back? I thought you said you were happy the way things were?'

Robyn stared at David. There was that anxious look again.

'Don't you want me to get my memories back?'

'Well … um … of course.'

'You don't sound too sure.'

He moved towards her, taking both her hands. 'Look, about what I said last night …'

She waited for him to go on. He'd said a lot of things the previous night. They both had at dinner, and then in the throes of passion afterwards. Lying entwined in each other's arms, they had said how much they loved one another.

David continued. 'I'm talking about how worried I've been about you … about us.'

Robyn pursed her lips.

'Look, I've got to be honest with you. No, I don't want your memories to come back, because I'm afraid …'

Robyn said, 'Go on.'

'Well, I'm afraid that there's someone in your past, and if you remember … then I might lose you if you go back to them.'

'No, I'll never go back to them!' Robyn cried.

David sat back in surprise at her outburst. 'So, there is someone?'

Robyn put her hand to her mouth. 'Honestly, I don't remember.'

'Then why did you just say—?'

'I don't know! It's just a feeling.' A not very nice feeling, she thought. The same one of dread she had whenever she recalled sitting in a car outside the boathouse in the pitch dark.

'Now you see – don't you? Why I need to go back to the hospital and find out if someone can help me remember? I thought I could, you know, carry on as I am – without my memories. In fact, I wanted it that way. My life is here now. I don't want to look back. But I can't keep feeling this way, afraid of what's really in my past.'

'I understand. Robyn. It's the elephant in the room, isn't it? Sometimes it's better to just face your fears. I bet whatever it is you're afraid of is not half as bad as you think.'

Robyn hoped so. She had a sudden thought that came out of nowhere. It wasn't the doll's house that connected her to the Rosses. It was something in her past.

David took both her hands in his once again. 'So, you haven't been meeting anyone else while you've been away in London, apart from clients?'

Robyn let out a nervous laugh. 'Of course not.'

'No one from your past?'

'Well, that would be a bit difficult, seeing as I don't remember.' Robyn shook her head, pursing her lips, hating to lie. It was true, she didn't remember. Not everything. But she had found herself face to face with someone, and it had not been at all what she had expected.

24

'I'm just going to head down to breakfast.'

Robyn had just emerged from the shower, her hair wrapped in a towel, her face devoid of makeup. 'Right now?'

David was already marching to the door.

'Can't you wait until I've dried my hair and put on some makeup? Then we can go down together.'

David had already showered and dressed. He wanted to go downstairs first so that he had a chance to speak to Gayle alone. 'I'd rather head on downstairs, if you don't mind.'

'I don't mind. I just thought you wanted to spend every waking second with me now I was back – remember?' She grinned.

David laughed nervously. 'Oh, yeah.' He'd forgotten he'd said that. He walked over to the dressing table where she had sat down and stood behind her. He watched her as she unwrapped the towel and her hair fell around her shoulders. He kissed the top of her head. 'I like your hair now.'

'You didn't like me blonde?'

David knitted his brow.

'It was just a bit …' He tried not to use the word odd or strange. 'Surprising.' Robyn's decision to dye her hair had been most unexpected. But now it was back to her natural dark hair colour. He preferred it that way.

She glanced over her shoulder at him. 'Would you like another surprise? I was thinking of changing the colour again.'

'Why do you want to do that?'

Standing behind her, David caught the look on her face in the mirror as she turned away from him. She wasn't smiling. She was looking anxious. Something wasn't right.

He'd had his suspicions when he'd asked her if he should be worried about the two of them. David was no fool. Now she was talking about wanting her memories back. All these months, since he'd known her, she'd never once talked about getting her memories back. In fact, she'd admitted it was the last thing she wanted. So – why now? Despite his own anxieties over what would happen when she remembered her past, he had reassured her that whatever she was afraid of would not be half as bad as she thought.

David was only saying that to make her, and himself, feel better. She'd said herself that she was afraid of what was really in her past. David couldn't get out of his mind the possibility that even though she couldn't remember anything, her subconscious was telling her something.

He kissed the top of her head once more. 'If you want to dye your hair again, then go for it.'

'Really?' She turned to look up at him, smiling.

He swallowed and forced a smile. Whatever or whoever it was she had been running from on Christmas Day, when she had been driving like a bat out of hell on that snowy road out of Aviemore, it was still haunting her. The fact that she wanted to dye her hair again, hiding her identity, was not a good sign.

'I'm going to nip downstairs while you dry your hair.'

Robyn caught his hand before he left and planted a kiss in the centre of his palm. 'I love you, David Gillespie. You know that – right?'

David gently took her face in his hands, kissing her. He drew back. 'I don't want to lose you.'

She grinned. 'And you won't. That's a promise.'

'Good.' David got up. 'I'll see you downstairs.' He was just opening the door when Robyn said, 'Hey, let Gayle know that before I leave, I'd like a quick colour and cut – if she has the time.'

David frowned. 'All right,' he said tightly, and closed the door.

❖

'What's with the face? I thought you two had worked things out.'

David walked into the kitchen, thankful that Nick and Marty were not around. He'd forgotten that he and Robyn didn't have the house to themselves. Although Marty and Nick had made themselves scarce the previous night, he knew they could show up at any time. It was Saturday, which meant neither of them would be at work, although it occurred to him that Marty might be doing some gardening work at the weekend.

Still, he didn't hear any footsteps on the stairs, and Olive was nowhere to be seen. He asked after the dog.

'She's out on a morning jog with Nick.'

'Great.'

Gayle pointed her half-eaten toast at David and said, 'I thought you liked Olive?'

'I do. It's just that this morning I want to be left alone.'

Gayle put her toast down and wiped her mouth. She looked towards the kitchen door. 'Where's Robyn?'

'She's blow-drying her hair,' David said sullenly.

Gayle pushed her plate away. 'I see.' Gayle raised her eyes to the ceiling. 'Trouble in paradise?'

'We're okay.' Sort of, thought David. Now that he was in the kitchen, sitting in front of Gayle, he didn't know whether to confide in her or not. Was it the case that he was just making a mountain out of a molehill, and that he had nothing to worry about when it came to Robyn and her past? But something was definitely going on. She wanted her hair dyed again.

'You want something to eat?'

'No, not hungry. Besides, I said I'd wait for Robyn.'

'Coffee?'

'Yeah.'

Gayle brewed some coffee and joined David at the table. She put a mug of steaming black coffee down in front of him and said, 'Now, why don't you tell me what's going on? Perhaps I can help.'

'All right.' David heaved a sigh. 'She asked me to tell you that she wants a cut and colour before she leaves. If you have the time.'

'She wants her hair dyed again?' Gayle frowned.

'I'm not happy about it either,' said David, catching her frown.

'You prefer her natural hair colour.'

'Well, yeah. But that's not really it.'

'You're wondering why, after all this time, she wants to dye her hair again?'

David nodded. 'I find it odd that it's coincided with her trips to London. I just think there's something she's not telling me. But I don't want to push it, otherwise …'

'Otherwise …?'

'I'm afraid she might leave me and move back in here for good. And that's the other thing. She told me she wants to go and see Dr Jamieson at the hospital about her memory problems.' David kept his voice low, glancing the door, feeling bad for sharing their private conversation.

'She did?' Gayle said in surprise. 'I thought she didn't want her memories back.'

'Yeah, me too. But something's changed.' David stared at Gayle, and fell silent. Did he really expect that Gayle could help him with any of this?

Gayle leaned forward, elbows on the table. 'It seems to me that all this has come to the fore since you moved into the boathouse.'

David sat back in his chair, nodding his head and wondering if maybe it had nothing to do with Robyn's London trips at all. 'Yes, yes. I do keep coming back to that.'

'The boathouse,' they both said in unison.

'But why? She says it isn't me. She was happy to move in together. She says she loves the boathouse and where it is. So, I really do not get it.' He stared at Gayle, waiting for some words of wisdom – even if they came from one of her numerous self-help books on the bookshelves in what had once been her father's study but was now a room to relax in, with easy chairs, scented candles, soft lighting, and bookshelves filled with Gayle's library of self-help books. The stereo playing whale calls was thankfully switched off.

Gayle sat back in her chair with a pensive look.

'She's not happy because your house doesn't feel like her home.'

Gayle and David exchanged a glance before turning in their seats to look at Doris, who had suddenly joined the conversation from where she was sitting at the end of the table, eating a bowl of cereal.

David said, 'Pardon me?' He was aware that Doris's dementia was not improving, but the last he'd heard she was on a drug trial. Of course, there was no cure, but it seemed to have slowed her decline quite remarkably.

'Look at what she did with this place.'

David sighed. 'She really hasn't got time to go redecorating the boathouse. Besides, she said she likes it just the way it is.' David wondered if she was just being kind so as not to hurt his feelings.

Gayle regarded her mother thoughtfully. 'I think you're on to something.'

'But she hasn't got time to redecorate,' David said again. 'She's got the shop, and clients in London. And then The Lake House …'

'No, I'm not talking about redecorating,' said Gayle. 'Mum just said your place doesn't feel like her home. What do you think will make her feel more settled?'

At that moment they were interrupted by the sound of the front door opening and a familiar noise. They all knew what was coming – Olive bounded into the kitchen.

'Hello, girl!' David exclaimed, giving her a fuss. 'Well, don't you brighten up a room.'

'That's dogs for you,' commented Nick, walking into the kitchen, checking his smart watch, and looking quite red in the face. 'When they're not spreading muddy paws around your kitchen, chewing your furniture legs, or stealing food from the table.'

Olive's snout appeared up on the table.

'Oh, for goodness' sake, Olive.'

Gayle said, 'Don't worry about it. Good run?'

'Oh, yeah. Hi, David. How's things?'

David was busy giving Olive a stroke, grinning at the silly dog, when he suddenly had an epiphany. 'Things are fantastic!'

'Great. Where's Robyn?'

'She'll be down for breakfast soon,' commented Gayle, eyeing David.

'Wonderful. I'd love to catch up with her. It's been a while. Well, I'm going to hit the shower.'

Nick jogged out of the room.

Gayle turned to look at David. 'You've thought of something, haven't you? Something to make her feel more at home, more settled.'

David continued giving Olive a fuss. 'Yes. I'm going to get her a puppy.'

'A dog?' said Doris.

David grinned. 'Oh, yes. She loves Olive.'

'You're going to get an Old English Sheepdog?' asked Gayle.

'Well, I don't know what breed yet. Then I was thinking I actually haven't taken her out on the boat. I've got a small wooden rowing boat. The weather has been amazing. I also thought how she's kind of not into driving, really. I thought she might like a bike to cycle on the footpaths in the forest.'

'You could both get a bike,' suggested Doris.

Gayle leaned forward in her chair. 'Actually, I think you're on to something. You know, decorating is kind of what she does for a living. It'd be nice if there were things she could do, you could do together, that had nothing to do with work. In fact, when was the last time you two took a holiday?'

'A holiday? We've only been together since Christmas.'

Gayle said, 'But it's July! That's a lot of months with no break from work, from your usual routine.'

'You're right, Gayle. But I don't think Robyn wants to go anywhere else. She loves it here. And besides, I'm meant to be trying to make her feel settled in the boathouse. Taking her away on holiday isn't going to help, is it?'

Gayle grinned. 'So, you know what you need to do.'

David scratched his head.

'Have a holiday closer to home. In fact, in your new home together.'

'In the boathouse?'

'Yes – why not? Spend some time together there. You mentioned your boat, and getting bikes. Then there's this puppy. You'll both want to be around if you're getting a new family member.'

'You know, I think you're on to something.' David thought it was a fantastic idea, but he could already see a problem.

Gayle sighed. 'What is it?'

'She's got so much work on, what with her outlet in my dad's store, and all the other work she's taken on lately.

'I'm sure Annie will mind the store. It's the summer holidays. She doesn't have to do the school run. And Evie loves spending time with her mum at the shop, so she won't mind going there while Joe is at work. Robyn's other commitments will just have to wait for a week or two. Everyone deserves a holiday.'

'But what about my dad? I'm still working at the store doing deliveries.'

'Alec works part-time at the store as a Saturday job. I hear he's passed his driving test. Off to university in September. I'm sure he could do with the extra money from working more hours over the summer break.'

David smiled at Gayle. 'I think you've got everything covered.'

'Not quite.'

'What are you thinking?'

'About your puppy …'

'You don't think it's a good idea?'

'Oh, on the contrary. It's an excellent idea, but I was thinking …'

David knitted his brow. 'Yes?'

'Robyn threw a lovely party for me to celebrate the opening of Lark Lodge as a guesthouse.'

David thought back to the garden party at Lark Lodge. Robyn had even hired a marquee for the garden, just in case it rained, but that day in June had been all sunshine and blue skies. She couldn't have picked a better day. 'So, what are you suggesting?'

'A combined engagement party and housewarming party at the boathouse. You could spend time together planning it, getting the boathouse prepared. I think she'd really enjoy it – don't you?'

David was sceptical. 'I don't know.' He looked down at Olive, sitting by his chair, her head resting on his lap. 'She enjoyed organising your party, but that was here, at Lark Lodge. She loves this place.'

'Hmm. But what if she was organising the party for a special guest – someone in particular she was inviting?'

David looked up. 'Do you mean Jake Campbell-Ross?'

Gayle shook her head. 'Why would I mean him?'

'Well, she is doing up his house. She hasn't met him yet. And the Rosses are pretty important people. I guess it would be the talk of the town if one of them came.'

Gayle laughed. 'I guess it would. I suppose she could invite him to the party.'

'I could invite him as a surprise, keep it a secret between us.'

'Yes – why not? Hopefully he's coming back. I kept his room free. But it wasn't him I was thinking of.'

'Then who?'

'Look, Robyn hasn't got any family in these parts.'

David immediately took offence. 'We're her family now. You, me, Doris, my brother and his family. Then there's my father, and of course Nick and Marty—'

Gayle held up her hand. 'Alright, already! I know that's true. But I'm talking about her relations, obviously. Perhaps it's time she mended bridges with her mum. I'm sure it would help tremendously with her settling into her new life with you at the boathouse.'

David was aware that Robyn and her mum must be estranged. Robyn didn't talk about her mum much. All he knew was that her mum had sold up the family home and gone travelling. Judith sent cheques in the post every once in a while, asking Robyn to join her for a holiday wherever she was in the world, but Robyn had always declined, apparently.

But Judith knew nothing of her life now, nor her amnesia. It made him wonder if Robyn would even recognise Judith, unless her memories came flooding back when she saw her. 'I don't think she's even told her mum that she's dropped out of university. You know, Robyn contacted the university recently. Her deferment will be ending soon. They'll expect her to return in September.' David was so relieved when Robyn had told him that she wasn't going back. He'd assumed she wasn't, but hadn't been sure until he'd heard her say the words.

Gayle said, 'She's been saying she needs to contact her mum, tell her about her new life, but as far as I know, she hasn't.'

David shook his head. 'No, she hasn't.'

'But it can't go on, can it, David? She set up a redirection so that the letters from her mum, which were still being sent to her university accommodation, come here instead. But pretty soon she'll have to cancel that redirection. She'll have to tell her. It's got to be unsettling for her, keeping all this a secret from her mum. I think it's time there were no more secrets in her life.'

David agreed.

'So, wouldn't it be lovely if she returned from abroad, and Robyn introduced her to her new friends, to her new life – and to her future husband?'

David raised his eyebrows as something occurred to him. 'Does that mean she'll have to stay at the boathouse? She could stay here at Lark Lodge.'

Gayle shook her head. 'I think Robyn would want her mum to stay at the boathouse. Besides, this chat was about making her feel more settled, more at home there. It wouldn't do at all if her mum was here. What if Robyn decides to stay here so she can spend more time with her?'

'Ah, I see your point.'

Something else crossed David's mind. 'What if her mum … Judith … doesn't like me? I've lost my career. I work for my father, making deliveries.'

'Well, that's not all you do. You're a volunteer coach for a local youth sports programme, and I heard you're also working towards a certification and further training, which could lead to a paid coaching position.'

David nodded. 'That's true.'

'And then there's that part-time history degree you're doing.'

'That's just a hobby.'

'Yes, but you never know where that might lead. You might want to become a history teacher. You've got a lot going for you.'

David looked at her doubtfully. 'Yeah, I guess.'

'If you're still worried about what Robyn's mum will think of her future son-in-law, please don't be. She'll see that her daughter has a lovely home with you at the boathouse, and that you love her very, very much. I think that's the most important thing.'

'What's the most important thing?' asked Robyn.

David turned in his seat as Robyn walked into the kitchen. She looked from Gayle to David. 'Did I miss something?'

No more secrets, thought David. Although he rather wanted the puppy to be a surprise, and the bike. 'We were talking about how you're not feeling settled in the boathouse. Sorry, I didn't mean to talk about you when you weren't here.'

'Really? You were rather keen to head on down to the kitchen without me.'

Gayle said, 'I think David wanted my advice.'

Robyn took a seat at the table as Olive darted over to say good morning. 'Hello, you. I've missed having you around.'

David exchanged a smile with Gayle, both thinking the same thing. Robyn would love a dog.

She looked up. 'So, what do you advise, Gayle?'

'I think you should have a party.'

'A party?'

'Yes, at the boathouse.'

David added, 'A combined housewarming and engagement party. What do you think?' he asked nervously. She'd enjoyed organising Gayle's party, but that had been at Lark Lodge. Would she feel the same way about hosting a party at the boathouse? To his relief, her face lit up.

Robyn said, 'Can we invite everyone?'

'You can have whoever you like.' He exchanged a glance with Gayle who nodded.

Robyn caught the exchange. 'What are you two up to?'

25

'Don't you think it's time to get in touch with your mum?' Gayle asked.

'My mum?'

David nodded, glad that Gayle had brought it up before they left Lark Lodge that morning. He turned to Robyn. 'I know you've been meaning to write her a letter, tell her about your new life, and that you're not returning to college.'

Gayle added, 'Rather than tell her all about your new life, your business, and your new friends, why not show her?'

'Show her?'

David smiled at Gayle. 'Yes. We were thinking you could invite her to the party. She could come and stay at the boathouse with us and … you know, get to know me, and meet all your new friends.'

Gayle said, 'What do you think? It's a great idea – isn't it?'

'But what will I say in my letter?'

'Send her a party invitation, and tell her you've got the biggest surprise.'

David nodded enthusiastically. 'I know this is a big thing for you, telling your mum you've dropped out of college, but you've got a fantastic life here, with a good job, and great friends.' David avoided the touchy subject of Robyn's memory loss, and whether she'd even recognise her mum. If she didn't, that would be another big thing she'd have to tell her mum on top of everything else.

Gayle said, 'She'll be so happy for you, just you wait and see. Especially when she meets your wonderful fiancé.'

'Oh, I wouldn't say that,' David remarked.

'Well, I would,' said Gayle.

'Me too,' Robyn said emphatically. She looked at Gayle and David. 'Why do I think you're ganging up on me, and won't take no for an answer?'

David smiled. 'We're not ganging up on you. It's just that it must be on your mind, your mum and when you're going to let her know about your new life here.'

Gayle added, 'Wouldn't a party be the perfect time for her to meet everyone and get to know the real you?'

'The real me,' Robyn repeated, staring off into space.

David nodded. 'She could stay a few days. Perhaps having family stay will make you feel more at home.'

'You told Gayle I wasn't happy at the boathouse.'

'It's not surprising, Robyn, that you're finding it hard to settle. You've still got unfinished business.'

Robyn sighed. 'I'll say.'

David looked at her sharply. Then his face softened. 'I think if you had your mum come and stay, she'd help with your memory problems. By all means, go and see Dr Jamieson. Perhaps she can refer you to someone. But in the meantime, doesn't it make sense if someone who knows you best comes to see you, and you spend time together? I bet she'll help you remember. After all, no one knows you quite like your parents.'

Gayle and David sat there with bated breath, wondering

whether Robyn would agree. 'All right. I suppose it couldn't hurt.'

David jumped out of his seat. 'Fantastic!'

Gayle was out of her seat too, clapping enthusiastically. 'Oh, boy, I love a party.'

Nick walked into the kitchen and stopped. 'Did I miss something?'

'We're having a party at the boathouse!' David exclaimed.

'I hope I'm invited.'

'Of course you are. And Olive, of course. Where's Marty?'

'Late night out with his mates. I expect he's having a lie-in.'

'What's the party in aid of?' Nick asked, taking a seat at the table.

David replied, 'It's a housewarming and engagement party.'

Nick nodded. 'Sweet.'

'The guest of honour is going to be Robyn's mum, Judith.'

'I haven't met her,' commented Nick.

'No, none of us have. She's going to be staying at the boathouse for a few days. At least, that's the plan.'

'Ah, having the future mother-in-law to stay. Not so sweet.'

David slapped his arm. 'Hey, don't put the kibosh on our plans.'

Nick whispered, 'I think someone already has.' He cocked his head at Robyn's sour expression.

David's good humour evaporated. 'Robyn?'

'But what will she do all day while I'm at work?' Robyn asked.

David looked across at Gayle, who nodded her head and said, 'Tell her.'

Robyn sighed. 'What else have you two been planning before I came down to breakfast?'

David winced. 'Now, just hear me out before you say no.' He

took a breath. 'We should have a holiday.'

'A holiday? Are you serious? I've got my outlet in your dad's store—'

'Annie will cover that. I know she will.'

'But what about the deliveries you do for your dad?'

'Relax. I'm sure Alec will cover those, work some overtime, so he can save up some more money for college.'

'But what about my commissions in London? And then there's The Lake House. I've started work on it.'

Nick interrupted. 'I didn't know you'd been commissioned to work on The Lake House. What's the house like? Does it need a lot of work? What are they going to do with the house when it's finished?'

David and Robyn turned to look at him.

Nick looked at them sheepishly. 'Too many questions?'

They both nodded.

'Sorry. Like most people, I'm intrigued by that family. I can't help it.' He looked at Gayle.

David hoped she wasn't going to say anything about the surprise he had in store for Robyn. He just hoped that when he invited Jake Campbell-Ross, he would come – assuming he had returned to Scotland in time after the emergency he had been called back to London for.

'I think I'll cook myself some scrambled eggs,' said Nick, getting up from the table. 'Anybody want some?' he asked, walking over to the Aga.

Everyone shook their heads.

David turned to Robyn. 'The commissions can wait. We can't. We need more days, nights, like last night.'

Robyn's cheeks turned bright red.

'But,' David continued, 'it can't be that our best times were here, at Lark Lodge.'

Gayle stepped in. 'You need to make some new memories together at the boathouse.'

'But that's not going to happen if we're hardly ever there,' added David. 'I thought we could have a holiday there. Do some fun things, make some good memories in that place.' He could tell by the wisp of a smile that Robyn was warming to the idea.

'We could start by spending some time planning the party and getting the boathouse ready. What do you say?'

'I suppose I could take a few days off.'

'That's the spirit!' exclaimed Gayle.

David grinned. 'Yes, and then perhaps after we've had our little holiday, you could take a few more days off when your mum comes to stay, so you can spend time together after the party.'

'All right.'

'Did you just say yes?' David whooped and started do a silly little dance on the spot.

'Did I miss something?'

They all turned to see Marty, in his dressing gown, hair askew, rubbing the sleep out of his eyes as he trudged into the kitchen. 'Whoa, you guys are far too awake for this time in the morning.'

'It's half past nine,' said Gayle.

Marty was just lifting the kettle to pour himself a cup of tea. He stopped and turned to look at the others seated around the table. 'Seriously? I thought it was a lot earlier.'

'Someone had a good night – so good, in fact, that you don't know what the time is.'

'Hi.'

Everyone turned in their seats at the sound of a stranger's

voice. A young woman stood at the door, looking nervously into the room.

Marty said, 'I thought you were waiting in my room for breakfast in bed?'

'Oh, sorry. I changed my mind. I thought you might like some company, but I see that's not, um, necessary.'

Everyone introduced themselves to Marty's date from the previous night. She looked away, clearly embarrassed in the spotlight of Marty's friends. 'I think I'll have breakfast in bed after all,' she said, even though she was dressed. 'I'll, um …' she pointed to the stairs and promptly disappeared.

'Oh, dear, we frightened her off,' commented Nick.

'Well that's not too hard, is it? All of us scrutinising her.'

'What do you think?' asked Marty. 'Isn't she the most gorgeous thing you've ever seen?'

David disagreed on that one. He said as much as he smiled across the table at Robyn.

'Very funny,' said Marty. 'But seriously, guys. Do you like her?'

Gayle sighed. 'We don't even know her.'

'Oh, yes. Of course,' Marty said, disappointed.

'But she looks a nice sort.'

Everyone turned to look at Doris.

'Well, then,' said Gayle, 'If Mum approves, then I think that rather settles it.'

'We hit it off right away,' said Marty. 'Know what I mean?'

David smiled across the room at Robyn. He knew exactly what Marty was talking about.

'She should come to Robyn and David's party,' added Doris.

Marty raised his eyebrows. 'I hope I'm getting an invite too, although this is the first I've heard of a party.'

Nick said, 'David and Robyn are having a heartwarming – no, housewarming – and engagement party.'

'But you moved in last month, and you got engaged already. I don't get it.'

David's smile slipped. 'There's nothing to get. We've been really busy, which is why the idea didn't even crop up. But it has now. And we're taking a holiday.'

'Cool,' replied Marty. 'Where are you going?'

'Nowhere, just spending our time together at the boathouse.'

Marty shrugged. 'Okay, I'd rather go on a holiday somewhere, but, you know, whatever floats your boat.'

Nick laughed out loud.

Marty scratched his head. 'What?'

'You said, whatever floats your … oh, never mind.'

Marty shrugged and put some toast in the toaster.

Nick's mobile phone rang. He answered it. 'Hi Mum. Yeah, I'm fine. Yes, Olive is fine too.' Nick held his phone from his ear. 'Mum likes to give me a call and catch up every week. I'll take this in the lounge.' He walked out of the kitchen.

David turned to Robyn. 'I thought we could go boating on the loch, and have picnics by the shore, and—'

'Start making preparations for the party?' suggested Robyn.

'Yes, yes. That would be brilliant too. And preparations for your mum coming to stay. You're going to have to write to her as soon as we've set a date for the party.'

'I guess so.'

'You don't sound very enthusiastic about contacting your mum,' observed Marty.

'I don't think we get on, really. It's been … I don't know how long it's been since I saw her last.'

Gayle said, 'Well, this is your chance to mend bridges, and get to know each other a little better, don't you think?'

'Yeah.'

David said, 'I can't wait to get back to the boathouse and start planning that party. You could design the party invitations.'

Her face lit up. 'Oh, yes. I'd love that.'

David had thought she would.

'In fact, I can't wait to go home, and make a start.'

David stared at her. Had she just called the boathouse home?

Robyn noticed him staring. 'What?'

David grinned. 'Oh, nothing. I can't wait to get home either.'

Marty was buttering some toast. He looked at Robyn and David.

'I'm going to get packed right now.'

'Good idea.'

David stopped in the doorway. 'What about your hair?'

'My hair? I washed it this morning – remember? Maybe I should have used the straighteners.'

'No, I thought you wanted a cut and colour.'

'Oh, yes, I forgot. You know what? I don't think I need a cut and colour after all. What do you think?'

'No, definitely not. I like you just the way you are.' They both left the kitchen, each carrying a plateful of toast and a cup of coffee.

Marty put some more toast in the toaster and turned to Gayle. 'What's with them?'

'Nothing at all. In fact, I think things might just be coming together.'

'Well, let's hope so. I overheard Robyn when she arrived here yesterday, hiding in the bedroom, ready to surprise David.'

'Overheard what?' Gayle whispered.

'She was on the phone, saying that she had no choice but to come back last night, but as soon as she could, she'd return to London if she could do it without raising suspicions.'

Gayle frowned. 'Suspicions about what?'

Marty shrugged. 'How would I know?'

'Look, you mustn't tell anyone else what you overheard – all right? Not until I've had a chance to speak to Robyn and find out what's going on.'

'I thought you knew. She tells you everything.'

'Apparently not.'

26

Gayle was in the kitchen with Doris, doing the washing up after Marty had finished breakfast and returned to his room, when she heard someone walking down the stairs. She spotted David walking past the kitchen door carrying Robyn's cabin-sized suitcase, which she'd taken to London, and his own rucksack.

'You leaving now?' Gayle called out as Olive scampered out of the room, following David to the front door.

David appeared in the kitchen doorway without the case and bag. He nodded as he stroked Olive, who was standing beside him. 'Just left our things by the front door.'

'Where's Robyn?'

'She sent me ahead. Said she had some last bits to pack.'

Gayle frowned up at the ceiling, wondering if she was on the phone to that mystery person again, making plans to return to London.

David said, 'Something the matter?' He answered his own question before Gayle had to lie and say everything was fine. 'I know you'd like us to have stayed for the weekend, but this is for the best. She's actually looking forward to returning to the boathouse, would you believe?'

'Are you definitely having that holiday at the boathouse?'

'Yes, right away, actually. I phoned Annie after breakfast. It's all arranged. She'll work in the shop for the coming week, starting today. Oh, and Robyn is on the phone to her clients in London as we speak.'

Gayle nodded. 'That's good,' she said flatly.

'I know. I didn't expect her to agree just like that. It's great. She's going to write to her mum, invite her to come and stay. The last she heard, her mum was in Sicily … or was it Italy?' David shook his head, smiling. 'Oh well, whichever it is, it's only a short flight away. The only thing is that if she sends a letter, then her mum might decide to write back. That's going to take time, and we wanted the party quite soon.'

'She might just come when she gets the letter. Ask Robyn to include your phone numbers, the one at the boathouse and Robyn's new mobile number. That way she can get in touch as soon as she receives the letter.'

'Hey, that's a good idea. I suggested she could just send her a text or WhatsApp, but she hasn't got her mum's mobile number. It was stored in her phone that she lost in the car accident. It's a shame because I think it would have been good for Robyn to speak to her, break the ice, before she arrived.'

Gayle nodded. 'Yes, from what I gather they weren't getting along very well. Hopefully when they see each other, and talk, they can iron things out.'

David nodded. 'Let's hope so. I think she's worried what her mum's reaction will be when she finds out her daughter has dropped out of university and not told her.'

'When is she sending the letter?'

David sighed. 'I asked her that. She just said soon. I get the feeling she's going to procrastinate, and keep putting it off, so I got her to promise that before she leaves, she sits in your dad's old study and writes that letter. Otherwise our guest of honour will miss the party we're planning.'

'That's a good idea, David.'

'Have you got any writing paper and an envelope by any chance?'

Gayle grinned. 'Of course.'

David said, 'Will you do one more thing for me? I don't know if you've heard whether Jake Campbell-Ross is returning?'

Gayle had answered the phone a moment earlier, before she'd started the washing up. 'Now, it's funny you should bring that up …' she said. Jake had phoned to say they'd found Natty safe and sound. Gayle had been so relieved to hear it. And they were planning a week away together to Scotland. He'd wanted to leave straight away, but his friend, Faye, had a course module she had to attend the next week for a headship qualification she was doing. It meant they couldn't leave for Scotland until the next Friday. They wouldn't arrive in Aviemore until late that afternoon. Gayle had said she would pick them up from the station.

There was just one thing – he'd needed to book an extra room for Faye and Natty, and was hoping she had vacancies. Gayle had just the room. It would mean turfing Nick out of the other bedroom in the attic, but she was sure he wouldn't mind moving into the room Robyn and David were vacating that morning. That way, Jake, Faye and Natty would all be on the same floor. Although it was an interconnecting room, which was handy for families, the internal door between the rooms was presently locked. Gayle wondered if they'd prefer it if she unlocked it.

David was still standing in the doorway. He glanced up the

stairs and lowered his voice. 'Look, I still want to invite Jake to the party, like we talked about, as a surprise for Robyn.'

'I know. The thing is, he's arriving next Friday, and only staying for the week. Any chance you can organise it soon?'

'I'll talk it over with Robyn – the party, I mean, not the surprise guest.' He grinned.

Gayle smiled. 'Perfect. As soon as you've set a date, let me know and I'll ask him.'

'Ask who?' Robyn was walking down the stairs, and caught the tail end of the conversation.

Talk about déjà vu, thought David, thinking of earlier that morning when he'd nipped down first while she was blow-drying her hair. He turned to her. 'Oh, never mind. Look, Gayle is going to fetch some writing paper and a pen so you can write your letter. We'll stop off in Aviemore and get a stamp, and post it.'

'Oh, okay. Do I have to write it now? Why don't we go back to the boathouse?'

'But where will we get a stamp?'

'On the way through Aviemore, like you said.'

'But when will you post it? I was rather hoping we could spend our week at the boathouse without venturing out.'

'Ah.'

Gayle and David exchanged a glance. Robyn was clearly putting it off.

Gayle opened a kitchen drawer and handed her a notepad, pen and envelope. 'Go sit in the study, why don't you?'

David mouthed thank you to Gayle. Robyn left her handbag with David and walked across the hallway to the study door. She glanced at them briefly before walking inside and closing the door.

Gayle walked back to the washing up. David followed, picking up a dry tea towel and wiping up the dishes.

Gayle said, 'Now, I've got a favour to ask you.'

'Anything, Gayle.'

'I went to do Rose's hair the other day.'

'David smiled at the mention of her name. He knew Rose and George, the retired couple, who had sold their old house in Aviemore and moved into a new-build on the development where Nick worked as the site manager. They had been Robyn's first clients. They had been the start of her business when she had changed their bare, soulless estate house into a cosy home.

'Well, the thing is,' continued Gayle, 'a dear friend of theirs, a widower, has gone to live in a home, but he can't take his pet with him. In his case, a dog.'

'A dog?'

'Yes. His son has taken the dog for now, but he's got a family, and they are far too busy with work to take care of a pet. The thing is, he really doesn't want to send it to a dog shelter if he can get it rehomed. Unfortunately, Rose and George can't take the dog. They're far too busy socialising, and besides, they said it wouldn't be fair for him to go to another elderly couple.'

David nodded. 'They're fit and healthy right now, but I see their point. They wouldn't want him to have to be rehomed again because they become too infirm to look after him.'

'Yes,' agreed Gayle. 'I'd love to take Percy, and although he'd really be no bother, that would mean two dogs living at the guesthouse. I've got to think of my guests.'

'Hold on. Is this favour you're asking to do with the dog?'

'Yes.'

'Are you asking me to take the dog?'

'Oh, god no. But I was wondering about Duncan …'

'My dad?'

Gayle nodded. 'He's on his own now, living in the flat above the shop, and he must be lonely up there … I know a flat isn't necessarily ideal for a dog, but Percy isn't a puppy who needs house-training. Puppies are hard work, a bit like having a baby. He just needs two walks a day, somebody to make a fuss of him, and he'll be no bother during the day when Duncan is at work. I'm sure he'll just doze in a corner like Olive does when she visits Robyn's outlet in Duncan's store.' Gayle looked at him hopefully.

David shook his head. 'We've already suggested to my dad that he could get a pet, a dog for some company, but he said no. And besides, he won't have dogs in his shop around food. He's worried it will put off his customers.'

'But what about Olive?'

'Olive stays in Robyn's side of the shop.'

Gayle sighed. 'I guess Percy will have to go to the local shelter to be rehomed. Such a shame. He's only three years old. Apparently, they told their parents not to get another dog when their old dog died, but would they listen?' Gayle shook her head sadly. 'This is exactly what they could foresee, apparently. That not too long down the road, their aged parents would have to give him up.'

David sighed too. 'That's just sad.'

'Yeah.'

David furrowed his brow. 'You said puppies are hard work.'

'That's right. Chances are that the first few nights in their strange new house they will cry, then there will be the dilemma of whether you bring puppy into your bedroom, or leave him downstairs. Then, of course, there will be several trips to the toilet in the night.'

'Pardon?'

'You know, they're still little, and can't hold themselves the night, they have to be taken outside in the cold and dark to do their business. They'll probably need paper training too, just so they don't go all over your nice hardwood—'

David held up his hand for her to stop.

'Floors,' concluded Gayle.

David gave her a sideways glance, and lowered his voice to a whisper. 'Are you trying to put me off my idea of getting Robyn a puppy?'

'Of course not. I haven't put you off – have I?'

'No, I'm not put off getting a dog. But a puppy … I hadn't thought through the reality.'

'I imagine most people don't, and they get a bit of a shock when they bring a puppy home.' Gayle's face lit up. 'Now, adopting an adult dog is a whole other ball game. Already toilet-trained. No accidents indoors. Comes with all their bits and bobs, like bed, blanket, and toys.'

David stared at Gayle. 'What sort of breed is Percy?'

'A beagle. Very sweet boy. Rose showed me a photo. He is rather fond of water, apparently. Loves a good splash around. Now, if his new family happened to live near water, in, oh … I don't know, a boathouse …' Gayle grinned. 'He loves long forest walks and swimming, but he's equally content cosying up to you on the sofa in the evening. Does he sound like a pet made in heaven, or what?'

David eyed her. 'You're doing a very good job of persuading me to consider taking Percy on.'

'Am I?' Gayle said innocently. 'You know, you'd be giving Percy, who has lost his home through no fault of his own, another chance. I think Robyn would like that too, the thought that she'd rehomed a dog.'

Gayle wiped her hands dry on the dishcloth in David's hands and took out her phone from the back pocket of her jeans. 'Shall I call Rose? Check Percy still needs rehoming?'

David replied, 'I can't believe I'm doing this.'

27

Robyn emerged from the study across the hall and walked into the kitchen. 'What are you two looking so pleased about?'

David exchanged a smile with Gayle and pointed at the letter. 'All done and ready to post?'

'I think so.'

Neither of them asked what exactly she'd written to Judith. Gayle was just relieved she'd finally written the letter. It was something she had been putting off.

Gayle hoped that spending time with David at the boathouse, and inviting her mother to stay, would help Robyn settle there – for both their sakes. But what Marty had overheard – Robyn on the phone in the bedroom soon after she'd arrived, saying she would return to London as soon as she could – was troubling. Gayle had told Marty she'd speak to Robyn and find out what was going on, but just then, it didn't seem a good time to try.

She looked from Robyn to David. With all these plans in place – having a holiday, spending time in the boathouse, and inviting Robyn's mum – Gayle hoped that whatever was really pulling her back to London – and she had a feeling it was more than simply work – would be put on the backburner for good.

'You did tell your mum you want her to come and stay with us at the boathouse?'

Robyn said, 'Yes, I told her. I even wrote our address in the letter, and told her I'm engaged, and that I'm living in a boathouse.'

'Wow.' David was taken aback. 'You told her everything in your letter, then?'

'Not everything.'

David raised an eyebrow. 'What do you mean?'

Robyn looked at the letter in her hands. 'I didn't tell her about dropping out of college, or my new career.'

'Oh, that.' David sighed, clearly relieved. Gayle could see that he'd wondered what she'd meant for a moment. He obviously still had the London trip on his mind.

'I think some things are best said in person,' Gayle said.

Robyn turned to Gayle. 'Yes, I thought so too.'

Gayle asked, 'What about your memory loss?'

Robyn shook her head. 'I didn't want to worry her. Besides, I phoned the hospital this morning to speak to Dr Jamieson.'

David turned to her. 'Really – when?'

'When I was getting some last-minute bits together after you'd taken our bags downstairs. I just rang on the spur of the moment.'

Gayle smiled in relief. 'You were phoning your doctor.'

'Yes.'

'Did you speak to her?' David asked. 'What did she say?'

Robyn frowned. 'I did speak to her, but …'

David looked concerned. 'What? But … what?'

'I've had scans. There's nothing wrong with my brain, not physically, anyway. She can refer me to a couple of specialists.'

'What specialists?' asked Gayle.

David glanced at Gayle. She'd been a nurse for years.

'An occupational therapist. Not sure what they do, exactly.'

Gayle nodded. 'They can help with memory loss, by providing interventions, strategies to maintain independence …' She trailed off when she caught Robyn and David looking at her blankly. 'My mother sees one, and she's a great help, but they tend to help people whose memory loss is related to age or illness, so they can continue to lead independent, fulfilling lives, and find strategies to cope with their decline.'

'But I'm not old or ill,' cried Robyn.

'Yes, your memory loss is … different.' Gayle paused. 'What other specialist did she recommend?'

Robyn pursed her lips and looked away. David looked concerned.

Gayle sighed. 'Did she book you an appointment with a psychiatrist?'

Robyn nodded. 'I'm not crazy.'

Gayle walked over and put an arm around her shoulders. 'Nobody thinks you're crazy.'

Robyn turned to her. 'Isn't there somebody else who can help? I don't want to see a shrink.'

'There is one possibility …'

'What is it?' Robyn asked.

Gayle shook her head. 'Oh, never mind. You'll probably think it's a silly idea.'

Robyn turned to her. 'Gayle, nothing is a silly idea if it will get my memories back. Tell me, please.'

'You could see a hypnotherapist.'

'A what?' Robyn and David said in unison.

'There. I told you it was a silly idea.'

'How would hypnotherapy help her?' David asked.

'I read about it in one of my books. Apparently hypnotism is just one tool in their toolbox. I can show you one of my books, if you like.'

David shook his head.

Gayle turned to Robyn. 'Look, hopefully your mum is coming home soon, and seeing her will trigger your memories. Then you won't need a therapist.'

David smiled. 'I agree. Wait for you mum to return, and take it from there. On that note, we'd better get going. The sooner that letter is in the post, the better.'

They all left the kitchen, saying their goodbyes at the front door. Robyn knelt down and gave Olive a hug, telling her how much she was going to miss having a dog around.

Gayle and David exchanged a knowing smile.

Gayle stood at the door, Olive by her side, watching them walk to the car. She heard Robyn ask, 'Are we stopping in Aviemore first?'

'Yes, we'll need to get a stamp to post your letter. And don't be thinking you need to stop by your shop. As I said before, Annie has got things covered. As of today, we are on holiday.'

As David opened the car door, Gayle overheard him say, 'After we've posted your letter, I've got one more pitstop on the way home.'

'Oh, right. Where's that?'

'You'll see.'

Gayle smiled knowingly as she watched them both get in the car. She got out her phone and looked at the photo of the sweet beagle. 'Percy, you are a lucky boy.'

28

Jake was woken by the sound of voices coming from the kitchen. He was pretty sure he'd heard Natty badgering her mother to wake him up, and Faye telling her to quieten down. He hoisted himself up to a sitting position. He checked the time and was shocked that it was almost ten. It was little wonder that Natty wanted to wake him up. The only time he'd stayed over at Faye's, and had slept on the couch, was when he'd babysat Natty while Faye was on a course and she'd got held up getting home.

This time, he wasn't babysitting. He and Patrick had hung around, anxious to see Natty when Faye returned home with her. Patrick had been so nervous; worried that as soon as Faye returned and found him still at her house, she'd tell him to leave. He hadn't been the only one feeling nervous. But Faye hadn't told them she wanted them gone before she returned. All she'd said was that she was collecting Natty from the bus station on her own.

When Natty arrived home, there was an awkward moment when she ran into Jake's arms, rather than her grandfather's. It was understandable; Jake had been a fixture in her life recently, far more than her grandfather.. Patrick was desperate to change that. And, as it turned out, so was Faye. They'd all had dinner together, and Patrick had stayed until Natty's bedtime, reading her a bedtime story before kissing her goodnight.

Natty had wanted a bedtime story from Jake too, and a promise that Jake would be there in the morning. She had not made her grandfather promise the same. It hadn't bothered Patrick. He'd walked out of the door on cloud nine about the fact that as soon as they returned from Scotland, he knew he could head round for dinner and read his granddaughter a bedtime story again.

Jake listened to Faye and Natty, who were still bickering in the kitchen. He hadn't been able to promise Natty the previous night that he'd still be there in the morning – it had been up to Faye to decide whether she wanted him to crash on her couch. The problem was that Natty had been up and down the stairs until late, checking he was still there. By the time she had gone off to sleep, and then he and Faye had sat chatting until late about their plans to go on holiday to Scotland, it was so late that Faye insisted he should stay. It was just as well, as Jake was too exhausted to walk to the tube station and get a train home.

Jake stood up, stretched, and folded the spare duvet that Faye had given him. Faye had decided not to tell Natty the previous night about the holiday to Scotland. Natty had been too excited as it was, both with Jake's unexpected arrival back from Scotland and with finding her doting grandfather waiting for her at home too. The news that she was going on holiday with Jake to Scotland too would have been a recipe for an overtired and overexcited nine-year-old to end up getting very little sleep – which would not start the first day of the school summer holidays on the right note. Faye was right when she'd said that Natty had had enough excitement for one day.

Now, Jake was wondering whether, in the cold light of day, all the talk of them going on holiday together to Scotland was going to turn out to be just that – talk.

Jake swallowed. He'd been so excited at the thought of returning to Scotland with them, making plans for what they could do together when they arrived, and thinking about Patrick's advice – make sure they have a bloody good time, get back in her good books, and lastly … don't screw it up. He'd found it difficult to sleep. Now, he was wondering why Faye hadn't woken him. Was she putting off the moment she was intending to tell him that she'd changed her mind?

Disappointment washed over him at the possibility. Perhaps the real reason she hadn't told Natty the previous night about the trip was because she was already having second thoughts. She'd suggested it in the heat of the moment, and now she'd had plenty of time to think it through and probably thought it was a bad idea.

Natty had disappeared all because of him. Jake wondered if Faye had only suggested it because Natty had planned to go to Scotland to find Jake, so in the spirit of proving to Natty that she'd definitely taken back what she'd said to her about not seeing Jake anymore, she was proving it by going on holiday with him – and to Scotland to boot.

Jake frowned. He was convinced that was it. He stepped out of the lounge and walked up the stairs to the bathroom. He was just opening the bathroom door when he happened to glance into Faye's bedroom. He saw two suitcases. He did a double-take. Was Faye already making preparations for their holiday, even though the plan wasn't to leave until Friday?

It was Saturday, and Jake would have loved to go that day, but even though it was the first week of the school holidays, Faye still had one of her courses to attend the next week for her headship qualification. The upside to hanging around London for the week was that he would be babysitting Natty while Faye was on her course.

Jake stood outside the bathroom door, staring at the suitcases in disbelief. Was it really happening – the three of them going on holiday to Scotland?

Jake flushed the loo and headed back downstairs. He heard Natty in the kitchen as he approached the door.

'Are you getting me a phone just like yours?'

'Not exactly sweetheart. It will be a basic phone without WiFi or internet, but we'll go shopping and you can choose one.'

'Oh Mummy, you're the best.'

'I know.'

'But will there be time before we go on holiday?'

Jake was about to open the kitchen door when he heard Faye say, 'There will be plenty of time to shop for a mobile phone. You've got all week.'

'Please can we wake Jake up now? I can't wait to talk to him about our holiday. He is coming too. Mummy, you won't change your mind, will you?'

'Oh, sweetheart. Rest assured, we are not going anywhere without him.'

Jake felt a lump in his throat. He had his heart set on showing them the country of his birth, and the place he would always think of as home, but in that moment he realised that although it would have been wonderful, he didn't actually care all that much where they went, as long as he was with them.

Jake couldn't wipe the smile off his face as he opened the kitchen door. Natty immediately flew into his arms. 'Jake!'

Jake threw Faye a sheepish look, suddenly afraid of how

spending a holiday together would work. Would it draw them closer? Would she start to feel the same way about him that he felt for her? Or would he find his relationship with her daughter getting in the way? It wouldn't get in the way of them physically being together, but what if Faye were to feel jealous and threatened by his presence in Natty's life, after being a single parent for so long?

Patrick was right: it had always been just the two of them before Jake had come along – she'd made sure of it by keeping distance in her relationships, keeping the guys she'd dated out of Natty's life. But she hadn't counted on a guy she wasn't dating, who she'd invited into their lives, capturing Natty's heart. Oh, how he wanted to capture Faye's too.

Jake held his breath.

'Jake,' said Faye, smiling, 'Natty and I have a surprise for you.'

'For me?'

Natty nodded. 'Yes.'

'You know I told you last night that I wanted us all to go on holiday together to Scotland?'

Jake nodded. He didn't let on that he'd already overheard them talking and had guessed that perhaps they weren't going to Scotland after all. He wasn't surprised. It was quite a distance to drive, unless they flew, and with the school summer holidays having started, and their plan to go at such short notice, he imagined the flights might be fully booked, unless he paid first class. Knowing Faye, she wouldn't want him to go to the expense. There would be plenty of other destinations in the UK that didn't involve a flight or such a long car journey.

He smiled. Wherever she wanted to go was fine by him – perfect, even. He'd have no quibbles whatsoever with her plans.

He looked at Natty. 'What's the surprise?'

'It was Natty's idea. Early this morning when she'd woken up, I told her the plan to have a holiday together in Scotland.'

Jake nodded. 'You know, it's absolutely fine not going to Scotland.'

'Who said we're not going to Scotland?'

'Um … I thought maybe you'd changed your mind about the destination.'

'Why would I do that?'

'Because it's a long way by car.'

'Well that's what holidays are for. To get away – a long way away.'

Jake grinned.

'But we don't have to travel by car,' said Faye. 'Natty and I talked about it, and I gave Natty a choice as to how we travel there – plane, train or automobile.'

Natty chuckled into her hand.

Faye smiled at her. 'Sorry, it's a bit of an in-joke. You know that old eighties movie she likes …'

'Oh, yeah.' Jake smiled. 'So, what did you choose?' Jake couldn't stop smiling. He still couldn't believe this was really happening – they were all going to Scotland together.

Natty ran up and gave Jake a slip of paper. 'Here – we printed yours out.'

'You booked already?' Jake said in surprise casting a glance over at Faye.

Natty said, 'Yes, while you were still asleep. We wanted to surprise you.'

Jake took the ticket. He was surprised all right. He gave Natty a hug.

'It's a train ticket,' said Faye.

Jake looked at the train ticket with a sinking feeling. 'Well, that's just … wonderful, Natty.'

Of all the ways to travel, why had she needed to choose the train? Jake tried hard not to think of Eleanor, but it wasn't working. They had always gone to Scotland by train. In the beginning, they hadn't. They had gone by car, but the car journeys had been long and monotonous. It had been Eleanor's idea to go by train. And it had stuck. They had always got the sleeper train. Jake looked at his ticket. At least it wasn't a sleeper.

'Mummy always says that trains are very romantic.'

Jake peered at Faye.

'Er … no, I don't.'

'Yes you do.'

'Well, um, not in this scenario, sweetheart.'

'What does that mean?'

'I mean this is a holiday, not a romantic break.'

Jake looked across at Faye, disappointed.

'Why not?' said Natty. 'You two could smoochy-smoochy on the train.' Natty puckered her lips.

'Natty!' Faye exclaimed. 'No one is doing any smoochy-smoochy on the train – or anywhere else on holiday.'

'Shame.'

Faye turned swiftly in Jake's direction. 'Pardon?'

'I said, er … same, no one is doing the … smoochy-smoochy.'

Faye looked at him for a long moment.

Jake wondered if she thought he was taking the mickey. He kept his expression neutral.

'Well, good. I'm glad to hear it.' Faye turned to Natty. 'Why don't we go shopping for your phone this morning?'

Jake noticed she'd quickly changed the subject.

'Can Jake come too?' Natty asked.

Jake turned to Faye expectantly. He wanted to spend the day with them. He wanted to spend every day with them until they all left for Scotland. They could go shopping for her phone, then get some lunch out, and take Natty to one of the London parks, and perhaps to a museum in the afternoon.

'Oh, Mummy, please say Jakey can come too. Please, please.'

Faye turned to him. 'Jake, would you like to—'

'Absolutely.'

'All right. Natty, go and clean your teeth.'

Natty was out of the door like a shot.

Jake smiled after her, thankful for pester power. He had the whole week already planned out in his head. There were lots of things they could do together each day in London: museums, the zoo, parks. Perhaps Patrick would like to join them and enjoy some days out together before the three of them headed off to Scotland on Friday.

He stole a glance at Faye. Of course, whether they invited Patrick would be up to her.

Natty's head reappeared round the door. 'Mummy says she fancies you.'

'Natty! I did not.'

'Did too, when I asked you if you like Jake.'

'Yes, but I didn't say—'

Natty slammed the door shut. Jake heard her thundering up the stairs. When he turned to Faye, she was furiously wiping up. 'Right, I've got a ton of things to get done before we go shopping this morning. Do you need to go home and, you know, shower and change?'

'I've got my bag right here.' Jake pointed towards the hall. Patrick had taken it out of his car and left it the previous night. 'I've got clean clothes. Would you prefer that I go home to shower and change?'

'No, why would I prefer that?'

Her back was still to him, he noticed. She was avoiding eye contact. Her reply was short, abrupt. Jake sighed. He really hoped this holiday was not going to turn out to be a bad idea. Natty clearly had plans for him and Faye to get together. He did too. But he wasn't a nine-year-old child with no filter, who wanted things now. Jake could wait. He'd wait and wait and wait, and hope that one day Faye might just feel an inkling of what he felt for her.

29

Faye put the kettle on.

Jake sat down at the kitchen table. There was a bowl, some milk and a box of cereal. He poured some cereal and eyed his train ticket. He still wished they weren't going by train. They were getting the early morning train from London Euston to Glasgow Central, which took four and a half hours, followed by another train from Glasgow to Aviemore. All in all, a train journey of over seven hours. It did beat doing it by road, but Jake would have preferred to fly.

He looked at his ticket and had to ask, 'It was very thoughtful of you to make the travel arrangements. Was the train really all Natty's idea? I know it's cheaper than flying, but I don't mind booking us a flight. That way, we wouldn't lose an entire day of our holiday travelling.'

Faye had boiled the kettle and made two mugs of tea. She turned around and put one in front of Jake, then sat at the table. 'I suppose I kind of nudged her in that direction. I was thinking of a bus, because that's cheaper, but neither of us wanted to revisit that bus station any time soon.'

Jake understood. 'So, do you want to cancel the train tickets, and I'll book us a flight?'

Faye shook her head. 'Patrick might be offended.'

Jake frowned 'What's it got to do with Patrick?'

'He offered to pay for the holiday. Insisted, actually. I told him I felt bad not inviting him to come with us, but he said he didn't want to get in the way, and that when we get back, he hopes he can have a day out with Natty, just him and his granddaughter.'

Jake was surprised Patrick had paid for the tickets. But then again, maybe he wasn't. When he'd told Patrick about Faye's idea for the three of them to go on holiday to Scotland, Patrick had seemed over the moon with the idea. Jake knew the reason – he could see his granddaughter was very fond of the babysitter. And he knew she'd called him Daddy. Natty's real father wasn't coming back. Patrick could see Jake as very, very good husband material for his daughter. Jake, and clearly Patrick, were hoping that during the course of this holiday, Faye would start to see that too.

'I've already got the accommodation sorted, so he doesn't have to worry about that.' Jake suddenly realised that wasn't true. His arrangement with Gayle had been made on the proviso that they would be returning shortly. Now they wouldn't be arriving until Friday. He made a mental note to phone Gayle, hoping she had vacancies. He had to organise two rooms – one for himself, and a family or twin room for Natty and Faye.

Faye took a sip of coffee and commented, 'Yeah, my dad said we wouldn't have to worry about booking accommodation.'

Jake was getting his mobile phone out to call Gayle. 'Oh, really? I didn't mention whereabouts we'd be staying in Scotland when I got off the phone to you yesterday before you collected Natty.'

'I guess he presumed we'd be staying at your holiday home.'

Jake's head shot up. 'Excuse me?'

'He gave me and Natty pocket money, which was kind of funny. I haven't had spending money for a holiday off my dad for years.'

Jake sat there staring at Faye. 'Look, about The Lake House…'

'The Lake House?'

He realised she didn't know the name of the Ross family's holiday home, nor that it was, in fact, his house. For some reason, Jake didn't feel inclined to tell her. He didn't know why. Or perhaps he did. Jake couldn't take her to The Lake House even if he hadn't had the excuse that it was in the throes of being redecorated. Even without that, being back there with Faye, the woman he'd fallen in love with, in a place that would just remind him of Eleanor …

'Jake – what is it?'

'The family holiday home, The Lake House, is being redecorated, so we can't stay there I'm afraid.'

'Oh, I see. That's a shame.'

'Yeah. But I know this amazing little guesthouse. Gayle, the owner, is lovely. She makes you feel right at home.' Jake really hoped she had vacancies. 'Natty will love it. There's a rather special guest that I'm sure she's going to make very good friends with. Her name is Olive.'

'Oh, she'll love to have someone to play with. I hope she likes ball games. Natty insisted on packing her ball.'

Jake grinned. 'Olive loves playing ball.'

'Oh, and Natty loves board games. We could all play, but having someone around her own age to play with—'

'Oh, no, I didn't mean another child.'

'Oh, then what—'

'Olive is a dog.'

'A dog?' Faye shook her head. 'I don't think that's a good idea.

You know she'll be pestering me big time for a puppy. She already has been.'

Jake really hoped that all this – the plan to take the train, then Patrick putting it into Faye's head that they were staying at the Rosses' holiday home, and now his own faux pas in mentioning the dog – wasn't a harbinger for things going south on their first holiday together.

Don't screw it up, Patrick had said. Jake was determined not to. But some things were just out of his control.

Faye surprised him by reaching across the table and taking his hand. 'You know what? Forget what I said about the dog. Hey, maybe I will get her one.'

'You will?' Jake said in surprise, although he was pleased. 'I can look after it when you're busy. Take it for walks to the park with Natty,' Jake quickly said.

'I know. I can't believe I'm even thinking about it. But after nearly losing her, doing things like that just doesn't seem a big deal anymore. I'm going to turn into you, aren't I? Spoiling her rotten.'

Jake grinned. 'Sounds like it.'

At that moment, Natty burst into the kitchen and caught them holding hands. She looked wide-eyed at both of them and offered up the biggest grin. 'This is going to be the best holiday ever.'

Faye eyed her daughter as she let go of Jake's hand. 'I hope so, because you haven't been on holiday for years. You won't remember the last holiday we had together, which was with your grandfather when he took a holiday to Ireland, and we went too.'

Jake eyed Faye. Nothing was going to get in the way of him making sure this was the best holiday ever. And that was precisely the reason they couldn't stay at The Lake House. Natty didn't understand. He was still married. He could not court the woman he now loved at that house.

That was what he realised this holiday was all about for him; an opportunity to court her. The Lake House held too many memories of the past. As much as he loved the house, he was back to thinking that once the redecorating was complete, he might have to let it go and finally move on from what had happened the previous Christmas.

'Have you cleaned your teeth, Natty?' Faye asked.

She nodded her head.

'Good.'

Natty ran up to Jake. 'Come on, Jake. Hurry up. Finish your drink.'

Jake smiled at Natty, then finished his coffee and cereal in double-quick time. 'I'll just go and shower and change.' He left Natty looking at a website on holidays in Scotland, grabbed his bag, and headed upstairs.

When he returned a short time later, the clean dishes and cutlery had been put away, and the laptop was closed down. He followed Natty and Faye out of the kitchen. He was waiting for them by the front door as they both slipped on jackets – it looked like rain – when Jake heard his mobile phone.

Faye turned around, glancing towards the lounge. 'I think you left your mobile in there.'

Jake ran into the lounge and picked it up. He looked at the number and frowned. He'd forgotten the promise he'd made to Marcus that as soon as he returned to London, he'd return to the Ross Corporation and step into Marcus's shoes temporarily, so that Marcus could check himself into the rehab clinic.

Marcus wouldn't know he was back. He'd left him at the airport on Thursday afternoon. It was only Saturday. He wouldn't expect him back so soon, after he'd told him that he had unfinished business relating to finding Martha's son. That business was still unfinished, along with the discovery that Marcus had been right – someone else had been on that mountain with them on Christmas Day. Before he told Marcus, he wanted to find out who that someone was, but just then he had something a lot more pressing and important to focus on – winning Faye's heart.

If he told Marcus that he was back in London already, he'd have to return to the Ross Corporation – and who knew how long that would be for, while Marcus was in rehab? Jake couldn't be in two places at once. Jake not only wanted to spend the week with Natty and Faye on days out in London, but he didn't want there to be any chance he'd have to cancel their week in Scotland at the end of the week.

Jake's finger hovered over the green icon. All he had to do was answer it, tell Marcus he'd be just a few more days – well, two weeks. Could Marcus wait that long? Jake had made a promise that he'd be back. He would. Just not right now.

But what if Marcus was on another spiral downwards, and needed to check into the clinic ASAP? Then he'd tell him to check in. The company would have to do without him.

Marcus would not do that. Jake knew that. He would not leave the company unless Jake was at the helm once more.

Standing by the front door, Faye called out, 'Jake?'

Jake was already torn, and he hadn't even answered the phone. That very thought made up his mind. He had to choose. 'Yeah – be right with you.'

'Everything okay?' Faye asked as he joined them. They stepped outside.

Jake thought, god, I hope so as he put his phone on silent.

30

'Are you okay?' David asked. 'You're a bit quiet this morning.'

Robyn didn't think that was surprising. She had a lot on her mind. She couldn't believe that it was Friday already. The week had gone surprisingly quickly since they'd left Gayle's on Saturday morning. Too quickly. And now she was sitting on the lawn, in front of the boathouse, watching David hanging the last of the paper lanterns she'd ordered online.

She'd been shocked at how much she'd enjoyed the holiday that, at first, she'd felt railroaded into. She'd thought she wouldn't enjoy time away from the work she loved. She had been wrong. She'd thought she wouldn't enjoy spending an entire week there at the boathouse. She'd been wrong on that score too.

She'd imagined that she'd find it hard doing nothing all day but mooch around the boathouse with David. But that wasn't how her week had turned out at all. In fact, she'd been extremely busy. That was probably the reason the time had flown. She hadn't realised how lazy days on holiday were not lazy at all, but filled with fun things to do.

It made her wonder about her childhood; her mother was off travelling, had been for months, but Robyn had a feeling that childhood holidays had been scarce. Perhaps her mother was making up for lost time.

Of course, those fun-filled days during her first holiday in months had all been down to David. She'd thought it rather strange at first, having a holiday at the boathouse rather than going away. But she knew what his game was. She hadn't been feeling at home in the boathouse, so he'd gone out of his way on their holiday week to make their time together there something special.

Some activities weren't really her thing; he'd taken her fishing on the loch in his little rowing boat, which she hadn't really expected to enjoy. She'd imagined this was a bit like what married life would involve – compromises. But she had made the best of the day; it had been beautiful weather, so she'd packed a picnic in a large hamper, together with a picnic blanket, a bottle of wine, and two wine glasses. They'd landed on a deserted little stretch of pebble beach across the loch from the boathouse, and had sat with the picnic, enjoying the views and their tranquil spot for lunch in the sunshine. They'd lain together on the blanket, holding hands, staring at the beautiful blue sky and listening to birds and the lapping of the water on the shore.

On the way back, David had insisted she try her hand at fishing. Surprisingly, she'd actually enjoyed herself and, much to David's chagrin, had caught a fish on her very first fishing trip. She'd insisted on throwing it back, saying she wanted the fish to live to swim another day. He'd bought her presents too. She looked at the bike with its baskets on the front and back. It was strange, but Robyn had a feeling that nobody had ever bought her a bike before, even when she was a child. She didn't know that for sure – how could she? She didn't remember. It was certainly something she was going to ask her mother.

Robyn had asked the hypnotherapist, whom she'd made an appointment with that week, if she'd mentioned a bike when she'd been under hypnosis. Apparently, she had not. Robyn was still pleased she had arranged that appointment to see the therapist. Although she was meant to be on holiday, she realised it was the perfect time to get the ball rolling, especially if she didn't want to wait until her mum arrived. She hadn't told her in the letter about her memory problems. And she didn't want to get into all that when her mum arrived. Robyn would prefer it if her memories came back first; then she could put the accident and her memory loss behind her.

David hadn't been too keen on her going to therapy sessions during her week's holiday. At first, she'd only made an appointment to see Dr Jamieson, who had been quite surprised that, after so many weeks, her memories still hadn't resurfaced. She'd said it was very rare and had agreed that it was high time Robyn had some help. She'd also agreed with Robyn that this would be the perfect time – while she was away from work and had free time to spend on herself. The fact that her mum was returning had galvanised Robyn to take the plunge and finally face her past.

Despite David's initial disappointment that it was taking time out of their holiday together, he understood her reasoning and supported her decision. That didn't stop him putting his all into their holiday together at the boathouse, though.

As well as buying her a bike, he'd dug his own bike out of storage and had had it looked at by a local bike company in Aviemore. It meant they could take rides together along the forest tracks surrounding the boathouse, and they'd also ridden along the single-track road that brought them out on to the main road and a small petrol station and convenience store. Robyn had enjoyed stopping there to buy fresh bread and croissants, filling her baskets before returning to the boathouse to sit upstairs on the balcony overlooking the loch with a pot of freshly brewed coffee and a delicious croissant warmed in the oven. It was all rather heavenly.

In the evenings, they'd sat by the log burner in the lounge, and for an entire week, they'd seen hardly a soul, save for some walkers in the forest, and of course the old chap running the petrol station and store. And Robyn's therapist. Dr Jamieson had given her some options, surprising her by recommending hypnosis along with some psychotherapy sessions. The doctor had said it was recommended for patients with Robyn's condition – dissociative amnesia disorder.

Robyn recalled that when she'd been in hospital she had been somewhat relieved that a name had been given to her condition. Although she hadn't been pleased to hear that, once brain injury or dementia had been ruled out as causes, people who couldn't remember things about themselves or what had happened to them in the past had often experienced some traumatic or stressful event.

But putting a name to her condition meant she could move forward with a professional when the time came and she was ready to get to the bottom of what exactly had led to her dissociative amnesia. That time had arrived. Her qualified hypnotherapist, a kind lady called Marnie, ran her practice from home. It was a lovely little bungalow, on the outskirts of Aviemore, with a large home office at the bottom of a long garden. Built in pine, the interior reminded Robyn of a log cabin, with warm pine floors, walls, and ceiling, a sofa with matching armchairs opposite, Aztec-style rugs, cushions, and a log burner with a chimney that stretched up into the vaulted ceiling.

It didn't look like an office at all, but an extension of her house – like a second lounge. There were framed pictures of tranquil landscapes – rolling hills and misty forests – hanging on the walls. Potted indoor plants with thick green foliage were dotted about the room, and there were scented candles on the coffee table. Apart from the laptop on the coffee table in front of them, nothing suggested it was an office at all, or a treatment room. Robyn was so thankful for that. It had taken a lot of courage to return to the hospital to see Dr Jamieson. Although she was a lovely doctor, Robyn wanted to steer clear of clinical environments again, if she could.

Although it took Robyn a couple of sessions to feel comfortable enough to get into the relaxed state needed for hypnosis, Marnie was now confident she was making progress and that soon there would be a breakthrough with her amnesia; soon, she'd recover her memories.

Robyn wished she could have said time had stood still that week, but instead it had rushed on. David had been very pleased to hear it. Not because he wanted to get the week out of the way and get back to normal, but because he'd thought it was a good sign that she felt that way – it meant she was having a good time. The only thing was that she still needed more time with her therapist.

When she'd left her session just the previous day, Marnie had said that the breakthrough could come any time – perhaps during the next session. Robyn hoped so. All she wanted now was to remember what had happened to her – and then she could look forward to her future with David, with no possibility of anything untoward appearing from her past to throw her life off course.

She looked over at David and smiled. She couldn't thank him

enough for her presents – one in particular, which was about to get her covered in loch water, yet again. 'Oh no!' The ball being dropped at her feet was always a precursor to what was coming next. She held up her hands to shield her hair from getting wet as Percy shook himself.

'Oh, Percy, you silly boy! Why do you always miss the ball when I throw it, and it ends up rolling down the slope into the water?'

She'd learned that Percy loved water. When she threw the ball, he wouldn't fetch it unless it went into the loch. Then he'd run into the water, nudging the ball that was floating on the surface, and have a lovely swim.

Robyn picked up the ball. 'You know I'm going to have to stop throwing it in that direction.'

Percy barked.

'Come here,' she called.

Percy ran straight into her arms, and Robyn didn't care if she got so wet she'd have to change her clothes. 'I love you so much – do you know that?'

Percy wagged his tail furiously. She looked over at David and then whispered to Percy, 'It was love at first sight when I met you.'

Percy woofed and licked her face.

Robyn laughed. 'I know you feel the same way about me.' She gave him more fusses. She whispered, 'Now, it's our secret. Otherwise, David might get jealous.' That wasn't far from the truth. Despite what Gayle had told David, which he'd passed on to Robyn – that Percy would be just as comfortable out on long walks, and accompanying David in his boat, fishing, as he would curling up on the sofa – it had turned out that Percy had immediately chosen his person the moment Robyn and David had walked through the door of the couple who were hoping to rehome him. Percy had darted straight over to Robyn. And that was the way it had been ever since they'd brought Percy back to the boathouse. Wherever Robyn was, Percy wanted to go too. He was her shadow.

Robyn threw the ball towards the water again and thought of the pitstop David had mentioned he needed to make the previous Saturday after posting her letter. She hadn't understood why they were stopping at some stranger's house in Aviemore. Had he needed to make a last-minute delivery before he had a week off?

It had turned out that it wasn't a delivery at all, but a pick-up – potentially, Sitting in the car, David had explained that they were there to meet Percy. He'd wanted to buy her a dog, a puppy, but then Gayle had told him about Rose and George's friend, and a little dog called Percy who needed rehoming. He'd showed her the photo on his phone that Gayle had sent him. Her reaction when he'd told her all this was not what either of them had expected. Robyn had burst into tears. Ten minutes later, they had been in the car with Percy and all his things. He was wagging his tail and trying to climb into Robyn's lap, licking her face and barking all at the same time. He was so excited that he couldn't contain himself. Percy knew he was going to his new home.

As for Robyn, she'd sat in the back seat with him, absolutely stunned that she had a dog all of her own. All her dreams were coming true.

She found it hard to believe that it was only the Friday before that she'd returned from London and surprised David at Lark Lodge. Now, there she was, just one week later, having had a fantastic holiday with David, and the boathouse was all prepared for the party that evening. Party invitations had gone out earlier in the week, and everybody who'd been invited had replied to say they were coming. The food she'd ordered online was laid out in the kitchen ready to go in the oven. Robyn was cooking her guests a meal. They would arrive after work. She had already baked a cake and a rhubarb crumble for dessert.

She looked up at the blue sky, with not a raincloud in sight, and sighed in relief. She hadn't wanted to check the weather forecast in case it was not going to be kind. The plan was that after dinner, everyone would wander outside with a drink and watch the sunset over the loch. That was when the party would begin. Duncan had friends who were in a traditional Scottish folk band. The band were coming along some time after dinner.

Now, she had nothing to do but sit and throw a ball for her dog, and watch David finish off the decorations outside, while she waited until it was time to leave the boathouse and collect their very first guest from the airport. Her mum was flying home.

'There – all done!' David climbed down from the ladder and admired his handiwork. The back of the boathouse, fronting the loch, was now festooned with lanterns, along with the several strings of fairy lights stretching along the jetty where David's small rowing boat was moored. He walked over and joined her on the grass in front of the loch. 'You're thinking about Judith, aren't you?'

Robyn glanced up at the balcony overlooking the loch, outside the lounge on the first floor. The previous evening, she'd wandered out on to the balcony, a throw covering her shoulders, a glass of wine in hand. She'd been standing there, looking up at the stars, and thinking of David proposing on bended knee back in June, soon after they'd moved into the boathouse together. It was then that she'd finally realised something.

David had joined her, and before saying a word, she'd looked about her, seeing her dog asleep in basket. She associated having a dog with being settled; with permanency. She'd turned to David and told him what she imagined he'd been dying to hear – not because it was what he wanted her to say, and she wanted to make him happy, but because she truly meant it. 'I've got exactly what I want, David.'

He'd joked, 'A devastatingly handsome fiancé?'

She'd shaken her head, surprising him, even though he'd said it half in jest.

His gaze had fallen on Percy. 'A dog?'

She'd shaken her head again. 'No.'

That was when he'd frowned. 'A bike?'

'Uh-uh.'

David had stared at her, looking worried.

'A home, David.'

'The boathouse?'

She'd smiled. 'I love this place, but of course I love it more because my devastatingly handsome fiancé, along with Percy and Lottie are here.'

'Who's Lottie?'

'My bike.'

'You named your bike?'

'Of course. Haven't you named yours?'

He'd laughed at that. 'No. But I did name my sports car.'

'Sorry about that.'

He'd taken her in his arms and said, 'Don't ever apologise for the accident that totalled my car. If it wasn't for that, I would never have met you.'

Robyn frowned when she recalled that conversation.

'What is it?' David asked, taking her hand and following her gaze up to the balcony.

'I was thinking of last night.'

'You don't regret what you said, do you, about this being home now?'

'Of course not. It's just … I'm scared about my memories coming back,' she confided. She wondered if she'd done the right thing, seeing the hypnotherapist. She'd been afraid it wouldn't work. Now she was afraid it would. 'What if you don't like the real me?'

'The real you?' David scoffed. 'I know the real you. Whatever happened in your past, whoever you were before you came here, I know you, Robyn Parker, and I will always love you.'

Robyn bit her lower lip.

'Robyn?' He gently lifted her chin.

'I wish the week hadn't flown by.'

David grinned. 'Well, so do I.'

What Robyn also wished was that her mum wasn't on her way to see her.

Judith had left a message on the answerphone to say she was on her way and would be with them on Friday, giving the time her plane would land for them to collect her. Robyn had written in her letter that they would be at the airport to collect her. All they'd need to know was when.

Robyn didn't think it was ideal, her mum arriving on the day of the party. She wanted to spend some time with her, just the two of them, but for some reason David had insisted the party was that week – on Friday night, preferably, when he was sure everyone could make it. Besides, he'd said she would have plenty of time to spend with Judith in the days following the party.

Robyn was thinking about that phone message. It was the first time she'd heard her mum's voice since … well, she couldn't remember. They'd been out when she'd called. Robyn had been strangely nervous about talking to her, so she had been relieved that she'd left a message. What would she say? How would she explain her memory loss? Gayle had suggested that seeing her mum might trigger her memories. But it did not bode well that, despite playing that message over and over, there was no inkling of recognition; all she heard was a stranger's voice.

31

Robyn stood in the airport, feeling anxious. The plane had landed some fifteen minutes earlier, but they were still waiting for Judith in the arrivals hall. David stood beside her, holding her hand reassuringly. 'She's still got to collect her luggage and go through passport control, so we'll just have to wait. I'm sure she won't be long.'

Robyn took a deep breath when she saw passengers start to trickle into the arrivals hall. She watched as some ran into the arms of their waiting relatives and friends, reuniting with their loved ones. She smiled. That would be her and her mum at any moment.

'Is that her?' David asked.

A tall, slim, middle-aged lady, looking tanned and wearing blue chinos, a white blouse, strappy sandals, and sunglasses on her head, had walked into the arrivals hall carrying on old suitcase covered in stickers. Robyn thought it looked familiar. 'That suitcase looks just like yours, Robyn. It's her – isn't it?'

Robyn watched as the lady stopped in the middle of the arrivals hall and put down the heavy old brown leather case. She had a small handbag over one shoulder and stood holding a large, bright pink sun hat.

Then David was no longer by Robyn's side but striding up to the lady with the sun hat, a welcoming smile on his face.

No, wait! Robyn wanted to say. She had the sudden impulse to bolt right out of the airport. She watched from afar as David greeted her stepmother. Robyn hadn't filled David in on the fact that Judith was her stepmum. She'd only discovered this in the past few days, and was just digesting the fact herself. She had planned to tell him, but stupidly she'd left it, and then hadn't felt at all talkative on the way to the airport. Robyn hadn't just spent the past week having a holiday and preparing for the party that evening. Seeing her therapist had encouraged her to search through all her belongings, and find her old diary, the one kept in an old shoe box, thinking that after all these months, since she'd looked at it last, something might jog her memory.

The last time she'd looked at it was when she'd left the hospital with Gayle months earlier to go and live at Lark Lodge. When she'd gone through her things and found the diary, it hadn't been quite what she'd expected. It was just full of sketches of things she'd done, places she'd been, and in some cases her feelings. She'd taken a cursory glance through it until she came across a pencil sketch that stood out – it was a sketch of Wilbur's Bookstore, with two women sitting in the window.

Gayle had taken her to visit the bookshop, which had been closed over Christmas, but it wasn't until she'd revisited the bookshop when it had reopened after Christmas that a memory had resurfaced. At least, she'd presumed it was a memory. She'd sat in the window of the bookstore the previous Christmas with a woman – she was sure of it. Beyond that, she had no clue. But she had avoided the place after that, avoiding her memories.

Now, seeing her stepmum, whom she did not recognise, she

desperately wanted them to come flooding back. She'd thought that perhaps her old diary might have helped together with the hypnotherapy sessions. She'd spent ages going through the diary entries, scrutinising the sketches she'd made as a teenager. Then she'd discovered something she'd missed – the word stepmum alongside a rather unflattering sketch of a woman, and a further entry scribbled in faint pencil: wish she was dead, instead of my mum.

Robyn wondered if that was why she hadn't used any of the money from the cheques her stepmum had sent her so that she could join her abroad for a holiday. She assumed that they just didn't get on. Robyn understood; she imagined that she'd never accepted her late father remarrying. But that wasn't Judith's fault. She'd obviously gone to some lengths, sending money for Robyn to join her abroad, but Robyn had not reciprocated the effort.

Robyn looked at Judith – the only family she had, as far as she was aware – and thought that it was time to change that. She was a grown-up now, not a sulky teenager who wouldn't accept her father remarrying. Robyn wanted to put all that behind her and make this relationship work. She'd put on her favourite outfit, a knee-length, fitted sleeveless dress in a light green colour with a delicate rose pattern. The dress matched her sandals. She also wore a light green cardigan.

Robyn had spent an afternoon, after one of her therapy sessions, meeting up with Gayle to go shopping for the dress. She'd wanted to look her best for her stepmum's arrival, to make a good first impression, almost as if to say, look – my life is on track, and I've made the right decision to give up university. Gayle had cut and styled her hair and had asked her if she wanted to dye it blonde again. Robyn had decided against it. She might not recognise Judith, but she didn't want to make such a drastic change to her appearance that Judith might not immediately recognise her.

Robyn smoothed down her dress and took a deep breath. She could see Judith chatting to David, her eyes darting about, looking for her.

Robyn, feeling absurdly nervous, forced herself to put one foot in front of the other and walk the few paces towards them. She stopped beside David and said, 'Hello—' Robyn halted abruptly realising she couldn't remember – did she call her mum or Judith?

'Ah, there you are, Robyn.' David put her arm around Robyn's waist and smiled at her.

'What the …?' Judith said in surprise, not taking her eyes from Robyn.

Robyn shifted uncomfortably. 'What is it?'

'What have you done with my stepdaughter?'

'Pardon?' David said. 'Your stepdaughter?'

Robyn pursed her lips wishing she'd told him. She mumbled, 'Sorry, David, I didn't tell you she's my stepmum,' before turning to Judith. What did she mean – what have you done with my stepdaughter?

'I'm right here,' replied Robyn, thinking it was lucky she hadn't dyed her hair. 'Do I look so different?'

Judith studied her intently. Robyn felt shy under her gaze. Judith finally said, 'Where's the little girl with the long, matted hair, those black clothes with heavy boots, and the thick eye liner that made her look like a goth?'

Robyn smiled, pleased by Judith's reaction, realising that she must look quite different to the grungy student Judith had left at university before she went on her travels. Robyn recalled those clothes in her suitcase that she had found, but that she had hated. It made her wonder if losing her memory had changed her somehow. She wouldn't be seen dead in those clothes. Or maybe it was something else …

'I think maybe I grew up these past few months,' said Robyn. Her life had certainly changed –she had gone from being a student to running a business. She was in a serious relationship. She had a home. Yes, Robyn concluded, she'd matured. She'd changed. And Judith could see that.

'Wow!' Judith stared at her. 'I go away leaving behind a stepdaughter who still acts and looks like a teenager, and I come back to a beautiful, sophisticated woman.'

Robyn looked down at the outfit she had spent ages choosing to wear to welcome her stepmother home. When she looked up, there were tears rolling down Judith's face. 'I didn't expect this. It's a bit of a shock.'

'Oh, Mum – don't cry.' Robyn said, stepping forward to give her stepmother a hug while wiping a tear from her own face. 'Can I call you Mum?'

Judith looked taken aback. 'Oh, er … yes, I suppose.'

Robyn put her arms around her. 'I'm so glad you're home.'

'Your hair, Robyn – you've had it cut.'

Robyn nervously fiddled with her shoulder-length hair.

'You know, I haven't had a decent haircut since I've been away. Guess I didn't really need to bother, what with wearing hats all the time.'

Robyn said brightly, 'I can recommend a great hairstylist. She's also a good friend. She used to do some mobile hairdressing but now runs a guesthouse, so she only cuts hair for friends and family now.'

'Where you had yours done?' Judith asked, appraising Robyn's haircut as they walked towards the exit.

Robyn smiled. 'Yes.' She glanced over her shoulder at David, who was following behind, carrying Judith's suitcase.

Judith caught sight of her appearance in a mirror as they passed a beauty counter. She stopped and stared at her reflection. Robyn looked into the mirror too, staring at her stepmother beside her. Judith was taller than her, with blue eyes and blonde hair, which Robyn guessed was her natural colour. But her blonde bob was dry and frizzy. It had obviously seen too much sun.

Robyn caught Judith looking at her in the mirror strangely, an expression on her face Robyn couldn't quite read. For a split second, Judith's ready smile was no more.

Judith turned to her, the beaming smile back. 'You said it was a friend of yours that did your hair?'

'Yes, her name is Gayle.'

'In that case, I need to book an appointment straight away.'

'Straight away?' Robyn said, surprised. Judith had only just arrived. She'd assumed her stepmum would want to go back to the boathouse and spend time with her after all these months, not prioritise going to have her hair done.

She turned to look at Robyn. 'I can't go around looking like this, can I? And there's the party this evening and I'm the guest of honour.'

Robyn nodded. 'Yes, that's true.' She'd also told her that she was engaged, and she was inviting her to an engagement and housewarming party, but so far her stepmum hadn't congratulated her on her engagement. Perhaps she was saving that for the party. Robyn hadn't mentioned the fact that she'd dropped out of university and was running her own very successful business. She'd just added that she wanted her to come home to see her. She had some important news.

'I shall want to look my best,' added Judith.

'Yes of course. I have her number. I can give Gayle a call, see if she's free.'

'Does she live locally? Can we just go there now?'

'I suppose.'

As they fell in step, nearing the exit, Judith said, 'You mentioned that Gayle runs a guesthouse. Are there vacancies?'

Robyn stopped in surprise. 'You don't want to stay with us?'

'Well, of course I do, but have you got the room? I don't want to be a bother or put anyone out.'

'Oh, I'm sure we'll squeeze you in somewhere.' She took her stepmother's arm and glanced over her shoulder. 'Won't we, David?'

David looked at her curiously.

She winked at him. It was a joke. They had plenty of room. She was looking forward to surprising her stepmum when she found out Robyn was living in a gorgeous place.

'Oh right, yeah – of course we will.' His face brightened and he winked back.

Good grief, thought Robyn, rolling her eyes at how long it had taken David to get her little joke.

They exited the arrivals hall and made their way to the parking area. 'This is us,' David said, opening the passenger door.

'What a beauty,' Robyn's mother breathed. 'I see I'm travelling in style.'

'I've not long had her.' David beamed.

Robyn rolled her eyes when she saw his hand tenderly wipe off an imaginary speck of dust. Robyn gave David a look before they all climbed into the car. It hadn't originally been David's car, but had been his dad's. Duncan had given it to David, saying he really had no use of it now he'd moved into the flat above the shop. Duncan had everything he needed in Aviemore, and if he really needed to go somewhere, he could always use the delivery van.

Robyn hadn't realised how much David loved the old car until his dad gave it to him. The car was very old, and she got the impression from Judith's reaction that it must be some sort of classic – not that she'd recognise one herself. She'd always assumed that it wasn't the car per se, but the fact that it was a gift from his dad that had made it so special to him. Perhaps it was a little of both.

'Where on earth did you get her?' Judith cooed from the front seat as they joined the flow of traffic from the airport.

Robyn wanted to lean forward and tell her not to encourage him, but she bit her tongue and looked out of the side window, taking in the scenery. The drive from Inverness Airport to Aviemore was an hour at most, depending on which route David chose. There were plenty of things Judith could have seen on the way, if they'd stopped en route; there were waterfalls and castles, museums, and even a famous battlefield called Culloden, all involving just a short detour. These were things that Robyn would love to see too, like the historic fortress, Urquhart Castle, on the shore of Loch Ness, along with the Loch Ness Centre dedicated to the loch's most famous resident – the Loch Ness Monster.

Judith hadn't mentioned how long she was intending to stay. Robyn was considering whether to take the next week off work too, and plan some special things to do with Judith. She knew her stepmum loved travelling. It would be a brilliant opportunity for them both to explore the touristy attractions of the Cairngorms –

something Robyn really hadn't had much of an opportunity to do over the past few months.

It was the school holidays, so she was sure Annie would be okay minding the shop for another week. The work at The Lake House and in London would just have to wait a little bit longer. This was more important – spending time with her stepmum.

As she looked out of the window, taking in the beauty of the surrounding scenery as they drove along the A9 to Aviemore, Robyn was enjoying the route she'd never travelled before – at least as far as she could remember. She frowned at the thought. She glanced at Judith in the front seat. She was chatting amiably to David about her recent sojourn in Sicily. So far, nothing awkward had come up in conversation about their shared past. She was dreading the words, 'Robyn, remember when …'

Robyn had hoped that coming face to face with Judith would have some sort of profound effect whereby her memories would suddenly come flooding back. Marnie had said that it was always a possibility. It hadn't happened. Nothing had happened. That was why Robyn had insisted that Judith sit up front with David during the journey home.

Very soon, she'd have to come out with it and tell Judith about the car accident and her new permanent life there in Aviemore. She wasn't going back to university in September. This was her life now: a successful career, new friends, and a beautiful home with David, Percy and Lottie. What more could a girl want? Robyn bit her lower lip and stared at Judith. She wanted Judith's blessing. She was desperate for her stepmum to be happy for her, support her in what felt like one of the biggest decisions of her life – to marry David and live with him at the boathouse.

'It was a present,' said David.

Robyn rolled her eyes. David was back to talking about his car.

'A present,' Judith repeated, turning in her seat to glance at Robyn. 'Well, it's some present. You must have a very good friend.'

Robyn settled back in her seat for the inevitable re-telling of a familiar story about his dad gifting him the car after the party at Gayle's to celebrate the opening of Lark Lodge as a guesthouse.

'No, it wasn't a friend. My dad gave it to me after the car accident. My sports car was a write-off.'

'You had a car accident? Oh my goodness! What happened?'

Robyn jerked her head, suddenly realising where this conversation was going. She hadn't told Judith anything about what had taken place at Christmas. As far as she was aware, her stepdaughter had returned to college after spending the Christmas break in Aviemore. Now, Robyn wished she'd written about all that in her letter too. At least her stepmum would have been forewarned.

32

They travelled the rest of the way along the main road in stony silence, punctuated by David trying his best to make conversation with Judith. Eventually, he gave up.

Robyn would have preferred it if Judith had said something – anything at all – rather than blank her after she'd been forced to tell her all about the accident, her amnesia, and deferring university, eventually deciding to drop out for good. It was the amnesia bit that was bothering her. Did Judith believe her, or did she think she was faking it to garner some sympathy?

Robyn stared out of the window, trying to enjoy the scenery once more, but it was impossible. She kept being drawn back to the passenger in the front, wondering what she was thinking.

They neared Aviemore. It reminded Robyn that she had been intending to phone Gayle to see if she had time to do something with Judith's hair before the party.

Robyn pursed her lips. She imagined Judith was now not interested in having her hair done or coming to her party. Unfortunately, this was exactly what Robyn had feared might happen when her stepmum found out she'd made such huge decisions without at least talking them through with her first.

Robyn took a deep breath and said, 'Judith, we're coming into Aviemore. This is where Gayle lives. Do you still want your hair cut for this evening, if she has the time?'

Robyn held her breath, hoping that Judith was still coming to her party. Judith turned in the seat to look at her. She said, 'You mentioned that Gayle is a good friend.'

Robyn nodded. 'The best.'

'Is that where you stayed, at her guesthouse, after the car accident?'

'Yes.' Robyn tried to keep her smile in check and not get her hopes up. Judith was speaking to her. That was a good sign – wasn't it? Robyn tried to put herself in Judith's shoes. It must have come as a huge shock to not only discover her very changed appearance, but how much her life had transformed in the last few months. She should have written to her months earlier. But what if Judith had read about her amnesia, and the fact that she'd dropped out of college, and had chosen not to visit? As things were, at least she was still there and hadn't asked David to turn the car around and take her straight back to the airport.

'I should like to see this place, Lark Lodge, and speak to the woman who took you in.'

'It wasn't a guesthouse when I moved in with Gayle.'

'It wasn't?'

Robyn shook her head, smiling to herself, thinking how wonderful it was that Judith wanted to meet her friends. There would be no shortage of those at her party.

David glanced at Judith. 'It was Robyn's idea to turn it into a guesthouse. She did it up for Gayle. My fiancée is really something, isn't she?'

Robyn caught Judith staring at David for a long moment as he faced forward, keeping his eyes on the road.

Robyn said, 'I'm going to phone Gayle and see if she's free to do your hair.'

Judith flicked her hand. 'Don't bother.'

'You don't want your hair done for the party?'

'Yes, of course I do.'

Robyn was so relieved to hear it. That meant Judith was definitely still planning on attending. She got out her mobile phone. 'It will be a wasted trip to Lark Lodge if she doesn't have enough time free.'

Judith shook her head. 'It won't be a wasted trip if I get to meet her. Like I said, I'd like to speak to her.'

What about? Robyn had it on the tip of her tongue to ask. But it was obvious. Judith wasn't going to take Robyn's word for it. She wanted to check with her friends that her life was working out, and perhaps ask them about the man she was marrying. Robyn had no problem with that – no problem at all.

'So, we're going straight to Gayle's?' David asked.

'Yes, please,' Robyn said enthusiastically. She just hoped Gayle did have time to do Judith's hair while they were having a chat. She wanted her to feel and look her best so she would enjoy the party without feeling self-conscious.

They had just reached the outskirts of Aviemore when Robyn's phone rang. She looked at her phone and commented, 'Oh, what are the chances?' before answering it. 'Hi, Gayle! We were just talking about you …' Robyn listened and smiled. 'It was all good things, I promise.'

She was about to ask Gayle if she was free to do a haircut for her special guest, when Gayle said, 'I'm out shopping in Aviemore. I thought I'd just phone you in case there were any last-minute odds and ends you needed for your party. I know you're picking your stepmum up today, so I thought I'd check, in case you couldn't get to the shops.'

Robyn looked at Judith. There was something she needed, but Gayle wouldn't be able to get it at Mr Gillespie's store. 'Are you going to be home soon?' Robyn asked.

It turned out that Gayle was milling around in town, waiting for Doris to finish having tea and biscuits with old friends. They all went along to the community centre to sessions run by volunteers, giving people like Gayle some respite from caring for their relatives.

Robyn was disappointed that Gayle wasn't home and wouldn't be for at least another hour. 'No, I don't need anything last-minute, apart from one thing ...' Robyn asked whether she could spare an hour to do Judith's hair. It would mean taking Judith straight to the boathouse, and then going out again to Lark Lodge. It wasn't ideal. Robyn wanted to get the dinner on for her guests.

'I can take Judith to Gayle's myself while you're getting the dinner on,' David offered, listening in to the conversation.

Robyn nodded, although she'd rather hoped that she and Judith could spend some time together before the other guests arrived. Perhaps she'd like to keep her company in the kitchen, having a chat with a glass of wine, like she imagined mothers and daughters might do.

'Why don't I come along a bit earlier, and do Judith's hair before everyone else arrives?'

Robyn hadn't thought of that. 'Oh, would you?'

'Of course. And if I brought my mum along a bit earlier too, we could get her settled into a nice armchair, so she can acclimatise to her new surroundings before everyone arrives.'

'That's a good idea, Gayle.' Robyn had wanted Doris there too. Gayle's neighbour had offered to pop in and keep an eye on her so that Gayle could go out for the evening, but Robyn at least wanted Doris to join them all for the meal. They'd come to a compromise. After dinner, Gayle was going to run her home and put her to bed, leaving the neighbour with her, while she returned to the party. If there were any problems, Gayle was just a phone call away.

Robyn added, 'Judith is really looking forward to meeting you, and all the rest of my friends.' They weren't just friends to Robyn; they were family – but she felt a little awkward referring to them as such in front of Judith. She hoped that once Judith got to know them all, she'd grow to love them as much as Robyn did. They were all part of the fabric of her new life now. She hoped Judith would become part of her life too from now on.

Robyn put her phone in her bag and smiled, letting Judith know the plan.

David said, 'So, we're heading straight home?'

Robyn looked at her phone, thinking of the call. Perhaps it was for the best that she wasn't taking Judith to Gayle's. Lark Lodge would always have a special place in her heart – it was where her new life, with her new friends and the man she loved, had truly begun – but it wasn't her home. Not anymore.

'Robyn?' David's eyes locked with hers in the rear-view mirror.

'Yes, take us straight home, please.' She couldn't wait to show Judith the boathouse.

33

Not far along the main road, David took the turn on to the single-track lane by a brown sign indicating a loch. Robyn could now do this journey with her eyes closed, after countless times up and down this country road. She knew exactly what was coming. Soon, they'd pass a detached cottage, then a couple of detached bungalows, and lastly a farmhouse. After that, it was a couple more miles until they reached the loch and the boathouse.

'Wow, this is quite remote,' said Judith.

Robyn heard her voice waver. She seemed nervous, for some reason. Robyn said, 'When I first did this journey with David's father, Duncan, to the boathouse …' Robyn did not want to get into the falling-out she'd had with David when he'd left the hospital after his knee operation, and how she'd ended up travelling with David's father to the boathouse instead.

Robyn said, 'I remember Duncan telling me it was a bit out of the way. But it's not really. It isn't that far from the main road, and there are other properties along here. Once we've passed the last property, a farmhouse, then it's only a couple of miles and we're there.'

She heard Judith exhale in relief. Robyn rested her hand on

Judith's shoulder, wondering why she seemed so nervous. There was nothing to be worried about. 'Not long now.'

Robyn frowned as her mind wandered back to the drive there with Duncan and what had happened when they'd arrived. She'd wanted to put that to the back of her mind. The problem was that every single time she turned up at the boathouse after dark, a troublesome memory resurfaced. Fortunately, they wouldn't be arriving after dark that day. It was the height of the summer, although the weather had changed – it was now cloudy and overcast; not the sort of weather she'd wished for Judith's arrival. But at least she was there, and it wasn't dark.

David had a house alarm fitted. When she'd first arrived with Duncan, he'd forgotten the alarm code, and had inadvertently set it off. Robyn remembered that. How could she forget? The sound of that alarm had sent her heart into her throat, and she'd immediately turned around and raced back to the car.

Duncan hadn't been best pleased, telling her to come over and help him fix the alarm. They'd figured out the keycode that Duncan had forgotten. It was the date that Robyn and David had first met, and incidentally the date of the accident – Christmas Day – when their cars had collided on the road while she appeared to be fleeing from Aviemore.

It turned out that wasn't the only unfortunate event that had befallen David last Christmas. Robyn hadn't been able to understand why David had had a house alarm fitted all the way out there, but then Duncan had told her what had also happened to David last Christmas.

David had been burgled on Christmas Day while he was out on a walk before he was due to visit his brother and sister-in-law for Christmas dinner. It was the reason he'd had the alarm fitted.

Robyn had thought how awful it must have been to be robbed over Christmas. She had wondered how someone would even know a house was there, in the pine forest, by a loch, two miles from the nearest neighbours.

Duncan reckoned that the burglars had got lost down the country lane and happened upon the house. It was unfortunate nobody was in. Duncan told her later that he had already been at Joe and Annie's house, spending Christmas Eve, as well as Christmas Day, with them and his grandchild.

The burglars hadn't touched the Christmas presents under the Christmas tree, because they'd found a lot of cash instead.

Robyn had been surprised when Duncan had told her that. It sounded as though David had cashed in some investments. But Duncan was right when he'd wondered aloud why David had left that amount of cash lying around. She'd been shocked to discover that it had been thousands of pounds. Of course, it wasn't David's fault he'd been burgled. It wouldn't have been. It was just really bad luck. But Duncan had been right when he'd questioned why David had taken such a risk. Robyn remembered asking Duncan what David had needed the money for. Duncan didn't know. His son hadn't wanted to talk about it.

And he still didn't. He hadn't mentioned it to her. She guessed he wouldn't. Why bring up the fact that he'd been stupid leaving all that cash around and had lost it? She imagined there was another reason he wouldn't tell her. He'd noticed she wasn't feeling settled in her new home. The week off on holiday, spent together at the boathouse, had been intended to solve that problem. She guessed he thought it would be really unsettling if she knew strangers had turned up and burgled the place.

He had no clue that Duncan had already told her, and she

found it all very unsettling, but not for the reasons he might think.

Robyn remembered asking Duncan a question she really wished she hadn't: how much cash there had been. When Duncan had told her the amount of money that had been stolen, Robyn had felt faint. She'd thought again of the car accident on Christmas Day. When she'd been discharged from the hospital, and Gayle had taken her back to Lark Lodge, Robyn had looked through her belongings that had been in the car – an old suitcase and a rucksack. At the bottom of the rucksack, under some clothes, she'd found cash – a lot of cash. She'd counted it, and the amount had matched the amount of cash that had been stolen from the boathouse. And now all the cash was gone, spent on her shop outlet, buying materials, helping Duncan out with redecorating and furnishing his flat, and paying him rent for use of part of his shop for her business.

All she could think was that it was a massive coincidence. How could she possibly have burgled David's house? She wasn't a thief. She was a student at university – until she had dropped out, anyway. And besides, she didn't need the money. She glanced at Judith. Her stepmum had sent her all these generous cheques, which she'd put into a savings account.

Robyn wouldn't have thought any more about it, if it hadn't been for the memory that kept resurfacing every time she returned to the boathouse: of sitting alone in a car in the dark and cold outside. It made no sense because when she'd followed Duncan inside the boathouse for the first time, she'd stood in the entrance hallway and had realised that nothing was familiar. No memory resurfaced when she caught sight of the large stuffed fish in a glass case on the wall, or the modern glass-panelled open-tread staircase that rose to the next floor, or the impressive kitchen and study she'd seen from the hall. She remembered the wave of relief that had swept over her when she'd realised she had most likely not been into the house.

When she'd ventured up to the next floor, and had seen the lounge with its exposed brick walls, log burner, beamed ceiling, and double doors out to the wooden balcony, with stunning views of the loch and the snow-capped mountains beyond, she knew she'd never been inside the boathouse until that moment.

Then a horrible thought had come out of nowhere. She hadn't been inside the property because she'd been the getaway driver. Robyn had no idea why she'd thought that – she still didn't. She was convinced her imagination had run wild simply because of the huge coincidence over the money in the rucksack. There had to be a logical explanation. Perhaps it was money she'd inherited from her late father. Maybe she'd taken it out of a bank for a reason. David must have had his reasons for taking such a large sum out of his bank. I must have had my reasons too, thought Robyn.

She turned to gaze at Judith sitting in front of her. Would she know? Could Judith tell her where the money had come from, and perhaps what her intentions had been for it?

Robyn had just opened her mouth to ask, when a thought occurred to her. Was she taking a risk asking Judith? What if Judith didn't have a clue where the money had come from? But it wasn't just that thought that kept Robyn from asking. Her gaze shifted to David. He had no clue about the cash she'd discovered in that rucksack. It clearly wasn't the time to bring it up, in front of him.

Robyn shut her mouth, wishing again that her memories would come back. As it was, she'd noticed the change in Judith towards her when she'd mentioned the amnesia. She wished David hadn't brought up the car accident. But I'd have had to tell Judith some time, thought Robyn miserably. It was bound to become obvious that she couldn't remember things in her past. She couldn't even remember Judith.

Robyn sighed. She didn't want to think about that, or where the money in the rucksack had come from. Instead she turned her thoughts to their imminent arrival. She hoped Judith loved her new home.

'The scenery is gorgeous – isn't it?' Robyn commented, focused on the forest of pines either side of the road, looking forward to Judith's first glimpse of the boathouse through the trees.

Judith nodded her head. 'I guess so. Is it far now? It still seems quite a distance from the main road.'

'Not far at all,' said David reassuringly.

Robyn frowned. Why was she so concerned about how far it was from the main road? Why wasn't she just enjoying the scenery?

David said, 'People come here to walk around the loch and fish. My dad used to bring me and my brother and take a boat out fishing.'

Robyn smiled when she remembered Duncan telling her this. She had been surprised to learn of those fishing trips with his sons. David had given her the impression that growing up, it had all been about the game – ice hockey – and that all he'd done in his spare time was get taken to ice hockey practice. But David had clearly loved those fishing trips to the old boathouse that Duncan had rented each summer. It came with an old rowing boat that they used for fishing, and a room in the eaves which provided very basic accommodation. They'd had to take sleeping bags and a cooking stove.

Robyn recalled that trip in the car with Duncan to the

boathouse. She'd been surprised to hear that, despite the very basic accommodation, David had obviously loved those trips so much that he'd gone ahead and bought it. Somehow, Robyn hadn't been able to imagine David living in an old, rundown boathouse. And she'd been right. He'd had the place demolished and a modern, architecturally designed boathouse built in its place, with some olde-worlde charm added inside, including faux beams and exposed brickwork.

'There – can you see it, Judith? Look, through the trees.'

Judith turned her head to look to her right, where they could just catch a glimpse of a pitched, tiled roof with a chimney. A few minutes later, they rounded a bend in the road. They could see the boathouse clearly now.

Judith remarked, 'It doesn't look like a boathouse. It looks like a house.'

Robyn smiled. 'That's exactly what I said when I first saw it.'

David glanced at Judith. 'The back of the house fronts the loch. I've got a jetty and a small rowing boat.'

Robyn added, 'There are double doors from the lounge upstairs on to a wooden balcony with fantastic views. You'll love it.' Robyn felt a little bit as though she was selling the place, especially as Judith wasn't exactly oohing and ahhing about the house. In fact, she'd said very little on the journey. 'You know, David proposed to me on that balcony. It was very romantic.'

'That's nice,' Judith commented.

Robyn frowned. She had expected Judith to ask her if they'd set the date for her wedding and to say that she'd put the date in her diary. They hadn't set a date, but during her week off, Robyn had started the planning side. When they'd stopped in Aviemore on Saturday morning to get a stamp before returning to the boathouse for their week's holiday, David had nipped out of the post-office while she was in the queue, saying he'd meet her back at the car. When she'd posted her letter, she'd returned to the car to find David sitting there grinning. He'd had something in a bag on his lap. He'd been shopping. Robyn had recognised the motif on the plastic bag. He'd been into the local paper shop which sold newspapers, birthday cards and the like.

He'd passed her the bag, saying, 'I thought this might come in handy.'

Robyn couldn't believe it when she'd looked inside. It was a gorgeous wedding planner book. She'd flung her arms around him and said she couldn't wait to get started.

Robyn would have liked to show Judith her wedding planner, and thought that perhaps her stepmum would enjoy helping her with some more planning during her stay. Robyn frowned. She didn't get the impression Judith would be that enthusiastic to help her. In fact, she didn't appear enthusiastic about anything so far.

Robyn's shoulders slumped. She'd really thought that Judith would be happy for her. She'd told Judith in her letter that she was engaged and had planned to show her the engagement ring when she met her at the airport. She was still waiting for Judith to congratulate her on her engagement, and ask her more about it; how she'd met David – that sort of thing. But Judith hadn't mentioned it at all.

As they approached the end of the drive, and David pulled up outside the boathouse, Robyn frowned. This reunion wasn't really turning out as she had hoped.

She looked up at the boathouse as she exited the car and thought that perhaps she was being selfish. Judith must still be getting over the shock of the revelations about Robyn's life. She hadn't exactly had much of a chance for it all to sink in – that her stepdaughter was no longer at college, but was getting married instead, and was running a successful business.

Robyn got out of the car, feeling a lot more positive at the thought that she just had to give Judith time. She still thought it was a bit unfortunate that she'd arrived on the day of the party, so they wouldn't be spending an awful lot of time together before everyone arrived. She looked at her watch. Gayle would be arriving soon to do Judith's hair. At least they could all go and sit on the balcony for a cup of coffee after she'd shown her around. And hopefully Judith would spend the following week with them.

Robyn realised that although she'd been to two hypnotherapy sessions, and Marnie had been quite positive that she felt they were making progress, and Robyn might turn a corner soon, her memories were still evading her. This was her opportunity to get to know her stepmum all over again. Perhaps that wasn't a bad thing. It didn't sound as though they'd got on in the past. Robyn was still intent on changing that.

34

'Come on, let me show you around,' said Robyn, racing ahead to the door and quickly punching in the key code for the alarm.

Judith came up behind her. 'What are you doing?'

'Just switching off the alarm.'

'Why do you need a house alarm all the way out here?'

Robyn pursed her lips. She did not want to talk about the reason, especially as David had no clue that Duncan had told her about the burglary.

She turned around, smiling at Judith, and shrugged. 'I don't know,' she said, and left it at that.

David followed them into the house, carrying Judith's luggage.

Robyn was just saying to Judith, 'Let me show you around,' when Judith rushed into the kitchen before Robyn even had a chance to start the grand tour. Judith then reached for the study door.

'Wait – I didn't tell you about—'

Too late. Judith had already opened the study door, only to be met by an excited beagle jumping up at her.

'Percy – down!' Robyn had left Percy in the study with his dog bed, toys, and a chew, and with the door shut, so that he didn't get under their feet when Judith first arrived. She had decided not to mention that she had a dog until they arrived home.

She'd wanted to take Percy with them to the airport, but hadn't wanted to leave him in the car on such a warm day while they met Judith in the airport terminal. The only option had been to leave Percy at home alone. Robyn knew they'd only be gone three hours. She wouldn't have left him any longer than that.

'Sorry, Judith. I hope you don't mind dogs. I should have told you about—'

Judith walked into the study, ignoring the dog at her heels, before Robyn had even finished what she was saying.

When Judith reappeared, David said, 'I'll take your suitcase up to one of the bedrooms.' He was just about to take the stairs when Judith pushed past him and took the stairs two at a time.

Robyn and David stood at the foot of the stairs and exchanged a look of surprise.

Even Percy sensed something was amiss. He stood beside Robyn and David, looking up the stairs, whining.

Robyn said, 'What's with her?'

David replied, 'Guess she's eager to see the place.'

Robyn smiled. 'Yes, I guess she is.' Robyn gave Percy a reassuring pat on the head before starting up the stairs. When she got to the lounge on the next floor, with the log burner, exposed brickwork, faux beams, and the gorgeous view out of the double doors to the loch, she presumed that was where she'd find Judith, keen to get out on the balcony and soak up the amazing views.

Robyn stopped in the lounge with Percy at her heels. The patio doors leading out to the balcony were still shut. 'Judith?'

Percy ran out of the lounge and stopped at the foot of the next flight of stairs up to the bedrooms.

Robyn followed Percy and met David on the landing, about to take Judith's case up the next flight. She said, 'I think Judith is upstairs.'

'All right. She can choose one of the spare bedrooms.'

Robyn leaned in and whispered, 'I wanted to show her the view from the balcony.'

'There will be plenty of time for that.' David glanced up the stairs. 'Perhaps she wants to unpack first, and get settled in.'

Robyn nodded. 'Of course.' She hadn't thought of that. 'Will you tell her that I'll be in the kitchen. I need to get the dinner on …' Robyn was keeping an eye on the time. She'd already prepared a homemade lasagne – she just needed to put it in the oven to bake, and then make up a rocket salad, and some homemade skin-on chips.

She'd debated what to cook for the party. She'd wanted a sit-down meal, and had come up with so many different recipes online, she didn't know what to choose. But whether she could pull off the ambitious recipes or even find all the ingredients in the local shops in Aviemore, she had no clue.

David told her not to make a rod for her own back, and to make something easy but tasty. He'd suggested Italian. She had settled on lasagne – one meat-based and one vegetarian. Robyn had also prepared a large pizza, buying the pizza base and adding her own toppings. She knew Annie and Joe's little girl, Evie, loved pizza. Although she'd be the only child at the party, and wouldn't eat a massive pizza all to herself, Robyn reckoned that a few of the adults might help themselves to a slice too. It would be a strange combination with lasagne, but Robyn didn't care. She thought of the pizza, ready to go in the oven about ten or so minutes before people arrived, and decided she'd definitely help herself to a slice.

'Will you tell Judith I'll put the kettle on, so when she's ready we can all have a cuppa together before Gayle arrives?'

'Will do!'

Robyn watched David hoist the old suitcase up the stairs. She looked at Percy, who was sitting by her feet. 'Come on, let's go downstairs and leave Judith to her unpacking.'

Percy woofed.

Robyn frowned at him and gently tapped his nose. 'Quiet! Remember – indoor voices. We talked about this.'

Percy licked her pointy finger.

'Well, I talked about it, and you just looked up at me with those adorable eyes, didn't you?' Robyn smiled and gave him a fuss, before heading downstairs. She heard Percy's paws on the open-tread stairs as he followed her.

In the kitchen, Robyn opened the enormous American-style fridge and got out two large Pyrex dishes containing the pre-prepared lasagne. It wouldn't take long to heat up in the oven.

The pizza was on a tray on the worktop near the oven and the chips were ready to be cooked. Next, she got out the rocket salad, some tomatoes, a cucumber, and a jar of the French dressing. She decided not to add the French dressing to the salad, but leave the jar on the table so that her guests could help themselves.

She turned around with the jar and looked at the table she'd set up with a tablecloth and place settings. It was a large table, which was just as well. She'd only invited close friends, but there would be eleven, without herself, David and Judith. Fourteen people at the meal. She'd had to jig around the place settings to fit everyone around the table. And then David had let her in on a little secret. He hadn't even planned to bring up that he'd invited a surprise guest until he'd seen her doing the place settings at the table. But it wasn't just one extra guest – it was three!

One was a child, so Robyn had brought in the small garden table for two, with two chairs, and put that in the corner, where Evie could sit with whoever was coming and hopefully make friends. She could just about squeeze in two more people at the table.

Robyn had tried to find out who the surprise guests were, but David would not tell. She had told him in the past that she didn't like surprises, but he had assured her that she'd like this one. Still, it was on Robyn's mind. She didn't know all David's friends, and supposed that perhaps it was an old friend from high school, along with a partner and child.

Robyn had even written out little cards for the table so that everyone knew where they were sitting. She thought that although it was a bit formal, it was a nice touch, and saved any awkward moments if people had a preference about whom they were sitting with.

She looked around the table and checked the seating arrangement for the umpteenth time. Joe and Annie would be seated together. Next to them would be Duncan and Alec, who planned to come straight after work in Duncan's van. Alec would be off to university in September. Robyn would miss him. He hadn't long started work in Duncan's store part-time while he was studying for his A-Levels. Robyn had found out that Duncan really didn't have the money to pay for him, but he'd hired him on the spot when his mother had said she desperately needed the money. It didn't take long for Robyn to realise that underneath Duncan's gruff, no-nonsense, and sometimes quite short-tempered exterior, there was a caring, gentle soul. If only he'd mellow and let people see that part of his nature once in a while.

She'd put her friend Melissa and her partner Brodie on that side of the table too, next to Duncan. Brodie now ran Wilbur's Bookstore. She remembered Melissa and Brodie moving in together in the flat above the bookstore after they both graduated from university. They were now settled into their new home, and were engaged. Robyn wasn't surprised. Melissa had confided that she'd set her heart on marrying Brodie before they'd even started dating.

Gayle, Doris, Marty and Nick, along with Judith, would be sitting together on the other side of the table. David would be at one end of the table, and she would be at the other, with Judith sitting to her right. She'd just squeezed in the two other surprise adult guests, one on either side of the table down at David's end. She'd placed them there because David knew them, with the letter 'A' on the cards for 'anonymous'. She had also invited Rose and George, the couple who lived on the new-build estate where Nick worked. They had been the first people to hire her services as an interior designer and were good friends. They'd passed her name on to all their new friends who'd moved on to the development.

She had been disappointed, but not surprised, when they'd sent their apologies – they'd already had a prior engagement. They were away with friends on a short break to Edinburgh to celebrate Rose's birthday. Apparently they were travelling back late that evening.

When Robyn had heard, she'd made a mental note. While she'd been planning for their wedding, she had already been thinking of where they might like to spend their honeymoon. Although it was very tempting to stay right where they were – the Cairngorms had everything they could possibly want for a fabulous holiday – they had their whole lives together to explore this glorious part of the world and make special memories in the place they called home. But Robyn also fancied making some special memories in another lovely part of Scotland, and Edinburgh sounded just the place. She was looking forward to catching up with Rose and George on their return and hearing all about their trip.

She was seeing them tomorrow afternoon. Although George and Rose had to miss her party, George had more than made up for it by booking something for Robyn which she'd always wanted to do. Robyn and David would be joining Rose and George for a special treat – afternoon tea on a steam train from Aviemore as it meandered through the breathtaking Scottish countryside.

Robyn returned her attention to the place settings. Melissa and Brodie were nearest to Robyn, on her left. She'd purposely put them there, as far away from David as she could. Robyn wondered if she had done the right thing by inviting Melissa.

They'd first met in the public library and had become friends. Robyn had gone there to see if she could find any old newspaper articles about David and the accident that had left him with an injured knee and had ruined his promising ice hockey career. He'd refused to talk about it, so she'd thought she'd try and find out for herself. She'd met Melissa, a law undergraduate, who had been working in the public library during her holidays.

Robyn had found out a lot more than she'd bargained for. She'd assumed he'd had an accident on the ice during a hockey game, and that was how he'd injured his knee. But that hadn't been it at all. There had been a burglary at Duncan's store. David had been on a night out with friends when he'd noticed a light in his father's shop and had found himself face-to-face with two intruders, who were robbing the cash till. One had been armed.

According to the reporter, a scuffle had ensued. David had been shot, but he'd managed to get hold of the gun and it had fired, shooting dead one of the intruders. He'd been arrested and charged, but had successfully pleaded self-defence.

As a law student, Melissa had been intrigued by the story that Robyn had uncovered. Things like that didn't happen in the small town of Aviemore. It was quite unheard of. Melissa had offered to look into it. Robyn had readily agreed. But then she'd started to get cold feet over what exactly Melissa might uncover.

Robyn's fears weren't unfounded after a conversation with David's sister-in-law, Annie. Robyn had discovered that it wasn't actually David who had shot the intruder, but Annie. She'd been on a rare night out with friends when they too had passed Duncan's store and had noticed the light. She'd ventured inside to discover David bleeding from a gunshot wound, and surprised the burglars, one of whom had dropped the gun they were carrying. Annie had picked it up and fired the gun. The question was: why had David lied to the police?

It was obvious. David was protecting his sister-in-law. She was a mother of a small child, his niece. She couldn't go to prison. So David had stepped up, and lied to the police that he had fired the gun when he had not. He'd risked a conviction and a prison sentence for Annie. Luckily, neither of those things had happened. David's brother, Joe, was none the wiser as to what had really happened that night.

And neither was Melissa. Not yet, anyway. But worryingly, when she'd asked Melissa to drop it, she'd suspected she would not, especially when it had turned out that the small law firm in Aviemore she'd started working for as a trainee solicitor after graduation might have handled David's case. Robyn didn't know for sure. All she knew was that when she'd let slip to him that she knew what had happened, David had told her – I was charged with manslaughter, but a very, very good lawyer got me off – self-defence. It had sounded as though it was a local firm of solicitors.

Robyn remembered her response. She'd been so relieved. She'd then asked him if that had been the end of it.

He'd hesitated before answering, saying yeah, of course, but avoiding eye contact. Although she'd said to him she didn't want any more secrets between them, she still had a strong suspicion that there was more to the story – something even Annie didn't know about.

And now Robyn had been worried that if Melissa was working for the same local firm, she now had access to those files, and could look through past cases.

Robyn hoped she didn't look at David's. It was still playing on Robyn's mind that there was something David hadn't told her. Whatever it was, she didn't want Melissa to find out first.

Robyn stared at the place-setting with Melissa's name on. She made a mental note to ask her not to bring up anything to do with the robbery at the party – especially not in front of David, who had no clue she'd looked into the circumstances surrounding his so-called accident. She did not want anything ruining the lovely meal she was having with friends, and the little party on the lawn by the loch afterwards.

'Robyn!' David called out. 'Are you making a cup of tea?'

Robyn switched on the cooker and stepped out of the kitchen, calling up the stairs, 'I'm doing it now.'

'Good, because Judith has come over a little faint.'

'What?' Robyn ran up the stairs to find Judith sitting on an armchair in the lounge, David fanning her with an old newspaper.

'What happened?' Robyn ran over and knelt down beside her. 'Are you all right?'

David said, 'I suspect it's been rather a long day, and I bet the food on the plane was rubbish.'

'There wasn't any food on the plane,' said Judith, gulping down air.

'No food? Did you have lunch?' asked Robyn.

Judith shook her head, staring at her.

'Well, that's it then,' said David confidently. 'What you need, Judith, is a hearty meal.'

Robyn ran downstairs as soon as she heard the kettle boil. A moment later she reappeared, carefully carrying a steaming mug of sweet tea across the lounge to where Judith was sitting.

Percy was being very good and had retreated to his dog bed to one side of the log burner.

Robyn handed her the tea. 'Sip this. It will make you feel better.' Robyn hoped it would. The last thing she wanted was for Judith to miss the party, and meeting all her friends. Thinking of meeting friends, Gayle would be arriving any minute to do Judith's hair. Surely, Judith wouldn't be up for that. Robyn said as much.

Judith lowered the mug. 'You're right – I'm not up for that.'

Robyn got her phone out from the back pocket of her jeans. 'I'd better let her know that you won't be—'

Robyn halted at the sound of a car turning up in the driveway. 'Oh, dear. I think that's her.'

Judith sat up. 'I want to meet her.'

Robyn frowned. 'I thought you said you didn't feel up to having your hair done?'

'Never mind that,' said Judith. 'I need to speak to her.'

Robyn stared at her. 'Well, all right. I'll go and answer the door.'

On her way out of the room, Robyn motioned for David to come with her.

'What did she mean, she needs to speak to her?' Robyn asked David in a hushed voice as they walked down the stairs.

'She just wants to meet your friends. I mean, I reckon she's just concerned about you. That's probably why she had a funny turn. It's a lot to take in. This is all completely new; not what she was expecting. She doesn't know us from Adam, does she?'

'Speak for yourself,' Robyn chided as she walked over to the front door.

He laughed. 'Yeah, you know what I mean. You told her you were living with Gayle for quite some time. She obviously wants to meet her, probably to thank her for taking you in.'

'Oh, right. I hadn't thought of that.'

'And besides, isn't it nice she wants to meet your friends? I bet she can't wait to meet everyone else. She'll feel better when she realises you're okay. You've got lovely friends, all looking out for you.'

Robyn brightened. 'You're right. I just hope she's going to be up to meeting everybody.'

David put a reassuring hand on her shoulder as she opened the front door. 'I'm sure she will be. Look how enthusiastic she is to meet Gayle.'

'Hi, Gayle.' Robyn stepped into Gayle's embrace. She was holding Doris's hand. Robyn gave Doris a hug too. Gayle handed David a bottle of something bubbly, and Robyn a large bunch of flowers.

Robyn said, 'Oh, you shouldn't have.'

Gayle smiled. 'Let me fetch my bag.'

'Oh, you needn't do that. Sorry, change of plan. Judith came over a little faint. She's not up to having her hair done. I was just going to phone you, and let you know, when I heard you arrive.'

'Do you need me to take a look at her, put my nurse's hat on?'

'No, not at all. We think it's all been a bit overwhelming for her.'

'Yes, that makes sense.'

'And she hasn't had anything to eat since breakfast, by the sound of it,' added David.

Robyn looked at David and nodded. She turned to Gayle. 'But she wants to meet you, have a chat. Is that okay? Sorry, you've come earlier than you needed to.'

'That's all right, Robyn. I'm looking forward to meeting your stepmum. It will give us a chance to get to know one another before everyone arrives.'

Robyn smiled. 'I'll make you and Doris a cuppa. Go right upstairs.'

David followed Robyn into the kitchen. 'There, you see? There's nothing to worry about.'

Robyn took two mugs out of the kitchen cupboard. It was still playing on her mind how strangely Judith had been acting since she'd arrived – and why did she *need* to speak to Gayle?

35

'Oh, you should see what Robyn's done with the place. I couldn't have set up Lark Lodge as a guesthouse if it hadn't been for Robyn redecorating the house. You'll have to come round and visit ...'

Robyn was just walking up the stairs to let them know it wouldn't be long until dinner was ready. The other guests would be arriving very soon. She smiled when she heard Gayle chatting. It sounded as though she and Judith were getting along.

She was going to pop her head in the lounge, but changed her mind. She didn't want to interrupt the conversation, and besides, they'd hear the doorbell soon enough.

Robyn returned to the kitchen. She was just putting on some oven gloves to check the lasagne when she heard Gayle. 'I'm just going to spend a penny.'

There was a bathroom on the top floor with the three bedrooms, and a cloakroom on the ground floor with a sink and loo across the hall from the study. She heard Gayle walking down the stairs.

Robyn checked the lasagne and had just taken off her oven gloves when Gayle walked out of the loo. Robyn walked over to the door before she headed upstairs. 'Sounds as though you two are getting along.' Gayle didn't offer up the ready smile she was expecting at that comment. 'What is it, Gayle?'

'Oh, it's nothing … really.'

Robyn frowned. That meant it was something. Robyn grasped her hand and pulled her into the kitchen, closing the door behind them. 'What is it?'

Gayle breathed a sigh. 'It's probably just me reading too much into things.'

'What do you mean?'

'Well, she's been asking some odd questions.'

Robyn sighed. 'She's been acting a little … odd since we arrived here. What's sort of questions?'

'Robyn, your guests are going to be arriving any minute. Really, it's so silly.'

Now Robyn was getting worried. Why was Gayle being evasive? 'Gayle, please tell me.'

Gayle sighed. 'She said that if you've lost your memory, how do you know that you're …'

'I'm …?'

'Well, that you're … you.'

Robyn was taken aback. 'What sort of question is that?'

'Well, exactly. I mean I told you it was so silly. You were driving your car. The police traced your licence through the DVLA.'

'Did you tell her that?'

'Well, of course.'

Robyn stared at her. 'I don't get why she would ask such a thing.'

Gayle turned her head at the sound of a convoy of cars turning up outside the house. 'By the sound of it, everyone has arrived.'

They both heard the clunk of several car doors slamming shut, quickly followed by the doorbell.

Percy started barking.

'I'll answer that,' David said, poking his head into the kitchen on the way to the front door.

'Don't look so worried.' Gayle put a gentle hand on Robyn's arm. 'Look, I'd ignore it. Judith has clearly had a bit of a turn. It's been a long day for her. Don't forget, she's just got off a flight, returning from abroad. This all must have been quite a shock – your new life. She's just got to get her head around it.'

Robyn smiled. 'You're right.'

'Why don't I go and fetch Judith?'

Robyn nodded.

'Robyn!' Evie came running into the kitchen, carrying a present.

She grinned. 'Hey, what's this?' she said, crouching down.

Percy bounded over and sniffed the wrapping paper.

Evie moved the dog's muzzle away from her present. 'This is not for you, Percy.'

Robyn smiled. Evie had come over during her week off with Annie to meet Percy, and Annie had given Robyn an update on how things were going in the shop, much to David's annoyance.

'Oh, you didn't have to bring a present.'

'But I wanted to. It's an engagement present.'

'That is so sweet of you, Evie.'

'Mummy helped me choose it.'

Five minutes later, there was a crowd of people in the kitchen, all talking at once and handing Robyn more presents. They started to take their seats around the table. 'Fancy,' said Duncan when he picked up the little card with his name on. 'I feel as though I've just stepped into an episode of Downton Abbey. I hope this is silver service and I'm going to have my own personal waiter,' he joked.

Robyn rolled her eyes at him as he guffawed and took his seat next to Alec. Joe and Annie pulled out a chair and were joined by Melissa and Brodie, all taking their seats on one side of the table.

Marty and Nick sat down the other side of the table, joined by Gayle and Doris. Judith appeared in the doorway, looking a bit overwhelmed.

Robyn immediately stepped forward. 'Judith, come and sit here.' She showed her the seat next to Gayle. That left four empty chairs – hers and David's at either end of the table, and two for the mystery guests.

'Oh, Evie, darling,' said Robyn, 'You're sitting at this little table just over here.'

'But I don't want to sit on my own.'

Robyn glanced at David.

He looked at his watch. 'I'm sure they're going to be here any minute.'

'Who?' said Duncan.

Robyn replied, 'Apparently we have three mystery guests.' She turned to Evie. 'I heard one of them is a little girl not much older than you.'

'Really?'

'Yes, would you like to make a new friend?'

Evie shook her head up and down.

'Great.'

Evie took her place at the little table while David looked out of the kitchen window and frowned.

Robyn joined him while everyone chatted at the table. 'Well, where are they?'

'I don't know.' He turned around. 'Gayle, they definitely said they're coming?'

Robyn whirled around. 'You're in on this?'

Gayle grinned. She looked at David. 'They're guests at Lark Lodge. They haven't long arrived. I was going to pick them up at the train station this afternoon, but they'd managed to hire a car in Aviemore. They'd just settled into their rooms, but left before me. I think they were quickly stopping off in Aviemore. I suspect they're buying Robyn a present.'

'Wait – did you just say they are guests at Lark Lodge?'

Gayle nodded.

'Who are they?'

'You'll see!'

Robyn turned to Marty and Nick, who were avoiding her gaze. 'You two know too, don't you?' Robyn rolled her eyes. It was a stupid question. Of course they did. They lived there too.

At that moment, another car turned up outside the house.

David grinned. 'They're here.'

Everybody got out of their seats.

Gayle said, 'Hey, everyone stay seated. You'll see who it is soon enough.'

Robyn held back, lingering in the kitchen. She did not like surprises.

Gayle guessed what she was thinking. 'Robyn, you'll love this surprise.'

She heard David answer the door. 'Hey, so glad you could make it.'

She heard the front door close. Then a couple with a child appeared in the kitchen doorway.

Behind them, David said, 'I'd like you all to meet Faye Ames, her daughter, Natasha, and their good friend, Mr Jake Campbell-Ross.'

There were gasps from the people in the kitchen. They were all delighted to meet an actual Ross in the flesh. All of them apart from one. 'Oh, my god,' said Robyn.

36

Robyn slunk into the background as everyone got out of their seats – everyone apart from Judith, who probably had no idea who Jake Campbell-Ross was. They all gathered around, welcoming the three new guests, eager to speak to Jake Campbell-Ross and shake his hand. One of the Rosses.

Robyn glared at David, who was looking very pleased with himself as he welcomed the mystery guests and thanked them for coming to his humble abode. Robyn rolled her eyes when she heard him say that, like he was in the presence of a celebrity, or royalty. Annie had been right, back when Robyn had thought she was meeting a Ross at The Lake House after finding out she had that commission, when she'd told her not to be intimidated by their wealth. It hadn't actually been their wealth that she had been concerned about, but the fact that she'd plagiarised those designs in the old doll's house in the basement of The Lake House and had recreated them in Lark Lodge.

She stared at Jake Campbell-Ross, who was busy chatting and shaking hands with the other guests, and thought that he must know what she'd done. He'd been in Lark Lodge. This was just what she had been afraid of. Was she in trouble? She guessed she was about to find out. Any minute, David was going to introduce Jake to her.

Robyn caught the time on the clock on the wall. The lasagne and pizza were ready. She had to get them out of the oven.

She was about to put on her oven gloves when she saw the large bowl with the side salad sitting on the worktop. Robyn picked it up off the counter to put it on the table. She turned around and was surprised to find Judith standing directly in front of her; clearly she wasn't interested in talking to Mr Campbell-Ross either.

'Oh, that was good timing. Could you just put this on the table?' Robyn held out the salad bowl.

Judith's arms remained resolutely by her sides. She opened her mouth to speak but it seemed to take her several seconds longer to formulate the words. Finally, she said, 'What do you want?' Her voice was flat, toneless, oddly devoid of emotion, as though she were a robot.

Robyn glanced at the other guests, who were still gathered around Jake. Evie had made a new friend. They were both seated at their little table, chatting. Robyn looked at Judith. 'If you could just take this and put it—'

She was cut off in mid-sentence by that strangely toneless voice again. 'Whatever you want, you can have,' she said. 'Anything.' Her eyes pleading. 'Just stop.'

'I don't …'

'I just want her back.' Her voice was hushed, but full of emotion this time. 'I played along with your little game at the airport, thinking, isn't this just like Robyn? Never straightforward.'

Robyn knitted her brow. Judith's behaviour was getting even stranger. She said, 'Mum – what's wrong?'

She stepped back. 'Stop it,' her voice was no longer hushed.

Robyn stopped where she was, wondering what had happened, what had got into her. She looked over at the others. Gayle was looking her way.

'Stop it. Just stop it. I've kept up the charade, but I can't stand it another minute.' Her voice grew louder as Robyn grew more concerned for her stepmother's wellbeing. Was she having a breakdown?

'Just tell me what you want!' she demanded. 'I thought I knew what your game was. I thought you were Robyn's friend, and she'd asked you to do this, to play some silly prank on me, and I'd arrive here, and she'd be here.'

'What are you talking about?'

This time she yelled, 'Where is my stepdaughter?'

The room suddenly fell silent. Everyone was looking her way. Worse still, so was Mr Campbell-Ross. Then the room started to spin. Robyn remembered the feeling from when she was a child. It was a game she had played, spinning around and around as fast as she could with her arms outstretched like a spinning top. She was with another child, younger than her. They were spinning together. Then, when she stopped, suddenly the ground violently tilted until she couldn't keep her balance and she fell, clinging to the floor for dear life.

She faintly heard the sound of a bowl hit the floor and shatter. Distant voices were calling her name. The last thing she heard quite clearly was Judith saying she was going to call the police.

❖

Someone was holding Robyn's hands. She opened her eyes. Gayle was beside her, patting her hand. Annie was holding a glass of water to her lips. When she had sufficiently gathered her senses, she realised that David must be kneeling on the floor, her head in his lap, the palm of his hand resting gently on her forehead.

She stared up at David. 'What happened?'

'You fainted,' said David with concern.

'Help me up.'

'Perhaps you should just lie still,' David began, but Robyn was already trying to stand, even though her legs felt like jelly. She felt David's hands under her arms as he lifted her to her feet.

'God, I don't know what came over me. Oh no! I dropped the salad.'

'Robyn, we need to talk,' said David with a note of urgency in his voice.

She glanced at her friends, feeling embarrassed. What would everyone think? But nobody was looking at her. Robyn followed their gaze to Judith, who was standing in the hallway, speaking on her mobile.

David turned to his brother. 'Joe, why didn't you stop her? You're the police, for god's sake. She's wasting their time.'

'What do you want me to do – arrest Robyn?'

'No, I meant stop Judith making that call!'

'And how do you propose I do that? Confiscate her phone?'

'Well – yeah.'

Judith lowered her phone and turned around, looking into the kitchen. 'They'll be right over; I've told them everything,' she said angrily.

'Who'll be right over?' Robyn looked from Annie to Gayle, still too embarrassed to look at anybody else in that kitchen. She knew all her guests who'd been seated around the table were still in the kitchen, most likely looking her way. She saw Judith leave the doorway.

Robyn called out, 'Judith?'

'I'm waiting outside for them to arrive.'

The next thing she heard was the front door slam shut.

Annie turned to her husband. 'Joe, you need to go and speak to her, or phone your colleagues, and tell them it's going to be a wasted trip – probably both.'

David took Robyn's hand. 'Robyn, I think your stepmother isn't quite well.'

David told Robyn what Judith had been saying to them shortly after Robyn had fainted, while they were trying to bring her round.

'She says it's a conspiracy. We're all in on it, and she just wants to know what we want, and if we won't tell her then we can tell the police.' David paused before whispering, 'I wish you could have warned me that she had a screw loose, but obviously you couldn't because you can't remember.'

Robyn stared at him wide-eyed. 'Oh god, I've invited a nutter into our lives.'

'Yeah, looks like. But you weren't to know. I wasn't expecting an easy ride from the mother-in-law but this kind of takes the biscuit, don't you think?'

'Are you seriously making a joke right now?' Robyn elbowed him in the ribs. 'This isn't funny. Something's wrong.' Robyn was trying to remember what Judith had been saying to her when she had fainted.

'Just don't think about it.' He looked over at his brother. 'Joe, can you step outside and sort this out?'

Annie pushed Joe towards the door. 'Did you hear your brother?'

Joe looked at the oven. 'Something smells delicious. I didn't want to miss my meal.'

David said, 'We'll leave some warm in the oven. Now go, sort this out will you before things get really out of hand and she ruins our party.'

Joe made for the door.

Annie clapped her hands. 'Right, folks – let's eat.'

Gayle asked Robyn if she wanted to cancel the party.

David said, 'I don't know what her agenda is, but don't let her ruin our evening, Robyn.'

Robyn nodded. 'I won't.'

As they took their seats at the table, with her friends asking her if she was all right, Annie and Gayle got the food out of the oven, which fortunately was not as overdone as Robyn had feared.

They'd just put the large casserole dishes full of lasagne, along with the large pizza, on the table when a car turned up outside.

David glanced out of the kitchen window. 'Oh, thank god. The police have come to rescue us from this mad woman. I hope Joe makes sure they take her down to the station for wasting police time and find out what her game is.'

Robyn had just picked up a plate, about to dish up the first slice of lasagne and pass it around the table, when Judith burst into the house.

Robyn froze. David turned in his seat and looked at his brother, who was following in Judith's wake. 'Seriously, Joe. I thought you were sorting this out?'

One of Joe's colleagues stepped into the kitchen, looking apologetic.

'It's them!' Judith pointed into the room. 'I'm telling you, they've done something with my stepdaughter. It's a conspiracy.'

'Hi, Sean,' said Annie to the familiar face of her husband's colleague.

'Aren't you going to arrest them?' Judith's voice was shrill.

'What for?' said Sean. 'A conspiracy to make friends with Robyn?' He winked at the group.

Judith glared at the officer. 'You're not listening to me. That woman there,' she pointed at Robyn, 'who claims she's lost her memory—'

'Now, look here,' David said, stepping forward, 'don't call Robyn that woman, and she has lost her memory.'

'That woman,' continued Judith, 'is not my stepdaughter.'

Gayle said, 'I don't know what your game is, Judith. We know who she is.'

'Really? Why don't you enlighten me, then? Because she is not Robyn Parker.'

David glared at her. 'Are you insane? You didn't say this when we picked you up from the airport. You're jealous of her new life. I bet you've never got on with your stepdaughter, and you've come to ruin it for her. Well, it's not going to work.' David turned to Sean. 'She didn't say any of this earlier. She was perfectly fine when we greeted her at the airport and on the way back to the boathouse.'

Robyn stared at Judith. She hadn't been perfectly fine. Robyn had caught her in the mirror at the beauty counter in the airport throwing her a strange look, and she'd been oddly quiet on the journey to the boathouse. Then, when they'd arrived, she'd rushed around the boathouse, looking in all the rooms as though she was … Robyn swallowed … looking for someone.

Judith turned to David. 'I told her, before she conveniently fainted, to stop.'

David shook his head. 'I don't understand – stop what?'

'This charade. I want her back. I told her,' she pointed at Robyn, 'and I'm telling you, that I played along with your little game at the airport, thinking isn't this just like Robyn? Never straightforward. I thought I knew what your game was. You were her new friends—'

'But we are her new friends …'

Judith rigorously shook her head. 'I thought she'd asked you all to play some silly prank on me, and when I arrived I'd find her here, at the boathouse.'

Robyn glanced over at David. Their eyes locked. He'd seen it too, her rushing around the place, frantically looking in every room.

Judith opened her handbag.

Sean stepped forward and said, 'What are you doing, Judith?' as she put her hand in her bag. 'What have you got in the bag, Judith?'

Judith's hand emerged from her handbag with her purse. She got out a small photo, and showed it to the officer.

Sean took a cursory glance. 'Very nice. Now, are you going to join these good people for their meal, or do I need to arrest you for wasting police—?'

'This photo was taken on the university campus before I left on my travels.'

'That's nice,' said Sean, glancing over at Joe and David, and shrugging.

'And this person next to me,' said Judith, pointing at the photo, 'is my stepdaughter – Robyn Parker.'

That got Sean's attention. 'Let me see that.'

Judith handed him the photo and stood there, arms folded, glaring at everyone in the room, her eyes eventually settling on one person in particular.

Robyn stood there, her heart pounding.

Sean's expression changed. Gone was the ready smile. In its

place was an officer on call. He looked at Judith. 'Can I keep hold of this?'

'Be my guest,' Judith said smugly. 'Are you going to arrest her now?'

Joe said, 'Let me see that photo.'

Sean passed Joe the photo.

'Joe?' David said, looking across at his brother.

Joe passed the photo back to Sean without a word, but nodded at his colleague.

Robyn gulped as the police officer walked over to her. 'I need you to come with me,' he said flatly.

No sooner had he spoken the words than an uproar ensued. Everybody wanted to know why she was being taken to the police station. Sean held up his hands for them to quieten down. 'I'm sorry to tell you that this woman is not Robyn Parker.'

There were gasps around the table.

'Come with me, please.'

'But I … I am Robyn!'

'No, you're not.'

Robyn looked around the table. Everyone was staring at her, but nobody made a move to stop the officer arresting her.

She looked at David. 'David …?'

He pursed his lips and looked at his brother.

She followed his gaze. 'Joe …? Tell him there's been a mistake.'

Joe heaved a sigh. 'There's been a mistake all right. Who are you – really?'

'I … I'm Robyn Parker.'

'No, you're not,' said Judith adamantly.

'But … but if I'm not Robyn, then who am I?' She searched the faces of the people sitting at the table, her friends – or they had been, only a moment earlier.

'Suppose you tell us,' said Sean.

'But … but I can't remember.' She looked around the table. 'You do believe me, don't you?' But she could tell by their expressions that they all thought she'd deceived them. All apart from the mystery guests.

Jake Campbell-Ross suddenly stood up.

Robyn looked at him in surprise. 'Do you know me?'

He shook his head. 'I'm sorry, I do not. I've never set eyes on you before today. Do you know my wife?'

'Your wife?'

'Eleanor Campbell-Ross. Have you ever met her?'

'I told you. I told all of you, I don't remember anything.'

'Are you sure about that?' he asked.

As Sean approached her, that episode came to mind, the memory she'd had when she'd visited Wilbur's Bookstore and had remembered sitting at the table in the window. She had been sitting with someone at that table – she was sure of it.

As she was led out of the kitchen, she glanced over her shoulder at Jake Campbell-Ross, who was staring at her intently. Had the person she'd been sitting with been Eleanor?

She overheard Judith saying, 'I can't stay here. I'm getting my bags and leaving.'

Gayle said, 'Where will you go? It's the summer. A lot of places are booked up.'

'Well, what do you suggest?'

'Come and stay with me at Lark Lodge.'

Robyn overheard that as she walked out of the door, feeling herself getting emotional over losing her friends and the life she thought she'd built. She turned to the officer as he led her out to the waiting police car. 'Can you tell me who I am?' she pleaded.

'Well, that's what I'm taking you to the station to find out.'

37

Robyn sat in the police station, at a desk opposite Joe's colleague, Sean, and nervously kneaded her hands, wondering what he'd find in their database. She was thinking of all that cash in the bottom of the rucksack. Oh, god! I'm a criminal on the run. It all made sense now. She'd burgled David's house, and then by a bizarre twist of fate, they had collided on the road as she was speeding out of Aviemore. And very soon all her new friends, whom she'd unintentionally deceived, would find out.

She looked at the police officer and thought that it would have been good if Joe had accompanied her in the police car. He was David's brother, and her friend. Or David himself could have run out of the house to go with her. She didn't know whether they would have been allowed, but as she sat there, feeling so very alone, she realised that it was a moot point. Not one of them had made a move to accompany her for moral support – not one.

She looked at Sean, searching through his database, her mind focusing on that rucksack full of money and the burglary at David's house on Christmas Day. She thought she knew exactly what had happened, and why she'd been on that snowy road, all alone, the previous Christmas. But that didn't explain how she had come to be in Robyn Parker's car with her suitcase. If she wasn't Robyn Parker – which clearly she was not – then who the hell was she, and why did she have Robyn's belongings, and her car?

'Hmm.'

Robyn looked at Sean wide-eyed as he turned away from his PC screen and looked at her.

She thought she was going to be sick. 'What is it?'

'Nothing – is what it is.'

'Pardon me?' Robyn stared at his computer. 'So, I'm not in your database?'

Sean sat back in his chair. 'No.'

Robyn looked at her hands. She could still see smudges of black on her fingertips where they'd taken her fingerprints. She hadn't wanted her mugshot taken either. It made her feel like a criminal. But they'd needed both to run checks on her identity and see if she came up in the police database.

She'd kept saying to him on the way in the police car that it wasn't what it looked like. She hadn't been impersonating Robyn Parker on purpose. It had been just as much of a shock to her that she wasn't who she thought she was as it had been for Judith – and everyone else in the room. She'd lost her memory in the accident. Dr Jamieson could vouch for that.

The problem was that although she'd had a bump on the head, and a mild concussion, Dr Jamieson had told her there was really nothing physically wrong with her. But how could she prove that she wasn't faking it?

'So, who am I?' She really hoped that he wasn't going to reply, *You tell me.*

Instead, he said, 'I've looked at the report of the car accident you were involved in on Christmas Day. You have no idea how you came to be in possession of Robyn's car?'

'I told you. I don't remember anything.' Robyn dropped her eyes from his gaze. She did remember two things: sitting in Wilbur's Bookstore with a young woman, and sitting in a car in the dark outside David's boathouse – neither of which she had any intention of sharing. She was not going to share the latter because of the money she'd found in the rucksack and the burglary at David's. The last thing she wanted to do was implicate herself in a crime. She was in enough trouble as it was. She was not going to share the former because she really couldn't see how it was relevant – sitting in Wilbur's Bookstore with a woman. She suddenly sucked in a breath. Was that Robyn she had been sitting with in Wilbur's Bookstore? The real Robyn? She remembered the sketch in Robyn's diary of two women sitting in the window. It was her and me, she thought. But if Robyn had let her borrow the car, why would she have left her suitcase in the car?

Robyn stared at Sean. There was only one logical explanation. She'd taken Robyn's car – stolen it. Oh, god … so I am a criminal!

'Are you all right?' Sean asked. 'You've gone awfully pale.'

'Have I?' she asked, feeling a little lightheaded.

'Let me get you some water.' He stood up and walked over to the water cooler. He'd just turned his back to her, about to pour her a glass, when he swiftly did an about-turn. 'I don't need to lock the door, do I?'

Her shoulders sagged. They were in a small interview room. She'd waived her right to free legal advice before being questioned. She didn't want to sit in a prison cell waiting for a lawyer to arrive. She just wanted to get on with finding out who the hell she was.

She glanced at the door. 'Where would I go?' She thought of Judith going back to Lark Lodge. Gayle had been quick to disown the fake Robyn, as, no doubt, had everyone else. She had absolutely nowhere to go. Until she found out who she was, she had nobody.

She looked at Sean. If it turned out she had broken the law, then she'd just have to face the consequences. All she wanted at that moment was to know her own name. 'Will you help me, Sean?' she pleaded as he handed her a paper cup of water.

'Yes. But you've got to help me.'

She frowned. 'I don't understand.'

'Where is Robyn Parker?'

'I … I don't know. I told you, I can't remember what I was doing on that road on Christmas Day. I woke up in hospital and didn't even know my name. The police did a DVLA search on the vehicle and assumed I was the owner of the car. And I believed them. I had no reason not to.'

Sean nodded. 'Yes, I know. As I said, I read the report.'

Robyn realised something just then. She wasn't in handcuffs, but she wasn't free to leave.

Sean leaned forward in his chair. 'We want to know your identity.'

'As do I!' And she knew just the person who might be able to find out. It didn't appear that the police were going to be much help. She just needed to contact the person she had in mind. 'I still get a phone call – don't I?' They'd already offered her a phone call, but she'd declined because she hadn't known who to call until that moment.

'Yes, you can make one phone call. May I suggest you consider who you choose to contact wisely.'

She looked at his earnest expression. 'What do you mean?'

'I would suggest contacting a lawyer.'

She smiled. 'That's exactly what I intend to do.' She wished she'd thought of it when they'd first asked her.

She sighed in relief when she got straight through to Melissa. She was nervous about making the call, thinking that Melissa wouldn't be the slightest bit interested as she would be thinking she'd been deceived. But on the contrary, Melissa was very worried about her and relieved she'd phoned her. Melissa was going to get straight on her case.

When she got off the phone, Sean was looking at her thoughtfully. He leaned forward in his chair. 'I do have an idea about how you might get your memories back – if you're up for it.'

38

She sat in the interview room, waiting to find out if Marnie would be prepared to see her at such short notice for another hypnotherapy session – and so late in the day, after office hours.

She'd been surprised by Sean's suggestion. She didn't think it would be something the police would entertain, but as Sean had said, he wanted to help her get her memories back.

While they waited for Marnie to pick up the message and phone back, she said, 'My friend, Gayle, suggested seeing a hypnotherapist too, but she was hopeful that seeing my stepmum would trigger my memories instead.'

Obviously that hadn't happened, so it was just as well she'd decided to start the therapy sessions beforehand. Under the circumstances, she couldn't imagine just walking into a stranger's office to attend her first session in her current circumstances. At least now she already knew Marnie, and what to expect. Who knew, perhaps today, if Marnie could see her, there might be the breakthrough she needed. Of course, that didn't help when she thought of all the wonderful friends she'd probably lost that day. She couldn't believe her fantastic week with David at the boathouse had culminated in this – the end of the amazing life they had been planning to have there.

'Except she's not your stepmother,' said Sean, interrupting her thoughts.

She looked at him. 'No, she's not.'

'So, are you okay having another session, if it can be arranged?'

She nodded. She was lucky that there had been someone qualified locally.

The phone rang. Sean took the call. Robyn listened. It sounded as though Marnie would do the session, but not surprisingly, she wanted to conduct the session in her own office, even though Sean had told her there was a missing person – Robyn Parker – and just then they had a woman in custody who might know her whereabouts, if only she could remember.

'I'm up for anything that will get my memories back, and reveal who I really am, even if I have to see her here,' she interrupted the call. 'Will you tell her that?' She remembered thinking before her first session with Marnie that she'd rather see a hypnotherapist than Dr Jamieson's suggestion – a psychiatrist.

Sean waved his hand in the air for her to be quiet.

She mouthed, sorry.

Sean said, 'I see. Yes, I understand. All right, I'll bring her to your office.'

She raised her eyebrows, saying a silent thank you that Marnie had persuaded him.

Sean put the phone down. 'Your therapist said there was no way she was doing the session here, at the police station. It wouldn't be at all conducive to achieving the state of relaxation required under hypnosis that she'd need to enable those memories repressed deep down in your subconscious to come to the fore.

She said the session would be a waste of time for her, and for you.'

Although she was definitely up for another session, looking around the sparsely furnished and rather depressing little interview room with no windows and harsh lighting, she realised that Marnie was absolutely right – she'd be wasting her time.

Sean said, 'She asked if you'd like a chaperone.'

'She asks me that each time.' She recalled what Marnie had said: You are welcome to have someone else present in the session. In fact, I recommend it. I make notes, but it's always helpful to have another pair of eyes and ears. And for moral support if you wish.

But every other session, she'd been happy to attend them alone. She looked at Sean. 'Do you have to attend?'

'No – only if you want me to.'

'But what about finding out what's happened to Robyn – the real Robyn?'

'You would need to give your consent to divulge what takes place, and what, if anything, you remember in your session.'

'Oh, okay.'

'Do you want me to sit in on the session?'

She nodded her head. For some reason, this time it seemed important. Not because she'd been taken into custody, but because she had a feeling that the previous sessions with Marnie had been building up to … something. Marnie had said she was making progress. The very fact that she could get into that hypnosis-induced state was a massive positive when it came to accessing the memories buried deep in her subconscious.

She looked at Sean. If something were to come to light today, she wanted someone she knew to be in there with her, hearing it all first hand – even though she had only known him for a short time. At that moment, she realised with a heavy heart that she didn't have another living soul who would support her.

There was a knock on the door. Sean frowned. 'I'd better go see who that is. Sit tight.' He looked at his watch. 'We'll be leaving soon.'

When Sean returned, he opened the door a crack, and said, 'Can you come here?'

She stood up, joining Sean at the door. 'What is it?' She hoped to goodness that something unexpected hadn't come up and they couldn't go, or Marnie had cancelled.

'The thing is,' said Sean, 'they're all being a right pain waiting in reception, demanding to see you.'

'What are you talking about?'

'My superior wants them all out of his station …' Sean opened the door wide to reveal a group of people waiting outside the door.

Her eyes went wide at the sight of them, and her hand flew to her chest. She started choking up. She stepped outside the room.

'Robyn, we're all here for you,' said Gayle.

There were nods of agreement from David, Joe, Annie, Nick, Marty and Melissa.

'Oh, aye!' said Duncan.

Percy woofed.

'You brought my dog?' She knelt down and gave him a fuss before she got a group hug.

'Did you think we'd just abandon you?' said David.

She wiped tears from her eyes. 'But I'm not Robyn. You heard Judith.'

Behind the group, someone else stepped forward. The last person she'd expected to come. Judith said, 'That's right.'

She swallowed. 'Oh, Judith, I am so sorry. I swear I'm telling the truth. I was in Robyn's car driving out of town when the accident happened. When I woke up I didn't know who I was. The police said I was Robyn Parker. Her licence was lost in the crash, so they just did a search on the DVLA. I should have questioned it.'

'Why would you?' said Gayle.

Judith stepped forward and smiled, taking her aback. 'It's all right. I had a lengthy chat with all your friends while you were being questioned. I'm convinced that you're telling the truth.'

She flung her arms around Judith. 'Oh, Judith. I'm so sorry about all this, and what I put you through.'

Gayle said, 'That's just like her, thinking of everybody else before herself.'

She immediately stepped back from embracing Judith. 'Sorry, I shouldn't have hugged you. You don't even know me.'

'Ah, but I think I do.'

She looked at Judith wide-eyed. 'Huh?'

'You're just what Gayle described – kind and thoughtful. My stepdaughter could learn a thing or two from you, I'm sure.'

She didn't know what to say, apart from the truth. 'When I arrived at Gayle's to stay there for a bit after leaving hospital, I found Robyn's journal with sketches inside, amongst her things. There was a sketch of Wilbur's Bookstore in Aviemore where I … she … was working over the Christmas holidays.'

She recalled having a coffee in the bookshop with Melissa. She realised now that Melissa must have had no idea that it was a woman called Robyn who had been working in the bookshop over Christmas. Melissa hadn't ventured into the shop at that time. If she had, she would have realised that the young woman she'd met in the library, calling herself Robyn, was not the person who had worked in the bookshop, and disappeared so suddenly on Christmas Day when she was meant to have been working at the shop until the New Year.

She realised, in hindsight, it was unfortunate that Melissa, or Brodie, hadn't met Judith's stepdaughter when she was working in the shop, or that Wilbur had not returned to run his store after Christmas.

Melissa's boyfriend, Brodie, had been away over the Christmas break with his family, including his grandfather, Wilbur. When she'd met him too, Brodie had never brought up the fact that Robyn had left her position in the bookshop so suddenly. Perhaps he didn't want to pry or maybe his grandfather had never mentioned her by name.

'I think I had some sort of flashback or memory. I was sitting at the table in the window with a woman. I didn't know who the woman was, but now I believe it was Robyn.' Judith smiled. 'Thank you for sharing that with me.'

'But that's all I remember.' She frowned. That wasn't all she remembered. She looked at David.

David said, 'What is it?'

Sean butted in before she had a chance to answer. 'Look, she has a therapy session booked, and I'm sure her therapist does not want to be waiting around all evening for her to arrive.'

David said, 'You're having another session with Marnie right now?'

She turned to look at David. 'Yes, I have to go.'

'Not without me, you're not.'

'Or me,' said Gayle.

Everyone stepped forward.

Sean stopped Duncan. 'Not the dog.'

'Oh, right.' Duncan handed the lead over to a custody officer.

Sean turned to her. 'Are you okay with this?'

She looked at the friends she loved, and the man she was in love with, and couldn't believe they were all there. 'Oh – yes.'

David grasped her hand. 'Do you want me to call Dr Jamieson? I know that you've been going along on your own, but I'm understandably worried this time. We're not talking about you just getting your memories back this time; we're talking about your identity.'

She squeezed his hand reassuringly. 'I know. But there's nothing to worry about, and do you know why I'm so sure?'

He shook his head.

'Because I'm going to have you guys with me.'

'But are you sure you want to do this?'

She smiled at David. 'I want to know who I am.'

'But I know who you are,' he whispered. 'You're the one I love.'

Robyn squeezed his hand. 'Come on. Let's put a name to the one you love, eh?'

'Funny.' He smiled. 'All right.'

39

She opened the door, and her moral support trooped in. When she closed the door and turned around, she found Marnie sitting in her usual seat, in the home office in her garden, ready for the session, but looking slightly perplexed. She looked around the room. 'Now, I realise I always recommend a chaperone for moral support, but just how much moral support do you need?'

Sean said, 'Do you have some extra chairs?'

She smiled at Sean, thankful that he'd agreed to her wishes and let everyone follow in their cars to Marnie's house. She hadn't forewarned her. She didn't want Marnie to refuse to let them all attend. But it was what she wanted. She hadn't deceived her friends on purpose, but she still felt she owed it to them to be honest. And how much more honest could she be, other than to let her best friends in the world sit in on her hypnotherapy session and finally hear the truth? She had to have them there. It was non-negotiable.

Marnie said, 'There are my dining room chairs, and some folding garden chairs inside the garden shed.'

Sean nodded. 'We'll all go and fetch a seat.'

She looked at her friends, trooping out to fetch a chair each, and said to Marnie, 'I know this is quite unusual …'

'It's not just quite unusual, it's a first.'

She looked at the paperwork in Marnie's hands. She'd been given the police report of the car accident. Marnie said, 'I appreciate your circumstances are unusual too, though.'

She nodded in agreement. 'I want my friends here. I need them here. They are the loveliest people, who let me, a perfect stranger, into their lives. They've got a right to know everything. And if, by chance, I remember today, I want them to hear it firsthand.'

Marnie smiled. 'It's fine.'

Once everyone had returned, and sat down, Marnie said, 'Shall we begin?'

Robyn took a seat on the sofa opposite Marnie, just as she had done before in their sessions. She was feeling anxious; both anxious that it might not work, but also bizarrely anxious that it would. It had only just occurred to her that she might not like her real self. She cast a glance at her friends. They might not like her either.

Marnie caught her attention. 'Don't look at your friends. Just focus on me, okay?'

She nodded, putting her hands in her lap, trying to relax.

'Good.'

'Now, I want you to repeat these words.'

'Wait.' David's voice cut in.

Marnie rolled her eyes. 'I'm afraid you will have to leave if you are going to interrupt the session.'

'Sorry. It's just …'

Marnie said, 'What is it?'

David hesitated. 'This is probably a stupid question, but there's no risk involved with this, is there?'

'Well, hypnotherapy is relatively safe, but it doesn't work for everyone. And there are instances where it does work, perhaps a little too well, and triggers suppressed memories.'

'But that would be a good thing,' said David, 'in the case of Ro … I mean my fiancée.'

'Perhaps. But some of those memories might be suppressed for a reason. They may be traumatic memories that she's protecting herself from.' Marnie paused. 'Does that answer your question?'

David nodded. 'Are you sure you want to do this?' he asked Robyn.

She nodded. 'Yes, I told you I do.'

Marnie looked around the room. 'Anybody else have a question before I proceed?'

Gayle raised her hand. 'Hi, I'm Gayle. How long will this take?'

Marnie replied, 'I can't answer that.'

'No matter,' said Gayle. 'My neighbour said she could look after my mum for as long as needs be. And by the way, this is Marty, and Nick …'

'Hi,' they both said in unison.

'They're staying with me at Lark Lodge at the moment. Have you heard of it?'

'The new guesthouse in Aviemore, backs on to the Rosses' holiday home, so I heard.'

'That's right.'

David spoke again. 'I forgot to tell you that I'm David, her fiancé, and this is Joe, my brother, and Annie his wife.'

'I'm Duncan – their dad,' Duncan added.

Marnie stared at them all. 'Well … er, thank you for introducing yourselves. Has anyone got anything else to add before

I begin?' There was a hint of weariness in her voice.

When nobody answered, she said, 'Good. Let's begin.' She turned to her patient again, but as she began to speak, her voice was drowned out by a ruckus coming from outside the office.

'What on earth …?'

Everyone turned towards the door as it opened. It was Sean. 'Sorry, but there's a guy out here, Jake Campbell-Ross. He said he was going to meet all you guys at the police station, but then got a text to come here.'

David said, 'Oh, he texted me. Sorry, I should have asked you before I told him about the therapy sessions. He says he needs to be here, that he thinks you might know something about Eleanor, and what happened the day of her accident on Christmas Day.'

She looked at David. 'Why would he think that?'

'I don't know.'

She looked around the room at her friends. Mr Campbell-Ross obviously had something unresolved he needed to find out.

'It's your call,' said Sean.

'I think if there's any possibility I met her, then he needs to be here.' She looked at Marnie and winced. 'Can I have one more?'

She threw her hands in the air, clearly getting exasperated. 'Come in, come in. It's already like a zoo in here.'

Jake walked in and thanked Marnie's patient for letting him join her therapy session. Sean provided another folding garden chair. Jake walked up to Marnie, shaking her hand, and introducing himself.

She looked at him sideways. 'Please,' she said, securing the return of her hand, 'just sit down. Now I'm going to try this one more time, and if I get one more interruption it may be best for you all to leave. Do … you … understand?'

Every head nodded. There was not so much as a whisper.

Satisfied, Marnie turned to her patient and started the hypnotherapy, getting her to relax to the point of a hypnosis-induced state. She said softly, 'We are going to go on a journey, a journey into your past,' she paused. 'Will you take me there?'

'I will,' she said in a dreamy voice.

'But before we go, we must get better acquainted, you and me. Can you tell me your name?'

There was a pause. 'Yes, I can tell you my name … it's Bonnie.'

40

'Bonnie?' Marnie looked at her in surprise. This had never happened in their previous sessions. She cast her glance around the room and held her finger to her lips. Everyone realised the enormity of what had just happened – she was remembering.

'Yes?' Bonnie replied.

'Now, let's journey into your past, all the way back to last Christmas. Can you do that?'

'I'll try.'

'Good. It's Christmas Day. Can you tell me where you are, Robyn?'

'Quit calling me Robyn. I told you my name!'

Marnie apologised. 'Of course. I'm sorry.' She'd made a genuine mistake after the previous sessions, where she'd obviously grown accustomed to calling her client Robyn. Although Marnie had been aware the young woman had lost her memories, she, like everyone else in that room, had had no clue before that day that her client's name wasn't really Robyn.

There was still a collective gasp and murmurings from her friends upon hearing her say, quit calling me Robyn. Marnie shot them a warning look and pointed at the door. Absolutely nobody moved a muscle. Everybody wanted to stay to hear this. She'd have to physically throw them out now.

Marnie turned back to her patient. 'It's Christmas morning. Where are you?'

'Where do you think I am?' came the retort. 'Same place as yesterday, same place as every day.'

'And where is that, Bonnie?'

'I try and make it pretty, you know. We've got no money, so I made curtains and cushions from fabric I bought cheap at a charity shop,' she paused. 'I like things to look pretty. Sometimes I see the magazines in the newsagent with big pictures of celebrity houses, you know, with … and everything!'

Marnie said softly, 'Have you got a house, Bonnie?'

'I wish!' She didn't give Marnie time to ask a further question. 'I keep saying to him, one day I'm going to live in a real house instead of a caravan.' Bonnie smiled to herself, as though imagining just what her dream house would be. Then her expression changed, and she pointed, lowering her voice, 'Don't be stupid, woman!' as though she was impersonating someone. She smiled again. 'So I don't say it anymore, but I think it all the same.'

'What did you do on Christmas Day? Were you in the caravan?' Marnie probed.

'Yes. I remember I was feeling ill, like a really bad hangover, except I don't drink.' She let out a laugh.

'Did you go see a doctor?'

'No doctor. Logan says I'll be fine.'

'Who's Logan?' Marnie asked.

'My boyfriend.'

Marnie lifted her eyes and looked across the room at David.

His eyes were riveted on Bonnie, his expression pained. She wasn't the only one who had turned to look at him. His friends and family had too. They were looking worried.

'Logan wants to go out, to the pub to see his mates, and get drunk no doubt, but I don't want to. I just want to stay home. That's what ordinary people do. They stay home and unwrap presents, and watch the King's speech.'

She touched her face. 'Funny thing …' She started to laugh, but caught herself, putting her hand to her mouth.

'What's funny Ro … Bonnie?'

'Well it's not funny, it's kinda weird, because I'm always saying to Logan *not my face*, because I don't want him to get into trouble, but now I'm saying *my face, my face*.'

Marnie frowned. 'Bonnie, I don't understand.'

'What d'ya mean – you don't understand? Just look at me, look at my face.' She touched her face gently and flinched at her own touch. 'I knew I shouldn't have fussed, and just gone out with him straight away.'

'Does he physically harm you, Bonnie?'

'Isn't it obvious?'

There was a sudden scrape of a chair as someone in the room abruptly stood up. Everyone looked a David, standing there, fists clenched as though he wanted to punch someone – punch Logan.

Gayle reached for his hand and slowly coaxed him to sit back down.

Marnie waited to be sure there wouldn't be another interruption. 'Is that why you say to him not to harm your face?'

'Uh-huh.' Her voice sounded so sweet, so innocent, so young yet so vulnerable.

'So what's changed? Do you want him to get caught now?'

She shook her head.

'Why not?' David's voice suddenly rang out.

She seemed not to notice the change in questioner and answered the question. 'What would I do? Where would I go?'

Marnie jumped in quickly before any of the others got the idea that they could interrupt the session, and ask their own questions, 'Haven't you got some family you could confide in – a mother, a sister, or an aunt maybe?'

Bonnie let out a hysterical laugh. 'I've been kicked around worse by that lot. Logan was my ticket out.'

'Some ticket,' someone murmured.

Marnie ignored the comment, although she silently agreed with it, and continued with her line of questioning. 'So, why … would you rather the bruising on your face?'

She said quietly, 'I don't want him to harm the baby.'

Everyone took a sharp intake of breath at that revelation, except Marnie and Gayle, who'd known the young woman who had thought her name was Robyn had been pregnant before the accident. When Marnie had first started the sessions, it had agreed that Dr Jamieson could discuss her patient's medical history, such as it was – stemming from her stay in hospital on Christmas Day after the car accident.

After a minute's silence, while everyone, especially David, digested this news, she began again. 'So Logan persuaded,' she emphasised the word, 'you to go with him.' It wasn't a question.

'Oh, yeah. He's good at persuading.'

Marnie frowned. 'I can imagine.' And she could well imagine that there were a few murderous thoughts swinging around that room to do with Logan at that very moment. She avoided the temptation to look at anyone.

'Can you tell me what happened when you went out in the car on Christmas Day? Remember, you're witnessing these events like a movie, except you're the star of this movie. All you need to do is tell me what you see – can you do that?'

'I wish it was set in England. I do so love those old black-and-white movies. You know, those Edgeware movies.'

'I think you mean Ealing. And no, this one is set in Scotland. So, where are you now?' Marnie prompted.

'In a lovely little town where I've never been before. It's dark, but there's twinkly lights, and Christmas decorations in shop windows, and … and there's an old-fashioned train station.'

'Sounds like Aviemore,' said Marnie.

'It's sooo cold. How could I be so silly, leaving my coat in the car? I know why. I'm in a hurry to escape …'

'Escape?' repeated Marnie. 'Are you running away from Logan?'

Suddenly Bonnie stood up. She flung her arms around herself frantically rubbing her arms up and down, and stamping her feet.

Everyone's eyes were on Bonnie. Something wasn't quite right.

'What's happening?' David whispered. 'Is she … sleepwalking?'

Marnie stood up slowly. She spoke quietly, glancing at her patient. 'Sometimes this happens. I have tried to access her memories as though she is just an observer, but this time she is in deep. Obviously I have taken her back to that day. She's re-living those events in real time, like they are actually happening.'

'Pull her out. Now.' David's voice was insistent.

'Wait.' Jake intervened. 'She's still OK, right? I mean, if we let it go on a little further, you can pull her out any time?' he asked in a hushed voice.

Marnie thought about this. 'I see no reason not to continue a little further. However, as you've seen, she is no longer answering my questions, so it is up to her now to see what she reveals about that Christmas Day.'

Marnie resumed her seat.

Everyone waited and watched as she cast a furtive glance behind her, as though she was checking she wasn't being followed.

'Can you tell me what you see?' Marnie asked.

'It's so dark. There's no shops open. Everyone's gone home for Christmas.' She cupped her hands and blew into them as though trying to warm them up. 'Now I'm free I don't know what to do, where to go.'

'Are you no longer in Logan's car?'

'I … I tried to start the car and drive off when he got out, but the car wouldn't start.'

She suddenly raised her eyebrows, as though something had caught her attention. 'Oh, my god.'

'What is it?' Marnie asked.

'I see a light on in a shop.'

'On Christmas Day?'

She didn't reply, but glanced over her shoulder, eyes darting around the room as though looking for someone. 'It must be a security light they leave on to deter people from breaking in. Not that it would deter Logan.' She stopped abruptly and put her hand to her mouth. 'I shouldn't have said that.' She spoke so quietly the others could barely hear. 'You won't tell anyone I said that, will you?' she whispered.

'It's just you and me, Bonnie,' Marnie whispered back, suppressing a smile at the absurdity of that statement. Just you, me, and a bunch of people who want to know who you really are.

Bonnie said, 'But it can't be just a security light because I see, I see …'

'What do you see?'

'There's a woman sitting at a table in the window of Wilbur's Bookstore.' She craned her neck. 'She's looking right at me and she's pointing. No, wait … she's not looking at me. She can't even see me because it's pitch black out here. She's drawing on the window … yes, in the misted-up window she's drawing something.'

The same thought was going through everyone's mind; the person sitting in Wilbur's Bookstore on Christmas Day must have been Robyn – the real Robyn. And what everyone wanted to know was: if the person sitting in front of them was not Robyn Parker, which she obviously wasn't, what had happened to the real Robyn?

'Can you describe her?' Jake broke ranks and spoke out of turn.

Marnie was about to admonish him, but to everyone's surprise, she answered his question. 'She's a young woman, but the window is too misted-up for me to see her clearly.' Her eyes moved to her left. 'I'm going to try the door. It says it's closed, but I'm going to try it anyway.'

'What's happening?' Jake whispered to the shrink.

Marnie whispered, 'She's going into the shop.'

Everybody leaned forward in their seats as she held out her hand and tried the door in her memory. 'It's locked!' She held up her hand, appearing to knock on an imaginary door. She suddenly stopped, lowering her hand.

Then she looked down and seemed to be studying what she was wearing. 'What will they think?'

They? Jake mouthed, looking around the room at the others, who were exchanging confused glances.

Marnie said, 'Is there someone else in the shop with the young woman?'

She didn't seem to hear the question; she was too busy looking down at what she was wearing. 'I'm standing here in a flimsy dress with no coat,' she touched her face, 'and a face like a punch bag. I don't know what I'm going to say if someone answers the door. I'm not here to buy a book. I'm trying to hide from Logan. Oh, the girl, the one I saw in the window, is coming over. I'm scared she's going to tell me to leave, but she surprises me when she says, Hi, we're having tea, want to join us? Like I'm just an ordinary person who's strolled in to look for a book on Christmas Day. I know the shop said Closed in the window. And she doesn't ask me questions that are going to make me embarrassed, like why I haven't got proper winter clothes on, or a coat, and what I'm doing here all alone on Christmas Day. Somehow I feel I'm good company. Like they understand.'

Bonnie smiled before she continued her story …

'The lady speaks with an accent. I know straight off that's she's from England. She speaks with this posh English accent that I recognise from all those wonderful old black-and-white movies that I love. And suddenly I'm feeling so sick of my life, like I've completely had it, you know? I always wanted just to be able to step into one of those old movies, just step out of my old life and into some place different, be somebody different.'

She paused. 'Is that so very bad? To want something more out of life?'

She didn't wait for an answer, although given the chance, every person in the room would have answered no in unison.

'It was kind of like a dream, finding that old bookstore on Christmas Day.'

Marnie said, 'Can you tell me what you mean by that, Bonnie?'

She nodded. 'I felt like I'd just stepped into a movie, having tea with a girl with an English accent, not questioning what I was doing there, and the other girl, who'd been sitting with her, letting me take her seat, and serving us drinks. Suddenly I didn't want to be me anymore. When I was alone in the caravan, I'd stand in front of the mirror and talk to myself as though I was one of those English ladies with a proper education from university. It's silly, I know, but it kept me going when Logan ... when things got bad.'

'Not at all,' said Marnie.

There were whispers of agreement around the room.

'I was making plans. I didn't know how I was going to do it or where I would go, but I sat in that bookshop, and I thought, no way am I going back to Logan. No way.' She hesitated. 'It was my chance.'

'Your chance?' Marnie said.

'Yes. I just wanted to be like her, be like the girl in the window, be educated and know about books and not be me. We felt like kindred spirits, us three girls, all there on Christmas Day to get away from the people in our lives, although nobody spoke of them.'

'What happened next?'

'Tell me what the English woman looked like,' Jake interrupted.

'Logan? I thought you said we were alone. Did you tell Logan where I am?'

Jake raised his eyebrows and his hands in a conciliatory gesture.

'There's … um, nobody here. Just you and me, and your memory of that day,' said Marnie.

'But I heard a man's voice. I thought it was in my imagination before, but now I'm sure …'

Everyone in the room, including Marnie, saw her getting

increasingly agitated. Marnie took her hands. 'It's just you and me, Bonnie.'

She pulled free. 'I don't believe you!'

Jake said, 'Please, at least tell me her name? Do you know her name?'

Marnie swung round to Jake. 'Quiet!'

David said, 'I think we need to bring her out of it – right now!'

Marnie agreed. 'Bonnie, it's time to return to from your journey into the past …'

41

It was just as she'd feared; she didn't much like who she was … and she imagined that neither would they.

She wasn't even sure she liked her name – Bonnie. She knew why. She felt she was now a different person. She wasn't living her old life anymore – Bonnie's life.

She looked sheepishly around the room. Oh, god – they hate me. She turned to David. She expected he'd hate her most of all after what she was about to reveal.

She'd finally remembered everything – her rubbish life before she had unwittingly stepped into someone else's shoes; someone else's life. But very soon, David would know who she was – the getaway driver who had been sitting outside his boathouse the previous Christmas morning, waiting for her boyfriend, Logan, who was a no-good thief, to collect his money.

She could barely look him in the eye. The trouble with the hypnosis was that although it had worked – she knew who she was: Bonnie Stewart, a young woman of no fixed abode, who had grown up in a tenement in Glasgow with a mother who was an alcoholic. She had dropped out of school and had hooked up with a young man who had turned out to be no good. Although she had not told the whole story under hypnosis, the session had worked, and her memories were back in all their horrible glory.

From what Marnie had just recounted, she had skipped over much of her life to her and Logan's arrival in Aviemore and her escape from him. But there were pieces of that day she had not described. She hadn't recounted in the session what had led up to her arrival at Wilbur's Bookstore. Doing so would mean she had to tell her friends things she'd really rather not. It meant they would have to hear things they didn't want to know. But she'd made a promise to herself that she would tell them everything.

Marnie said, 'Bonnie, are you all right?'

She looked at Marnie sharply. Of course she wasn't all right. She could see the way they were all looking at her, in shock. But she was determined to finish what Marnie had started – telling them what had happened the previous Christmas in Aviemore – all of it.

'Logan promised me he wasn't stealing again. He hadn't long got out of prison after that attempted robbery at your dad's store two years before.'

Duncan sat forward in his seat. 'What are you saying? It was your boyfriend who broke into my store and shot David?'

'I thought that name sounded familiar,' murmured David.

'No … yes. It was his older brother who came with the gun.'

'Oh, and that makes it okay, does it?' Duncan said.

Bonnie shook her head vehemently. 'Of course not.' She lowered her eyes. 'I'm sorry.'

Gayle said, 'Don't you be apologising for your rubbish boyfriend's actions, Robyn. I mean Bonnie.'

'Did you know he was going to rob my store?' Duncan asked.

'Of course not! We were living in the caravan, parked illegally in a back street in Inverness, and he said that he was going out last-minute Christmas shopping. I thought it was odd. What shops would be open that late on Christmas Eve? But that was the point, wasn't it? He was out to rob somewhere. And what better place than the sweet little town of Aviemore, less than an hour away?' Bonnie grimaced. 'The next thing I knew, I'd got a phone call from the police station. He'd been arrested for burglary, and then he told me his brother was dead, and some guy had been arrested for shooting him.'

She cast her gaze over to David. He was staring at her intently.

'I went back to live with my mum when he was in prison, but things were getting worse at home. She went out every night to the local pub. She'd arrive home in the early hours, blind drunk, leaving my two younger siblings to fend for themselves, get themselves something to eat before going to bed. I knew my mum drank, but I hadn't realised how bad things were until I returned. The place was a tip. I started to look after my younger brother and sister. They're twins. I cleaned up the flat, made sure their clothes were washed and ironed before school and that they had something proper to eat, even though I could only afford simple meals like jacket potatoes and beans – things like that.'

Everyone in the room was very quiet, listening.

'I didn't want to go back to my mum's. When Logan went to prison, I wanted to leave, run away, get a place of my own. I thought I'd return for a short time to figure out what I was going to do, but I realised even if I had the means to get a place of my own, I couldn't leave the children. I tried to take care of them and myself as best I could. But mum often stole what little money I earned to spend on drink. I felt trapped, but I was determined that when he got out of prison, I'd tell him we couldn't just pick up where we left off. I didn't want that life. We couldn't be together anymore.'

Bonnie frowned. 'One night, mum brought some bloke home – they were both drunk, falling about, laughing hysterically. The twins were asleep. I'd been asleep. I told them to keep it down. They were acting like teenagers. Mum lashed out at me, telling me I had no right to tell her what to do in her own home. She told me to get out. It was terrible. The twins had woken up, hearing the almighty row, and begged me not to leave them, but mum was shouting get out, get out, and physically threw me out, grabbing my stuff and tossing it out of the door. So I left – and went back to the caravan.'

Marnie said softly, 'Logan came back – didn't he?'

Bonnie shook her head. 'One of his friends must have told him I was living in the caravan again. I had no choice. I had nowhere else to go. Then Logan got out of prison. But when he came back, it was like he'd turned over a new leaf. His brother's death had changed him, made him see the error of his ways. He said he was going straight. No more thieving, no more prison stints.' She trailed off. 'I really thought our lives would be different.'

Judith said gently, 'Then what happened, Bonnie? Can you tell us how you came to be in Aviemore last Christmas, two years on from the robbery at Mr Gillespie's store? Sorry to ask, but that wasn't really explained in your hypnotherapy session.'

'Yes,' Bonnie said in a small voice. 'He told me he'd booked a fancy hotel.'

'In Aviemore?'

She nodded. 'We were checking in on Christmas Day, and going to have Christmas dinner in the restaurant. I couldn't believe it. I could just imagine a fancy hotel decorated for Christmas. He said there was a log burner, and it would have real atmosphere. Oh, my god – I was so happy at the thought that this marked the beginning of a new life together.'

Bonnie halted. She didn't want to go on with this. She looked around the room. 'All I ever wanted was for things to be different. I wanted a little house, and a dog, and more than anything a normal Christmas, with Logan out of prison and on the straight and narrow. On the way to Aviemore, he told me we weren't returning to the caravan. We were going to start over, just the two of us.'

She paused, and smiled. 'I remembered being so happy, thinking that this was just the start, and all my dreams would come true. And I would find the twins, who had been taken into care the night I'd been chucked out of the flat, after a neighbour had reported what they'd seen and heard. I wanted to have them come and live with me. We would be a proper family. I didn't mention that to Logan. He wouldn't have been happy with that idea. He didn't much like kids. They weren't babies – my siblings were ten – but I didn't want them to spend the rest of their childhood in care. I thought that things were different now, though – he might welcome the twins, and we would all have a new start together.'

Bonnie dropped her eyes to the floor. 'I should have known I wouldn't be that lucky.'

Marnie said, 'Bonnie, you don't have to do this now, telling us what happened, if you don't feel able.'

She looked up. 'I want to.' She took a deep breath. 'After feeling elated about where we were spending Christmas, on the journey there, I started to worry about where he was getting the money to do this. He hadn't long got out of prison, and he had no job.'

'Where did he get the money?' Duncan asked.

'He told me he had to make a stop before we checked into the hotel. He said he had some money to collect that was owed him. I asked him if it was for a job, but he wouldn't tell me. I knew he'd been involved with shady people. I felt scared. I thought … I thought he was going to see a criminal to collect his share of the money from something dodgy he'd done. Worse still, I thought if that wasn't the case, then he might be going to rob someone again on Christmas Day to pay for our hotel. I told him that he had to turn the car around. I wasn't going to spend Christmas in a fancy hotel if he'd robbed someone else on Christmas Day to pay for it. He reassured me that wasn't the case. He wasn't robbing anyone, and I'd see that for myself.'

She stopped abruptly and looked sheepishly at David, lowering her eyes as she admitted, 'I haven't been completely honest with you.'

David raised his eyebrows.

She continued, 'The first time I arrived at the boathouse with Duncan, I had some sort of flashback. I knew I'd been there before, but all I remembered was sitting in a car, in the dark, outside your house, and feeling very scared. I didn't know what I was doing there, or who I was with. I just couldn't remember anything more.'

'But now you can,' said Duncan.

Bonnie avoided Duncan's gaze and nodded. 'He said he was collecting what he was owed.' She looked over at David. 'I didn't know what he meant. I was afraid he was lying to me, and he was going to break into this house all the way out in the middle of nowhere. I was very scared that what had happened to his brother would happen to him. But I sat there watching him knocking on your door, and you answered, David. I saw you hand him a bag and shut the door. That was it.'

Duncan said, 'Excuse me? What did you just say?'

'David handed Logan a bag and shut the door.'

Duncan said, 'What was in the bag?'

She stole a glance at David. 'Money. Lots of money.'

Duncan slowly turned his head in his son's direction. 'David? What the hell is going on? You knew this Logan?'

'No … yes.'

Joe stepped in and exclaimed, 'Marnie, this session is over.'

Bonnie immediately understood what Joe was doing – protecting his brother. She hadn't realised that by telling her story, she might implicate David in a crime. She had no idea why he'd handed over that money.

Marnie slowly closed her notebook. 'As with all therapy sessions, obviously it goes without saying that all this is confidential and won't leave this room.'

Bonnie looked at her. Marnie wasn't stupid. She was probably thinking the same thing. Marnie said, 'However, that isn't up to you, but my patient.' She turned to Bonnie.

Bonnie looked at Joe, her eyes roving to David. Whatever had happened that led to David voluntarily handing over the money, David did not deserve to get into trouble for it.

'I'd like to end the session please, Marnie.'

'Are you sure?'

'I am, but thank you, Marnie, for getting my memories back.'

Marnie said, 'Would you like a moment here alone with your friends?'

She nodded. Her therapy session was over, but she still had things to tell them about that day.

Marnie rose from her chair. 'I'll be in the house, if you need me.'

Marnie paused at the door and turned around, looking at everyone in the room, her eyes finally settling on her patient. 'If you don't mind me saying, you've had a rough time of it, with your mother, and your two younger siblings taken into care, and ending up living in an old caravan. I don't know what I would have done without my lovely, supportive family at that age.'

Bonnie would have preferred it if she hadn't brought that up. It made her feel sad, and embarrassed in front of her friends.

Marnie looked around the room. 'I hope things work out for you, Bonnie. Despite your rough start in life, you are a kind soul who deserves so much more.' Marnie walked over to Bonnie and gave her a hug. 'Take care, Bonnie.'

Bonnie was surprised to find tears welling up.

'You've got my card with my number,' Marnie added. 'If you need anything, just call me.'

'Thank you, Marnie.'

When Marnie opened the door, Sean was outside. 'Ah, is the session over?'

'Yes, it is.'

Sean was about to step into the room when Joe strode up to him. 'We're not quite finished.'

'Oh, but I thought—'

Joe said authoritatively, 'I'll take it from here.'

Sean stood for a moment, eyeing Joe.

Joe said, 'Please, Sean. There's a … a family matter that needs resolving privately. Can you wait in the car?'

Sean nodded. 'All right, Joe. Just come fetch me when you're done.'

Joe was about to close the door, when Sean said, 'Oh – does she know where the real Robyn Parker is?'

Bonnie heard that, as did everyone else in the room.

'We'll get on to that, I'm sure.'

Bonnie caught Sean looking her way. 'Are you okay to answer Joe's questions without a chaperone?'

Bonnie was about to say that she was fine, and didn't need a chaperone; that she was among friends. But she wasn't among friends. They were the friends she'd made masquerading as Robyn, albeit unintentionally. But that didn't excuse what she'd done in her past – hooking up with a criminal and accompanying him to the boathouse. Did it make her an accessory? She hadn't committed a crime herself, but wondered if she was guilty of something by association.

She tried to keep her emotions in check when she realised that when her friends all walked out of this room, they'd probably walk out of her life, and she'd never see them again.

Bonnie nodded. She wanted to get it all over with. 'I'm fine, Sean.' She wasn't, but she imagined nobody in the room cared one bit.

42

Joe shut the door and swiftly turned around. 'David – what the hell …?'

David wasn't looking at Joe, but staring at Bonnie. 'You were outside my house with Logan?'

She wasn't surprised in the least by his reaction.

'I swear I didn't know what we were doing at the boathouse – I still don't, apart from him collecting money off you.'

Duncan was now on his feet. 'David, I want to know why you handed over that money to Logan right now!'

Bonnie caught David glancing Annie's way before he said, 'I can't tell you.'

'What do you mean – you can't tell me? You mean you won't,' Duncan shouted at him.

Bonnie was staring at Annie when suddenly she knew what Logan meant when he'd said, I'm collecting what I'm owed. Logan had been there when his brother had been shot. Had he seen who had pulled the trigger? If he had, why hadn't he told the police? Because he'd hatched a plan instead to blackmail David, who had taken the fall for Annie. David had paid for Logan's silence.

But Joe didn't know. He was a police officer. That was his job.

Neither David nor Annie wanted him to know that it was Annie who had pulled the trigger and shot Logan's brother. Ultimately, they were both protecting Joe from the truth.

And so was Bonnie, when she said, 'Isn't it obvious?'

David shot her a look.

She continued, 'Logan had read in the paper about David being arrested for shooting his brother. He wanted payback for that. He wanted what he felt was owed to him – compensation for losing his brother.'

It was a load of rubbish what she'd just said. Logan and his brother hadn't got along. He had just used the situation to blackmail David.

Joe looked at David. 'Is this true?'

Before he had a chance to answer, Duncan said, 'Why pay him? Why didn't you go straight to Joe and tell him what was going on? Logan would have been arrested again.'

Bonnie saw David steal another glance at Annie before looking at Joe. 'He lost a brother. I felt guilty.'

'But it wasn't your fault,' said Joe in exasperation. 'They attempted to burgle Dad's store, and brought a gun. Logan had to live with the consequences.'

Bonnie stepped in again. 'Well, he handed over the money, so it's all water under the bridge now, isn't it?'

Duncan sat down. 'I suppose that's true.'

Bonnie sighed in relief until she caught Melissa staring at David, her expression suggesting she might have guessed there was more to it than that. Bonnie thought, please, please don't start thinking of digging around, Melissa. She'd already told Melissa she didn't want her looking into what had happened with David and his knee injury any further. Now she wished she hadn't called her from the police station.

'Besides, he knew where I lived,' David explained. 'I was … I was afraid of what might happen if I didn't hand over the money. I didn't know what he was capable of.'

Joe looked at his brother. 'All right, so we've cleared that up.' His attention turned to Bonnie. 'So what happened to the money?'

All eyes fixed on Bonnie. She knew exactly what had happened to the money in that rucksack. It was all gone. At least she could now replace it with the money she was earning. But that wasn't the point. She'd taken the money, the stolen money, with every intention of keeping it for herself.

'I'm sorry to interrupt,' said Judith. 'I'm a little confused. You were with Logan in his car outside the boathouse when he collected the money.'

Bonnie nodded. 'That's right.'

'So, can you tell me, Bonnie, how you came to be in Robyn's car that very same day?' She paused. 'Can you tell me what happened to Robyn, where she is?'

All eyes were on Bonnie.

Suddenly she didn't know where to start. She hesitated.

Gayle leaned forward in her chair. 'Take your time. Why don't you just talk us through what happened when Logan returned to the car with the money?'

Bonnie began. 'When he got back in the car with the rucksack, he said he could take care of me now … me and the—' Bonnie stopped short.

Gayle sat back in her chair. 'You don't have to talk about that.'

Bonnie and Gayle's eyes locked. Aside from Dr Jamieson and Bonnie, Gayle had been the only person who knew, until Bonnie had got her memories back and remembered telling the two women she'd met in Wilbur's Bookstore on Christmas Day – Robyn and Eleanor.

Bonnie knew she didn't have to tell David, and she didn't have to tell him there, but what was the point of keeping it a secret? She wanted him to know, even though she guessed it was over between them.

'I was pregnant with Logan's child.'

She thought she'd hear gasps from everyone in the room, shocked by that revelation – especially David. She was surprised by the lack of reaction.

Gayle said, 'Honey, you mentioned the pregnancy in the session.'

'Oh, did I?' Bonnie avoided David's gaze. 'I lost the baby in the car accident.'

'Oh, Bonnie,' said Judith, 'I am so sorry.'

'I found out in the hospital. Dr Jamieson told me. At least I know who the father was now.' She quickly moved on. 'I want to tell you, Judith, about Robyn, and how I came to be in her car a short time later.'

Bonnie continued. 'We'd returned to the main road and were headed for Aviemore. It had started snowing. I was so relieved that Logan had been telling the truth and that he'd turned up just to collect some money. I was still worried that he hadn't told me everything, but I tried to put it to the back of my mind. I was cold and hungry. I was looking forward to turning up at the hotel, having a hot shower, and changing for Christmas dinner.'

The memory of that Christmas Day came flooding back …

❖

'Oh, it's such a magical place, isn't it Logan?' She'd never visited

Aviemore before. She was surprised he'd decided to stay there, in that town, on Christmas Day. She would have thought that after what had happened in one of the shops there when he'd burgled the place, he'd never return in a million years.

'There's just one more thing I want to do in Aviemore before we arrive at our hotel.'

'Okay. Will it take long?'

Logan glanced at her, and grinned. 'Not at all. I'll be in and out before you know it.'

'Are you doing some last-minute shopping?'

'Yeah.'

Bonnie looked out of the car window as they drove slowly through the town. 'I don't see any shops open. The town is deserted.'

'That's what I'm counting on.'

Bonnie was about to ask him what he meant when he suddenly swung the car over and stopped by the kerb. They were parked outside Gillespie's General Store. She stared at the shop front. 'Is this where you and your brother—'

'Yep.'

'What are you doing?' Her eyes drifted to the rucksack on her lap. 'Are you leaving some money for Mr Gillespie for Christmas?' She knew it was the shop he'd robbed two years earlier – or had tried to when he and his brother had been caught red-handed.

Logan turned in his seat, and looked at her. 'Why would I do that?'

'To say sorry for what happened two years ago, breaking into his shop on Christmas Eve.'

Logan started to laugh.

Bonnie frowned. 'What's funny?'

'Sometimes I think you're just too good for me, you know that?'

Bonnie smiled. 'I know.' She started to open the rucksack. 'How much do you think would be enough to compensate Mr Gillespie for—?'

Logan closed his hand around hers. 'Are you that stupid? I'm not here to give him money.' He looked at the shop. 'I'm here to finish what me and my brother started.' He opened the car door.

Bonnie looked at him, wide-eyed. 'You're going to do it again – break in and … and … rob the place?'

'Oh, yes. I'm going to take any cash that's in the cash register. It won't be much, hardly worth the effort. I've already had my payday.' His eyes drifted to the rucksack.

'Then why do it, Logan?'

'Let's call it getting even. While I'm in there, I'm going to give that Mr Gillespie a lovely surprise all right, but it won't be a penny from that rucksack.'

Before he got out of the car, he reached over and picked up a hockey stick.

'What's that for?'

'Let's just say I'm going to take a few swings in there. By the time I've finished, it's going to look like a whole hockey team has trampled through his shop, leaving a tsunami in their wake.'

Bonnie grabbed his arm. 'Oh, Logan, please don't do this! Not on Christmas Day.' Not on any day. 'I thought you were turning over a new leaf, for me … for the baby?'

'I am, and I will.' He leaned over her, reaching for the glove compartment. She sat there rigid when she saw what he had in his hand. 'Oh, my god, Logan!' she grabbed his arm.

'Are you mad, woman? I've got a loaded gun in my hand.'

Bonnie immediately let go. 'Please, Logan. Please don't do this. Why have you got a gun?'

'In case anyone happens along. This time, I'll be prepared. Now, just sit tight. I'll be right back. Then we can check into our fancy hotel with even more cash.' He paused when he got out of the car. She thought, for a moment, that he was going to change his mind. He said, 'Get in the driver's seat.'

'What – why?' He never let her drive his car. He never even left the car keys in the ignition when he left her sitting in the car.

'Just do it.'

Bonnie left the bag on the passenger seat and scooted over to the driver's side. The keys were still in the ignition.

'Now, if you see anybody – anybody at all – start the car and honk the horn.'

Bonnie thought she was going to cry. Now she was his getaway driver.

'Bonnie! Do you understand?'

She slowly nodded her head, tears streaming down her face. What she understood in that moment was that for all the promises he'd made to her, Logan was never going to change. He wasn't going to turn over a new leaf, settle down and get a job. When he'd spent the cash, he'd be out doing this again.

She sat in the car, staring at him as he scoped the street, checking nobody was around. It was dark. The streetlights were on, casting a hazy white glow as the snow fell. It was getting heavier. There wasn't a soul around. Why would there be? thought Bonnie. It was four o'clock in the afternoon on Christmas Day. She imagined everyone had eaten their Christmas dinner, and friends and families were sitting together, perhaps watching the King's speech. Children would be playing with their new toys, and parents would be washing up the dishes from Christmas lunch.

She looked at Logan, who was standing in front of the shop, looking through the window. 'I deserve more than this,' she said. She rested a hand on her stomach. 'You deserve more.'

She cast a glance over at Logan. He was trying the handle of the shop, trying to force the door. She opened the rucksack and looked inside. At the bottom were wads of cash. She stared at the money. Enough for her and her baby to disappear, start over, as far away from Logan, and this town, as possible. She swallowed. This was her chance.

Her heart was pounding in her chest as she reached for the car key. Logan had disappeared down an alleyway between the general store and a shop next door, presumably to see if he could force a back door instead.

Bonnie took a deep breath and turned the key in the ignition. The car didn't start. She'd never driven Logan's car. Her first thought was that she was doing something wrong. She put her foot on the clutch, this time, and then tried again. The engine turned over a couple of times as she stared wide-eyed at the lane between the shops, thinking that Logan was going to hear the car and come running. He would assume she'd spotted someone.

Then the car engine died. 'Oh, god! Don't do this now!' She tried again, but the same thing happened.

Without a second thought, Bonnie left behind her suitcase, grabbed the bag full of money, and ran.

43

She wiped tears from her eyes and looked around the room.

Duncan said, 'But my shop wasn't robbed the Christmas just gone – was it, Joe?'

Joe pursed his lips and looked at his hands.

David turned to his brother. 'What are you not telling us, Joe?'

Joe breathed a heavy sigh. 'Look, after what happened two years ago, I'd asked one of my colleagues just to pass through Aviemore on Christmas Eve.'

'Keeping an eye on my store?'

'Yeah, Dad. It was a stupid thought. Why would the guy who lost his brother that night return to the scene of the crime or attempt another robbery? I knew that the thief, Logan, had been released from prison a month earlier. But why would he return? Of course nothing happened on Christmas Eve, but imagine my shock when I found out he was back, and had been spotted by the police officer as he cruised through town on Christmas Day, running along the road with an illegal firearm and carrying a crowbar. He recognised Logan, pulled over, and arrested him on the spot. And outside Dad's shop was a car – stolen. It was obvious what he'd returned to Aviemore to do.' Joe turned to David. 'I had no idea he'd blackmailed you.'

David looked at him sheepishly.

Joe continued, 'But after what had happened at your store before, I didn't want to ruin our family's Christmas by bringing up the fact that he'd come back to finish the job.'

Nobody spoke for a moment. Then Gayle asked Bonnie, 'So, after you ran from the car, did you go to the hotel?'

She shook her head. 'I didn't know which hotel he'd booked, and even if I had, that would have been the last place I'd have gone. I couldn't check into the hotel. He'd be looking for me there. So, I ran through the town, towards the train station, thinking that would be a refuge from the cold, and maybe there might be a train. But it was Christmas Day, and there were no lights on. There were no lights on in any shops – apart from one.'

'Wilbur's Bookstore,' said Judith, 'where Robyn was living and working over the Christmas holidays.'

'I ran up to the bookshop and couldn't believe it when I saw a young woman sitting at a table in the window. Although the bookstore said it was closed, I banged on the door. I was so cold, and getting wet from the snowfall, and I couldn't carry the bag full of cash for another second. Oh, the relief when she opened that door.' Bonnie remembered the young woman ushering her inside.

'I told them my car had broken down on the way through Aviemore. I didn't want to tell her that I'd run away from my rotten boyfriend who was, at that moment, robbing one of the stores. She appeared genuine and kind, and … and I should have told her to phone the police, but …' She looked at her hands. 'I had all that money. I didn't know whether it was drugs money, or what it was, but I was sure I'd be arrested too as an accomplice. I felt so bad for lying, but this was my chance to escape – don't you see?'

She barely looked up, too embarrassed to look them all in the eye. 'I know I did the wrong thing, but all I was thinking about was my baby, and getting away.'

She gathered herself and looked up. 'Robyn explained that she lived there above the shop. She sent me upstairs to change out of my wet clothes and choose something to wear of hers. Even my shoes were soaked from running along the slushy pavements. She gave me a pair of her Doc Marten boots. They weren't the sorts of clothes I'd normally wear – the clothes she dressed in weren't me at all – but I didn't care. I was warm. I was dry, and the two women were keen to help me.' Bonnie frowned when she remembered that while she was changing, she'd also stuffed a few of Robyn's clothes into the rucksack to hide the cash.

'Who was the woman with Robyn?' Judith asked.

'She said her name was Eleanor.'

'Eleanor?' Jake stared at her, wide-eyed. 'Are you sure? Are you absolutely sure?'

Bonnie looked over at Jake Campbell-Ross. 'Yes, she said her name was Eleanor.'

'So, that's where she went on Christmas Day. She said she was doing last-minute shopping. It didn't make sense to me. What shops were open on Christmas Day?'

Bonnie said, 'There weren't any shops open. Didn't she tell you she was meeting a friend?'

'Robyn was her friend?'

'Yes. They'd only met the day before, on Christmas Eve, when Eleanor had stepped into Wilbur's Bookstore. While Robyn was making me a hot drink, I sat with Eleanor at the table, and she told me that she'd invited Robyn to have Christmas dinner with her family in Aviemore, but that Robyn had refused. She hadn't wanted to intrude. So Eleanor had come to see her on Christmas Day instead.'

Jake stared at her. 'Thank you, Bonnie, for telling me that. I've always wondered where she'd been that afternoon before she arrived at the ski slopes.'

Judith said, 'Bonnie, do you know what happened to Robyn?'

'She'd been in the middle of packing her things, said I could help myself to whichever clothes I wanted from her suitcase. Then she shut her suitcase and put it in her car, ready to leave the next morning. I guess she was returning to university. She said I could stay the night, and in the morning she could phone a local garage, see if they could come out and repair the car. That seemed like a good idea, unless Logan had decided to sleep in the car. But I couldn't see that in sub-zero temperatures. I imagined he would check into that hotel and return to his car in the morning. Either way, I knew I had to abandon the idea of leaving town in his car. I couldn't explain that to Robyn, but she came to my rescue and said she doubted they'd be any car mechanics working on Boxing Day, so if I wanted, she'd take me where I wanted to go the next day.' She sighed. 'I didn't know where I was going, and I didn't care. All I knew was that I needed to get out of Aviemore, away from him.'

Judith said, 'But I don't understand … you were driving out of Aviemore in Robyn's car, alone, when you had the accident.'

'Yes.' Bonnie halted. She knew she had to tell them. She felt her resolve slipping. Bonnie took a deep breath and forced herself to continue. 'Robyn asked me if I'd do her one small favour in return. Her friend, Eleanor, wanted to go skiing, but she had some things she still wanted to do in the shop before she left the next day. Would I drive Eleanor to the ski slopes? Of course, I said yes.

It was such a small favour to ask. It was the least I could do. They both went upstairs, Eleanor to change into her ski stuff, and Robyn to tidy up the flat.'

'So you drove Eleanor in Robyn's car?'

Bonnie looked at her hands. 'Yes. She looked like some sort of professional skier in her lovely ski wear. I had no idea you needed so much kit. She had dark reflective glasses on, a large cosy bandana type sleeve wrapped around her head and ears, and a silk scarf that she'd pulled up to her nose.'

She stole a glance at Jake. 'I'm so sorry about what happened on the ski slopes. I wish … I wish I'd never driven her there.'

Jake shook his head. 'Don't say that. It wasn't your fault. She'd have got there one way or the other. Obviously Robyn was going to drive her there before you appeared.'

Bonnie looked at him. It didn't make her feel any better – not after what had happened after she'd dropped Eleanor off.

Judith said, 'But you didn't return to the shop, did you?'

Bonnie shook her head, avoiding Judith's gaze. 'We drove through Aviemore, on the way to the ski slopes, and we passed Logan, standing by his car, scratching his head with the butt of his gun, not even bothering to conceal it. I couldn't see a broken window, but he had a crowbar in his hand, and the boot of the car open. I guessed he'd returned to his car for the crowbar to prise open the shop door, when he realised I was gone, along with the money.'

Bonnie had left her mobile phone in the car, so he'd had no way of contacting her, or tracing her whereabouts through his phone. She'd also had the presence of mind, in the split second that she'd fled, to take his keys so that he couldn't get the car started.

'He spotted me, in her car, and quickly jumped in his own car, but there was no key. So I saw him in the rear-view mirror, running along the pavement with the gun in one hand and the crowbar in another. That was when I realised I couldn't return to Wilbur's Bookstore. He was still in town. He'd find me. I needed to get out of Aviemore immediately.'

'So you stole my stepdaughter's car?'

'Yes, it's true. I … I'd made up my mind before we even arrived at the ski slopes that I wouldn't return to the shop. But I wasn't going to keep her car, not at all. I'm not like Logan. I don't steal stuff. I was desperate, and I just needed to borrow it to get out of town. There wasn't time to explain. But as soon as I got someplace else, I was going to phone Wilbur's Bookstore, let her know where her car was, pay to have it returned to her.'

'And that's why you were speeding out of Aviemore,' said David, 'on Christmas Day.'

'And you had the accident in Robyn's car,' Judith added.

'But you never made it past the town limits,' said Gayle.

Bonnie looked at each one of them in turn and nodded.

Judith said, 'So, where is Robyn?'

'I … I don't know.'

Melissa's boyfriend, Brodie, who'd taken over running his grandfather's bookshop said, 'Last Christmas, when my grandfather, Wilbur, returned from his Christmas break, expecting the young lady he'd employed to still be there minding the shop, he found the keys to the shop posted through the letter box, and her things gone. I never thought to ask her name, but then he didn't seem all that bothered, to be honest. He just said she was a student at university, and had probably changed her mind about the holiday job, and returned to campus early. He'd decided to retire anyway. I think he'd lost interest in the shop, and was just biding his time until I took over the place.'

Bonnie looked over at Brodie. 'Robyn said she was leaving. I don't know where she was going, but her things were packed up in the car, ready to go.'

'The car you … borrowed,' said Gayle.

'Yes.'

'So, the question is,' said Joe, 'What happened to Robyn Parker when you didn't return to the shop with her car? She obviously left the shop, just like she'd planned. But where did she go?'

It was a rhetorical question. Nobody in the room knew. The only thing that was obvious was that she'd locked up the shop, put the keys through the letterbox, and disappeared.

44

Joe opened the door to the hypnotherapist's garden office and stepped outside. Bonnie could see Joe and Sean talking in hushed voices, just outside the door, as everyone inside the room rose from their chairs. Everyone apart from her. She didn't know whether she was free to go. She imagined it was more likely she'd be arrested for stealing Robyn's car. She had confessed to it, after all. And if she was free to go – where would that be? Her friends, the people she knew and loved, were filing out one by one. Nobody was speaking to each other – let alone to her.

Joe and Sean stepped into the therapist's office. They stepped aside to let David past. He was the last to leave.

'David?' she called after him.

He stopped at the door and turned around. 'Those London trips …'

'Yes?' She didn't see what relevance that had now.

'That last trip, a week ago, when you asked me not to come with you …' He paused, as if trying to gather his thoughts. 'You weren't meeting Logan, were you?'

Bonnie saw Gayle, who was milling around outside with the others, step forward and stare at her through the open doorway.

'Logan?' She looked at him wide-eyed, suddenly realising that Logan could be out of prison, looking for her. What if he came back to Aviemore, the last place he'd seen her, to find her?

Joe spoke. 'That's not possible, David. I stepped out during the hypnosis to find out if Logan is still serving time for the attempted robbery the second time round, which he is. It was a longer sentence. He had a firearm. It will be a while yet before he's released.'

'Oh, thank god,' Bonnie and David said in unison.

David said, 'I don't know why … I thought you'd discovered someone from your past, and that was why you didn't want me to go with you – because you were meeting someone in London.'

She looked at him sheepishly. She'd made a promise to herself that she'd tell them everything, but she couldn't – not right now. She had discovered someone from her past in London. It was true. But she wanted to keep that to herself – for Jake's sake.

She'd found out something by chance on her last visit to London. Eleanor Campbell-Ross was alive. But Jake hadn't been to visit his wife yet – not since the accident. None of his family had. How would he feel if he found out that a virtual stranger had discovered this fact, and knew Eleanor's whereabouts, even though she hadn't actually set eyes on her? David didn't need to know about that. Neither did anybody else who'd been in that interview room – least of all Jake.

She watched David leave the room without another word, along with his brother, Joe. Bonnie slowly rose from her chair, and as Joe closed the door on all her friends, and the beautiful life she'd had, her heart felt like it had broken into a million pieces.

'Bonnie, please can you take a seat.'

Bonnie's eyes dropped from the door to Sean.

She sat down. 'Are you arresting me now?'

'No.'

'But I stole Robyn's car!'

'Yes, Joe has filled me in on everything that has been said in this room. When he comes back with the paperwork, you need to read it through and sign it.'

'Joe is coming back?' She felt so relieved that one of her friends wasn't abandoning her.

'Yes.' Sean looked around Marnie's office before fixing his gaze on her. 'You've been through a bit of a session, haven't you? Rather than taking you back to the station to do the paperwork, we thought that under the circumstances, Marnie would be happy for you to remain here until Joe returns and we wrap this up. He is also going to file a missing person's report for Robyn Parker.'

'But her car—?'

'Robyn is not here to corroborate your story—'

'But I'm admitting—'

Sean held up his hand. 'In any case, in the absence of Robyn Parker, her next of kin, Judith Parker, is not pressing charges.'

'Really?'

'Yes.'

'But what about the money?'

'What money?'

'The money that David handed over to Logan that I then took out of his car and ran away with?'

'Joe told me you'd bring that up. David never handed Logan any money.'

'What?'

'Just what I told you.' Sean sat back in his chair and crossed his arms. 'But, theoretically speaking, if you had had a rucksack full of money, might you have spent that on setting up Robyn's Interior Design, and paying Duncan a lot of rental money that saved his shop, and his livelihood, drawing in more customers, not to mention the financial help setting up his flat above the shop for him to move into?'

Bonnie understood. She couldn't believe that David and Joe, and Sean, had colluded so that she wasn't going to be charged in connection with the stolen money or as an accessory to Logan's crimes. 'Theoretically speaking, yes.'

'Good. That's what they thought – theoretically speaking, of course.'

For the first time since she'd been arrested, Bonnie managed a small smile.

'So, once you've signed the paperwork, you're free to go.'

'But go where?' she blurted.

Sean sighed. 'Now that, I cannot help you with.'

By the time Marnie appeared with two cups of tea, and they had finished their drinks, there was another knock on the door. Joe had returned from the station.

'Ah, Joe. I'll let you finish off.'

'Thanks, Sean.'

Bonnie watched Sean leave Marnie's office and turned to Joe as he took a seat. 'Joe, I want to thank you for—'

Joe held up his hand. 'Not necessary,' he said, very businesslike. 'Now, if you could read through this paperwork, then sign it, I can go back to the station and file the missing person's report.'

Bonnie didn't bother reading it. She trusted Joe. She wanted to get it all over with. She signed it.

'Good.' Joe picked up the paperwork, put it in a file, and rose from his chair.

Bonnie pursed her lips. She remembered once overhearing Duncan warn David that he didn't know what he was getting himself into with this stranger from out of town. He didn't know her from Adam. Duncan had been right to be wary of her. They all should have been. She'd done just what they were afraid of – broken David's heart. Now they were closing ranks, and probably thinking it would be good riddance when she finally left town.

She looked at Joe as he waited at the door. This wasn't the friendly, easy-going Joe she was used to. This wasn't her friend. This was Joe doing his police duty and escorting her out of Marnie's office.

As they approached the door, she suddenly had the most wonderful thought. Were they all waiting behind that door, in hushed silence, read to surprise her?

When Joe opened the door, there was no one there – just the view down Marnie's lovely garden with the neat lawn, prim rose bushes, and tall privet hedging shielding her garden from the neighbours.

Joe said, 'I'm taking you back to the boathouse.'

She frowned. 'What? Why?' That was the last place she wanted to go, to remind her of the life that would never be.

'To collect your things.'

'Can't you just take me back to the police station?' That was the second last place she wanted to return to, but she'd much rather that than the boathouse. 'I'd like you to go and get my belongings for me.'

Joe was already shaking his head. 'Look, I wouldn't want to pack your things myself.'

Bonnie understood. David had probably gone to the pub to drown his sorrows. She expected he didn't want to return to the boathouse just then either. It would be awkward for Joe, packing up her clothes, her underwear, her personal things.

'Of course.' She grimaced. As they walked down the lawn to the patio outside Marnie's dining room, a little part of her thought, just for a moment, that they might still all be waiting for her with Marnie in the house. But of course, they weren't. It was just Marnie, giving her a hug before she left, and wishing her well.

As they stepped out of the front door, she stopped and looked about her. 'What about Percy?' Sean had been looking after Percy because Duncan couldn't bring him into the hypnotherapy session.

'Who?'

'My dog!'

'Oh, the rescue dog.'

As soon as he said the word rescue she knew she had to give him up too. He'd just found himself a wonderful home in the boathouse. Just because she'd screwed up, it didn't mean he had to pay for her mistakes too. She said as much to Joe. 'I want him to stay with David, if he would be so kind as to keep him. If not, please can you ask Duncan, or Gayle – or maybe you could take him? I really, really don't want him ending up homeless in a shelter all because of me.' She could feel the tears rolling down her cheeks at the thought. 'He is such a sweet boy. He doesn't deserve that.'

'David won't give up on Percy – I can assure you.'

Bonnie stared at Joe, wishing with all her heart that David felt the same way about her.

Joe looked at her for a long moment.

She was about to ask him what was on his mind when he said, 'Right, let's get on the road, shall we?'

Perhaps it was just as well that she didn't ask. Bonnie breathed a heavy sigh. She was not looking forward to returning to the boathouse. She couldn't fail to see the irony. Now she had her memories back, thanks to Marnie, returning there would no longer fill her with dread. She'd quite happily live there now, forever.

At least the saving grace was that nobody would be there when she arrived to pack up her stuff and leave.

45

They drove down the single-track lane in silence. She thought Joe might at least ask her where she'd go once she collected her belongings or what she'd do about her interior design outlet, which wasn't actually her shop. She realised with a start that everything was in Robyn's name, from the business to the money in the savings account from the cheques that Judith had sent.

She looked at Joe and suddenly realised why he was accompanying her to the house to collect her stuff. Her stuff. The clothes she could pack into the old rucksack. Not the suitcase that belonged to Robyn. Not the keys to Duncan's shop where she ran Robyn's Interior Design, not the savings account containing Robyn's money, and certainly not the keys to the boathouse.

She realised something else with a start. She would leave Aviemore just as she had arrived on Christmas Day, penniless and homeless. But this time she'd be alone too. Bonnie didn't care about Logan. She was glad to be rid of him. But she'd cared about the baby so very much. She remembered when she'd woken up in the hospital after the accident, and Dr Jamieson had broken the news that she'd been pregnant and that she'd lost her child. All she'd hoped was that one day, she might – just might – be so very lucky as to start a family with the man of her dreams.

She had thought that it would happen, with David.

A wave of nausea suddenly hit her. 'Oh, god. I need you to pull over. I think I'm going to be sick.'

'Hold on.' Joe slowed down to a stop. He'd barely put the handbrake on when she opened the car door and leaned over, retching. 'Oh, god, I'm so sorry,' she said before another bout.

Joe said in a gentle voice. 'Are you all right?'

She sat up in her seat, and wiped her mouth.

Joe was frantically trying to unscrew a bottle of water. 'Here.'

She took several sips.

'Feeling better?'

She didn't, not really, but nodded anyway. 'Sorry.'

'Please don't apologise, Roby— I mean Bonnie.' He paused. 'That name is going to take some getting used to,' she heard him mumble as he set off in the car.

Bonnie stared at the scenery. She couldn't believe it had just been a few hours ago that she'd been driving down this road, sitting in the back of David's car, excited about showing Judith her home and the wedding planner. And now she was back, in Joe's car, going to collect her belongings and be escorted from the boathouse. It could be worse, she supposed. At least she wasn't arriving in a police car.

She looked at Joe. 'Will you do something for me? Will you tell David I'm sorry?' She realised she wasn't the only one whose life had changed forever that day.

Unsurprisingly, Joe shook his head. 'No.'

Bonnie peered out of the window. 'You're right. You don't have to do anything for me, and I wouldn't expect you to.'

'That's not it, Bonnie.'

She continued staring out of the window at the pine forest. 'What do you mean, Joe?'

'You have nothing to apologise for.'

'That's just not true. I was Logan's girlfriend, the man who robbed your dad's store, robbed David.'

'That wasn't you. That was Logan.'

'But you all welcomed me into your homes, your hearts, and I was living a lie. I'm not the person you all thought I was. I'm not Robyn, I'm Bonnie.'

'What's in a name?'

'What's in a name?' she repeated, getting angry. 'What's in a name? Everything, as it happens – at least for me.'

'Ah, you see, that's where you're wrong. So wrong. We got to know you over the last few months, and you're still you, whether you call yourself Robyn or Bonnie.'

As Joe turned down the driveway of the boathouse, she was expecting it to be deserted, but there was David's car, and other cars parked haphazardly in the driveway, as though people had arrived in a hurry to vacate their cars.

Joe pulled the car up outside the house.

'What's going on?' She recognised the cars – Gayle's, and Brodie's, Duncan's delivery van. And a rental car that Jake, Faye and her daughter must have arrived in earlier that evening.

Joe turned in his seat to look at her.

She stared at him. 'I don't understand …'

'I wanted to tell you – I really did.'

'Tell me what?'

'Why don't you go inside?'

'Aren't you coming with me to check I don't steal anything? Are they all here to make sure I don't take anything that isn't mine?

Well, Bonnie's, I mean.'

Joe got out of the car and whizzed around to the other side, opening the car door for her.

She reluctantly got out. She had not expected everybody to be there, making it all so, so much harder. But where were they?

Joe walked up to the front door. He didn't have to punch in the alarm. The door was ajar. They were expected.

He walked in, but she didn't follow. He turned around, walked back, and took her by the hand, saying softly, 'You're going to be okay. Everything is going to be okay.'

He led her up to the kitchen door and opened it. The door swung wide open.

Joes whispered, 'They all swore me to secrecy. Sorry, I wanted to tell you. Whether you call yourself Robyn or Bonnie, that doesn't change the fact that we all love you.'

She stared around the table. Everything was as it had been before, except it wasn't her by the kitchen counter turning around with a large bowl of salad, about to drop it when she was confronted by Judith. It was Judith herself. She walked over to the table and put it down.

Everyone was looking a little flustered, as though they'd only just taken their seats.

Her homemade pizza and lasagne were in the centre of the table.

Judith said matter-of-factly, smiling at Bonnie, 'Let's start over.'

David stood up, walked around the table, and pulled out her chair. 'Please, take a seat.'

Bonnie slowly sat down, not sure what to make of it all. Was she dreaming?

She felt David's hand rest gently on her shoulder, then the

feeling of his lips kissing the top of her head.

She watched Joe take a seat and then raise a glass. She looked around the table, stunned that they were there – her friends who were, to her, family. They were all there, in the same seats, raising a glass – the two children, raising a glass of squash – as though all that had happened when Judith had called the police had just been a horrible, horrible nightmare.

Joe said, 'To the happy couple. Congratulations on your engagement.'

David stood by her chair, a hand on her shoulder, raising his glass.

Duncan said, 'Hear, hear!'

Percy woofed twice, which made everyone laugh.

'Shall I be mother?' asked Gayle, rising from her chair.

'But I'm mother,' said Doris.

Gayle smiled as the plates were passed to her one by one and she started dishing up the homemade lasagne. Conversation rose around the table.

David was about to walk over to resume his seat at the other end of the table when Bonnie grasped his hand.

He looked down at her, concerned. He whispered. 'Is everything okay?'

'Oh, David – everything is more than okay. It's just … I didn't expect this.' She'd tried very hard not to cry in front of everyone, but now tears were streaming down her face.

He knelt down by her chair and reached up, gently wiping away her tears. 'Did you think we'd all love you any less?'

'I thought … I really thought I was coming back here to collect my things and leave.'

'I know. Joe really wanted to tell you, but we just wanted to surprise you. I'm so sorry, it was a stupid, stupid idea. I didn't mean to make you cry. We were all in on it, obviously. Gayle did think that after what you'd been through it was too much, surprising you, and continuing with the meal, and having the party, but we all wanted to be here to welcome you home. Can you forgive us?'

'Can you forgive me?'

'What for? Having a raw deal in life, and trying your best to make a go of it with the rotten cards you'd been dealt?' He took her hands gently in his and whispered, 'Tell me it's all too much and I'll send everyone home. They'll understand … we can do this another time.'

She smiled at him, then looked around the table at everyone chatting, and eating, as though nothing extraordinary had happened that day. But something extraordinary had. She wasn't thinking about the fact that after so many months, she had her memories back. What she'd discovered was far, far more important to her; finding out where she truly belonged, right there in the boathouse, with the people who knew her, the real her – the young woman who had started life with absolutely nothing, and nobody in her corner, but through a twist of fate had ended up with everything she could ever wish for.

'I love you, David Gillespie.'

'And I love you, Bonnie Stewart. Now, how about we eat, finally?'

Epilogue

She'd been standing on the balcony, looking over the loch and watching the sunset. In the back garden below, the lanterns and fairy lights had come on. It was now dusk, and the party had spilled outside. The band had arrived, lively folk music getting people in the mood to dance. She saw Melissa dragging Brodie into the middle of the lawn near the band, and with some encouragement he started to dance.

She smiled when she caught sight of Evie and Natty. Evie was showing Natty how to tie ribbons in Olive's fur. On the way back from the hypnotherapy session at Marnie's, Nick had made a detour to Lark Lodge and collected Olive so that she wasn't left home alone. Percy was a little jealous of Olive getting all the attention from the girls. He kept stealing the ribbons and running off with them, burying them in the garden.

She turned as David reappeared with a throw from the lounge. He put it around her shoulders.

'Thank you. It was a lovely sunset, wasn't it?'

'Yes, it was.'

She turned to look at him. 'Will you do something for me?'

'Yes, of course. Anything.'

'I want to help Judith find her daughter.'

'I know.'

She cast her gaze down at Judith, who had a glass of wine and was chatting to Gayle. Although Gayle had vacancies, Judith would be staying at the boathouse for a while. Judith had said that she didn't want to speak ill of her missing stepdaughter, but in the very short time she'd known the young woman calling herself Robyn, she'd grown fond of her, of the fact that she had the qualities – kindness and compassion – that she felt her stepdaughter lacked.

Bonnie had been honest in turn and had told her that she wished she was her stepmum for real. In that instant, a friendship had been forged, and while Judith was searching for Robyn, Bonnie had insisted she stay with them in the town where Robyn had last been seen.

'There's something else, David.'

'What is it?'

'I'd like to do a trip down memory lane.'

He raised his eyebrows.

'Return to where I grew up. My two younger siblings, the twins, who were taken into care – I'd like to find them too.'

He put an arm around her shoulders and pulled her close. 'We'll find them, I promise you.' He paused. 'Will you do something for me?'

'Of course, anything.'

'Will you tell me why you're still lying to me?'

She looked at David, shocked. 'What are you talking about?'

'I just know you haven't told me everything.'

She lowered her eyes, remembering the conversation she'd had with Gayle in the kitchen alone, while the two of them were washing up after the meal, before she headed upstairs and out onto the balcony. Gayle had said to her, whoever you were meeting in London, you need to tell David. No more secrets.

She'd told Gayle, 'It really isn't of any consequence in terms of him and me.'

'Even so, just tell him. It's something that's obviously been playing on your mind,' she'd replied.

She took a deep breath. 'All right, I will.' She looked at David in the eye, and said, 'There's this guy.'

'Oh, my god – I knew it!'

'No, no – it's nothing like that. It's an older guy. It was him who employed me to redecorate The Lake House.'

'Jake Campbell-Ross's house?'

'Yes.'

'He had some extra work for you in London?'

Bonnie smiled. 'Yes.'

'Oh, thank god!' he grinned at her. Then his smile dropped. 'There's something else – isn't there?'

'The job in London … I promised to be … discreet.'

'Discreet?'

'Well, actually, it was written into my contract not to tell anyone.'

'Who is this guy who employed you? Is it William Ross?'

'No, his name is Aubrey Jones. I'm not meant to tell anyone. I shouldn't be telling you.'

'Telling me what?'

'About Eleanor Campbell-Ross. That's why I couldn't say anything in front of everybody at the police station or at my therapy session.'

'What about her?'

'After the accident, they didn't tell the press what happened to her, did they?'

David shook her head. 'They seemed to close ranks, no press conference or press release. Nothing. I don't think anybody knows what really happened to her after that.' He stared at her. 'You know where she is, don't you?'

She nodded, thinking there but for the grace of god go I.

'You don't have to tell me anything more.'

She smiled at him. 'Thank you, David.' She trailed off when she caught sight of Jake walking towards Faye with two glasses of champagne. It was obvious he was besotted with her.

David followed her gaze. 'I was talking to my father, and he'd mentioned to Jake in conversation about the body found on the mountain when the snow thawed.'

Bonnie looked at him in surprise. 'What body?'

'Oh, it was in the local news. I forget the name of the guy who died up there on Christmas Day.'

'You didn't tell me.'

'You'd just had your accident, and were stuck in hospital, so it wasn't exactly something I wanted to talk to you about. In fact, I'm sorry for bringing it up right now, at the party. It's just that seeing Jake reminded me that Dad said he wanted to talk to me about it, see if I knew anything more about the poor fellow.'

'And do you?'

'No, not at all. But I wonder if it has something to do with that accident up there on the mountain last Christmas, and what happened to Eleanor Campbell-Ross.'

She closed her eyes. She didn't want to think about it.

She felt David's arms wrap around her as they stood on the balcony, listening to the music and to the sounds of their friends having a wonderful time on the lawn below. Her thoughts turned to the Rosses and what had happened on the mountain the previous Christmas. She turned to face David. 'We should count our blessings.'

'I'm certainly counting mine.' He kissed her, then drew back. 'Shall we go and join the party?'

'Oh yes.'

'But before we do, I want to toast our new life together in the boathouse.' He turned around and picked up two glasses. He gave her one.

'What's in the glass?' Bonnie asked.

'Silly question – champagne, of course.' He saw her expression. 'Don't you want to make a toast?'

'Well, yes. But I was thinking I might prefer squash.'

'Why?'

'Just in case.'

'In case of what?'

She stared at him. 'It's just possible …' she glanced at her dog on the lawn below, and was so relieved to see how gentle he was with the children, even when he was being naughty. 'I think I might be—'

She didn't even get to finish her sentence. David looked at her wide-eyed, gulped down his drink, put the glass down, and scooped her into his arms. 'You know what this means – don't you?'

She shook her head, wondering what he was going to say.

'I'll have to get you another planner.'

She remembered when he'd stopped off in Aviemore on the way there, before their week's holiday together. She'd bought a stamp, and he'd nipped into another shop and surprised her with another gift – a gorgeous wedding planner.

'You're going to have your hands full, what with planning the wedding, and baby showers, and all that.'

She grinned. 'Yes, I am.'

'Mind you, you'll have no shortage of helping hands.'

'That's true.' Bonnie smiled at her friends, her family down below. She was still thinking of another family, the Rosses, and counting her blessings, as David took her hand, and together they joined the party that would mark the start of many happy family celebrations to come in her forever home – the boathouse by the loch.

The Scottish Highlands Series continues in

Coming Home to Aviemore

Paperback and Kindle eBook coming soon.

If you enjoyed *The Boathouse by the Loch* I would be grateful if you would leave a review on Amazon.

For further details about the author and her novels please visit the author's website.

www.elisedarcy.com

Also by Elise Darcy

The Sunrise Coast Series

New Beginnings at the Harbour Inn

The Secret of the Summerhouse

The Cottage by the Sea

The Guest House at Shingle Cove

The Houseboat by the Quay

Return to Willow Tree Cottage

The Bookshop of Memories

The Beach House

A Summer to Remember

The Living Apart Together Series

Living Apart Together

It Takes 2 to Tango

Dear John

Love on the Rooftop

Standalone Novels

Lola & The Man

A Mallorcan Affair

We'll Meet Again

The Villa in Sicily

Printed in Dunstable, United Kingdom

65974476R00234